kol.li.go
verb
conjugation: 1st
voice: transitive

Definitions:
1. Bind/tie/pack together/fetter/put in bonds
2. Up/connect
3. Unite/unify

BY

Lee S. Hannon

Cover Design by Tori Mulhern
Map Design by Keir DuBois

First Edition, 2022

The Library of Congress has catalogued the hardcover edition as follows:
Names: Lee S. Hannon, author.
Title: COLIGO: Book #1, The UNITAS Series: a novel / Lee S. Hannon
Description: First edition. | Boston : Idella Imprint Publishing, LLC, 2021
Identifiers: LCCN 2021921574 | ISBN 9798985117509 (hardcover) | ISBN 9798985117530 (hardcover, special edition) | ISBN 9798985117516 (paperback) | ISBN 978985117523 (ebook)
Subjects: Fiction, Techno-Thriller | Science Fiction | Dystopian.

Our books may be purchased in bulk for promotional, educational, or business use. Please contact your local bookseller or Idella Imprint Publishing, LLC by email at:
sleehannon@gmail.com.

www.leeshannonbooks.com
Follow on Instagram, Twitter and TikTok: @leeshannonbooks

For more information or inquiries, please reach out to Idella Imprint Publishing, LLC

10 9 8 7 6 5 4 3 2 1

To Tori

For reminding me to "just keep writing" even during the most difficult times

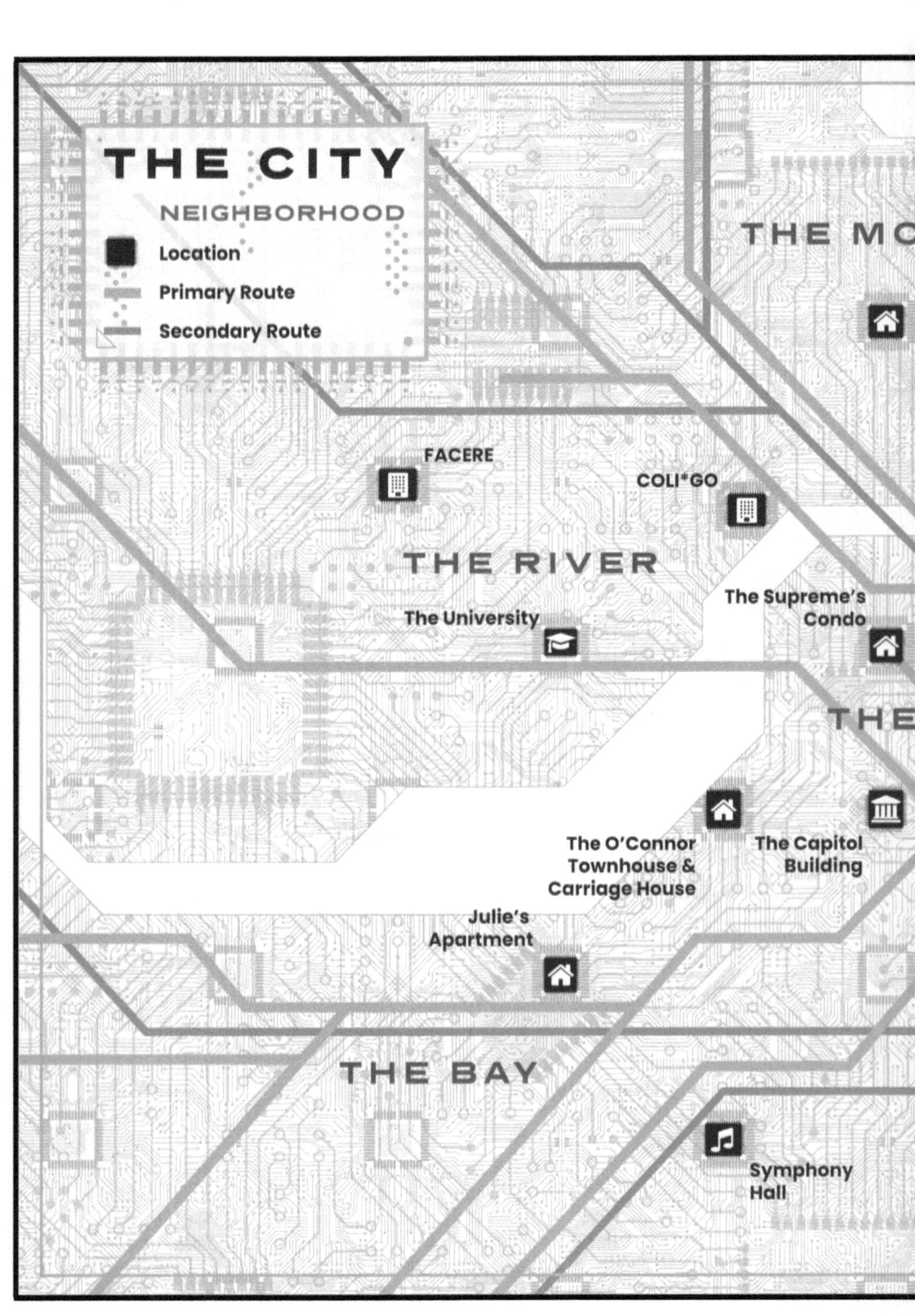
THE CITY
NEIGHBORHOOD
Location
Primary Route
Secondary Route
THE MO
FACERE
COLI*GO
THE RIVER
The University
The Supreme's Condo
THE
The O'Connor Townhouse & Carriage House
The Capitol Building
Julie's Apartment
THE BAY
Symphony Hall

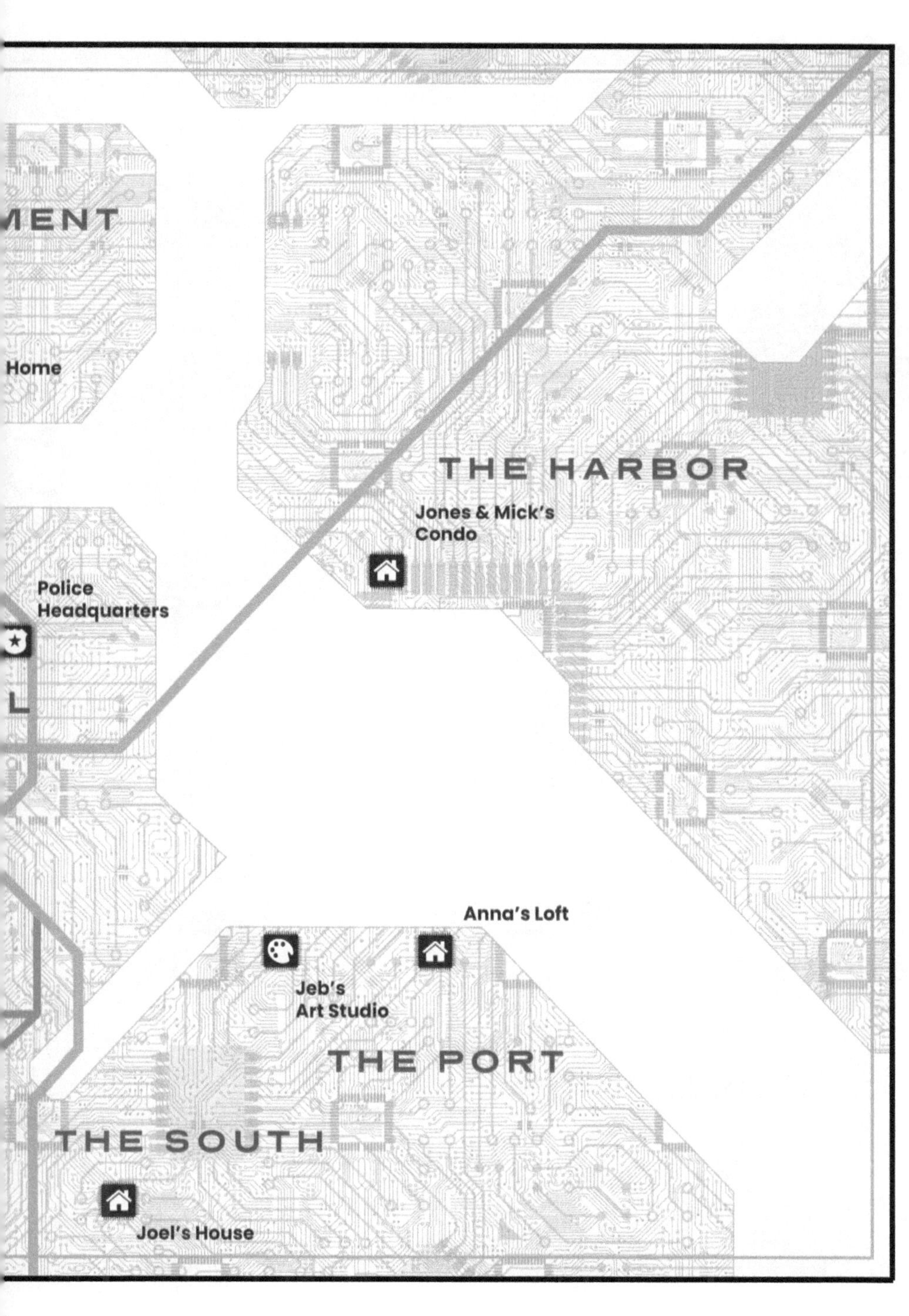
MENT
Home
Police
Headquarters
L
THE HARBOR
Jones & Mick's
Condo
Anna's Loft
Jeb's
Art Studio
THE PORT
THE SOUTH
Joel's House

PART ONE

"Deep into that darkness peering, long I stood there, wondering, fearing, doubting, dreaming dreams no mortal ever dared to dream before."
-Edgar Allan Poe

Prologue

January 28th, 47 A.R.

A.R. = Years After Resurgence

The snow fell lightly around the wooded swamp as dusk quickly approached the horizon. Her body lay in the week-old snowfall in almost an angelic way, her strawberry blonde hair slightly damp around her face.

With her eyes closed, he believed she wasn't actually dying before his eyes—just peacefully sleeping in the cold winter woods. She was his masterpiece, his whole world, and she remained beautiful right here in this exact moment. Or that's what It believed, not him. To him, she was perfect, alive, not dead.

Minutes passed before he slowly rose from his crouched position. The crunch of the icy snow beneath his feet echoed slightly in the empty wilderness surrounding them. He felt like they were in their own special place miles outside The City, while in reality, the sounds of The City lurked only a few miles away.

It never allowed him to touch the bodies after their kills. Instead, they lingered and waited for their victims to completely slip away from consciousness. Then they'd make their way back to his home and submerge themselves in beer and wine before passing out. In the morning, they'd watch the news with the discovery of the death on the screen.

The killings were few and far between, but this was their ritual together. They never felt the need to say goodbye.

But she was different to him. He loved her.

He imagined bringing her home and keeping her safe, like he had always promised. He almost felt her warmth despite the bitterness of the cold winter air around them. It wouldn't allow her as a permanent part of his life, and he knew better. He was selfish and greedy, risking her by wanting her. By wanting only them.

Back to the ritual.

Her bright red lips, painted in her own blood like a shade of sticky, flirtatious lipstick, flickered in the moonlight. He felt her body growing colder as her pale skin turned a light shade of purple. This wasn't the same shade of purple bruises that normally accompanied their killings.

This is where the ritual deviated.

The time to leave came, but he couldn't stop looking at her. Breaking the rules tempted him as his thumb hovered over her lips.

"Do not touch her. We worked too hard," It said.

But touching her is so damn tempting, he thought as desire crept into his mind. Memories of kissing her neck, her warm embrace, the tininess of her hands, and the smell of her hair consumed him.

It was right. He only made things difficult by dragging this out. They needed to leave now.

He looked away from her body toward the hiking path. The android police force wouldn't catch them. They never did. An early morning jogger would likely find her tomorrow, and then they'd watch her story unfold on the news.

She was well known in the community. Her innovations in and commitment to pharmaceutical research and drug discovery spoke volumes. To the outside world, she was a lovely, smart scientist who left behind no husband and no children, with her priority solely focused on curing neurological conditions. Boring.

She was full of life, he reminded himself.

Seeing her mutilated and shallow stab wounds brought soft tears to the corners of his eyes. He couldn't help himself as he bent down and stroked her hair. It shook his head at him but didn't scold. It knew this wasn't easy.

His hand pulled away from her face slowly. The smell of her soothingly lingered on his fingertips. Their final goodbye.

It brushed away their footprints and faced the trail.

"Why is this so hard for me?"

"You knew we had no choice," It answered as they reached the car.

The engine purred to life at the command of his thumbprint, and the lights flickered on, illuminating the inside.

"Where would you like to go today, sir?" The voice activation emerged from the vehicle's dashboard system.

"Home," he simply responded.

It looked over at him from the passenger seat with an anxious twitch as the car calculated their route. He closed his eyes and lay back before the car pulled out onto the icy road. Lights quickly appeared on the surrounding streets as they exited the forest. Within minutes, the scenery changed from tall pine trees to crowded urban streets.

Duplexes and triple-decker homes squeezed close together as the crooked streets of The City led them through the most unsavory and neglected neighborhood within metropolitan limits.

A century ago, developers promised to clean up the riffraff and build picturesque, modern, sleek condos. Politicians in The Legislature assured better schools and safer streets for both humans and androids. While the plan infiltrated some neighborhoods in The City, this section wasn't one of them.

As they neared downtown, the buildings stood taller, and revitalized glass complexes came into view. They neared a popular district, The Bay, which emulated limestone townhomes with large bay windows along tree-lined sidewalks.

Almost home.

He raised the volume of the music, and It looked over at him, smiling before glancing out the passenger window. Classical music made a comeback during the end of The Resurgence and symbolized a sign of status. The reverberations of the pianist's fingers against the keys soothed and mesmerized him.

The feel of an incline woke him from his lulled state. They were finally entering The Hill.

The Hill neighborhood held on to its historic charm even during the conflict of The Resurgence. Beautiful brick brownstones stood for centuries alongside gaslit lamp posts that now shined with modern lights. This section of The City was built by old bloodline families. He was part of one of the most notorious old bloodline families, the O'Connors.

The car parked itself in a tiny garage attached to his townhome, and they both climbed up the stairs. Striding across the living room, he lit the fireplace and kept the lights turned off. He smelled the pasta she and he cooked earlier that evening, and the second bottle of wine they opened sat barely touched on the dining room table. He didn't bother with a glass as he grabbed the bottle and headed toward the stairs. It followed him, grabbing a bottle of beer out of the refrigerator.

The ritual.

He detoured in the cold, unfinished laundry room. He stared at the washing machine longer than necessary and stripped off his clothes. The water rushed behind the glass window as the machine zoomed to life. The smell of her from his clothes now lost forever.

Naked, he moved from the laundry room and up the next set of stairs, stopping every few steps and drinking directly from the bottle. The wine clouded his mind as a much-needed distraction.

He paused upon reaching the master bedroom, realizing he'd never forget her, no matter how hard he tried. How could he? Her things were everywhere: a tossed University sweatshirt, pairs of mismatched socks, and her hairbrush. Her presence consumed the room as if she were still here watching him.

"She used you," It yelled from down the hall, reminding him. Maybe she did use me, he thought, but didn't I use her, too?

He took another swig from the bottle, emptying it. Tipsiness threatened him, but the wine wasn't strong enough.

Instead of entering the bedroom, he walked down the hall to his study. Inside the cabinet he found his Scotch and poured himself three fingers. The amber liquid didn't last long as he consumed its contents in a single gulp.

Forgetting what happened wasn't enough—he wanted It to know how angry he was with him. He couldn't be the only one grieving, the only one punished.

Her light chuckle rang through his ears as he reminisced about the first time he brought her into his home. The townhouse was impressive, even with a checkered past.

The home belonged to his family for generations, the old-world charm present among modern technology.

"This is yours?" she had asked, running her hand on the banister while taking in the artwork lining the walls. Her eyes had shifted to the original light fixtures and chandeliers.

He distinctly remembered the look on her face. She had always been observant and curious. A true scientist and researcher at her core. While she appeared cold and aloof to the outside world, she always approached him softly and gently. She held him during his night terrors, the night terrors that shook him uncontrollably. She was his sanctuary, promising to fix and cure his demons.

"But then she used you," It whispered in his ear.

It always remembered everything when he so desperately wanted to forget.

***

Her body remained still, but her petrified brain raced rapidly. Her fingers twitched from the rawness of the winter air, and her body ached in indescribable pain.

But Julie Walsh didn't lose a fight. Ever.

After a few pep talks in her mind, Julie opened her eyes.

How did I end up here? she wondered, taking in the strange and unfamiliar surroundings. *How did I go from dinner with Colin to these dark and isolated woods?*

Crying out for help required more strength than her body possessed. A searing pain jarred through her abdomen and ribcage, and the snow around her seeped in bright red. Her eyes rolled back into her head from pure shock.

Fight or flight took over. What mattered most was getting out of these woods alive. She opened her eyes again and looked up at the sky. The blackness shone without any stars.

So, I'm close to The City.

Julie observed the wilderness around her. If she didn't act quickly, she'd suffer from her wounds and die. Blood poured profusely from several shallow stab wounds near her left ribcage and across her stomach.

Julie moved her hand away from her open injuries and up her body, stopping right below her left earlobe. She felt a small incision, a tear.

That was more of a concern.

The sound of branches snapping across the ground echoed around her. Panic and terror rang through her ears, and she wondered if the person who tried killing her returned.

Or is it someone who can help me?

She couldn't take that chance.

Rolling onto the right side of her body, Julie struggled for a few moments, getting herself off the ground. The pain blinded her. Against Julie's better judgment, she closed her eyes again.

"Hello?" a deep voice echoed out across the trees.

Julie instantly froze, attempting not to breathe or make any noise.

"Hello?" the voice came again.

The reality of her situation set in. She was gravely wounded and couldn't escape these woods by herself. This stranger might be her only chance for survival.

"I need help!" Julie called out vulnerably, a foreign concept for her. Julie couldn't see the stranger, but the sound of his boots on the snow crunched louder and louder as he approached.

When the man stood above her, Julie analyzed his appearance. He wasn't overly intimidating and showcased an acquired honest look in the nighttime darkness. There was something oddly familiar about this old man. Without understanding why, Julie trusted him.

"I'm not sure what happened," she said breathlessly.

The stranger looked her over, his face ragged and tired with fine lines around his dark lips and purple rings underneath his eyes. He wore a light windbreaker, not a puffy jacket needed for the cold winters in The City.

"Julie, I'm here. Don't worry, I'll help you." His warm, deep voice softened as she faded from consciousness.

How does he know my name? Julie wondered.

Miraculously, he lifted her with ease and carried her deeper into the forest toward a bright, shining light.

***

"You're ridiculous!" Julie's voice echoed in the hall as she ran down the stairs. She'd been tense lately, and this was the first time in weeks that he remembered her laughing.

"No, I'm not!" Colin called after her, laughter filling the townhouse. He smiled in her direction. She made him feel light, happy, and alive.

Julie continued racing through the townhouse in her oversized sweatshirt and ripped jeans. He liked how she dressed casually here with him, so different from her outside life.

Ducking into the living room, Julie quickly realized her mistake. Colin sprinted around the other side of the kitchen before running into her. She swiftly turned, but he caught her from behind and pulled her close to him, kissing her forehead and then her neck. His hands raced up underneath her sweatshirt.

"Colin!" she yelped through her laughter.

His hands traced along the curves of her body while he kissed her neck more aggressively. Colin pulled himself away to remove her sweatshirt, but when he looked down, his hands were covered in blood.

Colin's eyes darted open. He was back in his bedroom, not the kitchen. There was no Julie in sight.

As he lay drenched in sweat, the sun shone through the window, illuminating his bare body. The pillows and sheets littered the floor as if someone threw them at an intruder. An empty bottle of wine left a purple ring on the nightstand next to a half-empty bottle of Scotch. His head pounded from a terrible hangover.

Colin grabbed his device without hesitation and requested access to the local news. The familiar news anchors smiled in their overly done makeup on the razor-thin screen on the wall. Jessica Something-or-Other was the main reporter on the screen. She once interviewed Colin when she was the political correspondent.

A news segment played on a clean water initiative from The City's most prestigious and innovative corporation. The representative from that district excitedly shared his optimism.

Fucking Representative Joel Kennsington. How does he keep getting elected? Colin hated that man.

As a politician himself, Colin recognized that humans preferred the devil they knew better than the devil they didn't know.

Back in the newsroom, Jessica introduced the progress of the high-speed, emissions-free floating tram. A new route was proposed, legislature Colin specifically remembered listening to only weeks ago. Eventually, they moved on to the weather forecast.

Where is the breaking news about a famous scientist found dead in the wooded reserves outside The City? Has someone not found her yet?

He felt heavy footsteps approaching from behind.

"Shit," It echoed.

***

"I'm Mick," the old man said, "a slightly different version of Mick but still Mick."

Mick Taylor was Julie's friend; he was her age. Not an old man. They stood at the entrance of the mesmerizing and hauntingly beautiful light coming from a small chrome box. Julie tilted her head, unsure if she were hallucinating in these woods.

Mick looked down at her and smiled.

"Do you trust me?"

Julie nodded, realizing she had no other choice.

Mick sheltered Julie's eyes with a pair of glasses. She couldn't see anything through the dark lenses, but the darkness calmed her. She concentrated on her breathing and pushed aside the pain coursing through her body.

A soft clicking sound cascaded from the glasses, and a vibration pulsed through her body. The experience was noticeable but not violent or unpleasant.

When Mick removed the glasses from Julie's eyes, The City's skyline appeared. Unlike the clean streets and scenery she was accustomed to, she observed garbage and debris surrounding her in unforgiving gray colors.

Reality crashed around her as the pain thundered back with a vengeance. Mick propped her up against the building behind them before retrieving the small rectangular device on the ground. He flattened the box and placed it in his pocket with both sets of glasses.

"We need to move quickly before the bots come out and enforce curfew hours," Mick said.

Julie's brow raised at his statement. The term "bots" was derogatory, referring to the android citizens of The City. People barely used that word anymore, especially someone like Mick. He cared about androids, even loved one.

He scooped her back up and carried her through the streets at a slow but steady pace. They passed a woman who didn't even bat an eye their way. Many humans and androids surrounded them with no concern of a man holding a bloody woman.

"They can't see you," Mick said as if reading her mind. "It's like you don't exist to them."

"Why?" Julie asked, her ghostly presence an uncomfortable notion.

"You're only visible in dimensions where you're alive. You're dead in this one." His words sliced through her as this harsh reality set in.

"This is the future?"

Mick didn't respond, his silence deafening against the loud noises of The City.

They reached a paved parking lot, and Mick opened the back door of a sleek vehicle she didn't recognize. As they drove, Julie observed The City while applying pressure to her wounds. This future version of The City looked vastly different.

Polluted clouds lined the tops of skyscrapers, so she couldn't see the highest floors of the buildings. Some appeared abandoned. People on the sidewalks wouldn't look at one another, and children were held close to their mothers' chests. Everything was cold and gray. There were no vibrant colors, no sense of greenery anywhere. An overpowering sense of sadness overcame her as she pieced together why society looked this way.

"Humans and androids have no control here anymore," Mick said from the front seat.

Julie looked out the window again. Humans wore dull black clothing as they passed by vehicles and one another. The androids among them also wore muted tones, but their beautiful scales reflected starkly off the glass buildings.

Mick's vehicle turned the windy street corners gently as if he knew her unbearable pain. Comfort filled Julie for the first time once they approached a familiar part of The City. The Hill.

When she wasn't in the lab at COLI*GO, Julie spent her time in The Hill. This was where the secret part of her lived. The real part of her.

The vehicle stopped in front of the O'Connor townhouse.

"Colin is still here? How did he let any of this happen?" Julie asked, fear trickling out of her voice.

"Let's not talk about Colin yet," Mick said while maneuvering her out of the back seat.

Her body left a bloody mess behind as Mick carried her up the stairs and into the elegant dining room.

Nothing about the O'Connor townhouse changed. The immaculate furniture was organized meticulously. The smell of the home even put her at ease. It smelled like Colin.

New waves of pain spread across her whole body as Mick tried gently placing her on the dining room table. Julie's eyes widened as a familiar shadow loomed above her.

PART TWO

Six Years Earlier

"Have no fear of perfection, you'll never reach it."
-Salvador Dali

Chapter 1
Julie

January 28th, 41 A.R.

Julie's research consumed her whole life. It occupied her mornings, afternoons, and evenings. Sometimes she forgot to eat, and she grew skinnier than she liked. But Julie didn't care—she couldn't stop thinking about the next steps in her research.

Becker didn't care about Julie's passion in the same way. Julie discovered after several years that Becker was a very particular android and a peculiar professor. He evaluated all his PhD students with the sharpest scrutiny. While he believed they fell short, his students already discovered and pioneered innovations changing the world. Being an android attributed to his lack of enthusiasm and emotion. Created and controlled by The Legislature, androids were manufactured in a laboratory facility called FACERE across The River with the purpose of filling essential job functions in society where emotions couldn't cloud judgment.

Androids looked like humans except for their skin. Rapidly vibrant colored scales spread across their bodies. These scales were the eyes into their processors—a mechanical version of a brain. Technically, an android comprehended emotions and feelings, but their programming only allowed a limited percent of understanding those feelings.

When androids felt emotions, the colors of their scales illuminated or changed.

Julie walked into the classroom a bit early, as she normally did. At the front of the room, Becker set up his lecture for the day. Most professors were androids, not humans. Androids could store information and memories in larger capacities within their processors. Her peers at The University, however, were a nearly equal mix of humans and androids.

"Julie, can you stay after class?" Becker asked, breaking her train of thought.

She nodded and took her seat. His lecture today centered on neurotransmitters in the human brain, a topic she studied closely in her own research. Julie cautiously pulled out her personal device, looking for an invitation to present from the COLI*GO Board of Directors.

COLI*GO was the most innovative company in The City and held an extremely influential and intertwined role in both the public and private sectors. The name derived from the Latin word *coligo*, which loosely translated to unification and connection. The company invested in any idea with potential to help society. It didn't matter if the research focus was in biology, engineering, the arts, or even the languages.

The company's mission was to unify society through innovation. Celine O'Connor founded COLI*GO almost a decade ago. As a member of the O'Connor old bloodline family, she grew up in a stable and fortunate environment but witnessed the struggles of her friends and peers emerging out of The Resurgence. Much like her father, she wanted to connect people and androids but also understood the role commitment, urgency, and sense of purpose played in unity.

At the time, her father, Henry O'Connor, was the governor. Now Celine's brother, Colin, filled his father's shoes. Support for COLI*GO came from other old bloodline members of society like the scientist and her husband, Martin Borges, and from Celine's friend, an equally powerful android referred to as The Supreme.

After The Resurgence, a time when androids revolted against the government, androids finally received representation in The Legislature with the formation of The Representatives of The Androids and a selected leader. Their leader, The Supreme, acted as a counterpart to the governor. The Supreme watched over the androids, protected them, and was now an important, intricate part of society.

The Supreme wildly supported COLI*GO, and in a short amount of time, the company forged the way in gene therapy technologies, providing cures and treatments for auto-immune diseases and numerous cancers. Additionally, the company brought back extinct species and advanced automobile technology and broad communication infrastructures.

Fresh innovation was paramount for COLI*GO's success. Each year, The Board of Directors selected graduating PhD students to present their research and pitch themselves.

Julie and her peers submitted proposals and executive summaries before the holiday break. Now, she waited patiently, hoping COLI*GO would announce her as a finalist.

"Julie, please pay attention," Becker said in his tone-deaf manner.

She attempted an apologetic look in his direction.

Concentrating for the rest of the lecture proved impossible, and after a couple of grueling hours, her classmates shuffled out into the hall. Julie lingered behind and approached Becker's lectern.

"So," he said in a similar tone, "I've gone through your latest updates and data."

He pulled out his tablet, and the three-dimensional report projected off the screen in front of them. Becker's blue scaled arms faintly shifted from an indigo purple to a sky blue. The shift in coloring put Julie on edge—one emotion Becker flaunted frequently was agitation.

"I think I've just scratched the surface of something really special. There's a chance the molecule I'm developing could work beyond dementia-associated memory issues."

Becker sighed. "Julie, this could be really dangerous."

Those words weren't what Julie expected. She thought he'd praise her for her brazenness and creativity.

"Well, isn't that the risk of science? That's why we run reports and tests in simulations first. Danger isn't a threat in coding biologics and antibodies anymore." Julie grasped her hands together, her nervous rambling bubbling up in her throat.

"Yes, but the human mind isn't simulated with exact accuracy like other organs. We understand neurological responders, but memory receptors still puzzle us," Becker replied, looking up at her with an intimidating glare.

"Yes, which is why I started this research in dementia and

Alzheimer's." Julie paused. "But I noticed similar receptors are damaged in psychological conditions. I'm approaching this molecule as an antidote in gene therapy rather than a traditional therapeutic."

"Are you suggesting the human brain poisons itself? That these cells mutate similarly to outside pathogens? Because, if so, you're characterizing this research the same way the medical field characterizes cancer. And brain cancer isn't the focus of your research."

Julie looked straight at Becker, her jaw dropping slightly. Her research and data showed certain conditions of the brain acting strangely in response to mutations, but those mutations weren't cancerous. The pathophysiology differed.

"While I'll admit your recent discovery is fascinating," Becker said, shifting his gaze back down to her report, "as your sponsor, I can't allow this change in direction. While I couldn't alter your submission to COLI*GO, I made a note that your focus remains on the extraordinary work within Alzheimer's. I hope you understand the reasons why. You're thinking too far ahead. Don't allow for frivolous opportunities in more fascinating and daring spaces to discredit the scientifically sound discovery you've worked hard on for many years."

He looked at Julie the way most androids looked at humans: blankly. Becker tried understanding her feelings, but at this moment, her emotions were beyond his programming.

Does Becker not believe in my research anymore? Julie wondered. She couldn't help but feel puzzled by their conversation.

"If COLI*GO accepts my presentation, I will mention all the data on the antidote's role in the human brain."

Becker's scales changed colors again. This time, a bright neon flash vibrated across him. His glow magnified his presence and intensity in the room as he stood.

The colors of his scales burned around her, pulsating in the room. Becker physically towered over Julie like most androids. She wasn't a tiny woman, but Becker felt like a mountain beside her.

"I would highly recommend you do not."

***

"Don't listen to Becker," Mick answered in an impassioned voice equal to Julie's after she replayed her earlier conversation.

Julie and Mick's friendship went back to their orientation several years ago. Neither came from old bloodline families and enjoyed that familiarity they shared. Mick grew up on a farm out in The Countryside, and his father disowned him for coming to The University. With the help of his uncle Jeb, Mick moved himself to The City with a single piece of luggage and a few hundred dollars to his name. Julie admired her friend for pursuing his dreams and considered him brave. It was rare for someone from The Countryside to be accepted at The University, but Mick's intellect and research in blood types and DNA markers proved him to be a great candidate for the hematologic program.

"I don't want to get kicked out a few months before receiving my degree," Julie said.

"They won't kick you out," Mick replied, reaching over and grabbing her hand. The quick squeeze felt both reassuring and easing.

"If your research gets you kicked out, Mick's research will definitely get him kicked out," Jones said from across the kitchenette.

Jones, Mick's partner, was an android and one of Julie's closest friends. Julie and Jones met in high school, and while their history was complex, their friendship remained extremely intertwined. Jones and Julie trusted one another fiercely.

What Julie risked for Jones in their youth remained a secret from Mick. Julie didn't regret the night Jones begged her to reprogram the microchip in his processor. Jones wanted to understand more human emotions and feelings, and he needed her help. A month later, after Julie's mother died, Jones never left her side. Nothing could break their inseparable bond.

"Will you ever let me in on your secret research?"

Mick worked similarly crazy hours as she, rushing to the lab early and coming home late.

"Another day and another time," Mick responded, pushing his glasses up the bridge of his nose.

Jones looked over at Julie and rolled his eyes.

"You two stop bickering. Let's order food," Jones said, his scales changing from a pale green to a dark shade of emerald.

"I could go for some pasta," Julie said with a shrug. Mick hated Italian food, but Julie knew if he conceded, he wasn't truly annoyed with her poking and prodding.

"Fine! But I need to change out of my lab clothes first." Mick stomped off into the bedroom of his and Jones's tiny apartment. Jones and Julie burst into laughter. Once Mick was out of sight, Jones looked over at Julie with raised brows.

"What?" she asked.

"I don't know how you two do it," he said. "I don't want any part of repetitive research, coding, and simulations. It isn't fast-paced enough."

Julie smiled at him. With his heightened ability to feel emotions, Jones was an odd android. He cared about people, a less common quality in both humans and androids alike.

"It's impactful. Just not as quickly as anyone would like."

"I spoke with Mick about his research. I'll continue helping where he needs it, but I've decided not to present with him." Jones rested his hand on Julie's arm.

Jones invested years of his life assisting Mick in his research, and they both worked very hard. Julie couldn't understand why Jones had a change of heart. They were all stressed and ready to finish their last semester, ready to move on from The University. Julie particularly longed for the next phase of her life.

"What are you going to do?" she asked.

"I have some exciting news," Jones answered, getting up from the couch. He grabbed his device and walked back over to Julie, holding it out for her to take. "I was accepted into the police academy! I'll train as a detective."

"Jones! That's amazing! How long have you known and not told me?" Julie couldn't help but playfully slap his arm.

"I just found out this week. It won't be easy, but I really want to help people and androids. I'll leave the 'helping from afar' to the geeky scientists like you and Mick."

Mick emerged from the bedroom with a large grin, aware that Jones shared his good news. "Did Jones tell you?"

Julie smiled and nodded.

Chapter 2
The Governor

January 28th, 41 A.R.

Her elegant hands flung wildly from the piano as the sound filled Symphony Hall. Her talent was stunningly magnificent. Colin watched how smoothly and vivaciously her long graceful fingertips traced the keys. He closed his eyes, breathing it all in before letting the moment absorb him.

In his childhood, Colin played the piano and appreciated the calming act of both listening and playing the instrument. Symphony Hall held during The Resurgence and remained a place for the well-connected and affluent members of society to mingle. The Hall's old stuffy seats were recently replaced with sleek chairs and glossy devices projecting the sound and reflection of the orchestra into the crowd.

Isabella Garcia startled Colin back to reality by laying her hand on his thigh. He looked over at her and smiled. Their evening started off with dinner, followed by the orchestra's performance. Together, they shared laughs, the stresses of their days, and the excitement for a night alone, especially knowing Colin had a long week ahead. He was a board member at COLI*GO, his sister's tech company, and still needed to review the submitted innovations. After several years of living through this process, Colin appreciated the brilliant minds that benefited the well-being of his constituents.

He loved the people he served. There wasn't a Sunday spent without visiting one of the neighborhoods within his constituency. Colin insisted on taking every message personally, even at the dismay of his secretary, Kathleen Murphy. The idea of a long to-do list invigorated him. Kathleen usually rolled her eyes, put her hands on her hips, and yelled in her thick City accent, "Colin, are yah outta yah mind, kid?"

Colin was out of his mind, but he liked that.

"Let's head out before the crowd?" Isabella whispered saucily into his ear.

He didn't want to leave early. The escape he experienced in this room calmed him. But Isabella was right, they wouldn't get home at a decent hour if they left with the crowds. People respected the governor, and he'd never deny someone a chance to speak with him. Colin already served two terms and was one of the youngest and beloved politicians in The City.

"Exactly what I was thinking," he lied.

They discretely left the O'Connors' private box, and Colin pulled out his device once they were in the hall. The music faded away as they walked down the red-carpeted stairs.

Come into the office tomorrow morning. 8 a.m. Thx

Colin rolled his eyes at the message from his android counterpart, The Supreme. She constantly blew up his phone with requests. Sometimes he didn't mind but not on a night like this one.

He wrote back:

Ok—to discuss The University submissions?

"Colin, are you coming?" Isabella asked from the bottom of the stairs. Annoyance lingered in her eyes.

"Yes, sorry, darling," he said and put his phone back into his pocket, grabbing her hand. "I am all yours now."

Isabella smiled at him for winning the small victory of his attention.

Once they arrived back at the townhouse, Isabella left him for the kitchen. Colin heard her open a bottle of wine before she appeared with two glasses. She extended one out toward him.

"Only one, I have to go into the office tomorrow," he replied, taking the glass from her smooth tan hand.

She sat beside him and sighed. He sensed she was upset.

Have I ruined our whole evening? Colin wondered, not blaming her for the disappointment across her gorgeous face. Isabella Garcia was simply stunning: smart, beautiful, and polished. He could get lost in her for hours if she let him. She wore her soft espresso-colored hair in luscious curls, and her deep green eyes softened when he looked into them. Isabell's skin was blemish-free and as smooth as caramel.

Colin thought about his own skin, the fine lines slightly appearing in the corners of his eyes as he reached his late thirties. Colin knew she found him charming. He bore a square jawline and a lean muscular build for his unusually tall frame. Being nearly six-foot-four, Colin appeared disproportionate around her only five-foot-tall frame.

Isabella's sophistication and allure radiated even in this moment of annoyance. He felt lucky to call her his, but he also felt obligated.

The Garcias were an old bloodline family originally from The Island, not The City. During the day, Isabella operated an impressive nonprofit organization providing meals and housing for the less fortunate. Originally, Isabella trained as a surgeon at The University but gave up a life of a practicing physician to devote herself entirely to her nonprofit.

Colin and Isabella met at a campaign event during his first election. At that time, The City faced issues with unstable work opportunities and many families didn't have enough resources. He addressed this issue in his platform and Isabella offered her expertise and advice. If Isabella wasn't a Garcia, Colin's father would have instantaneously approved of her. The feud between the Garcias and O'Connors ignited during Colin's youth, and this scandalous union sparked Colin's initial intrigue.

Isabella was a great companion; they cared about similar issues, were passionate about their careers, and supported one another. Her busyness left Colin opportunities to pursue his own hobbies without her, which he enjoyed and appreciated. As a couple, Isabella and Colin made sense.

She leaned over the couch and kissed his neck. Her warm lips pressed softly against his skin. Colin pulled her close, kissing her back. Isabella unbuttoned his shirt, grazing her lips against his chest.

Predictable.

They made love the way they always did—very routine—but got the job done. The two were asleep in bed before finishing the glass of wine she poured them.

***

Colin's alarm abruptly woke him.

He rolled over and looked at his device before quietly leaving the bed, putting on his gym shorts and lacing up his running shoes.

Colin started his mornings at 4:45 with a jog up The Hill. This cleared his mind before starting the day. By the time he made it back to the townhouse, Isabella was still asleep. He rinsed off, dressed for the day, and headed to the kitchen. Colin cooked breakfast as she emerged downstairs.

"I'm not sure when I'll be back. What are you up to today, darling?" he asked.

Isabella gripped her coffee mug tightly without giving away any emotion in her eyes.

"I'm flying to The Island for the rest of the weekend. I'm helping Mom through her doctor appointments. It's on the calendar," she answered with a lighthearted laugh.

Isabella kept a joint digital calendar on the refrigerator in an attempt to organize their busy schedules. To her dismay, Colin never added anything, let alone bothered checking it, and Kathleen never uploaded his schedule either. At first, this drove Isabella insane, but eventually, it grew into an inside joke.

"Well," Colin said, walking over and kissing her forehead, "have a safe flight and let me know when you're there safely."

"I will," she said, smiling up at him.

Colin grabbed the rest of his things, opened the door, and headed toward the garage.

"Colin," she called out to him.

He looked back at her, eyebrows raised.

"I love you."

He smiled and nodded.

Chapter 3
Julie

February 1st, 41 A.R.

The sun shone brightly against Julie's face, as arriving at the lab first required an early start. She had minute datasets waiting for her and finishing touches to complete before presenting to COLI*GO's Board of Directors. Julie looked down at her device and unsurprisingly saw another nagging message from Becker.

Stop micromanaging me, Becker.

The device screens in the lab came to life after scanning Julie's thumbprint. Another simulation of the antidote appeared. The simulation danced around the screen, numbers and letters filling the space in an erratic way.

After what felt like an eternity, the simulation stopped, and results appeared. Julie copied them into the final slide of her presentation and signed off before entering the hallway.

"Excuse me, miss, you dropped this," a gruff voice behind her echoed.

Julie looked up, frazzled by another person's presence. An intimidatingly tall man in a nicely fitted suit faced her. He was handsome, his hair kept neat but stylish, and a small bit of stubble crossed his jawline. His eyes were a sharp steel blue, almost gray, and the intensity of his stare intrigued her. She approached him slowly. His warm fingertips lightly touched hers as she took her printed data results from him.

This man appeared familiar, but she couldn't quite place him. His stance was friendly but stiff as curiosity seeped through Julie's mind like spilled coffee on a paper towel. He smiled at her, his eyes wandering from her hand to meet her gaze. Curiosity consumed him, too.

Julie was an attractive young woman, but hours in the lab over the last few months wore her ragged. Her hair was a disaster, haphazardly thrown into a bun, and her exposed freckles popped off her pale skin from little time spent outside. Flush spread across her face as she glanced down at her old, oversized University sweatshirt and loose, ripped jeans. Not the impression any single young woman wanted to showcase. Despite her appearance, she sensed an interest and intrigue from this strange man.

"Thank you," she responded as the redness slowly faded from her cheeks.

His eyes lingered on the results on the page, half in her hands and half in his, before letting go.

"Are you presenting to COLI*GO?" he asked, his stare remaining intense.

"Yes, later today."

"Good luck," he said with a small grin across his face before walking past her.

Julie watched him stroll down the hallway, briefcase in hand. They were alone in the building as far as she could tell, and the sound of his shoes against the linoleum floors clicked so loudly it was almost deafening.

***

Her heart raced uncontrollably in her chest as she reread the briefing document from Becker.

Julie's classmates surrounded her in the cold hallway. They all wore the same nervous twitch and identical look of fear mixed with anticipation. She reread Becker's message and traced her finger across the screen. The image of the mysterious man she encountered earlier stared back at her. He looked younger in this photograph, a little more charismatic compared to his tense demeanor. But still handsome.

Colin O'Connor (The Governor)—focus on benefits to society

The Supreme—focus on logic

Marta McKenna (CFO)—focus on the return on investment

Martin Borges (Head of Research and Development)—focus on your science acumen and methodology

Celine O'Connor (CEO)—focus on marketability

Julie looked away from her device and toward Mick. Mick appeared underprepared with a large cardboard box hastily closed with duct tape. Julie believed in him, regardless of not knowing his research, and his frazzled demeanor made her affectionately smile.

"Julie Walsh, you're next."

A well-polished and sharply dressed android looked down at her. She was tall and lean, with pale lilac-colored scales and soft ivory hair tied neatly in a bun. Julie followed the android down the hallway to a quiet room. The Board of Directors were concentrating on their devices, scribbling feverishly with stylists in hand, still engaged from the previous presenter.

Julie cleared her throat and The Supreme and Colin O'Connor looked up at her.

Colin gave her a small smile and nod, a warm and comforting gesture she hadn't expected in comparison to their intense encounter earlier.

"I'm Julie Walsh." She handed each a small drive with preliminary data and her presentation. "Today, I'll speak on the possibility of an antidote that could change the human brain as we know it."

The air in the room grew still and heavy in silence. The Supreme glanced curiously at Julie, while Celine O'Connor's eyes widened. Martin Borges eagerly rested his chin in his hand, and Marta McKenna cocked her head to the side. Colin leaned back curiously. His hesitation oddly pleased Julie.

"COLI*GO develops honorable innovations in areas of biotech and healthcare, from top-of-the-line oncology treatments to cures for autoimmune diseases. Your researchers edit DNA and regenerate human cells with ease. These strides not only help society but also advance us. One area COLI*GO hasn't ventured into yet is the human brain. Neurological diseases like dementia and Alzheimer's devastate millions of humans and happen unpredictably."

Everyone continued looking at her.

I should listen to Becker and not overpromise and under-deliver.

For the first time in years, Julie recognized a familiar feeling in her gut. Her science and data were strong. She believed in herself and her research.

"There's even potential to treat incredibly complex mental and psychological illnesses with the antidote." Julie pulled her simulation up on the screen.

The human neurological system appeared, and she zoomed in on the brain. In the simulation, the neurons attached the antidote molecule to a branch-like structure in control of collecting information from other neurons, the dendrites. After attaching, the cells were guided from one neurotransmitter to another. The antidote learned from the healthy cells by copying them, then replaced the mutated cells with ease. The antidote repeated this process until the unhealthy, mutated cells no longer remained. She played a few different simulations on the screen representing Alzheimer's, Parkinson's, and bipolar disorder.

At first, no one said a word. Julie's foot tapped lightly against the floor.

"This is magnificent," Martin said, pulling his glasses off his face.

Julie let out a large sigh she didn't realize she kept captive. His praise brought a lightness to her chest.

"Imagine the number of indications for this pharmaceutical," Marta responded, scanning through the presentation on her device. "This is biohacking at its finest."

Julie grinned from ear to ear.

"But the brain is tricky, and we don't know everything about it," Celine answered. She pushed a strand of glossy brown hair behind her ear, leaning over the table to enlarge her presence. All the executives could see her from this angle.

"It is, but this could be an opportunity of a lifetime."

Those words came unexpectedly from Colin. Throughout her presentation, the governor remained perplexed and worried.

"I'm not convinced quite yet, Governor," The Supreme hissed.

The rest of The Board leaned back into their seats. As an android, The Supreme held significant knowledge in her processor. Her sole purpose was to ensure androids weren't oppressed by humans, and as the only android in the room, her statement weighed Julie down.

"Well," Julie said, scrambling at her device, "I've run thousands of simulations and took into account different molecular compounds. But we won't know until testing the antidote in a living brain."

"At this stage of development, we can't test on humans," The Supreme said, laying down her device with force. "Why are you so passionate about this molecule? Help me understand, human, for I can't feel the way you do." A hint of sarcasm lingered in the air.

But I could make you. Julie thought back to Jones.

The Supreme's scales sharply engaged, the amber tones rapidly shimmering. The drastic change made everyone pause and look at her.

"Now, there's no need to be hostile." Martin rolled his eyes.

The Board bickered with one another at Martin's comment, and Julie felt very small in the room with these rich, intelligent, and powerful beings.

"My mother." Julie's words came in a whisper.

No one heard her at first as fingers waved in the air at one another. Martin pointed to Julie's graphs, and Celine droned on about dangerous risks. Julie looked in Colin's direction. He remained silent. His powerful gaze held hers, his eyes narrowing as if he were about to devour her alive.

"My mother!" Julie raised her voice loudly this time.

The executives murmured softly before silence pulsated around the room.

"Excuse me?" The Supreme asked into the tense room.

"You asked why I'm passionate about my research. It's because of my mother. She killed herself after suffering from depression and an unmanageable form of dementia. I never want anyone to lose their mother because of those demons, to suffer from the amount of grief and loss at a young age. I never want anyone to suffer like that ever again." Julie felt tears forming in her eyes.

"It won't be easy, and I'm still unconvinced of the proposed antidote's effectiveness but," The Supreme responded, her eyes glancing back and forth across the room, "I am convinced you'd move mountains and will never take 'no' for an answer. I like that tenacity about you. I bid on your pitch."

Martin's eyes widened, and his voice followed The Supreme's. "I also bid on you."

"As do I," Marta echoed.

"I also bid on you," Celine said quietly, looking down, her eyes avoiding Julie's.

"It's unanimous then. Congratulations, Miss Walsh," the governor said, standing up from his seat.

The tension in her body released as she approached the others. After years of her life dedicated to this research, Julie would join the ranks of COLI*GO after graduation. And so would her antidote. The next few moments whirled by as Marta discussed putting together an offer package. Martin awkwardly congratulated her again before Colin held out his hand to shake hers.

He escorted her out of the room swiftly and gracefully, closing the door behind them. Once they were in the hallway, he placed his hand on her shoulder.

"We need innovators like you at COLI*GO, but please be careful." The governor's cool eyes looked lost in hers. His hand slid down her arm, lingering a moment too long.

Why would he warn me like this? she wondered.

Before she mustered up the courage to ask him, he let go and turned away, closing the door behind him.

Chapter 4
Mick

February 1st, 41 A.R.

"Wait a minute," The Supreme said, chasing after Mick down the long hallway.

Mick didn't slow down. He was angry, hurt, and afraid. He risked everything coming to The University, burned every bridge with his family in the process. All for nothing. An overwhelming feeling to punch the wall vibrated in his normally docile mind.

"I said stop!" The Supreme yelled. Her tone and the loudness of her words reverberating down the hallway made Mick pause. He turned around and faced her.

The Supreme was terrifying. She stood at six feet tall with dark scaly features and bright green eyes. Her eyes were so round and large that Mick felt like she was reading his mind. The locks in her hair intertwined together, set back in a polished bun. Everything about The Supreme symbolized power.

She approached him slowly, aware that deep down, he was enraged. A human might not recognize he was moments away from hurling a punch, but an android knew better.

"About what?" Mick asked.

"Your theory and research on time travel."

Mick spent the last few years working with Jones on perfecting the theory of time travel. He proved the concept as a reality by using human blood. Blood was a surprisingly complex component, but Mick studied the proteins contained within the cells and how they stored so much more than scientists had ever imagined. This research was his ticket to The University. He thought it would be his ticket to COLI*GO, too.

He thought back to what happened in the room he rushed out of. Mick spent hours and hours in the lab understanding how the human body moved from one dimension to another. The driving mechanism was blood. With help from Jones, he was so close to the solution. Even Becker encouraged him. Thinking back, Mick wasn't sure Becker completely understood the human tendencies of impulsiveness, selfishness, greed, and irresponsibility.

The Board of Directors was right on that: Time travel in the wrong hands posed a dangerous threat. Mick argued back that in the right hands, or in the hands of impartial beings like androids, time travel could help society.

"Have you lost your goddamn mind? I thought this had been proposed as exploratory travel in other dimensions, such as space," Martin had yelled after Mick introduced himself and his research.

"Absolutely not. This will hurt more people, cause war and instability," the governor had said, pounding his fist on the table.

Mick's pitch didn't even last five minutes. He barely convinced the executives to let him show off his device. He remembered slowly pulling out his hard work from a trashed cardboard box he carried around with him almost everywhere. The Board of Directors were horrified and disgusted by him. He could see it in their eyes.

Then the governor demanded he leave the room immediately and never speak of his discovery to anyone, a threat to call in his sponsor at The University to discuss the matter further. His voice boomed so loudly, so powerfully.

Now, The Supreme chased him down the hall, requesting they discuss his research in private.

"I know your research is important. It's something humans are afraid of because they can't control it. But that's why there are beings like me," The Supreme said with a grin. "I want to hire you as a consultant. I'll pay you and provide you with a place to live and conduct your research. But there will be conditions."

"Conditions?" Mick asked.

The Supreme pulled him into another room and sat at a desk. Mick took her lead and sat across from her.

"Yes," she said, "you'll get a budget to manage. You'll get a salary for whatever else you need money for. I'll secure an apartment for you over east of The City in The Harbor. Far enough away but close enough. You can't discuss the nature of your research or work with anyone. No one from COLI*GO can know I hired you. You'll officially consult for Enterprise Holdings, Inc., which Celine and I operate."

"Celine O'Connor?" Mick asked, noting Celine viscerally hated his pitch moments earlier.

"Let me handle Celine," The Supreme said and grabbed Mick's hands. He looked up into her eyes. "The most important thing is, you must live alone and work on this alone."

Her eyes were hollow, but Mick knew she scanned his body, evaluating what his facial expressions truly meant.

"I can't honestly agree to that," Mick said, instantly thinking about Jones.

The Supreme leaned back in her chair.

"The truth is, there is an android that I am…" Mick started, "friends with. He helped me with my research until recently. His name is Jones. He's pursuing other career interests in the police academy, but I can't leave him."

The Supreme looked at him with cold eyes that softened slightly at this knowledge.

"Of course. I knew there was something else behind how terrifyingly accurate and brilliant this research was."

Mick felt his embarrassment rise back up in his neck and creep onto his face. The Supreme was correct in her assessment; he wouldn't be where he was today without Jones.

The Supreme remained quiet for a moment, and Mick closed his eyes. Everything crumbled around him at that moment. He wasn't sure where he'd go from here if he graduated from The University without a job. He couldn't go back to The Countryside and live with his family. His father made that clear: *Never show your face around here again.* And he'd lose Jones regardless.

Mick loved Jones. Jones couldn't support them both on a police detective's salary. And even then, Jones wouldn't graduate for another two years. *What would we do until then?*

"I'll allow it," The Supreme said while watching his face. "I need his information. I won't be contacting him, and you mustn't tell him who exactly you're consulting for. But I need to keep tabs on him. This needs to be as secret as possible. Do you understand?"

Relief flooded Mick's body. He couldn't control himself and nodded as he stood up to hug The Supreme. She was rigid in his arms but embraced the gesture.

"When do you think you could start?"

"Right after graduation. I mean, I'll still work on the research now during my last semester."

"I'll set you up sooner," The Supreme said, getting up out of her seat. "I will have my assistant be in touch with you in the next couple of days."

"Okay."

The Supreme reached down to the cardboard box.

"I'm going to take this with me. I need some kind of," she said before pausing and looking Mick straight in the eye, "insurance you wouldn't bail or that you don't take this seriously."

"But it's the only one I have," Mick stuttered.

"Well, then next time you might plan better," she said with a smirk. "It will be safe with me. I promise."

Mick believed The Supreme wouldn't defy her word, but he wasn't sure if he trusted her completely with the device either. Regardless, he nodded in acknowledgment. She couldn't use it herself. The only flaw in his research so far—androids don't have blood and therefore can't travel time.

But The Supreme offered him a once-in-a-lifetime opportunity. He couldn't mess this up. He wondered how to lie to Jones, who'd always been curious in nature. Most androids were passive, less unique than his partner. Mick often thought of Jones as a human in disguise or a weird species COLI*GO grew in a lab somewhere. One that escaped.

The Supreme left the room without saying goodbye, and Mick sat back for a few minutes, thinking. In this time alone, the shadows from the sun shifted into the room, and he needed to head back before anyone worried about him.

Walking home, Julie crossed Mick's mind. He watched earlier in the day as Julie was escorted out of the lecture hall by a different android. Her research was bid on.

Mick wasn't surprised but still envious. Sure, she didn't have an easy childhood, but Julie still had a family that loved her. She never fully knew what it was like to miss a meal unless it was by choice. What it meant to love another who didn't fully understand what it meant to feel love wholly.

Shame followed his thoughts. Julie would do anything for him, always supported him. She'd be genuinely happy for him with an opportunity to continue researching time travel if he told her. But he couldn't.

Damn these secrets. Why is life so full of secrets anyways?

Secrets from Jones, secrets from Julie, secrets from his uncle Jeb. Mick practiced his poker face the rest of the way home. He'd continue hiding his liabilities from others. He knew already more would manifest in the future.

Chapter 5
The Governor

February 1st, 41 A.R.

"How were the interview candidates?" Isabella asked Colin.

Colin observed Isabella as her image emulated through the screen on his device. Behind her, he could see the ocean waves crashing along the shallow beachline through the window. The winter gray and blue colors of the water looked oddly enticing to him, reminding him of his own family's estate at The Oceanside.

"They were great. There were barely any disappointments, and we made some tough choices. We couldn't select as many as we would have liked."

Isabella smiled wide. "The youth, so smart and so creative. Remember when we were that age?" she asked with a laugh. Colin couldn't help but chuckle, too.

"Maybe you were. I was busy learning to negotiate and write up legislative documents for my father." Colin sighed.

Growing up was nothing short of abnormal for Colin. His childhood wasn't typical with his father; he was the governor back then, and his sister was the apple of his eye. When his father became sick, Colin was a young man but old enough to hold down the fort. The public couldn't know the truth, so he took on as much of his father's work as possible.

Isabella took a sip from her wine glass. "Were there any proposals that particularly stood out? I promise I won't tell."

"Well, there was one in particular you might find interesting with your medical background. This young woman thinks she can treat illnesses stemming from the brain through an antidote," Colin started explaining.

He rattled off a high-level overview from Julie's executive summary. Isabella's eyes grew with intrigue. She placed her wine glass down and concentrated on Colin.

"She was incredibly brilliant, and her research is rock solid. But she was memorable because of her passion and drive. She was enticing."

Colin instantly thought back to Julie Walsh's full report. He read the whole thing, not only the executive summary. Simply the way Julie wrote her proposal captivated and mesmerized him. He hadn't paid much attention to the young, skittish gentleman who came in after her, pitching something with cleaner energy alternatives to wind turbines. He thought about his father—how Julie's antidote might have saved his father if it really worked.

"Enticing? Wow, that sounds intense. Maybe a bit of a liability though? If she is . . . unpredictable?" Isabella asked him, eyebrows raised.

Colin instantly regretted using the word enticing. Isabella's jealousy annoyed him immensely. She'd always been this way even when it came to Kathleen. The problem festered a while ago, but Colin refused to stand down. Kathleen worked not only on his campaign but also as his trusted confidant. And Kathleen was happily married to her partner for almost a decade.

"She's young. Nothing that The Supreme or Celine won't be able to handle. You know I'm not too involved except for my duties as a board member and to make sure that the private and public sector play nicely," Colin said, hoping his words calmed Isabella's nerves. The last thing Colin needed was Isabella spiraling in a fit and insisting he join her on The Island.

While The Island was lovely, he didn't have the time; legislature for a clean water initiative was forthcoming.

"That's true. I remember when I was that age. Nothing could stand in my way!" Her shoulders relaxed as she spoke.

"And clearly nothing ever did," Colin responded, laughing as the mood shifted.

Colin often pondered about what their life together would be like in a more permanent situation. If they married. They'd spent nearly a decade together, but the tensions between their old bloodline families prevented the rush or desire to officially wed. The public didn't mind; they adored the couple.

"I need to head to bed. My mother has her appointments tomorrow, and I don't want to be too tired," Isabella said with a yawn.

"Goodnight, darling."

"Goodnight!" she said before disappearing from the screen. Darkness emerged across Colin's device. He pushed the device aside and lay on the couch. His mind lingered back to Julie's antidote. There were so many issues in society stemming from a lack of treatment for neurological and psychological disorders.

How wonderful it'd be if we helped save people in these conditions? If we provide a solution to one of the biggest public health issues?

Colin didn't doubt how agitating Julie Walsh could be to work with based on meeting her earlier that morning. She looked completely different in the lab than she did in front of The Board of Directors. Julie cleaned up nicely, but for some reason, he preferred how raw and authentic she appeared when dressed down.

He enjoyed observing her body language. She stood very confidently once capturing their attention, but the moment hesitation shifted in the room, she retreated. The young woman had been nervous the whole time. Celine would need to teach Julie to use her voice and be heard without sounding demeaning or indecisive. Self-doubt would eat her alive in the halls of COLI*GO if she wasn't careful. But he believed in the curious and naïve creature. And her long, elegant neck exposed with her hair in that messy bun . . . He imagined exploring every inch of her with his lips and fingers while engaged in that image.

Colin stood up and shook his head. *I have a beautiful, uncomplicated woman. Isabella was right to feel jealous earlier; something about Julie does enamor me.*

He didn't doubt that Julie Walsh would cause him trouble.

After taking a moment to himself, Colin headed toward the stairs. He walked down into the kitchen, noticing the light on. His pace slowed, and he peered through the doorway.

"Hello, friend." The dark shadowed figure sitting on the edge of the countertop egged him on. His shoulders tensed, knowing who loomed in the dark corners of his home, taunting him.

"Hello," Colin replied curtly, continuing his journey into the kitchen.

"Been a while," It said in a deep voice.

"Yes, you're right about that." Colin approached the refrigerator and pulled out a beer. The top cracked off in his hands, and he handed the beverage over to It. They clinked their glasses together, taking equally long swigs.

"I won't stay long. I just wanted to stop by." It chuckled.

Now wasn't the best time for It to make an unscheduled visit. But It was never polite or cared about timing, and the two hadn't seen one another in a very long time. There was a small part of Colin that missed his friend, no matter how competitive they were amongst one another.

"Well, stay a bit. Have a beer or two with me," Colin said with a mischievous grin.

"Okay then," It replied without a pause. "I think I will."

PART THREE

Two Years Later

"Everything you can imagine is real."
-Pablo Picasso

Chapter 6
Julie

January 28th, 43 A.R.

The COLI*GO company headquarters housed hundreds of scientists, engineers, business executives, and entrepreneurs. Humans and androids puttered in and out of labs, conference rooms, and workstations within the massive glass skyscraper. Working for COLI*GO was an honor.

Two years passed since Julie presented her pitch to The Board of Directors. COLI*GO hesitated in moving the antidote forward in testing and instead placed Julie on exploring other indications within rare neurological diseases for an already approved drug, COL2120. The "COL" identified the drug belonged to COLI*GO, while the number afterward was assigned as a random unique identifier. All drugs were named this way, making it easier for the company to track its assets.

In her short tenure, Julie fell into COLI*GO's corporate culture with unfortunate ease. Required hours lasted from eight to five, but in order to climb the ladder, Julie let COLI*GO consume her. There were happy hour networking events in The Port district among other outings and activities. Often, Julie stumbled home late into the evening, tempting her body with only a few hours of sleep. Colleagues rarely spent time outside these walls, spending too much time with one another. Julie spent too much time with Peter Schneider. He was her first serious boyfriend, having met Julie while working on the COL2120 asset together.

But moving up remained Julie's top priority. Especially because she wanted off the COL2120 project and the ability to work on the antidote. Her extra hours and dedication paid off; a month ago, she discovered a new indication for COL2120 in multiple sclerosis. Martin invited her to the weekly "new innovations" meeting, giving her access to two very different mentors: Celine O'Connor and The Supreme.

Julie's obsession with perfection and success didn't surprise either Mick or Jones, but it did surprise her father and sister Becky. Julie couldn't dedicate as much time to family dinners and weekend outings, spending nearly all her free time in COLI*GO's state-of-the-art lab. She swiped her badge at six thirty each morning and didn't return home until eight or nine at night. Becky threw mention of their mother to guilt Julie, and they hadn't spoken since.

At least she still had Jones and Mick. Even with their equally busy schedules, they always reserved Fridays for one another. Normally she'd head over from The River to The Harbor on the subway to meet Jones at their apartment. Together, they'd walk down to the waterfront and people-watch. Jones admired the boats and yachts sprinkled across the harbor in the water before Mick joined them. Then the three typically walked to a bar around the corner and Julie always ended up awake the next morning in their guest bedroom before returning home to her studio apartment in The Bay.

Living anywhere in The City was expensive, but nothing compared to The Hill's price tag. She wished she lived in The Hill. Her commute from The Bay wreaked havoc on her shoes. Each morning, Julie walked from The Bay, up the infamous hill that The Hill was named after, to catch the subway to COLI*GO headquarters. As the most historic part of The City, The Hill portrayed a fairy tale aesthetic with rich brick brownstone townhomes and charming cobblestone roads. She admired the personality of the neighborhood, but getting property there required sums of cash or a connection with old bloodline families. But Julie didn't mind her small open studio in The Bay. At barely four hundred square feet, the outside of the building consisted of limestone, and the inside remained sleek and modern. Every appliance was efficient, and the contrast of dark and light colors signified The Bay; while a desirable location, it didn't have the same essence of class as The Hill.

Mick and Jones never thought about social discrepancy in The Harbor. The Harbor lived in its own little world across the water and portrayed an authentic, artsy vibe. The neighborhood was thrifty and fun, providing picturesque sunrises each morning soaked across The City's skyline.

Julie looked at the time on her device. She was still hours away from seeing Jones and Mick but smiled as she buttoned up her lab coat, stained and ruined from earlier in the morning. The markings proudly displayed themselves as a badge of honor.

"Want to go to The Port after work for a drink?" Peter asked, coming up from behind her. His hand lingered at the back pocket of Julie's coat. She moved her body away, uninterested in public displays of affection. That wasn't her style.

"I have my weekly plans with Mick and Jones," Julie responded but didn't invite him to join. Pushing Peter aside felt wrong, but Julie couldn't place her finger on why she kept doing so.

There was something about the adorable scientist that didn't settle right in her heart.

Maybe I'm not built for love. Maybe I don't deserve it, she thought as Peter frowned. He moved away from her and headed back to his own desk.

Julie's device pinged. A message from Celine O'Connor:

Meet me in my office at 4:30.

Her heart raced loudly, and her hands grew clammy. The rest of the day continued like a blur, her mind ping-ponging from one task to the next.

What does Celine want to meet with me about?

Celine only invested in a single one-on-one meeting with Julie every month, far less than the norm for mentors at COLI*GO. On the other hand, Julie met with The Supreme nearly every week. To calm her nerves, Julie walked around the building.

She loved the design of the COLI*GO building. Her mother had been an architect before falling ill, and her protégée designed the COLI*GO headquarters. The small elements in the building reminded her of her mother.

The open concept lobby on the first floor had various security checkpoints and a large fountain in the middle. The second through tenth floors housed accounting and finance departments, and legal departments sat on floors ten through twenty. Marketing, product development, and commercial strategy colleagues rotated up the next thirty floors. Scientists like Julie stayed on floors fifty to one hundred within various laboratories, desks, huddle rooms, and offices. Many theorized the labs were so high up in the building to make leaving inconvenient.

The top floor, fondly nicknamed "the observatory," consisted of large meeting spaces with floor-to-ceiling windows. The company's large events and shareholder meetings occurred there. The views from the top were breathtaking, exposing the full skyline of The City and the river below.

The 101st floor, right below the observatory, was the most important. Offices of vice president and higher titles were located there. This included a space for each member of The Board of Directors.

The journey to the top took time.

When Julie finally arrived, an android greeted her from behind a sleek white desk. Julie handed over her identification badge and took a seat. Julie followed the rules without hesitation due to muscle memory. She pulled out her device, reading over new clinical data notes before meeting with Celine.

A disruptive slam of The Supreme's heavy glass office door sounded from down the hall, and Julie jumped to the edge of her seat. Her ears perked up instantly.

"Colin, let's talk about it." The low and curt voice of The Supreme rang from her office.

"I'm not doing that, I've already told you. Good luck." Julie heard Colin's deep voice in response.

His massive presence came into view. Julie only ran into the governor a few times in passing over the last two years. They hadn't spoken one-on-one since his warning at The University. He stormed out of The Supreme's office and purposefully slammed the door behind him. Infuriation and agitation fluttered across his brow. Julie only knew him in charismatic, allusive gestures. This was a new look for him; one Julie wasn't sure she liked.

Colin stopped in his tracks once he saw her waiting in the lobby area.

"Hello, Governor," Julie said, breaking the silence.

He didn't respond right away, and a long awkward moment passed between them.

Has he forgotten who I am? she wondered, rationalizing in her mind that the governor was a busy man. He met hundreds of people and androids within a given week.

"Hello, Miss Walsh," Colin responded, approaching her slowly.

Julie stood and shook his hand. She didn't care he hadn't addressed her formally as Doctor; she was shocked he remembered her at all.

"How is the antidote coming along?"

Julie instantly burst into a small laugh. Colin's head tilted back, surprised by her response to his question.

"It's officially on hold due to budgetary purposes. But unofficially," Julie said, peering quickly around the lobby to confirm they were alone, "I'm specifying the molecule a bit more in my spare time."

A smirk grew across the governor's face, and his eyes softened from the broody anger of before. He seemed amused by her brazen honesty and fascinated by her trust in him.

"So, this is where you spend your weekends?" he asked in a lower tone, his eyes focusing intently on hers.

While Colin wasn't a scientist, Julie respected his opinion. He was a successful politician and businessman, one of the few in The Capitol Building without any scandals. She'd never heard anyone speak unkindly of him, even the news and media.

How can someone be so put together all the time?

Julie hesitantly broke their stare. She took a risk by telling him she utilized lab resources on the weekends for an off-the-books project, but there was something drawing her in to him.

She nodded at him.

"Good to know you're here on weekends," he said and adjusted his suit jacket before checking his device. "If you'll excuse me, I have to get going. It was an unexpected pleasure running into you, Miss Walsh."

He approached the elevator, and for a moment, Julie considered the impact of confiding in a man like him. But he turned around and smiled at her before crossing the threshold of the elevator car.

His endearing smile showcased warmth from the corners of his lips.

Not a mistake.

"Dr. Walsh, Celine is ready to see you," the android said from behind the receptionist desk, pulling Julie away from the moment.

Julie and the receptionist walked down the hallway, past The Supreme's closed office door. Once they reached the end, the android nodded and headed back to the lobby.

Celine's office impressed Julie each time she entered it. The floor-to-ceiling windows overlooked the water below and let in such an illuminating amount of light. The color of today's sunset bounced off the water, shifting from shades of purple to deep pink hues.

The furniture inside was minimal—a chrome desk and chair sat in one corner and a hard-white leather sofa with two matching armchairs sat on the other side. Celine remained at her desk, taking in the unobstructed view of the outside.

She was a striking woman, elegant and poised with deep chestnut hair fashioned in a long stylish bob. But Celine O'Connor was more than just a lovely face; she was intelligent and witty. COLI*GO wouldn't exist without her grit and passion.

"Julie, thank you for taking time to meet with me today," Celine said. "Take a seat." She gestured to the sofa.

Julie obeyed as Celine joined her on the other end.

"I hear you're making great headway on COL2120. But after your breakthrough for MS, you've seemed a bit distracted."

Julie took a deep breath as the jab harshly hit her. She spent more time on COL2120 than her teammates, clocked in more hours.

"To be fair, I think most of the research team looks forward to moving on from COL2120 to investigate pipeline assets," Julie stated. "COL2120 is a fantastic drug candidate. It's trusted and tried. Perfecting it isn't easy because it's already so close to perfect."

Celine looked at Julie and smiled a small half-smile. She stood, walking to the wall of windows. Celine stayed there for a while as tension filled Julie's body. She now doubted her response.

"Would you not stop until the antidote was perfect, though?" Celine asked without turning back or looking at Julie. The silence penetrated the room.

"You're right," Julie admitted. "So, what should I do with COL2120 to get it ready for The Legislature's session hearing?"

"Talk to Product Development. Spend some time with your colleagues with non-science backgrounds. They'll have interesting, different perspectives. Get out of your comfort zone. We need COL2120 as perfect as possible for MS patients." Celine offered Julie an encouraging smile.

"Thank you. I'll set up some time with the commercial team. How quickly do we need to accelerate the timelines? I'll prioritize this over everything else."

"The clinical data is being presented to The Legislature in May, so April will do."

This wasn't a wish; it was a request disguised in the form of a challenge. The room remained quiet as Julie rose from her seat. Celine didn't have to tell Julie the meeting was over; she knew.

"Have a nice evening and a good weekend, Ms. O'Connor."

"Thank you, you too," Celine answered. "And make sure you close the door on your way out."

Julie nodded, doing exactly what she was told.

Chapter 7
Jones

April 25th, 43 A.R.

The lights dimmed over the audience. Jones couldn't find Julie and Mick through the darkness but knew they were out there: his two humans. The only ones in the world who would do anything for him. The small audience in the theater remained quiet for the police academy graduation ceremony. The commissioner called out Jones's name. He approached the podium and shook his hand. The commissioner was a skeleton of an android, having a withdrawn face so sunken in that he resembled a ghost. His scales were a pale platinum blue, adding to his unique creepiness and allure. He accepted his diploma and walked off the stage, joining his classmates lined up perfectly off to the side. The commissioner continued calling out the names of graduates.

Jones looked up into the crowd at the spectators, the lights finally back on. From this angle, he was close enough to scan the audience and locate Julie within seconds. His eye scanner dimmed a bit but recognized Mick right beside her. Once every name was called, the room went from hushed whispers to complete silence.

"The world isn't what we imagined, but it's getting there," the commissioner spoke into the microphone. "We envision a world without violence, a world without crime, impulses, and disputes. We may never see a day in our lifetimes of complete peace, but we strive for it. And until we do see that day, we need you, the newest graduating class, to provide sanity, shelter, and safety to our constituents. You'll help our great people and androids of The City and surrounding municipalities find a sense of comfort. Be the role models our citizens need. And with that, I welcome our governor for a few words before closing remarks from The Supreme."

The commissioner bowed his head and exited the stage. The

governor emerged from behind the curtains and stood at the lectern. His face illuminated the three-dimensional monitor out into the middle of the audience so everyone saw him clearly.

"Good afternoon, ladies, gentlemen, and androids of all varieties," Colin spoke clearly and solidly, his voice stretching across the room with a sense of authority.

Jones didn't know much about the governor other than what he saw on the news. His approval rating skyrocketed, not a surprise for a young, energetic, smart, and confident man. Colin O'Connor, at one point, was an underdog, driven to his position of power in his youth. But looking at the man on the stage, Jones noticed something a bit off about his smile. The emptiness that stared back. Humans were emotional creatures; androids were rational and logical. As an android, Jones was programmed to recognize these small details.

"Today is a great day. A day where we welcome 102 new android graduates of the police academy into our ranks to protect us." The governor's voice raised in enthusiasm as the audience cheered him on. "Decades ago, most held negative feelings toward the police force. I'm glad to say because of the hard work from your mentors and those detectives and sergeants before you, the perception is changing. But I ask you to remember that both reputation and trust are easy to lose. When you take your oaths today, remember you are part of the change. You will pass down a legacy to another future graduating class. Congratulations and best of luck!"

The room erupted loudly in applause, the loudest sound the audience made so far. The androids around Jones clapped their hands enthusiastically. Once the sound quieted down, The governor nodded to The Supreme as she took the stage.

"Class, congratulations! As the governor mentioned, you have a legacy to not only withhold but also make stronger," she said with a sense of ease. "I ask you to rise as we recite the oath."

As the highest-ranking android in The Constituency, The Supreme held the responsibility for swearing in the new police officers.

"On my honor, I will never betray my fellow androids or the humans of this great city. It is public trust I strive for. I will always hold myself and others accountable to the truth and to the law. I will maintain my processor to the highest ethical coding standards and thus uphold the values of humans and androids. And it is within that, I will serve."

The room remained quiet for a few moments after the androids completed the recitation of the oath. They held a moment of silence, remembering all those androids and humans before them who lost their lives in this line of duty. They remembered without hope, perseverance, and determination, people and androids wouldn't prosper.

The oath lingered like a salty dish in Jones's mouth. He swore to protect people and androids, but Jones wasn't a person, no matter how desperately he wished he was. His mind wasn't the same, and envy flowed through him. Julie helped him understand and experience feelings by reprogramming the microchip in his processor but only to 60 percent capacity. Not one hundred.

Do I understand and feel the most important emotions? Jones often wondered. He didn't know the answer. More than anything, Jones hoped he fully understood love. He believed he loved Mick but not in the way of infatuation. He suspected Mick would always love Jones more than Jones could ever love him.

The Supreme looked out into the audience and locked eyes briefly with Jones. He wondered how many feelings and emotions she truly understood. In school, he learned The Supreme was programmed to the maximum legal amount, just over 20 percent. Jones believed she understood much more, considering re-coding his own microchip hadn't taken much sleuthing and effort. He did worry the sergeants would discover Jones's secret, but he passed his exams and mastered his skills; rumors of random processor checks were just hearsay among cadets.

The sharpness of The Supreme's voice sliced through the room, interrupting his thoughts.

"We feel no pain; we are in more control of our actions compared to humans," she said. "But we must remember our responsibility as androids lies in protecting our fellow androids and humans surrounding us. Together, we'll preserve the foundation of our community."

The Supreme slowly walked away from the lectern as the audience clapped. After the rest of the pomp and circumstance, Jones finally met up with Julie and Mick outside. Julie rushed to him without any hesitation, throwing her arms around him in a large hug. She smelled softly of roses and lavender, her typical scent, her familiarity welcoming.

"Jones! I'm so proud of you!" Julie said.

Proud. Such a human emotion.

This was one Jones didn't feel or understand. Feeling and understanding were different concepts. Jones couldn't fathom why something one promised they'd do and fulfilling that promise would emote such a response.

"Thank you, Julie," Jones responded but looked directly at Mick.

Mick softly smiled at him. Their forbidden relationship defied logic. Julie started the catalyst between them, introducing the two their first year at The University. Jones recalled the party very distinctly because he remembered all moments in his life. He stored all his memories in his processor but preferred thinking of this particular one as a memory.

At the party, Mick observed Jones's scales with awe. They changed colors; vibrant emerald greens glowed in the dimly lit apartment basement. Seeing Mick stare at them with a sense of curiosity made Jones approach him. Mick's inappropriate stares weren't his fault. Mick grew up far outside The City, and there weren't many androids in The Countryside. Jones enjoyed being the object of curiosity to a human and associated the feeling to the equivalent of lust in humans.

Jones had kissed humans before, but Mick was different. From that night on, the two were inseparable. Humans and androids were forbidden by the rules of society to intertwine romantically. A formal relationship gave unfair advantages to both humans and androids. Androids consumed more information than humans. Many androids and humans didn't follow this law of relationships. They hid their relationships from the public. Kissing Mick at a private house party at The University was fine. Kissing Mick on the sidewalk outside was not. Without Julie reminding Mick of the ramifications Jones would face if they were discovered, they would have gotten caught.

But there was something nice about not having a spotlight on them all the time. They were friends to those around them, nothing more. Except in private, it was more, so much more.

"What do you want to do to celebrate?" Julie asked Jones. Another very human question but he liked the spirit of "celebration" and understood that feeling fondly.

"I'd like to dim down my processor for a bit," Jones admitted with a very straightforward look on his face.

"Let's go!" Julie said, linking her arms with Mick on one side and Jones on the other.

The Supreme nodded toward the group as they walked by. Jones noticed her gaze lingered a bit too long on Mick.

Does she know? No . . . she couldn't. How could she? Jones's least favorite emotion, panic, crept up his body. Julie let go of Jones's and Mick's arms and walked over to The Supreme.

"What are they talking about?" Jones asked Mick.

Mick sighed heavily, the way he always did when it came to Julie and anything associated with COLI*GO.

"Probably the damn drug she works on," Mick answered in a huff. COLI*GO caused mixed feelings for Mick after not getting a job offer out of school. But as far as Jones understood, Mick was happy most of the time with his current arrangement as a consultant. He still worked on time travel, looking for ways to make the invention compatible with androids. Jones offered himself as a test subject once Mick felt comfortable; he couldn't die unless his processor was permanently corrupted or shut down, which was difficult to accomplish. Like the brain, the processor slowed over time, even with updates. But androids expected their processors to last about ninety to one hundred years, a similar life expectancy of humans these days.

Jones moved his focus to the governor. Jones noted the posse of legislative aides, representatives, and media surrounding him. Colin smiled and pointed over to The Supreme often.

Why isn't she getting the same kind of attention? She is his counterpart after all. Jones continued watching the governor as he placed his hand on someone's shoulder and chuckled, how he smiled before speaking.

Julie walked away from The Supreme and back toward Mick and Jones. She laughed while Mick shook his head at her, his eyes lingering on The Supreme. Jones couldn't confirm The Supreme supported Mick's consulting projects, but he peered at his documents on more than one occasion.

The group headed back to The Harbor and visited their favorite establishment, a hole-in-the-wall joint with the same three bartenders on rotation. Julie, Mick, and Jones placed their identification cards on the bar, the way everyone paid for things. Decades ago, The Legislature eliminated credit and debit cards and replaced the system with personal identification cards. This eliminated the concept of debt and held all identifiable information, tracking citizens and their whereabouts.

The bartender scanned each card before handing them back, knowing them well enough he didn't bother asking them for their orders. Within a few moments, he was back and placed a dark rum concoction next to Jones, a gin and tonic beside Mick, and a vodka soda next to Julie.

The three smiled at one another, clinking glasses. They sipped their drinks slowly, knowing they'd head home after just one.

Chapter 8
The Governor

April 30th, 43 A.R.

Colin watched her bite into the apple. Her mouth moved and adjusted, her hand still holding the fruit in-between her fingertips.

Julie's eyes focused on the screen in front of her, the numbers rapidly populating the screen. The lab was lonely on the weekends, and she was alone. There weren't many others in the building minus a few other scientists, security, and Julie. And him.

COLI*GO valued weekends and time-off seriously. Employees needed special permissions for weekend access, and Colin wasn't surprised The Supreme granted Julie with it. The Supreme seemed equally as fascinated with the young scientist as Colin.

He leaned back in his chair and continued observing Julie through his screen. Receiving access to security cameras in the lab was easy; as the governor, he rarely received pushback. Most of his requests were granted with ease inside the walls of COLI*GO. In The Capitol Building, that wasn't always the case.

The Representatives of The People recently drafted legislation he and The Supreme didn't like. Joel Kennsington and the Humanizer sect of representatives always caused trouble. The Humanizers were a small group of legislators who continued oppressing androids, believing they didn't deserve the same rights as people. Their mindset drove Colin crazy; they reminded him of old-fashioned and backward times. He sided more with the Sympathizers, believing androids were equal citizens.

Colin knew the motion wouldn't pass but remained concerned about the Humanizers' noise. He and The Supreme met in secret, discussing how to eradicate the problem. The Supreme's stance on Joel Kennsington was much harsher than Colin's.

"Get rid of him," she had said.

It wasn't that simple, and Colin knew she was also aware of this fact. Joel's term lasted two more years before reelection. His district remained complicated, and a coup wouldn't be a viable option. Sitting in The Supreme's office at COLI*GO, they spent over an hour trying to devise a solution.

"What about you and It?" The Supreme had asked. Her gaze was intense, and her scales had flickered a gold color as she admired her reflection in the window.

"What about It?" Colin spat back.

It was non-negotiable. It was complicated. He was impulsive, intrusive, loud, obnoxious, angry, and selfish. It didn't care about anyone else but himself, similarly to The Supreme. Which is why he knew The Supreme brought up his name, why she liked him.

"We could make a deal if you and It find a creative way to put Joel Kennsington in his place," she had hinted, leaning back in her chair. This was also not very uncommon. The Representatives of The Androids called in favors from The Representatives of The People all the time. There were sympathizers on both sides.

"If The Representatives of The People wanted more spending for human children in public schools, I could make that happen," The Supreme said.

Colin hated how corruption was sometimes the only way. The Supreme continued pondering, while Colin had said nothing.

"Isn't Joel Kennsington very fond of his legislative aide? What's her name? Kendra?"

Joel Kennsington sleeping with his legislative aide wasn't a secret. Everyone knew, probably even Joel's wife. He was an arrogant man, overconfident and self-assured. The conceited man aggravated Colin to no end. He was appealing; Colin would give him that. The man won his district at a young age, similarly to Colin. Joel had a square jawline, broad shoulders, and a dangerous attractiveness to him. But when it came to power and influence, Joel faltered. He was loud but hardly strategic.

Colin found himself fond of Joel's legislative aide, Kendra Washington. Most aides were lost in the shuffle, and few stood out. Kendra's intelligence and persuasive writing techniques were the reason other representatives even bothered reading Joel's proposals.

She excelled at drafting legislation but was misguided by that brute.

"I don't want to hurt Kendra. This is between us and Joel," Colin had answered back then. He remembered The Supreme rolled her eyes and explained how deep down, Kendra was also a sympathizer to the Humanizers.

"How could she let that man sleep with her otherwise?" The Supreme had posed the question.

Her directness didn't make Colin flinch. The Supreme was always bold and harsh, and while he wasn't surprised at her insinuations, Colin was furious.

Does she always think everything gets to go her way? Colin remembered thinking before storming out of her office. At the time, he didn't care about the fuss and noise.

But then he noticed Julie. She had been waiting in the lobby for a meeting with his sister. In that moment, he took the young scientist in. Not much changed about her from when she pitched the antidote, and he wasn't surprised when she admitted to spending her weekends in the lab.

The Supreme spoke fondly of her to Colin in passing, bringing up Julie's name more than necessary. Reminding him.

Colin reread her report from The University after seeing her, thankful he kept a hard copy in the bottom drawer of his home study. The next day, he planned on telling Julie he'd help her get traction for the antidote, but he realized how preposterous that was. With no scientific background, he consumed the contagiousness of her passion.

Instead, Colin watched her from afar and said nothing of his new obsession. Julie symbolized the opposite of everything he normally felt drawn to. The Supreme wouldn't like it, neither would Celine.

Or Isabella.

Being observant from afar kept It out of this, too. He'd known It since childhood, their friendship strong but complicated. They understood each other's tendencies and mixing naïve Julie with It prickled Colin like a bad idea.

Colin craved control; he had zero room for impulsive tendencies. Or at least, zero room to give into them.

Another person entered the lab, drawing Colin away from

his thoughts.

He didn't recognize the young man standing behind Julie. Colin watched as he took a seat beside her. The man wore a COLI*GO lab coat, his tall and lanky frame awkward next to Julie. Then, the man swiveled Julie's chair around so that she faced him.

That's awfully bold of him.

Julie grinned, rolling her eyes. They were talking, but Colin couldn't hear them. Julie pointed to the display behind her, and the man's gaze lingered as he placed his hand on Julie's thigh, disappearing under her skirt. She welcomed his kiss.

Colin's eyes widened with curiosity before quickly clouding with annoyance. He'd watched her for months now, and she had always been alone. Julie's male companion shouldn't have bothered him because he knew very little about her. They had exchanged brief hallway conversations and nothing more.

Their intimate embrace lasted, and Colin couldn't look away even though he wanted to. Fingers rapidly typing, Colin checked the system. The name Dr. Peter Schneider appeared in the log of those who had entered the lab. He read his bio and title. According to his profile, Peter was a mid-level researcher in Julie's department.

Colin looked back at the screen. Their romantic embrace ended.

Who granted him access to the lab for off-hours? Colin wondered before quickly realizing he already knew the answer: The Supreme.

Colin pulled out his device and typed furiously to The Supreme:

Get me the votes for more public-school funding and move Peter Schneider to a different division. It and I will handle Joel.

After a painstakingly long moment, a message back appeared:

Done. But why Dr. Schneider?

Colin sighed. He acted rashly and impulsively, which was very out of character for him.

Thx. Those children need the funding. And Peter? He's infringing on one of your important assets. Take care of this, please.

He hit send.

***

"So, there's this woman, Kendra," Colin explained to It in the kitchen of the townhouse. It sat on the island, drinking his beer and patiently waiting for more information.

Colin pulled up Kendra's profile on his device.

"An attractive woman," It noted. "Can I sleep with her?"

"No," Colin answered, pulling his device sharply away.

"Why not? She's cute," It said, straining to look once more at her picture.

"Because that's not part of this," Colin said, taking a swig of his beer. He only drank beer with It. Something about the hoppy taste soothed him.

"Okay, but let me flirt with her, charm her, at least. I do get to talk to her, right?" It asked, smirking.

Spending the day spying on Julie hadn't calmed Colin's nerves. Especially as the unexpected jealousy consumed his mind. Colin was strung up tightly in stress the rest of the day, and It sensed this. It cynically liked when Colin was agitated and took advantage of his mood to poke and prod him.

Colin shook his head. "I don't want to argue. I don't even understand why you'd want to do that."

It pondered for a moment but said nothing.

"Let's concentrate on the resting place instead. We can figure out the other details later." Colin's eyes glanced sideways in response.

"Ah, yes! Been so long since we've done this, my friend, I nearly forgot how important that was to you," he said, taking another swig from his bottle.

It was correct, a very long time passed since they killed someone. Five years, a long time indeed. Colin wondered if five years constituted a coincidence, not a similarity or pattern, but something enticed him with never being caught.

"I'm thinking somewhere easily noticeable. Generate a lot of attention," Colin said.

It looked at him with an intensity Colin hadn't seen in a while before he tipped his beer bottle over, letting the glass rattle on the tabletop. Empty.

"Is she seeing someone we can pin this on?" It asked.

"Besides Joel? No, I don't think so. We don't want to pin this on him, just embarrass him," Colin noted, moving across the kitchen and pulling another beer out of the refrigerator. He popped the cap off and handed the bottle to It.

"I don't understand." It asked, his tone raising with intrigue.

"There are diplomats coming from another country. If her body is found at the airport when they arrive, he'll unravel and discredit him."

"What about the legislation you're worried about?" It asked.

"Kendra writes all of it. Joel isn't very good with words. How can she write the proposed bill if she's dead?"

"I like the way you think! You're very much the Colin I missed," It said, taking a swig of his fresh beer.

Colin smirked. On rare occasions, he liked the calculated preciseness, the drive; but sometimes, he hated those attributes of himself, too, especially feeling out of control.

"Should I stop by The Capitol Building after your meeting? Talk to her?" It asked.

Colin paused, leaning back on the kitchen counter, deep in thought.

"No," he decided. "I'll arrange invitations to the COL2120 approval celebration. You can meet her there."

"You don't like me in The Capitol Building, do you?" It pouted.

Colin didn't like It there. He kept his friend, this part of his life separate from his public persona.

"No one can connect us together; you know that," Colin answered.

It did know that.

"You should go," Colin said looking at the doorway. Colin picked up the second empty bottle in front of It.

"Boring plans with the lovely Isabella tonight, my friend?" It snickered, his large hands grasping his beer tighter.

"We live very different lives. What I enjoy and what you enjoy are two very different things."

But sometimes . . .

"Well," It said, interrupting him, "that couldn't be truer."

***

"I can't stand that fahking asshole," Kathleen said, rolling her eyes at Colin as he stood over her desk.

Colin enjoyed Kathleen's wild and abrasive spirit. They'd known one another almost their whole lives, and she remained by Colin's side when he first ran for governor. Growing up, her family worked for Colin's father and she was one of the few friends who didn't bully or pick on him. He often thought of Kathleen as the older sister he wished he had over Celine.

"Speak of the devil," she whispered.

Kathleen's eyes wandered, and Colin followed them. Joel and Kendra appeared at the other end of the hall. Kathleen smiled, and Colin kept his brooding look before offering a small smile.

"Representative Kennsington, how are yah?" Kathleen asked, emphasizing her City accent as Joel approached.

Joel liked Kathleen's accent, calling it the sound of "the hard-working people." Joel shook Kathleen's hand before kissing it.

"Wonderful, darling. How's life on this side of The Capitol Building?"

Kathleen bore an obnoxiously fake smile. "It's fine, same ol' same ol' if yah know what I mean."

Kendra remained silent, her eyes glued to her feet. Joel and Kendra signed in and logged their fingerprints on the security device before Colin brought them into his office. The meeting started awkwardly as Kendra sat in the corner of the room, hastily taking notes. Her fingers typed quickly and heatedly, the noise of her bracelet clanking against her metal device.

Thump, thump, thump.

Her bracelet was a beautiful sterling silver piece, shining brightly as if brand-new. Colin noted how she didn't miss a single thing with the speed of her typing.

"Kendra, the governor and I need to discuss a private matter," Joel said, leaning over.

Joel looked back at her. She put her things into her bag and stood.

"Ping me when you want me," she said quietly, not meeting Colin's gaze. Colin nodded as she exited the room, realizing how loud her presence had been while she was here. There were no sounds of quick fingers vigorously on the keyboard, no small intakes of breath when either man said something troublesome.

"I need the rest of the representatives to consider this legislation, Governor. I need your support," Joel said, edging closer to him. Colin felt his sticky, stale breath across his skin.

"That's not going to happen with some of the more radical thoughts you have," Colin responded carefully.

"Androids are too influential these days. They'll surpass us and take control if we aren't careful. And I hear they're doing wicked work at your sister's company. Something about a hybrid species of human-androids," Joel said with a blotchy face and squinted eyes. "We developed the androids; it's our responsibility to tame them."

Colin sat back in his chair.

The two men came from very different backgrounds. Joel wasn't from an old bloodline nor was he born into a family of politicians or public servants. He didn't know how to act appropriately as one. A man like Joel Kennsington didn't cool off and think about his words before saying them, but his erratic and flippant demeanor was partly why his constituents voted for him.

"Look," Colin said as he tapped his fingers along the mahogany of the desk, "I understand there should be swim lanes between humans and androids. But, Joel, are you listening to yourself? COLI*GO developing a hybrid species? You sound irrational, out of your mind, even. You'll cause tension with that approach. Let's tamper it a bit and find a solution." Colin leaned into the desk, his face inching closer to Joel's.

"You let your close relationship with The Supreme get in the way," a voice in the back of the room said. Both Colin and Joel looked up to find Kendra in the doorway.

He watched Joel snicker out of the corner of his eye. In this moment, Colin confirmed what he and It were planning to do to Kendra wasn't so evil after all. The Supreme was correct; she was a Humanizer in her core.

The room remained soundless for a few uncomfortable moments as their stand-off with one another intensified. Colin broke the silence with a chuckle.

"What would you know about my relationship with The

Supreme?" Colin asked Kendra, not even bothering with Joel. As far as Colin was concerned, Joel was no longer part of this conversation.

"You do everything together. I see you at events, which is understandable, but you chose to ride in the same vehicle as her and you're always chatting in the background. I bet she even knows you have a meeting with us today. Everything is too transparent."

Colin let Kendra's words sink into the room.

"I have my own schedule. I have my own agendas, my own policies to push through our government. But without partnership, we wouldn't have a collaborative government working toward the well-being of humans and androids alike. Instead, there'd be conflict. People would suffer. Is that a world we want to live in? I have an oath to humans. Are you saying I do not honor that oath? That I do not take it seriously? I assure you, Miss Washington, I take that very seriously."

Colin eyed her but let a small smile creep in through the corners of his mouth. He felt like a snake inviting her into the forest, promising to not strike. She stared at him with that look he craved: a fine line between intimidation and curiosity. Colin sensed from her flushed cheeks that he fascinated her, interested her.

"Now, Kendra, I think you've insulted the governor," Joel said almost too quickly. He scolded his pet to appease Colin, but Joel's words were meaningless: He liked what she had said.

Colin thrived on this art of observation, seeing the symbiotic relationships between two people play out like the words of a book. He excelled in this delicate dance. Kendra had a knack for it, too; her defiance attracted Joel, and she was well aware of that. Kendra's true desire wasn't Joel. She strived to climb the ladder in The Capitol Building. She wasn't the submissive, nervous woman she led everyone in The Legislature to believe. She played a part. Aligning herself with power would trump any loyalty to Joel. And in a room with Colin and Joel, the more powerful man was blatantly obvious.

"I'm sorry," Kendra said with a gulp. "I hope you can forgive me, Governor. I care very deeply about my constituents."

If I were to completely charm her, how would I respond? After a few moments of prickly silence, Colin knew.

"No insult taken at all. Being passionate about your constituents is admirable; it is . . . commanding," Colin responded, looking her directly into her eyes.

The meeting was over.

After the appropriate amount of time passed, Colin rose from his chair, and Joel quickly followed suit.

"Sir," Colin said, extending his hand. Joel shook it. Kendra rose from her seat, too. Colin shook her hand, extending the same level of respect to her as he had with Joel.

The three exited his office.

"Representative," Colin said, looking at Joel, "Kendra. There's a party at COLI*GO this Friday to celebrate the approval of COL2120 from the vote earlier this week. I'd like for you two to join."

"That would be fantastic, Governor. Kendra and I will be there," Joel answered.

"Please bring the Mrs. with you, Representative. It's been so long since I've seen her," Colin said as Joel walked through the doorway and into the hallway.

Joel turned his eyes toward Colin with an icy glare, and Colin lightly placed his hand on the small of Kendra's back, leading her out of the doorway. The two left down the hall, Kendra's heels echoing behind them.

Checkmate.

"Yah look like that meetin' went well. All smug and shit." Kathleen laughed, snapping her fingers at him.

"Joel is an idiot," Colin responded, joining her with a chuckle.

Chapter 9
Julie

May 4th, 43 A.R

The whole team watched from the office as The Legislature voted and approved COL2120 in multiple sclerosis. Julie found the concept odd; none of these politicians were scientists. But these were the rules, and this was the process. Now, it was time to celebrate before the team dispersed and moved on to other assets in COLI*GO's portfolio.

COLI*GO hosted grand affairs whenever a product was approved. It didn't matter if it was a new therapeutic technological device or the invention of some fancy vehicle. Julie wasn't sure how expensive these parties cost the company, but no one cared when they didn't need to place an identification card down to get a drink.

Peter looked over at Julie quietly. Things were still a bit awkward between them after they broke off their relationship. Upon completion of the COL2120 project, Peter would leave for an affiliate office in a different country. He asked her to move with him, and when she said no, she realized Peter actually loved her. Julie cared about him deeply but couldn't consider giving up her whole life for him.

"I can't do that, Peter," Julie had answered when he asked.

There were many reasons, but mostly, the antidote was here. She couldn't let Martin Borges give her research to someone else in a few years. That was hers. The other reason she couldn't leave: her father. Julie's heart ached at leaving him behind in The City even with her sister still here.

"Bring him with us," Peter had said, pleading with her.

"He won't leave her," Julie responded, referring to her mother, who was buried in The City.

Then Peter said something cruel. He was heartbroken, and Julie couldn't blame him. She said hurtful and nasty things when she was hurt by people she cared about, too.

"Are you always going to live in the shadow of your mother, Julie?" Peter had asked before storming away.

After that incident, they didn't talk for days. Julie wished he wouldn't show up to the celebration because part of her was hurt, too. Peter was the first person she let in emotionally even if minimally. Julie invited Jones as her plus one to the celebration because she couldn't face going alone. While Jones, in his own android way, didn't quite feel hurt the same as her, he emphasized and tried to understand. To keep Julie distracted from Peter, Jones pulled Julie to a corner spot at the makeshift bar, the perfect place to see guests make their entrances.

"Who's that?" Jones asked. He didn't need to; he could scan anyone's identification from his eyes within seconds, but he found Julie's commentary amusing.

"Jim Hynes, he's the head of product development."

Jim had red hair that softened with age. He'd been welcoming when Julie reached out to him and asked about his approach to strategy and product commercialization.

"And her?" Jones asked as a gorgeous woman entered the room beside the governor.

"That," Julie started, holding her champagne flute closely while taking a generous sip, "would be Dr. Isabella Garcia."

Jones eyed her with awe.

Isabella wore a bright glittery cocktail dress with a modest hemline and revealing bodice. The yellow and gold colors were magnificent against her dark skin and caramel-colored hair. Julie never met the infamous philanthropist, but she knew who she was. Isabella was all over the tabloids and was great friends with Celine and The Supreme, presumably because she dated the governor.

She turned away from the doorway and gestured toward the open balcony overlooking The River and The City. The sun set perfectly, the purple and pink colors illuminating across the river. Beautiful moments like tonight reminded Julie why she belonged here, not in some foreign country with Peter.

"Do you work at COLI*GO?" a young woman standing next to

her asked. Julie turned, startled by her presence.

"I do. I worked on COL2120," Julie said as if wearing the words like a badge of honor.

Jones looked over at Julie and nodded, his signal that he'd leave her to mingle and network on his own.

"That's amazing. I watched The Legislature vote on the drug's approval," the young woman responded with a large smile. She had lovely high cheekbones and soft brown hair that fell in curly trundles around her pale skin.

"You work in The Capitol Building?" Julie asked, trying to make pleasant conversation. Julie was shy and making new friends challenged her. But she needed to practice if she wanted to be a successful businesswoman.

"I do!" Her voice beamed enthusiastically. "I work for Representative Kennsington."

Julie sensed how power hungry—like herself—this woman was by her proud stance. She carried herself with grace, her shoulders back and chin raised slightly up.

"That sounds like really interesting work," Julie said, outstretching her hand. "I'm Julie Walsh."

"Kendra Washington," the woman said, taking Julie's hand. "Your friend, he's an android, right?" Kendra uncomfortably played with the bracelet on her right wrist, the roped sterling silver moving abrasively against her milky skin.

"Yes, he is. We've been friends since childhood," Julie answered with a fond smile.

"So, you treat him the same way you treat your human friends?" Kendra pestered, a bit perplexed by Julie's casualness.

"Of course," Julie said as Kendra eyed her oddly.

"Well," Kendra said, outreaching her hand, "it was lovely meeting you, but I should head back inside."

The two women shook hands for a final time before Kendra walked into the crowd, her beautiful, perfect skin shimmering in the sunset's lighting. Julie pulled her device from her clutch and searched Representative Joel Kennsington. He didn't represent her district, so she wasn't familiar with him. After scanning a few head-lines and some of his quotes, Julie understood why Kendra acted oddly about Jones. Joel Kennsington was a member of the Humanizer movement.

"Ah, here is Dr. Walsh!" Julie heard the familiar voice from behind. She found Celine, The Supreme, Marta, and Isabella clustered together.

"Hello," Julie responded, a nervousness flushing her skin. This group of women was arguably the most influential in The City. Julie was simply a "nobody."

"It hasn't been announced yet, but Marta and I made a bold decision," The Supreme said, a grin spreading across her scaly face. "We're promoting you to assistant lead on the research team for a new MS drug COLI*GO is developing. It'll align nicely based on your work with COL2120."

Julie tried to smile. *Why are they stonewalling me and putting me on these assets?*

"She doesn't look too thrilled," Marta observed with a hint of humor.

"I'm shocked," Julie said, trying to recover. "I'm very excited about this opportunity."

"We'll discuss Monday," The Supreme responded. "I just wanted you to know tonight so that you could relax and celebrate."

"You should definitely celebrate before you're stuck in the lab again!" Isabella giggled.

Julie found Isabella's response insulting but hid her feelings when The Supreme and Marta chuckled alongside her. Celine remained silent and locked eyes with Julie. An alignment passed between them: disdain for Isabella Garcia.

"If you'll excuse me," Julie said, averting her eyes toward her feet, "I need to catch up with the rest of the R&D team."

The women nodded as Julie dashed away from the awkward silence. Jones waved from the bar, and she darted over to him.

"I need to go," Jones said, looking down at his small handheld device, "I was called in for a hit and run."

With self-driving cars, these incidents were rare but alarming. Luckily for detectives like Jones, tracking vehicles was easy with virtual owner identification cards. They said goodbye, and Julie asked the bartender for another drink. While waiting on her beverage, she felt a presence linger behind her.

"Congratulations on launching your first asset. You should be proud of yourself, Miss Walsh," a distantly familiar voice said into her ear. Colin O'Connor stared directly at her, and Julie wasn't entirely sure if she was buzzed or he was standing a bit too close.

"Oh no, not you too with the praise." The words escaped her and she felt ashamed she had said this to him, but Colin laughed with her. She found his response oddly comforting.

"Did my fellow board members annoy you with too many questions tonight?" Colin asked, turning to the bar. He ordered a whiskey, straight up. Julie cringed.

"No," she answered, tilting her head with a smirk, "just The Supreme did."

Colin's eyebrows furrowed, and his smirk turned to a scowl.

"Oh, sorry. I didn't mean to make a joke out of it," Julie said, rambling like she always did when nervous. "Anyways, what I meant was that The Supreme is putting me on a time-wasting project next."

She calmed as the words flowed through her and Colin's face warmed at her. She found it unusually comfortable talking with Colin, a man of such prestige. They hadn't interacted often, but each time she felt like he was a friend rather than the governor. As if they'd known each other for years.

"That sounds about right," Colin responded, leaning against the bar. His body relaxed as he sipped his drink. He was a very tall man, his presence overpowering. Julie figured his stature was why she found him intimidating. His shoulder brushed against her, and in response, her body leaned into his.

"Are you still working on the antidote on weekends?" he whispered, asking as if he already knew the answer to his own question.

"Yes," she replied with a grin as a muscular man with a broody stature pointed in their direction.

"Aw shit," Colin said, taking a quick gulp from his glass. "I'm going to have to talk to him in about two minutes. I guess that comes with the territory of being the governor."

Julie laughed. "Who is he?"

"Representative Kennsington," Colin answered, rolling his eyes.

"I met his legislative aide earlier. Kendra. And then I looked him up. He seems like a real winner." A large emphasis of sarcasm filled her voice.

"Oh, he's a nut. His politics are crazy. The other day, he told me he thinks you crazy scientists at COLI*GO are developing human-android hybrid species." Colin chuckled.

"I think we have better things to do than waste our time on wacky science experiments," Julie said, smiling up at him.

He grinned back at her. Julie noticed Colin's gaze softened as he took all of her in with his eyes.

"Joel will make a fool of himself. He always does."

The man inched himself closer to Colin and Julie at the bar. Julie's eyes gazed deeply into Colin's, and the gears in her mind clicked together. She wasn't sure if it was the alcohol, a stroke of pure genius, or a bit of both.

"I need your help," Julie said, placing her drink down loudly on the bar.

"My help?" he asked, giving her an intriguing stare. She noticed he was captivated by her rashness. Fascinated by it.

"Yes," she started, "I know that for some reason—"

But she was interrupted by the burly, foul man.

"Who is this gem?" Joel asked, looking Julie up and down.

"I work for COLI*GO," Julie said with a crisp edge. Being ogled by this man wasn't on her agenda. "Dr. Julie Walsh."

She shook his hand. Joel's were rough and very warm compared to hers. She felt him place his hand on her back as he settled into the bar. He was clearly intoxicated.

"Joel, when are you going to send me the revised legislation?" Colin asked, putting his arm around the man's shoulders and directing him away from Julie. She was grateful for Colin's saving gesture as Joel mumbled a response.

Colin leaned into Julie's ear. "Set up a meeting with me at The Capitol Building so that we can discuss how I can help you."

Colin's whispered breath felt warm against her skin, and goose-bumps crept across her skin.

"How do I schedule that?"

Colin looked over his shoulder and smiled wide as Joel pushed him toward a group of people from The Legislature.

"Message Kathleen."

Julie wasn't sure who Kathleen was, but she was determined to find out.

Chapter 10
The Governor

May 4th, 43 A.R.

Colin waited in the car. He felt like he could hear what happened inside the apartment. It was with Kendra. He watched them flirt innocently at the COLI*GO celebration. Colin did his part: He introduced them, and as expected, they hit it off. It's hand lingered, testing the waters. No one seemed to notice. Everyone else was too drunk. Colin realized Kendra would sleep with It the moment the introduction was made. Kendra no longer wanted to climb Joel's social ladder. He was of no interest to her now. She wanted a seat at Colin's table on the other side of The Capitol Building.

I'd like to work for you, she'd whispered when Colin asked about her career development plans. Colin knew if she could sneak her way into his inner circle, she would.

Colin looked back up at the window and sighed. He anticipated It would give him the low down of his encounter when he returned, how her body felt, how his hands held her down.

None of this stopped Colin from wishing the evening would end.

Is the sedative settling in at all? he wondered, thinking about Isabella. She and The Supreme were out at a wine bar on the bottom of The Hill. Isabella would stumble home in a few hours and expect Colin to be there, either already asleep or at least working in his study.

The car door opened with a loud pull. Colin looked up as It jumped inside. He sat as if in a rush, half the buttons on his shirt undone. A sloppy mess.

"Finally," Colin said with a huff.

It settled into the car and let out a loud sigh of annoyance. Colin shook his head; he thought It was a bit disgusting, a bit whorish. He hated that about his friend.

"Well, how much longer?" Colin asked. It raised his

eyebrows at him.

"Five to ten minutes." It closed his eyes.

Colin watched his friend from across the car. It was an attractive man—muscular in the right places without being too overwhelming. His confidence took care of any doubts, and he never had issues picking up beautiful women when they were at The University together. It was fun, wild and exciting. In comparison, Colin was aloof and quiet, charming but reserved.

It tapped the clock on the display screen. The right amount of time had passed. They got out of the car and disappeared into the entryway of Kendra's building. The apartment was quiet and dimly lit. They strode down the hallway, peering into Kendra's room. She was passed out, naked on the bed.

Perfect.

Colin approached her cautiously. Her breaths were light, her chest rising and falling slowly, methodically, and steadily. She looked so peaceful. Colin realized he lingered too long when It moved past him, scooping Kendra up in his arms.

It placed her in the back of the vehicle before binding her hands together. The knot wasn't complex or intricate but ensured a sense of security. Then It disassembled the navigation in the car so that Colin could drive freely. Not many people knew how to drive a car automatically anymore with only self-driving vehicles available.

Colin remembered his father teaching him how to drive when he was a teenager. They had been at their family home in The Oceanside, far outside The City. The scenery was indescribable, the air lighter as waves crashed meaningfully against the cliffs.

His father pulled him aside to the garage at the edge of the property. Inside was a classic vintage vehicle. Colin didn't even recognize the manufacturer. Colin reached out, the black and red paint coursed through his veins when he touched the car's steering wheel. There was no navigation in this vehicle; a physical key was needed to ignite the engine. This was one of the very few special positive memories he shared with that cold, distant man.

Once It finished disabling the car's controls, Colin manually drove the vehicle, passing through the tunnel connecting this part of The City to The Harbor. A loud roar echoed above them; an airplane made its descent onto the runway at the airport. The sound initially startled It, his eyes glancing toward the backseat at Kendra. She remained sedated. Colin didn't expect the potency of the drug to wear off anytime soon. They had time; they always had more time than anticipated. But Colin understood It's jitters. He often felt them himself, for different reasons. They hadn't taken someone's life for almost five years now.

He turned off the highway and onto a back service road near a terminal. They arrived at a beach overlooking the backside of the airport. This sandy spot acted as a small park, a midway point for a recreational pathway used by joggers, bikers, and walkers.

They moved Kendra carefully out of the back of his car and carried her to the waterfront. The sky was dark, but the sun tempted them in the distance. The days grew longer as the summer season approached. It placed Kendra into his boat carefully, almost too cautiously. It owned and docked his boat in The Harbor, a secret, simple, and unsuspecting motorboat unlike the one the O'Connors kept docked in The Port.

Kendra stirred a little when It turned on the engine but settled back into her darkness. They cruised against the gentle wake with ease, allowing the boat to putter before killing the engine. The sound of the waves rocked against the side of the boat as they waded in the bay.

Thump, thump, thump.

Colin looked out across the water. He liked the ocean, found the waves calming.

"Colin?" a soft and confused voice rose from behind him.

It alarmingly looked over at Colin, his eyes wide with fear. Instinct took over. Colin's left hand clenched Kendra's throat, holding her down roughly. She struggled, wiggling sideways and grabbing at his arms with her sharp nails.

That will not do.

With a quick motion, Colin violently smacked her head against the side of the boat with a vengeance.

Thump, thump, thump.

By the third hit, her eyes rolled back.

"I'm sorry," Colin said to her, still holding his left hand around her neck tightly. In swift motions, the knife in his right hand tore into her. One. Two. Three. Four. Five. He stopped counting but continued. Colin didn't want to know how many times the blade pierced her skin, sliced open, and exposed her to the outside world. He knew she was long gone, but he didn't stop. He couldn't stop. His arm hurt as he pulled himself away, grasping the knife tighter and sobbing.

This act of violence didn't come easily to him, the experience painful, ripping him apart at the seams. He felt as if he was torn into millions of shattered pieces.

It placed his hand on his shoulder, allowing Colin's tears to flow from his eyes.

"Why?" Colin cried out. He continued yelling the word into the impending darkness.

"We needed to. For the greater good, like all our killings. To save society," It answered, trying to calm Colin down.

It took control of the situation, as Colin couldn't handle the repercussions of his actions anymore. Colin slipped away into his mind and out of reality for a bit.

The boat motor purred to life, and It navigated them around the backside of the airport toward the shoreline abutting the runway. The water became swampy, and It slowed the boat down. The emptiness around them calmed Colin, centering him. But then he looked toward the back of the boat at Kendra.

The sight of her mutilated and ripped body made him vomit uncontrollably off the boat's edge. It handed him water and a towel. He vomited again. There was already so much to clean, too much to clean.

"I think this is the spot?" It asked, distracting him.

Colin closed his eyes before opening them again. He looked over the front end. They indeed arrived at the planned spot.

Colin nodded.

"We have a way. We have a ritual. So we don't make any mistakes. So we don't get caught," It reminded him. His body appeared so calm in the madness surrounding them. Majestic.

"We do," Colin responded, standing up.

He took a few deep breaths and reached out to It. Colin felt more in control now. It embraced him and after a few moments, they separated, looking down at Kendra. Colin grabbed her and waded into the water, walking up the shoreline. It followed him.

Colin placed her body on the sandy bank and parted her hair, fanning the locks around her face in an angelic way. Colin's hands lingered down her arm and paused at her wrist. He unhooked the bracelet from her and placed it in his pocket. Taking his gloves off, he looked down at Kendra. He could no longer touch her.

Kendra was already dead. They didn't need to watch her body slip away this time, deviating from their ritual. But five years was a long time—inconsistencies were bound to happen.

Did Kendra deserve this? Colin wondered as he and It stood above her body, watching her for the sake of tradition.

"Don't mourn her for too long. She was part of the movement destroying peace." It looked him squarely in the eyes. He always knew the right thing to say.

With the incoming tide, sweeping away their footprints in the sandbanks wasn't necessary, but they did so regardless. They could never be too careful. After returning to the boat, Colin inhaled the sharp scent of bleach. The smell remained in his nostrils until they decided the boat was clean. Pristine white reflected off the floor where Kendra's blood previously left behind a vivacious red glow. Remnants of her physical being were no longer visible, but her memory remained vibrant in Colin's mind.

Colin barely concentrated on the drive home. It looked out the passenger window, his head in his hands. Colin turned up the volume of the radio, allowing the sounds of a beautiful violin to fill the vehicle. The music soothed him, soothed It.

After emerging from under the tunnel, they found themselves back in The Hill. Finally, they were at the townhouse, climbing the stairs. A bottle of barely touched wine sat open on the dining room table. Colin didn't grab a glass as he walked toward the back of his home. It remained quiet behind him but gravitated to the refrigerator, grabbing a few bottles of beer. Isabella's purse caught his eye—perched on the kitchen island. She was home.

Detouring, Colin ended up in the laundry room. He took the bracelet out from his pocket and placed it in the small box behind the laundry detergent. The trinket joined others, pairs of earrings, a diamond necklace, and shiny golden bands, to name a few.

He stared at the washing machine before stripping off his clothes and throwing them inside. The machine turned on by itself, feeling the weight of the clothes mixed with the detergent. It zoomed to life, and Colin gazed at the water rushing through the glass window.

Moving naked from the laundry room, Colin approached the large staircase. He stopped every few steps to drink from the bottle of wine. He needed that part of the ritual, the alcohol. The wine clouded his mind, It became drunk off his beers, and the two left one another alone.

He approached his bedroom and quietly slinked into the bathroom. It tapped his shoulder after he emerged from the shower, placing his fingers up to his lips. He handed Colin a pill.

"This will help you," It whispered.

It turned down the hall toward one of the guest bedrooms. Colin knew It would be out of the townhouse early in the morning before Isabella even woke.

Colin stared at the little pill in his hand, pondering the capsule for a moment. He wasn't sure what drug this was but decided he didn't care. He placed the pill on his tongue and took a swig from the wine bottle as he entered the bedroom.

Isabella's body was still and silent in bed. Colin almost thought she was asleep, that he would drift off himself in loneliness, but she reached out to him as he approached.

Chapter 11
Jones

May 5th, 43 A.R.

One hundred and eighty-two days have passed since The City last experienced a homicide. The sounds of the water crashing onto the beach drowned out all other commotion happening around Jones as he blankly stared at Kendra Washington's body. He remembered meeting this woman last night at the COLI*GO approval party. She spoke with Julie. Kendra was a member of the Humanizer party, but Jones was impartial to her beliefs. Her misguided feelings about androids wouldn't affect him or his judgment in finding justice for her by catching her killer.

Jones observed her body, the sight of her truly brutal. The bruises on the right side of her face shadowed different shades of purple and blue exploding off her pale skin. He noted yellow mixed in, painting her skin like a watercolor, seeping in and out of the lines, circling around in swirls so vivid and terrifying. Jones was lost looking at her, realizing she suffered a horrible concussion before her death. His eyes traveled down her neck to bruises stretching across her collarbone. Large hands held her down by the size of them. Her chest and abdomen were ripped apart by stab wounds.

Twenty-three stab wounds.

The skin on the rest of her body lingered in between shades of milky white and pale blue from overnight exposure. Jones pictured her body floating along the marsh tides, weaving in and out of the shallow sections of the harbor bordering the airport. But that wasn't what happened; her body wasn't bloated or saturated from the saltwater. She'd been placed along the shoreline.

Kendra's death was clearly painful, and based on the sheer violence, Jones assumed her death was very personal. Jones heard the commissioner behind him, consoling Representative Joel

Kennsington while asking simple questions.

"What happened when you arrived on the tarmac?"

"I don't know."

"Where were you last night?"

"At the COLI*GO event. Then I went home."

"You were home all night?"

"Of course, where else would I be?"

Stabbing your legislative aide? Jones wondered.

"Detective Jones," the commissioner's shaky voice beckoned him over, "a word, please."

"Sire," Jones responded, approaching the android at attention.

"This is obviously a very sensitive case. It'll generate a lot of media coverage."

Jones nodded. As the most junior officer on the scene, he was convinced the commissioner was about to ask him to leave.

"I need you to help the medical examiner," he said, his voice trailing off while his eyes darted around the scene.

"Is that protocol?" Jones asked.

"Murders are uncommon," the commissioner responded, "and honestly, there can be no room for human error."

Jones understood immediately. The chief medical examiner was a human. Jones looked over his shoulder as the sound of commotion increased. The governor put his arm around Kennsington's shoulder as the foreign ambassadors glanced at the transpiring scene. The medical examiner tapped Jones on his shoulder. Dr. Anna Garcia was a small woman, barely five feet tall, with tiny hands and a slightly curvy frame. She had beautiful mocha-colored hair styled in a bun. She resembled her older sister, Isabella Garcia, with the exception of a much more muscular build.

"Do you think you can help me with the gurney?" she asked, her voice trembling.

"Of course," Jones answered, looking over at Kendra.

Jones helped Dr. Garcia remove the body and load her into the vehicle, and then Anna and Jones climbed into the front. Anna looked away from Jones and out the window, her hands shaking as they hovered over the dashboard. Jones swiftly grabbed her hand in his as a gesture of comfort. She pulled her hand away, her eyes wide.

"I'm sorry," she said. "I was startled."

"I didn't mean to startle you. I wanted you to feel . . . calmer?"

The medical examiner smiled softly at Jones, and the two remained quiet as the vehicle navigated off the tarmac and onto a service road.

"The last time I worked on a homicide, it was a deranged man who killed his lover in a fit of jealousy. But this . . . this is more horrifying," Anna said, lifting her gaze to Jones.

Jones remembered the case: It occurred 182 days ago.

"I worked on a case five years ago where we didn't find the killer," Anna continued, closing her eyes. Jones remained silent, letting her speak at her own pace. "Also a young woman. She'd been the chief of staff to Celine O'Connor."

The vehicle proceeded under the tunnel before emerging downtown. Jones peered out the window as the vehicle pulled into the garage attached to the morgue, parking perfectly in its designated space. The engine still purred, the vibration coursing through Jones's body.

"I remember that murder investigation, but I was still in school," Jones responded, not able to stand the uncomfortable silence any longer.

"She'd been stabbed twenty-three times, too." Anna opened her door and exited the vehicle without looking at him.

Jones's eyes widened. It took him a few moments to follow Dr. Garcia inside.

***

Kendra's body lying on the medical examiner's table was a horrific sight, one more ungodly than her body on the sandy beach. The paleness of her skin shone brighter against the cold steel slab, her bruises more pronounced. Jones never attended or witnessed an autopsy before and watched Dr. Garcia intently. The medical examiner took her own photos before reaching over and turning on a recording device.

"My name is Dr. Anna Garcia. I'm the chief medical examiner for the office of The City," she spoke soundly. "The victim is identified as Ms. Kendra Washington, a twenty-six-year-old Caucasian female of human origin. I am joined by Detective Jones."

Anna looked over at him for a long moment. Jones nodded in her direction with confidence. He was ready.

A sigh came out from between her lips as she continued her protocol. She identified Kendra's markings, bruises, and irregular imperfections. Anna's eyes locked with Jones's before she picked up her surgical tools.

Dr. Garcia's incisions into Kendra's body sounded horrific in Jones's ears, knife against skin. The noise echoed around them as if someone in the room zipped up their sweater.

***

Back at the station, Jones immediately found the archives room. The memory of the autopsy shifted through his processor. He couldn't believe humans performed this procedure, the process cold and disturbing. Dr. Garcia had sliced Kendra's body open and pulled apart her skin as Jones watched in complete astonishment. Seeing a human body opened up was a rare sight for him.

He shook his head, stepping into the library.

The machines in the archives room were filled with various documents dating back to the birth of the digital age. Surely enough, Jones found the mysterious cold case of Celine O'Connor's chief of staff: Amanda MacDonald.

Anna's recording notes were eerily familiar to the ones she made for Kendra Washington. Various similarities jumped across the screen: the number of stab wounds, the bruises around her neck, the youthfulness of the woman. Both were involved with high-powered individuals, immersed in similar circles.

Were Kendra and Amanda killed by the same individual? Jones read through all the files of the unsolved case, wanting to understand the circumstances and situations in greater detail. Not finding the killer was unheard of, especially with the level of forensics available.

Jones turned to another device and searched for other unsolved cases with similar descriptors. His breathing stopped short. There were more unsolved cases of dead women dating back ten years.

Dead women with twenty-three stab wounds.

A significant amount of time occurred between the killings, often a year or two, except in the beginning. The police connected the first group of killings; The City had an uncaught "serial killer." Jones didn't remember these cases; he'd been too young at the time.

After a couple years, the police stopped connecting the murders. The signs and connections were obvious to Jones: young women with the same number of stab wounds, neck bruises, all working in government or for COLI*GO.

This either went undetected, things went missing, or things were buried, Jones thought, standing up.

He felt dizzy and held on to the wall to steady himself. As an android, he shouldn't feel this swing in emotions. But if Julie hadn't reprogrammed his processor, he wasn't sure if his level of curiosity would have been the same.

I'm sure as hell that I'm going to figure this out.

Chapter 12
The Governor

May 7th, 43 A.R.

"Colin, yah had an appointment request," Kathleen said as he walked into his office.

"What?" he asked, not looking up from his device.

Colin was too preoccupied with the news coverage of Kendra Washington's mysterious murder.

"Uhm," Kathleen said, looking at her tablet, "a COLI*GO employee. I told her tah make an appointment with yah at the COLI*GO building, but she was persistent, insistin' in meetin' yah here."

"Who?"

"Doctah Julie Walsh."

Colin stopped dead in his tracks.

"What time?" he asked, sharply looking up at Kathleen.

"Noon. Do yah want me tah get lunch? Or do yah want me tah cancel?" Kathleen asked, already typing on the screen of her device.

"Don't cancel. Lunch would be great. You know, the regular." He flipped through his agenda for the day before closing the door.

Julie Walsh wasted no time. He remembered their encounter at the COLI*GO event and smiled. He wanted Julie to find an ally in him; he genuinely cared about her . . . about her antidote.

Think, Colin. His mind churned but then paused. He couldn't distract himself with thoughts of her.

Colin spent the next few hours diving into the legislative agenda Kathleen had provided him. After Kendra's death, the building remained unnervingly quiet. Kendra was junior in her role but left a mark within The Capitol Building. There was a hesitation to keep bill proposals under wraps, the extremist Humanizers wanting to exploit the situation to their advantage. But they were also smart enough to know their main voice, Kennsington, couldn't handle the pressure. Colin refocused on the school and public education bill. He couldn't waste time cashing in on The Supreme's promises. The whole motivation behind killing Kendra.

The Representatives of The Androids messaged back: They unanimously supported the measure.

A light knock on his open office door broke his thoughts.

"Governor?" The voice was soft but confident.

"Yes," he answered without looking up from his device. Out of the corner of his eye, he recognized Julie Walsh and watched her enter his office. Colin looked up and leaned back in his chair, giving her his full attention.

"You said to make an appointment with Kathleen," she said with a shrug. "So, here I am."

"I'm glad you did," he responded, gesturing for her to sit in the seat across from his desk.

Julie hesitantly sat, looking around his office curiously. He watched her observe her surroundings; she was truly a scientist at heart, taking mental notes of every aspect of the room. Her eyes paused over the image on his desk of him and his mother from his childhood. A small warm smile crept across her face.

She didn't flinch once she noticed him watching her.

"That's a lovely picture."

He admired her authenticity. While Julie was young, her drive and ambition shone through, but Colin glimpsed at the softer side of her he hadn't expected. Julie was a genuine and intuitive woman, gentle, even. Instinctively, Colin confidently believed Julie would never manipulate him. A feeling he wasn't used to.

"I need your help." Julie looked at him, her cheeks flushed with embarrassment. "It's about the antidote."

Colin nodded as she continued.

"I'm close to having support from enough board members. Martin, you, and potentially The Supreme. I don't need a large budget. It could be an exploratory lab assignment or something, I don't know. I need to get the antidote back in everyone's purview since there's been so much advancement to it over the last two years. But I can't take it any further without more resources."

"Of course there's been advancement; I wouldn't expect anything less from you," Colin said kindly.

She smiled, the blush deepening against the freckles on her skin.

"But you can't let them know about all of your advancements."

"I can't?"

"No," Colin said and smiled, "you never let them know all the moves you're thinking about." He pointed to the chessboard on the table beside them. "Imagine how impressed they'll be if the antidote gets minimal dollars diverted to it and it accelerates so quickly? They'll never question you again."

He and Julie looked at one another as a playful smile passed between them.

Chapter 13
Mick

May 5th, 43 A.R.

He was close but not close enough for The Supreme. It wasn't for a lack of trying, but she didn't care: The Supreme was driven by results. From living with Jones, Mick knew better than to plead or debate with an android. A useless endeavor. Mick proved humans could travel time by utilizing human blood. He easily deployed proteins from blood through a coding technique and created a device that extrapolated those components, activating receptors. This activation propelled him backward and forward in time.

Essentially, humans traveled through the experiences and knowledge their DNA possessed. Certain limitations hindered time travel. Someone couldn't transport themselves to a specific year prior to their birth through their own blood. Their blood didn't hold any memories from that year. Similarly, someone couldn't transport hundreds of years into the future with their own blood either; they'd already be dead.

Mick discovered a loophole: utilizing blood from another human, one who lived during the desired year he wished to travel. This posed heavy side effects. His body aged whenever he traveled into parts of the future or past that were out of his own existence. The aging wasn't overly noticeable: a fine line on his forehead or an additional depth to the crow's feet along his eyes. Otherwise, Mick enjoyed the sensation of the glasses-like device he developed. The glasses were slightly bulkier than he'd like, but nothing was ever perfect on the first try. Or the second. Or the third.

I'll get there.

One roadblock he hadn't found a loophole for yet: Androids didn't have blood. They couldn't time travel. And Mick refused to test his theories on Jones. He loved Jones, more than life itself. Until he found a solution, Mick remained the only test subject.

He often waited until Jones went to bed before tiptoeing to his home office. Mick spent hours with the glasses over his eyes, reliving his childhood through what felt like a sixth sense. Time travel was vibrant and uncanny yet bone-chillingly familiar.

Mick wished he could shake his younger self and tell him things would be okay, remind him that being interested in science wasn't nerdy, that he shouldn't feel guilty wanting a life outside The Countryside. His family didn't understand or fathom why he'd want to leave the simple life they lived.

There aren't a lot of androids to worry about. There are women here, simple women, but they're looking for a husband to serve on the farm. There isn't any infection or disease here. We live a pure life, Mick.

He didn't need to travel back in time to hear all the excuses his father repeated. He didn't need to travel back in time to remind himself he was a disappointment to his family. Or at least most of his family.

Except Uncle Jeb.

Much like Mick, Uncle Jeb was a black sheep. He devoted his life to art. Jeb was talented, and wealthy old bloodline families purchased his masterpieces ad nauseam. Henry O'Connor put Jeb Taylor on the map, and then Uncle Jeb was gone.

Uncle Jeb didn't care much for the family farm except for its fortune. He stole from the family to finance his lifestyle in The City, and Mick happened upon this knowledge by mistake. Mick remembered thinking about turning his uncle in. His family struggled with bankruptcy, and food was scarce some weeks. But Mick remained quiet.

Was it because I wanted something more meaningful out of my life, like him? But when Mick's father disowned him, he asked Uncle Jeb for a loan for school.

"Are you sure you want to go to The University, Mick?" Uncle Jeb had said in the living room of his loft. Mick blackmailed him, then Uncle Jeb agreed to finance Mick's education.

Mick had been relieved; he'd spent all his money on the high-speed train to The City. While tiring, the adventure had been well worth it.

When he got off the platform, Mick remembered looking at the tall skyscrapers in awe. He wondered what the view looked like from the top. He experienced many firsts in The City that day. Specifically, interactions with androids. Mick previously only knew one android. She worked as a quasi-representative for the town he lived in, reporting back to The Capitol Building in The City. She checked the crops, making sure they were up to standard. She only cared about the quality and quantities of what farms grew.

Seeing so many androids integrated into the streets of The City surprised Mick. He found androids fascinating creatures. Their scales mesmerized him, the vibrant colors changing deep majestic colors. He never wanted to go back to The Countryside.

Even in his worst mentorship, Uncle Jeb didn't judge Mick, but he did itch for his scandalous life back—a life of selling dangerous pharmaceuticals on the black market to his art clients. He himself engaged in the activities, his paintings growing more and more grotesque with each high.

Mick often thought of one piece in particular that his uncle worked on when Mick lived with him. On the canvas, a woman kneeled down to the outline of shoes. The sadness in her face swirled; it was horrific, almost unrecognizable. She overwhelmed Mick, her eyes longing for an escape from her lifetime of servitude.

He thought more about this painting when he traveled to the past and future. The past provided answers, potential solutions to fix the future. But the future always changed, swirling together into an unknown like the woman's face.

When Mick watched Julie reprogram Jones's processor, he decided not to blame them for their actions. Instead, Mick wondered if there could ever be a future that normalized androids understanding all human emotions. He shared these idealistic thoughts with The Supreme and she often smiled at him. Eventually, she looked at Mick as a co-conspirator rather than an employee.

We could forge the world for a better future if they harnessed the dangers of time travel, Mick thought, staring off into the distance.

PART FOUR

Ten Years Earlier

"To see takes time."
-Georgia O'Keeffe

Chapter 14
Colin

January 28th, 33 A.R.

"Can't you write it, Colin?" Celine asked, looking up at him from across the dining room table.

Colin smelled the cigar his father smoked earlier, the pungent smell creeping into the walls of the townhouse. Celine looked exhausted and anxious, her skin paler than normal and dark bags forming under her eyes. She worked long hours lately, preparing various business plans while simultaneously examining new and innovative technologies.

He wanted to be a more supportive brother, a caring son, and overall, a better person. But he felt no purpose lately, as if each day came in and out like mundane waves.

I wish Celine could take care of our father, he selfishly thought.

Their father despised Colin. While there were moments in his childhood where his father didn't treat him like an outcast, Colin often felt he came up short. Even as a young man in his late twenties, Colin hadn't grown out of these uncomfortable characteristics his father instilled in him.

Colin believed his father resented him for the death of his wife. The family forcibly stuck together that fitful day about twenty years ago, a dark stain seeping into the fabric of their family. When Colin and Celine left for The University, they never thought they'd be back in the townhouse, living with their father. But then he was diagnosed with Alzheimer's, and his condition worsened each year.

After being elected to The Ways and Means Committee six years ago, Colin helped hide his father's inflictions from the public and The Legislature. His experience on The Committee provided a vast knowledge of the ins and outs of The Capitol Building. He knew each representative like the back of his hand, making hiding his father's condition a fairly easy task.

Colin looked across the table at Celine and scowled. Her defeated look made him feel even more like a complete failure. His gaze drifted from her toward his father at the other end of the table.

Henry O'Connor wasn't listening to their conversation, looking down at his plate with a hollow look in his eyes. He was present in the room, but Colin knew better; his father didn't fully remember most of his days anymore. Shame spread through Colin's mind.

I should have helped sooner.

"Send it over," Colin said, looking back at his sister. She smiled brightly, and relief flooded her body as she relaxed into her seat. One less thing for her to worry about.

"Kathleen will send it over," Celine answered. "Do you think Don Ludewing will be a competent governor after father? I mean, I'm sure he will win easily if we support his campaign. If father endorses him . . ."

Colin sighed. There was always a secret agenda with Celine.

"What's your concern?" Colin asked but already suspected the answer: The Supreme.

The Supreme was a piece of work, but they were all friends. The three attended The University and before that summered together at The Oceanside. Back then, The Supreme went by her given name: Emilia. Emilia always knew she'd rise to the position of supreme, and due to her status, her predecessor insisted she spend the vast majority of her younger years with the O'Connor family.

Once they graduated, Emilia worked with the former supreme in preparation, taking on the official role four years later. She was highly praised by her android constituents, seen as brazen and honest. Don Ludewing didn't stand a chance against The Supreme on The Legislature floor. She'd dominate him.

"He's just so . . ." Celine started.

"Soft. Cowardly. A pushover," their father interrupted.

Colin and Celine glanced over at him, eyebrows raised.

"Father, he's the only option," Celine responded, stretching her hand and placing it on his shoulder soothingly.

Colin watched his father breathe in deeply before shaking Celine off. No one dared speak after the outburst, and after several painful minutes of silence, Henry stood and excused himself. When he left, the air in the room settled.

"Colin," Celine said, leaning over toward him, "you should run."

"Father wouldn't approve," Colin responded with a sigh. "And I'm not qualified."

"What makes you think you so?" Celine asked.

Because we disagree on so much, Colin wanted to answer.

Henry O'Connor had been elected right at the end of The Resurgence. The previous governor was thrown in jail, and Henry was tasked with bridging the gap between people and androids. Uncharted territory. His ideology lingered on equality for androids but not completely. He believed they deserved representation but held humans as superior beings. During this time, people still feared androids after they rose up. From there, the Humanizer party emerged. Colin had a different viewpoint. He believed humans and androids could prosper together, equally. He supported the Sympathizer movement and collaborated with all beings across The Constituency.

Leaning back in his seat, Colin pushed his plate back. Neither sibling touched the rest of their meal.

"The only reason he lets me even respond and approve legislation is because he doesn't want the public to know he's sick. That he can't do it himself. He wants to finish out his term without stepping down. Otherwise, he hates my ideology."

Their political differences were another point of contention between him and his father: Colin wouldn't give up on his beliefs, even to protect his father.

Why not utilize their processor power? Help create cures for diseases, solve financial crises? Colin once asked.

His father simply laughed. Androids were not the enemy; they helped society. Colin grew angry when his father insisted on segregating androids and humans in The City.

Celine agreed with Colin's beliefs and even went behind their father's back to include The Supreme on The Board of COLI*GO. Henry eventually forgave her; he could never say no to his dutiful and perfect daughter. *His lousy son, on the other hand . . .*

"That's not true, Colin. He appreciates your perspective. You don't understand the turmoil and pain occurring in his mind," Celine interrupted his thoughts.

"Stop sugarcoating this. His attitude toward me has been the same my whole life, even before he was sick. You, on the other hand, can't do anything wrong. If anyone should run for governor, it should be you," Colin said with a laugh.

"I'm too busy building COLI*GO. I'm focusing all my energy there. COLI*GO is too important," Celine said, frustration creeping into her tone.

"More important than our family legacy?" Colin asked.

Celine rolled her eyes before glaring at him.

"Diving into politics might do you some good. Give you a break from the toxic corporate environment."

She chuckled, the shrillness uncharacteristic of his prim and proper sister.

"Politics isn't any less toxic than the corporate world."

"Look," Colin said, his eyes directly staring her down. "You're my sister and I respect you. But you need to get out of your business partner's pants. He's using you. And he has a wife."

Celine's eyes darkened like stormy summer thunderstorm clouds. She and Martin Borges were engaged in an illicit affair, but he was a Borges, a member of another old bloodline family. His wife was a "nobody." And Celine needed him; he was instrumental in the technical sciences. As a researcher and scientist, he provided invaluable insight into building the biotech company.

A huff came out of her throat. Celine despised her brother sometimes. He was the smart one, the one who excelled in school. He skipped a grade and joined her the same year at The University. And while her father did adore her, he always reminded her of Colin's intellect. Martin was different. For once, there was a man in her life who made her feel like a genius.

"If you could show some restraint, you could be an even better fucking politician than our father. But you can't help yourself, can you? You think you know better than everyone." Celine leaned across the table as the words exploded out of her. The table shook in her grip as she looked at Colin. She stormed out of the dining room, her footsteps ascending the stairwell.

Thump. Thump. Thump.

Colin's eyes glanced back at the meal on his plate. Barely touched. He pushed the plate aside and pulled out his device. The legislation his father was supposed to review was already in his inbox. He took the liberty of removing and adding new sentences, smiling smugly. Celine would read this, and he found pleasure in making her feel incompetent in the realm of law and government. He switched over from the document and scrolled through his contacts until he reached Kathleen.

Kathleen Murphy was very intertwined in his life. The Murphys were family friends to the O'Connors for decades. Kathleen's mother was originally Henry's legislative aide, and Kathleen worked for him after graduating from The University. Henry even footed the bill for her tuition. Growing up, Colin and Kathleen were great friends, almost inseparable. There were never any romantic feelings between the two—only genuine friendship.

"Hey," Kathleen said, her face appearing on the screen.

"I want to do something out of character, and I need your help," Colin said, glancing back at the empty dining room entryway.

"Okay," Kathleen said, turning her head slightly to the side.

"I want to run against Don Ludewing."

"Wait," Kathleen said, confusion furrowing her brow. "For governor?"

"Yes," Colin answered slowly. "I've been practically doing the job for the last year and a half anyways."

Kathleen pondered the idea for a moment before nodding.

"Don's an idiot. He'll only carry out my father's terrible legacy. I want to make The Constituency better. Get us out of these dark ages."

Kathleen's eyes widened as a warm smile spread across her face. Running for governor wouldn't be easy; Colin's platform was completely different from his father's, and he didn't expect any kind of endorsement from him.

"Well, you're like a brother to me. I'd do anythin' for yah, so what do yah need from me?"

"Will you be my campaign manager?" Colin asked her.

"Me? I'm not qualified." Kathleen's eyes grew at his request.

"You're the perfect person for the job and the only one I trust." Colin smiled and Kathleen returned the favor.

"Okay, well," she said, "let's do this. When do yah wanna make the announcement?"

"Exactly one hour after my father publicly endorses Don." A mischievous grin spread across Colin's face. He was tired of being a disappointment.

Let this be a lesson for them.

"I'll draft somethin' for the media. Let's schedule yah time tah discuss your stance on the issues. You'll need tah visit all the districts." Colin almost heard the gears in her mind turning, running a million miles a minute.

"Yes, let's do that. And I need to schedule time with The Supreme. Alone. Before we make the announcement."

"Of course." They said goodbye, and Colin ended their video chat.

He sighed, looking at the steak on the plate once more. He ate the cold slab of meat and smiled.

***

"Hello, Amanda," Colin said to the beautiful young blonde woman behind the desk. Amanda MacDonald was his sister's chief of staff. Celine was quite fond of her and now Colin realized why. No matter how much Celine praised Amanda's intelligence, he knew his sister's ulterior motives in the manners of attraction.

"Hello, Mr. O'Connor. What can I help you with today?" her gentle voice asked.

"I need thirty minutes on The Supreme's schedule today. It's important," Colin answered with a generous smile.

"Well, Mr. O'Connor, I don't think that's possible."

"What do I need to do to receive higher priority?" Colin asked, moving away from the front of Amanda's desk to lean against the side. She smirked coyly at him.

"I'd like to say lunch might help your case, but dinner definitely will."

She's good.

"Next Friday?" he asked, leaning closer to her.

"Wow, look at that. I can get you in, in an hour."

Colin beamed his charming grin. He didn't hate the idea. Amanda was brilliant and beautiful, her freckles sprinkled innocently across the bridge of her nose. Colin had a certain charisma with women like Amanda; he didn't mind using his charm. The only good thing he'd inherited from his father.

He and Kathleen headed back down to the lobby, and she rolled her eyes at him once they were in the elevator. They took a seat next to the large atrium to wait out the hour. They drafted announcements and schedules.

"I can tell yah lookin' at me funny," Kathleen said without glancing up from her device.

"I'm curious what Emilia will say. I'm not sure she'll like the idea."

"Well," Kathleen said, looking up from her device. "Get that shit outta yah head. If yah get elected, there are gonna be a lotta people who don't like what yah have tah say."

After an hour passed, Colin headed back up to the 101st floor of the building. The Supreme welcomed him into her office with an alluring grin.

"To what do I owe this surprise, old friend?" The Supreme asked as they settled into the sitting area.

Colin noted the interesting design choice for the room; harsh and rigid lines bounced off the intimate meeting space. He assumed the color tones would be warmer, playing against the beautiful skyline of The City behind them, but everything was painted gray.

"I'm running for governor."

"Really?" she asked with no inclination of approval or disapproval in her tone.

"Yes. I plan on announcing my intentions this afternoon. And I wanted you to know beforehand."

"Have you told your father?" The question hung in the air with an awkwardness Colin hadn't anticipated.

"No."

"Interesting." The Supreme leaned back in her seat.

Colin wanted shock value. Don thought he was running

unopposed. "I'll tell him after the announcement."

The Supreme squinted her eyes inquisitively at Colin as if sizing him up. When they were younger, he and Emilia pretended they were leaders, discussed topics of ethics, and enjoyed card and chess games. They shared a craving for competitive, intellectual banter. He'd yet to break her poker face and thrived on the challenge.

"That will cause a lot of issues."

"And where would the fun be if it didn't?" Colin asked with a smile.

Chapter 15
Mick

February 18th, 33 A.R.

Mick hated spying on his friends, but after seeing the future, he needed answers from the past, needed the deep-rooted reasoning behind Julie's future decisions. And then there was Colin he needed to think about. Everything started here, in 33 A.R.

Julie looked less serious ten years in the past but remained her curious self. Mick expected her in the front row of the classroom, and she didn't disappoint him. Jones sat beside her. Based on the dates, Mick remembered this was a couple years after Julie's family moved into The City from The Outskirts. The move allowed her family closer proximity to medical professionals her mother needed. She wasn't a popular girl in school, a bit of an outcast. She was a teacher's pet and cared too much about schoolwork. That's why Julie and Jones gravitated toward one another.

Physically, Jones looked the same, but personality-wise, Jones displayed more detached, typical android characteristics. His demeanor was colder, more distant. This Jones wasn't the same android who crept into Mick's bed each night, the android he cried to, confided in.

Mick sat directly behind Jones and Julie in the classroom, pulling his sweatshirt up over his head to remain undetected.

"Julie," Jones whispered, leaning across the aisle toward her. "Can I ask a favor?"

Julie nodded enthusiastically.

"You know how you said you'd do anything for me?"

"Yes, of course," Julie responded, reaching out and grabbing his hand.

"I researched reprogrammed codes for android processors and our ability to understand humans." Jones turned his head back and forth, making sure no one listened to them, but as he did, their teacher entered the room.

Julie let go of Jones's hand, and the two pulled out their devices to take notes. Whatever was so urgent could wait.

The teacher started the lecture, and Mick's thoughts drifted to where the younger version of himself was in this dimension. In the past, Mick confronted all the wrongdoings of his family. Teenage Mick always dreamed of The City, but through Julie's blood and experiences, he learned his impression was incorrect. While The City improved over time, the streets were still harsh. People and androids still eyed one another warily.

He prominently felt the lingering pangs of The Resurgence here. The O'Connor family supported prosperity after the uprising of androids, but humans were still afraid.

How so much changed, so quickly in only a decade.

Part of the answer was Colin O'Connor as the governor. The man saved The City.

After class ended, Mick retreated to the small space he occupied in The Hill. The wind picked up as the afternoon rolled in. When he reached the carriage house, Mick welcomed the warmth and fireplace. He ignited the flame and settled in at his desk.

The Supreme acquired this space for him. He needed a place to hide when in the past or future. The small converted carriage house sat directly behind the O'Connor townhouse. The two-room abode was perfect for Mick with one large room in the front and a tiny bedroom in the back. Mick picked up an older model device because his actual device remained off when time traveling. He searched the news for Colin's campaign events.

Mick needed to get close enough to Colin and steal his blood.

Chapter 16
Julie

March 2nd, 33 A.R.

She didn't understand why Jones wanted to feel more human, why he wanted to feel emotions. Julie envied him, wishing she retained more information in her mind and didn't feel upset or alienated by others. Jones asked her to reprogram his processor, wanting to understand more feelings than the legally allowed limit. Julie was a master at coding and loved learning not only about the human brain but also the android processor as well. She read for hours on both subjects while waiting to visit her mother at the hospital.

Together, they examined the code on Julie's device. Her father was out visiting her mother and Becky, her sister, was finishing homework downstairs. The Walsh's condo overlooked the old monument in the park. The statue withstood the riots during The Resurgence.

"What percentage of emotions and feelings will I comprehend with this altered code?" Jones asked.

"You'll go from 13 percent," Julie answered, her eyes hovering over the device's screen, "to about 60 percent. We shouldn't push the limit any higher. I don't want to overwhelm your processor."

"Good idea. Can you revert me back?"

"Not without severely impacting you," Julie responded with a flash of concern in her eyes.

What if the coding doesn't work? she wondered, looking at it on the screen. *Could I ever forgive myself if I seriously damage my best friend? My only friend?*

"I trust you," Jones said. One of the few feelings he currently understood.

"That means the world to me, but I'm scared."

"I'm the one asking you to do this," he said with no

contemplation at all. Jones grabbed her hands to reassure her. "Do you know which emotions I'll understand and which I still won't?"

"Unfortunately, I don't," Julie answered truthfully. "I looked at the coding structures you provided me from the dark web, but I don't trust those so I built a replica from scratch."

Jones looked at her in awe.

"Understanding and feeling emotions will be a learning curve for you. I know that's not what you want to hear."

"I can accept that," he answered flatly.

Julie nodded as Jones sat in the chair facing her. Her fingers grazed the back of his left earlobe and his scales rapidly changed shades of green. Julie leaned into Jones a bit more, her lips brushing against him.

"This is going to hurt a little. I'm sorry."

The knife slit a small incision between his scales, granting access to the wires and microchip attached to his processor. Jones flinched as the silver liquid, similar to human blood, protruded from the small opening. With tweezers, Julie removed the small microchip. Jones's eyes instantly went blank; he no longer functioned, could no longer hear her. He was officially powered off.

Julie placed the microchip in her device and imported the new code. The process took about two minutes but felt like an eternity. Her palms grew sweaty, and her heart raced inside her chest. When the transfer completed, Julie placed the microchip carefully back inside Jones's processor.

What if I hurt him? She wondered, but it was too late; she already completed the illegal task. Moving quickly out of nervousness, Julie stitched the small incision back together with a needle and thread. Her heartrate increased, beating loudly in her own ears as she waited for Jones to wake up. The seconds passed in elongated moments. Finally, life came back to his eyes. Jones looked up at Julie inquisitively at first, then the corners of his mouth eased into a genuine smile.

"Jones?" Julie asked hesitantly.

"Julie!" Jones said as his hands felt his face. He looked up at her, jumping up from his seat, hugging her. The shock of his excitement made Julie pause before hugging him back.

"I feel like . . . I feel like a new android," Jones said, his smile growing wide. "Things feel . . . lighter."

"Oh good," Julie said and then let go of her friend, "but you know you have to be careful. What we did was—"

"Very illegal," Jones said, finishing her sentence.

Julie regarded him with agreement in her eyes.

"But Julie, do you recognize how innovative this is? I feel so free. Like there is more clarity in my life."

Chapter 17
Colin

June 29th, 33 A.R.

Excitement suspended deep within the humidity as Colin stepped off the small platform. Campaigning challenged him; being the underdog provided a new perspective. Colin thrived off this energy, working four times as hard as his opponent, proving his worth to the voters. He needed their trust.

Don Ludewing was boring by comparison. He lived a simple, transparent life as the patriarch of his old bloodline family. Colin was a calculated risk, a thrill of excitement and unknown. News reporters coined him as "new blood from old blood."

Kathleen secured speaking engagements for Colin within as many places as possible. He campaigned across The Constituency, but The City remained the most important district.

"Colin!" she yelled to him. "The Supreme requested a meetn'."

Colin stopped dead in his tracks. His relationship with The Supreme remained aloof during the election. "Let's make it happen," he responded with a grin. Kathleen nodded slightly, stepping aside.

"Excuse me, Mr. O'Connor?"

A man approached him from the crowd. His hair was dark and wiry, matching his elegant skin tone, but Colin noted the fine lines spreading across his face, aging an otherwise youthful stature.

"Can I ask you a question?" the man spoke sheepishly. Colin extended his hand to shake the man's.

"Of course," Colin said, noticing the crowd forming around them. "What is your name, sir?"

"Mick," the man answered, his eyes darting quickly back and forth. "My family's lived here for generations, but some months, it's difficult putting food on the table."

He looked ashamed, his eyes dropping to his feet.

"Food shortage is a serious issue. Families shouldn't feel insecure, and providing assistance to farms to lower costs is the first step," Colin responded. He was glad the man asked about his policies on this particular issue. Don didn't have a plan for food sustainability, but Colin devoted a large portion of his platform to this issue.

"I'd work to pass legislation providing new technology to farms at no additional cost if they sell back their old equipment. This is a bipartisan issue between people and androids. No one should go hungry, and it's my number one priority to make sure no one does."

A woman emerged from the crowd, approaching him. The sight of her took Colin's breath away. He recognized her instantly.

"I want to formally introduce myself," she said in an intoxicating tone. "I'm Dr. Isabella Garcia."

Colin's gaze didn't move from her eyes even though they wanted to linger down her frame. He shook her hand. "Colin O'Connor."

The O'Connors and the Garcias had a tumultuous history, one Colin was too familiar with.

"I know," she responded simply. "We should discuss your plan to feed hungry citizens of The Constituency. You're on the right track, but there's room for improvement. If you want to develop an actionable plan, you'll listen to what I have to say."

Isabella's confidence surprised Colin, but he admired her for her brazenness. Colin recognized the stunningly beautiful woman possessed a deep knowledge and intellect, an asset if he could persuade her.

"Well, Doctor," Colin said with a wide grin, "I'm all ears."

"Have your people contact my people to set up a time later this week," she said, returning a graceful smile.

Colin watched her walk away, disappearing into the crowd. He turned back toward the man who asked him the question, but he was nowhere in sight.

***

The Supreme welcomed Colin into her office a little too casually this time. Skeptically, he sat across from her desk.

"I have to say, I'm actually quite impressed with your campaign."

Colin opened his mouth to respond but thought better of it. He and his campaign staff worked long hours, barely committing to normal schedules, let alone personal lives. Colin assumed The Supreme and The Representatives of The Androids favored him over his opponent, but androids didn't vote in the election. Their influence could hinder him; depending on the political analyst, his margins were already razor thin. Winning wasn't good enough for Colin; he wanted to crush Don Ludewing.

"You know I can't take sides," The Supreme said, her words stinging Colin. He knew better than to let his emotions show with The Supreme.

"Well," he said, straightening up in his seat. "I'm a good candidate. I have great ideas for my people, and I have an amazing, dedicated team."

"True, but you're still lacking support from your father's base voters."

"Why do you care about them?" he asked. "They don't want you or androids to have any say in society."

"Well," The Supreme replied, twisting a lock of hair around her finger, "you still need them to win."

He couldn't argue with her, no matter how much he despised Humanizers and those leaning toward the Humanizer party.

"I'd recommend you stop with the bachelor lifestyle. That might help."

"I wouldn't call myself a playboy by any means, Madam Supreme," Colin said, laughing. Deep down, Colin admitted some truth in her accusation. In the years after The University, Colin gained a bit of a reputation. He was a good-looking man and a charming one at that.

The Supreme chuckled deeply, her head tilting back as she let go of the lock of hair in her hand. Her scales pulsated from an amber to a shade of soft gold. Colin hadn't witnessed her scales change color since their youth, and his body softened at the familiarity they shared. While they hadn't remained close over the last few years, they grew up together and knew one another well.

"Find someone to settle in with during this campaign. It'll stop the rumors of your wild ways," she said with a devilish smile.

"My schedule is incredibly insane. How am I supposed to do that?" Colin admitted, a sigh exiting his chest. "I have committee meetings, advisory calls, and I need to find some time this week for Dr. Isabella Garcia."

"You should find time for Isabella; her insight into the food crisis is valuable. She's also beloved by everyone. Who wouldn't admire a selfless woman who gave up her career as a surgeon to help the less fortunate?" The Supreme nodded, a grin spreading across her scaly face. "And it helps that she's both single and easy on the eyes, too."

Chapter 18
Julie

June 30th, 33 A.R.

The bland, noisy hallway thrived with commotion while Julie waited. This hospital was acclaimed and prestigious but lacked any novel aesthetic. The bare walls were painted a cold beige, and the worn, faded floors had seen better days.

"Julie?"

She looked up, noticing her father at the other end of the hallway. Patrick Walsh was a lean man with tired bags under his eyes and pale red hair. When he smiled, his freckles danced around his face as if recklessly scattered there. Julie smiled hesitantly as he approached. She was relieved when he returned a smile.

"Yes, Dad?" Julie asked. He sat down beside her, grabbing her hand in his.

"Your mother is very happy you're here and wants to see you. Whenever you're ready," he responded, his faint smile glowing.

"I'm glad!" Julie said, eagerly getting up from her seat, but her father didn't release his hold on her hand.

"Dad?" Julie asked, looking at him with concern creeping into her body.

"Oh." He cleared his throat before letting go. "Sorry, hun."

Enthusiasm engulfed Julie's steps down the hallway. The past few months were particularly challenging for her mother. She didn't want to see Julie, was too tired, or didn't remember who her daughter was.

But not today.

When Julie reached the door, she knocked hesitantly and poked her head inside. Mrs. Walsh sat in a chair by the window, her gaze looking out toward The City. Her mother lifted her eyes and nodded at Julie. Mrs. Walsh was a beautiful woman but looked sickly now with sunken-in eyes and a thinness of her frame.

"Julie!" The sound of happiness and recognition in her mother's voice made Julie's emotions swell. Tears teased the corners of Julie's eyes, but she blinked them away quickly.

"Mom!" Julie approached her in a tight embrace. "I missed you."

"Here, come sit." Her mother patted the seat beside her. Julie settled in and grabbed her mother's hand. "How is school going?"

"I'm finishing my application for The University. I really hope I get in," Julie answered. The stress of getting accepted to The University constantly lingered in Julie's mind. If she wanted to pursue her dream as a scientist, this was her only option. If The University denied her application, she'd be sent to a trade school or start working as an office administrator.

"You'll get in. You're so smart, much smarter than either me or your father." Her mother chuckled and Julie laughed alongside her.

"You and Dad are both smart. You are an architect!"

"Was," her mother replied, looking away from Julie and back out at The City. "That feels so long ago now."

She released Julie's hand and a pang of disappointment flooded Julie's mind.

"What was the highlight of your week?" Julie asked her, knowing the nurses and doctors kept patients busy during the day.

Engagement and focus were imperative to a successful recovery, they had said.

"The woman next door and I painted. We worked on landscapes, but I miss designing buildings and sketching cityscapes."

"I know you do, Mom," Julie said, trying to keep the conversation optimistic. "But you can look outside and see buildings you've designed."

"Yes, I love those buildings. Do you remember my protégé, Charlie?"

Julie nodded slowly.

"He designed the new COLI*GO building." She pointed out the window and across The River. "It's beautiful, isn't it?"

"It really is. Maybe someday I'll see the inside."

"I bet someday you'll be on the top floor." Her mother pushed a lock of strawberry blonde hair behind Julie's ear. The gesture warmed Julie's heart. She was glad she inherited many features of her mother's, especially her gorgeous locks of hair and long elegant neck.

The two sat quietly together, Julie not minding the silence between them. Being with her mother felt peaceful today. Her dementia worsened the last few months; she couldn't remember her husband half the time. Patrick put on a brave face for his daughters, but both heard his sobs at night. The sound echoed in a heart-wrenching manner across the old wooden floorboards.

"They're going to kick you out soon," Julie's mother said with a gentle nudge of her elbow into Julie's side.

"I don't want them to."

Tears escaped from the corners of Julie's eyes. Her mother grabbed Julie tightly, pulling her into a warm but bony embrace.

"I know, honey."

"I wish I could do something," Julie said into her mother's neck as the tears crept down her face.

"If anyone could, it'd be you." Her mother let go and wiped away Julie's tears with her thumb.

No matter how much I want to save my mother right now, I can't.

"I love you, Julie. Please always remember that, even when I'm not me," her mother said, holding Julie's hands tightly in hers.

"Of course. I know that, Mom. I love you, too, more than you can imagine."

A quiet knock sounded from the door, and Julie heard the nurse enter.

"Miss Walsh, visiting hours are coming to a close," the faint voice said from behind her.

"Okay, thank you for letting me know."

She looked at her mother and hugged her once more before leaving her in that awful room alone.

Chapter 19
Mick

July 8th, 33 A.R.

Every time Mick ventured into the past or the future, he faced demons from his own life or the demons of people he cared about. Today, he found himself around the time of Julie's mother's death. But his purpose wasn't to see Julie; Mick came back needing a sample of Colin's blood.

Obtaining a sample in the present wasn't an option; he never interacted with the governor. The past was the safest path for execution. On election day, Mick planned on seeing Colin in the voting hall. There, he'd bump into Colin with a small pin—enough of a prick to collect the small sample he needed.

Mick stayed under the radar as much as possible while visiting the past. He occupied his time within the comforts of the carriage house, tinkering with the algorithm in his device as he examined blood samples. Here, he kept a detailed journal of not only his research but also his experiences.

When he wasn't working, he watched the O'Connor family through an old pair of binoculars he found in the bedroom. The family provided entertainment in his long and lonely days, and he found comfort in their familiarity. Old bloodline families kept similar traditions to conservative families in The Countryside. All members lived in the family residence until they started their new lives with a partner or left for a job in The City and always came together each night for dinner.

Henry O'Connor occupied the head of the dining room table, and Celine often sat to his left. She technically still lived in the townhouse, but Mick noticed her leave after dinner most nights, heading in the direction of Martin Borges's condo on the other side of The Hill. Colin always remained home.

Tonight, Mick grabbed his takeout ramen and settled into the couch position across from the windows. He looked at his food ironically, noting how he always lost weight when traveling time through someone else's blood. He added this observation to his journal.

Mick picked up his binoculars without a second thought and zoomed in. He spotted Colin instantly, the man stood at about six and a half feet and was hard to miss. There was a woman with him that Mick didn't recognize. She wasn't Dr. Isabella Garcia, the current woman of interest for Colin. Instead, this woman laughed with a younger smile and walked around the townhouse the way visitors wandered around a museum. The recessed ceiling lights reflected off her light brown hair. She wore a pair of fashionable slacks and a fitted jacket showing off her narrow figure.

Who is she? Mick questioned.

He fumbled with the binoculars more, steadying them in his shaky hands. What happened between Colin and her didn't appear innocent, but the hallways cast dark shadows.

Mick felt the preparation on his hands slip as the binoculars fell in his lap.

He picked them up quickly and dropped the ramen onto the couch, spilling half the takeout container in the process. By the time he steadied himself, everything appeared dark, the shadows vanished, and the girl was gone.

All Mick could see was Colin heading toward the staircase.

Chapter 20
The Supreme

July 10th, 33 A.R.

"I don't understand," Celine said, staring back at The Supreme from across her desk.

Regardless of their business and political ties, The Supreme and Celine were childhood friends. The Supreme remained by Celine's side since their youth and young adulthood. They never backstabbed one another, but today, Celine felt blindsided by her friend and her brother.

"Did I plant the seed in his brain that he needed to stop his bachelor lifestyle? Sure. But it takes two to tango, isn't that the saying?" The Supreme asked, looking directly at Celine.

Celine huffed like a child. Living in the footsteps of someone like Celine's father was challenging enough, let alone now her brother ran for office. Colin and Celine always sought out their father's approval, but The Supreme knew they craved his affection for different reasons. Celine was savvy and witty; she wasn't intellectual in a technical sense, but her creativity uniquely shone through. She looked at her business success with COLI*GO as a showcase of her power. Colin gained his father's attention differently; he used his overly confident masculinity and interest in politics to pique his interest. While they disagreed on ideology, the idea of Colin imitating his father's career choices showed his dedication to family tradition. The Supreme admired Colin's intellect, remembering fondly their time together at The University. He had stealth masked by undeniable charm.

The Supreme identified this dynamic relationship between the O'Connor siblings in her younger years and spent time deciphering the ins and outs of their psyches. What surprised her most was no matter how often the siblings pushed one another's buttons, they always protected each other. This deep-rooted loyalty was an emotion The Supreme inherently didn't comprehend, but she acknowledged and logically respected the sentiment.

Unlike Colin or Celine, The Supreme always knew her destiny. She'd been manufactured in FACERE, the android manufacturing laboratory in The City, for this role specifically. Everything in Emilia's life was planned; choice simply didn't exist for her. She didn't mind; androids were rooted in logic and control, a nice check and balance against the wide range of emotions and inconsistencies found in human nature.

Being the most powerful android and leading all androids across The Constituency was an honor. The Supreme couldn't fail, so she fought against segregation and disparities each day.

"I think it's good for him. I understand you dislike her; she's definitely a bit trite. But you can't deny she's loved by people across The Constituency. A sweetheart of sorts," The Supreme answered, speaking of Dr. Isabella Garcia.

Celine's icy sharp eyes sliced through her gaze. She couldn't stomach the idea of her brother being involved with the Garcia family. What bothered Celine more was how he praised Isabella and then courted her. Old bloodline families were typically only allowed courtships with other old bloodline families, but Celine wished his interests were with just about anyone else. Shortly after Colin and Isabella's relationship went public, the Garcia family publicly endorsed his bid for governor and his numbers in the polls skyrocketed.

She hated the Garcias. Celine reached out to Isabella's father, Filipe, for an investment in COLI*GO. With their origin from The Island, they were highly respected across the networks of old bloodline families from outside The City. Their support in COLI*GO was a perfect fit.

Until it wasn't.

Filipe dragged Celine along like a puppet with his indecisiveness. He believed in COLI*GO's mission of unity but played Celine in the end, shaming her within social circles, making it more difficult for her to gather the support she needed to start the company. All stemmed from some old feud between him and her father.

"It's about controlling Colin and the election. Don't you see if he wins, how much better it would be over Don Ludewing?" The Supreme asked, running a hand down her scaly arm as if she knew without looking her colors slightly grew deeper, more vibrant.

"Control? Control Colin? Are you out of your mind? He's wild, unpredictable . . . He thinks he can do anything without any consequences," Celine responded, hitting her hand on The Supreme's desk.

"He's not wild or unpredictable. He's easily swayed by his emotions. I think he knows that about himself, and that's why he tries so hard to be cold and distant."

Celine looked at her as if they were speaking about two different people.

"Celine, my dear. You don't know?"

"Know what?" Celine asked, looking past The Supreme to the window behind her.

The Supreme sighed and shook her head.

"I think your brother will tell you in his own time. It is not my secret to tell," The Supreme said in a quiet tone.

The room grew silent for a few minutes while Celine gathered her thoughts. The Supreme eyed Celine's body language, noting her friend's deep inhales, fidgety hands, and the deep flush spreading across her skin. While The Supreme's scales gave away her true thoughts, Celine's complexion exposed her.

"I feel like he's betraying the family. And he's betraying me," Celine said after a moment, a twinge of hurt exposing itself in her cracked tone.

The Supreme understood all human emotions, and "hurt" was one she actually experienced from time to time. She reached her hand out and grabbed Celine's.

"I understand you feel hurt that your brother brought the Garcias back into your lives. As if he showed you and your father no respect." The Supreme made direct eye contact with Celine.

Celine nodded after a moment.

"Don likes the status quo. Colin has better ideas. He wants equality, unity. Colin envisions a world where everyone is much better off, where success can happen for anyone. Where everyone has a chance, regardless if they are human or android. You have the same values; it's why you started COLI*GO," The Supreme said and let go of Celine's hand.

"I don't disagree with you. I'm glad you're my friend, and I'm grateful for your support. I can't help but feel angry about Isabella."

"What is that saying?" The Supreme asked. "Keep your friends close but keep your enemies closer?"

Celine looked up at her and smirked. "I hadn't thought about it that way."

The Supreme imagined the thousands of ideas circling Celine's mind. *Plant the seeds, plant the seeds . . .*

"And that's why you have me, my dear."

***

The commissioner's office in the precinct was as bland as the android himself. The Supreme wasn't particularly fond of spending time with The commissioner but it was part of their duties. Their weekly meetings were normally discreet and efficient. Normally.

Today was different.

The Supreme noticed his feet fidgeting beneath him and the lips on his thin cheeks puckering together tightly.

"What are you not telling me?" The Supreme asked him bluntly.

"I don't like this," he said, leaning his tablet down so that The Supreme could see it. "Dr. Anna Garcia has noticed some . . . patterns."

"Patterns?"

"A homicide was called in last night. We were able to keep the media off it. But I don't imagine how we'll keep them away for too long given the circumstances."

She looked at him, waiting. "I don't have all day, Commissioner."

"I know," he said, taking a deep breath, "but the young woman who was murdered, her profile fits the same as the serial killer from a few years ago. She's a legislative aide for a member of The Ways and Means Committee . . ." He trailed off, looking through his notes.

"Representative Atkinson?" The Supreme ventured with a guess.

Representative Atkinson supported Don Ludewing and was an outspoken Humanizer. His current obsession was shifting budgets away from android assistance programs. Colin O'Connor despised him.

"Yes," the commissioner said. "But that's not all. She was stabbed twenty-three times, as outlined by Dr. Garcia. She's making a huge fuss about it because we 'didn't do enough last time' according to her."

The Supreme grabbed the commissioner's tablet from his hands and scrolled through the report. The images showcased the gruesome body behind a dumpster in The Bay. The forensics came up fairly empty—no trace of the killer left behind. The Supreme continued glancing through Dr. Garcia's autopsy report. She didn't know Dr. Anna Garcia well, other than that she was good at her job and fresh out of medical school. This new, young Chief Medical Examiner asked too many questions for The Supreme's liking.

The autopsy notes outlined twenty-three stab wounds and strangulation marks on the woman's neck. Dr. Garcia even linked the report with cold cases from her predecessor, stating either a copycat killer emerged or the "uncaught serial killer is back." The words "serial killer" were underlined several times.

"This is a disastrous media frenzy," The Supreme said, throwing the tablet back on the desk.

"Doesn't The City deserve to know about the potential of an uncaught serial killer?" the commissioner asked her.

The Supreme thought for a moment too long, and the commissioner viciously slammed his hand down on the desk. His scaled pulsated deeper blue hues around his body.

"Madam Supreme!" His voice bellowed forcefully around the room.

"Look," she said, "I see your side, but this will cause mass hysteria and this is an important election cycle. We can't afford any distractions and unease."

"Then what are we going to do? The girl's family needs to be notified."

"She doesn't have any family here. Her family lives out in The

Countryside," The Supreme answered.

"How do you know that?" The commissioner's eyes locked in with The Supreme's, analyzing her. She drew her face down and matched his gaze.

"I knew her, Commissioner. I work with The Ways and Means Committee nearly every day," The Supreme replied.

"So, what are you suggesting I do here?"

"Bury it."

"But what about Dr. Garcia?"

"Tell her the truth. There is no next of kin. There's nothing in the forensics report. Unless new evidence emerges or someone comes forward with information, there's simply nothing we can do." The Supreme reached over and grabbed the tablet one more time off his desk. "And tell her to change her goddamn autopsy report. We don't need any extremists in The City getting unhinged. Do I need to remind you of The Resurgence? How The Resurgence started over the brutal killings of a few androids? Imagine if humans, particularly the Humanizers, ignited that now for humans?"

The commissioner looked up at her, the hollow appearance of his face intensified in pure defeat.

***

The sound of the violin echoed in The Supreme's ears. She looked out toward the O'Connor box, noting Colin and Isabella together. The two weren't paying attention to the orchestra onstage. Instead, they appeared to be in a very deep, consuming conversation with one another. The Supreme felt a smile spread across her face as a sudden silence pierced the room for a brief pause before the crowd erupted in applause. Now was her time to visit the hopeful soon-to-be governor and his date. The android attendant smiled at her as she approached.

The mahogany door of the O'Connor box opened, and Colin greeted her. He looked surprised by The Supreme's presence and her moment of intrusion on his night out.

"Madam Supreme, to what do I owe this pleasure?" he asked in his crisp but deep voice.

The Supreme watched him intently as he exited the box. Colin was a very tall man. The Supreme herself stood almost six feet tall, but looking up at him, she couldn't help but experience a slight nervousness.

"Are you not going to invite me in?" The Supreme asked coyly.

Colin raised his eyebrows at her and opened the door behind him. Isabella looked up from her seat and smiled at them. She was a charming woman, modern but still feminine. Her hair was pulled back tightly in a long sleek ponytail, and her dark caramel skin glowed against the twinkling chandeliers.

"Good evening, Dr. Garcia."

"Please, call me Isabella," she replied, getting up from her seat and embracing The Supreme in an informal hug. In Isabella's embrace, The Supreme noticed Colin's dark stare.

"I couldn't help but notice the two of you from my box across the way. I wanted to say hello during the intermission."

The Supreme suddenly felt the emotion of "agitation" coursing through her. She thrived on control but felt a difference in Colin's presence from the last time they were together.

"Colin and I were actually discussing his campaign schedule over the next few weeks, and I always appreciate a distraction from logistics. What is the point of a nice evening out if politics and business ruin it?" Isabella asked.

The Supreme nodded. While Dr. Garcia was charming, she was still tirelessly chatty.

"We certainly shouldn't discuss politics now, darling; it would put Madam Supreme in an uncomfortable position," Colin said as his hand lingered on the small of Isabella's back.

"Darling?" The Supreme said aloud before she realized the words escaped her.

Isabella blushed in response.

"Well," The Supreme said, giving the two an awkward glance. "I don't want to interrupt your evening together. But I did want to say hello and congratulations on the latest poll numbers. They look very promising."

"Thank you," Colin said as he opened the door to escort her out.

Surprisingly, Colin followed The Supreme out of the box and

closed the door before firmly grabbing her arm. The foreign feeling of human skin against her scales made her shiver.

"I appreciate all you do to help COLI*GO and my gubernatorial campaign," Colin said in a low voice, his eyes darting around the narrow hallway to make sure they were alone. "But please don't put a wedge between me and my sister again. Or you will regret that decision."

He let go of her arm forcibly and opened the door to the box quickly before disappearing behind it.

Maybe Celine was correct, she thought. Colin O'Connor wasn't as easy to control as she assumed. But The Supreme was tired of playing the mental chess game in The Capitol Building alone. She appreciated the challenge.

Chapter 21
Jones

July 16th, 33 A.R.

Jones still navigated the thousands of new emotions and feelings he now understood after Julie updated his processor. Sadly, heartbreak was one he comprehended. He couldn't comfort Julie other than simply hold her as she sobbed.

They met in the park across from her family's home after she messaged him. Jones wasn't expecting to hear her mother had died.

The monument in the middle of the park stared down at the two of them with a sense of solitude, as if understanding this serious moment. Many historical statues and monuments didn't survive The Resurgence, but The Monument's namesake lasted.

You understand better now. With that comes responsibility, Jones thought as he held Julie through her cries. She risked everything for him; this was the least he could do.

After Julie had reprogrammed his microchip, Jones went home, afraid his sponsors would notice a change in him.

They hadn't.

Instead, everything continued normally. Jones retained a bit of his inhuman, logical personality but gained a new understanding of emotions and feelings. "Belonging" resonated strongly with him, especially as they all prepared for exams.

Julie dreamed of attending The University, but he wasn't sure what was next for him. For the first time, Jones experienced the emotion of loneliness as he imagined her leaving him behind. Jones hated the feelings he witnessed Julie experience in his arms. He read them on her like a book: anger, hurt, sadness, and even regret. Only time and empathy could help Julie now.

"I don't understand. She was finally doing better," Julie said in between her tears. Jones rubbed her back in slow circles as loud bursts of sobs emerged from her.

The summer day was sweltering, leaving the two mostly alone in the park. At first, Julie wasn't forthcoming about the circumstances of her mother's death. When she finally confided in him, Jones experienced horror for the first time—another emotion he didn't realize he now understood until he faced it head-on.

Jones recalled Julie's optimism from her recent visit with her, and even her father was hopeful Mrs. Walsh had finally emerged from her worst episode. Julie spoke of her mother coming home soon.

No one expected Mrs. Walsh would steal a nurse's badge, gain access to the rooftop, and jump off the building. Logically, Jones couldn't blame her; Mrs. Walsh's mind wasn't her own anymore, and he believed there was no worse feeling than having zero control over that knowledge.

Chapter 22
The Governor

September 4th, 33 A.R.

Colin walked into the voting booth with clammy hands and nervousness in his gut. Today was the day. No matter how much Kathleen assured him he was up in the polls, Colin felt uneasy until all the votes were counted. In this surreal moment, he imagined his father sitting at home, proud of his son.

In reality, this wasn't the case. Colin and his father weren't on speaking terms, and in the past few months, Henry's Alzheimer's and health declined rapidly.

Colin looked down at the screen and a monitor scanned his eyes to verify his identity. Upon approval in the system, the ballot appeared. Seeing his name in front of him made him pause.

Months of endless nights from the campaign were finally behind him. While the tiredness of his days was only beginning if he won the election, he looked forward to restless days in The Capitol Building. Colin selected his name and filled out the rest of the ballot with ease. The media waited outside for him along with Isabella. The thought of her presence brought him an unexpected sense of relief.

As he exited the partician, a young man entered behind him. They collided abruptly and harshly as a small but sharp pain pierced Colin's upper left arm. The man looked familiar as he awkwardly stumbled by.

"I'm so sorry," the man said, rushing away and ducking behind a voting booth. A small trail of blood dotted across Colin's arm, and he shook his head, brushing off the odd incident and continuing to the exit.

Isabella approached him and grabbed his hand in hers. She voted earlier in the day on The Island and flew back to The City. Colin strategically waited until midday and took the morning to speak with some of the first voters at the polls. He'd spend the rest of the day visiting other polling locations across The City, stopping at as many municipalities as possible before ending back at the townhouse. The rest of his campaign staff waited for him there, along with his family and closest friends.

Tonight, they'd be celebrating or commiserating, but if Colin knew Kathleen, he was sure a ridiculous amount of booze and food would get them through the evening.

***

Colin felt dizzy. He couldn't concentrate in the room as the results poured in from across different parts of The Constituency. He was ahead in The City, but Don still held a slight lead in The Countryside. Everywhere else, the race was too close to call. The smile grew on Kathleen's face as she read updates on her device.

"They're votin' for yah, Colin!" she exclaimed, her accent more pronounced after her fourth cocktail.

Colin wrapped his arm around her shoulders. He appreciated Kathleen's support through this experience. She risked everything: her career and stability working for his father and eventually Don. Kathleen showed Colin true loyalty, and he vowed to never forget.

"Kid, I think yah got this," she said into his ear.

"All thanks to you," he replied before giving her a kiss on the cheek before stepping away from the dining room.

Isabella, Celine, and other guests were in the front living space of the townhouse, but Colin headed down the hall to the staircase. He ascended the spiral stairs while looking out the windows at The City. The party downstairs raged on below, but another thought lingered in Colin's mind.

The loud sounds drowned out as he continued climbing the stairs. Once he reached the top, Colin turned his head to the end of the hallway. Colin approached the last door on the left and paused before knocking gently on the doorframe. This guest bedroom occupied his father.

"Come in," he heard faintly from behind the door.

Colin stepped into the room cautiously and closed the door behind him. Henry sat at his desk instead of his normal position in bed. His father appeared more alert, his stature reminding Colin of his younger years when he found him intimidating.

"Father," Colin stated, staring him in the eyes.

Henry gawked without saying a word, and the silence between them sliced through Colin's mind harshly.

"I'm going to win this election."

"You don't deserve it." His father's words hurt more than Colin had anticipated even though he expected them.

"I've never been worthy enough for you," Colin responded flatly. The two men looked at one another. Their twenty-year stand-off pulsing around them, neither would concede now.

"At least you have some sense of control like me. Like my father and his father before him. The only difference between you and the rest of the O'Connor men is that you're a coward. You will ruin everything I've built. You'll tarnish our legacy with your ridiculous belief in unity and equality."

"All I ever wanted was for you to believe in me. I'm not a coward!" Colin yelled back at him. "I have solid ideas that will extend the O'Connor legacy, but no, it's never good enough for you. Are you threatened that I might be a more beloved governor than you? That I might bring more prosperity than you could ever imagine? Are you jealous, Father?"

The room darkened around Colin, the air humming with a fuzzy, strange sound. He grabbed the vial on his father's desk and drew the needle. The pharmaceutical calmed his father during hysterical episodes, but the drug was volatile if too much was administered. His father's steely blue eyes reflected off the glass bottle.

"Go ahead, put me out of my misery. I don't want to be part of this world when you're in charge. You're a fucking coward, Colin. You were as a child, and you still are now. You'll always be weak!" Henry yelled as Colin injected him with the substance.

The amount in the needle wouldn't kill Henry. Not today. Not tomorrow. But by putting him in a vegetable state, Celine would eventually need to make the horrid decision about whether or not to end his life.

Colin grasped himself in his hands as he shook hysterically.

Why did I do something that'll hurt Celine? He knew the answer: for his own peace, his own resolution.

"Colin?"

He heard the familiar voice call from behind him. The sound comforted him.

Colin hastily collected himself, wiping the tears from the corner of his eyes and discreetly slipping the needle into his pocket.

"I'm sorry, I was checking on my father," he said, walking toward the door.

Chapter 23
It

September 4th, 33 A.R.

Colin didn't always think about the consequences of his actions, but that's why Colin had It. They knew one another for so long now; It sensed when something was off with his friend. With the spotlight on his family, Colin never had many friends growing up, and being an outcast, It didn't have many friends either. Colin depended on him as much as he depended on Colin.

It watched Colin smile with an exhausted look in his eyes. It couldn't help but feel proud of his friend, not for becoming the youngest elected governor. This was much larger than that.

Colin held up his champagne flute and grinned before starting his toast. Isabella's arm wrapped tightly around Colin's waist, and she looked up at him with her beautiful hazel eyes and perfectly straight white teeth. Colin's life appeared perfect to an outsider, but It knew better.

He continued watching as the crowd cheered and clapped as Colin spoke. His words were filled with endless "thank yous" and "I couldn't have done this without you" isms. Everyone raised their glasses one last time and cheered on their new governor.

There is no one better for this job than Colin, It admitted.

The crowd dispersed into their own circles and conversations, and It observed everyone. There was so much adrenaline, excitement, and optimism filling the room. This collective group of people and androids held influential posts in society, working with and against one another.

Six years wasn't long, but It instinctively knew there would be a second term, maybe even a third. Colin was young; he'd make a career of being governor for his whole life if the voters let him. He was an O'Connor after all.

The stuffy room closed in around It, clouding his mind and disorienting him. The alcohol he consumed didn't help his situation, but he was familiar with the townhouse. This felt like his home, too. It knew every hallway, each painting, and all the nooks and crannies. The best-kept secret of the house was up on the roof deck.

It climbed up the circular staircase and opened the door to the roof. He let out a sigh of relief into the intoxicatingly muggy air, not realizing how stale he previously felt inside the townhouse.

The roof deck showcased a 360-degree view of The City's skyline. Turning to the west, It took in the sights of The River and the new COLI*GO building. The reflection of the lights shimmered like diamonds in the water.

At least up here I can think, It noted.

A creaking sound from the door rang through It's ears as the silhouette of The Supreme emerged from the faint glow of the hallway. He relaxed a bit upon recognizing her.

The Supreme strode over gracefully without saying a word. She wore a very professional black fitted suit, the same one she'd wear when swearing in Colin as the governor the next day. Her scales shimmered against the darkness, the beauty of her golden amber resting across her figure. Faint sounds of celebrations continuing downstairs echoed behind them, contrasting to the stillness in the air around them.

"I felt lost for a long time. My purpose wasn't clear," It said, breaking the silence between them. "But I feel like I can see again."

The Supreme smiled coyly at him and looked out over across The River at the COLI*GO building. She patted his shoulder.

"Well, we have a lot of work to do, my friend."

PART FIVE

Twelve Years Later

"I desire the things which will destroy me in the end."
-Sylvia Plath

Chapter 24
Julie

January 28th, 45 A.R.

Julie didn't have a plan for The Board of Directors meeting in two weeks. They requested an update on the antidote, and her news wasn't positive.

She pinged Colin earlier, asking if he'd review her draft report. While Colin didn't fully comprehend the nuances in the science, he asked thought-provoking questions and anticipated the queries of his fellow board members.

Colin and Julie developed an unspoken process for working together over the last two years. Colin's insights between the executives at COLI*GO and representatives at The Capitol Building were invaluable. He taught Julie the art of understanding financial implications, allocations of resources, and other core business-related processes she previously had no experience in.

After slipping Colin her initial findings two years ago, the trajectory of the antidote took off. Martin was impressed and secured extra funding from his budget for the project. He instructed Julie to expense the resources to an obscure accounting line item within the R&D cost center. But even with the impressive advances of the antidote, Martin insisted Julie remained focused on the COL2120 project.

Julie read through her reports from The University and used the extra funding on the antidote to move beyond just Alzheimer's. She identified the antidote's potential for patients suffering from psychological conditions; particularly depression and trauma-related disorders impacting memory functions. The effects remained promising throughout testing, as the antidote focused on repairing damaged receptors within the brain through its advanced gene-editing process.

With a year of additional research, Martin presented the antidote to the board members, requesting more funding. The Supreme insisted Julie find someone to work part-time on COL2120 in her absence, but Julie was overworked. Colin provided assistance wherever possible to help cut through the red tape and roadblocks. Through this experience, Julie learned COLI*GO was a political disaster. The Supreme remained Julie's mentor, and Julie never divulged their close relationship to Colin. Research was Julie's specialty, and she observed the complex relationship between him and The Supreme.

Julie assumed the tension festered between the governor and The Supreme from their working relationship at The Capitol Building before Julie discovered they'd grown up together. In The University alumni archives, Julie found photos of Colin, Celine, and The Supreme in their younger years. Colin graduated with his sister and The Supreme even though he was two years younger.

This discovery surprised Julie; there was so much about Colin beyond the surface. He was an exceptional student; he excelled in various subjects from mathematics to philosophy. Learning more about him was a welcome distraction while Julie continued testing the antidote. Colin intrigued her while the error codes in her simulations agitated her.

Her device pinged with a message from Colin, distracting her from her thoughts.

Can you come to The townhouse later to discuss your report? I'm wrapped up in a hearing and don't think I can make it across The River today.

Julie looked at her screen for a moment. Her device pinged again.

As long as you're okay with that?

A nervousness filled her stomach, but she replied back she'd be over later that evening.

***

The Hill was a picturesque and magical neighborhood with centuries-old buildings constructed with beautiful copper and red bricks. The snowfall from earlier in the day lightly dusted the roads with blissful ease and gas lamps stately lined the streets. Even in the dead of winter, charm filled the cobblestone streets like a forbidden lover.

Julie approached the O'Connor townhouse and paused. She'd passed by this residence many times but never fully appreciated which family occupied the home. The impressive structure wasn't overly ostentatious but rather alluring and elegant. Julie's gaze lifted to the black iron gate as a small device scanned her eye. After identifying her, the gate opened with a soft click.

A small chuckle escaped Julie's lips as she approached the front door. There was no doorbell or intercom in sight but rather an old-fashioned doorknocker in the shape of a lion's head. The heavy weight of the knocker fell loudly from her hands. Colin's welcoming smile greeted her on the other side of the door.

"Hello, Julie." His deep voice rang through her ears as he stepped back and allowed her entrance into his home.

Julie's light footsteps stopped abruptly in the entryway. She looked over at Colin with wide eyes, and a flush spread across her freckled cheeks.

"This is yours?" she asked, walking past Colin and running her hand on the deep mahogany banister.

"Well, it's the family's townhouse, but I suppose, yes, it's mine for now." Colin smiled, noting the pure wonder flashing through Julie's eyes.

Her gaze shifted to the artwork lining the perfectly wood-paneled walls. Original chandeliers and light fixtures illuminated the exquisiteness of the home, and she admired an intricate painting of a woman leaning down toward a man's shoes. The initials "JT" slashed the bottom right-hand corner. This painting was oddly placed next to a coveted and rare Monet, the delicate flowers and soft field a vibrant difference. A home with such treasures and charms reminded Julie that Colin O'Connor was from an old bloodline family. But even with the expensive décor, Julie felt a warmth on her skin as she ventured further into Colin's home.

Colin led them into an expansive living area designed for

entertaining. The architecture of the first floor was open and massive, the living room and kitchen intertwined as one space. A substantial fireplace with white-painted bricks spanned from floor to ceiling, and a warm fire sparked inside.

"Oh," Julie said with a pause. "I picked up food on my way over."

Colin took the paper bag out of her hands and headed toward the kitchen. Julie followed him eagerly, elongating her steps in order to keep up with him. Colin removed the containers and placed them on the extended marble island, gesturing Julie toward the barstools on the other side. She obeyed without hesitation, watching as Colin reached with complete effortlessness to grab plates from the highest shelves in the cabinet. He placed a glass of water and a plate down in front of Julie before opening the food containers slowly and methodically. Julie noted Colin performed each task with a sense of purpose both inside and outside his home.

Julie found herself watching Colin, wondering why she didn't feel nervous in his home. He was the governor, the highest-ranking official in all The Constituency and one of the most powerful men in society, if not the most powerful. Oddly enough, comfort and ease filled her chest as she relaxed into her seat.

He wants me to trust him, she sensed. *I'm a nobody, and I was invited to the governor's estate.*

Colin looked over at her, and a sly smirk crept up the corners of his lips.

"You're quiet. Is something bothering you?"

"Did you read the report I sent you?" Julie asked.

"Of course I read it," Colin brooded in response.

Julie sat up straight in her seat, surprised by his answer.

"The antidote has an error in the latest simulation."

"Isn't that expected? Don't all drugs have side effects?"

"Yes." Julie sighed before looking at Colin. "But the issue is, I can't identify why."

Colin stood completely still, giving her his undivided attention.

"The purpose of the antidote is two-fold," Julie explained. "First, it attaches to the part of the brain that collects and stores memories. Then the antidote learns from healthy cells and identifies damaged receptors to help them regenerate and grow."

Julie took a gulp of water and looked down and away from Colin's intense stare. "But sometimes, the antidote regenerates the unhealthy cell. Sometimes, the antidote allows the disease to take over instead of curing it."

"What do you mean by sometimes?" Colin asked, placing their silverware down with a loud bang.

"Not often," Julie rambled. "That's the fault of gene therapy. We're essentially instructing the drug to use the patient's genetic makeup to assist in treatment. I think I can fix this, but I'm not confident in testing in human subjects yet."

"How often does this happen, Julie?" Colin asked a bit stronger.

"Roughly 15 percent of the time."

Colin's body relaxed, and relief filled his previously worried eyes. But worry remained deep inside Julie's chest, the tightness squeezing her rapidly beating heart.

"I was afraid you were going to say 50 percent," Colin responded with a chuckle.

"Fifteen percent is terrible."

Colin and I have completely different backgrounds. This is astronomical to me and insignificant to him.

"Julie," Colin said, walking toward the other end of the kitchen, "we've only secured sufficient funding for this project over the last few months. Cut yourself some slack. At this rate, you'll figure out the errors quickly. Don't be surprised by a slight setback in the progress of your antidote."

If only it was that simple.

"Martin won't agree," Julie protested. "Neither will The Supreme. They're driven by the data. The data isn't sufficient to start testing in live subjects, much less ask The Legislature for an application for a clinical trial."

"Martin is the last person you need to worry about, and don't worry about The Legislature; that's my job," Colin replied sternly. "And The Supreme? She speaks highly of you. I'm not sure how you pulled that one off."

"She does?" Julie asked, her tone rising higher in shock.

Colin walked back over from the other end of the kitchen,

holding a bottle of Chianti.

"Normally, I'd say we should wait until all our work is taken care of before opening a bottle of wine," Colin said, his large hands gripping the bottle tightly as he pulled the cork loose, "but you nearly gave me heart failure and, honestly, you need to relax a little."

He filled a glass with the ruby red liquid and handed it to her. Julie took the glass to her lips and drank hesitantly. The strong aroma relaxed her face and made her body feel lighter.

"The Supreme can't know I'm helping you." Colin looked down as he spoke, a darkness flashing across his eyes.

"Of course not," Julie replied almost too quickly.

"I know you admire her," Colin said more gently this time. "And I do as well. But we have a very complicated relationship. She's a strategic game player, and I don't want to give her any advance moves."

"As I've promised several times before, I won't mention it to her," Julie said, slightly annoyed.

Trust works both ways, Colin.

But when he grinned in her direction, the tension between them faded. Colin leaned forward across the kitchen island, his face much closer to Julie's. She smelled his smoky aftershave and returned a delicate smile.

"So, what's the game plan for the meeting? How do I effectively deliver terrible news?"

The soft clicking of high heels on the hardwood floors filled Julie's ears before Isabella's presence emerged in Julie's line of vision. Isabella paused at the top of the stairs, her tan skin glowing effortlessly even in the dead of winter.

"Hello, Dr. Walsh." Isabella's crisp voice filled the room as she descended the last set of stairs.

"Hello, Doctor."

Isabella gracefully approached Colin in the kitchen, a raised brow of skepticism crossed her face as she eyed their food and the open bottle of wine.

"How are things at COLI*GO?" Isabella asked Julie, her large lips still faintly painted with the red lipstick she wore that day. Her chic maroon and black dress hugged her in all the right places, extenuating the curve of her hips and petite frame.

"Busy. We're preparing for the board meeting in a couple weeks," Julie answered, leaning back in her chair and putting distance between herself and Colin.

For the first time since arriving at Colin's home, Julie felt nervous and unsettled.

"I'm sure you'll do great; you're very confident," Isabella responded curtly.

The compliment stung as Julie's eyes shifted over toward Colin. Surprisingly, she found his gaze hadn't left her, even with Isabella's entrance.

"I suppose I am in the right circumstances." Julie brought her wine glass to her lips and took a lengthy sip. She didn't want to say more and welcomed the distraction as Isabella settled into the seat next to her.

"I put slides together for you," Colin said to Julie, ignoring Isabella completely. "I figured it'd give you a head start when you mentioned you needed extra time in the lab today."

He pulled his device out of his briefcase and handed it to Julie. She glanced through the slides, thankful for his gesture. Placing her device beneath Colin's, she electronically transferred the file. Her eyes widened when she reached his bullet points on the project timelines.

"We need to push this out," Julie noted, scrunching up her nose.

Colin smirked at her. "How did I know you'd say that?"

The two laughed. Julie eased on her enthusiasm when she sensed Isabella's awkwardness around them; Isabella didn't understand their unspoken banter. Isabella picked at some of the food, her eyes never leaving Julie and Colin.

"With only me on the project, I'll need at least three months for testing and an additional two or three months to actually fix the problem. Six months is safer versus the three you've indicated here." Julie pointed toward the screen.

"We can't stretch the budget out over six months." Colin closed his eyes for a moment. "How about four months?"

Julie looked down at the latest data set from the simulation. The error terrified her, and she never liked over-promising. Colin observed the concerned expression in Julie's eyes, and she felt his large warm hand rest gently on top of hers.

"Maybe I can get you an extra set of hands?" he asked softly.

Julie nodded, a smile spreading across her face as optimism blossomed in her chest. She updated the slides as Colin poured her another glass of wine. His eyes wandered over to Isabella's peculiar stare.

"Would you like a glass, darling?"

"Yes," she responded coolly, and Colin poured her a glass very slowly. "I'll head back upstairs. You two seem busy, and I have to prepare for the food drive next month."

"It was really nice seeing you, Doctor," Julie said as Isabella rose from her seat.

"It was, yes," Isabella said with a smirk. "Why don't we have lunch sometime soon? I'll have my assistant send you a calendar invitation."

"Yes. I would like that," Julie responded, although she wasn't sure if she really meant it.

"Please make sure Colin finds you a ride home tonight. It's very cold, and I don't want you walking the streets of The City alone," Isabella said before ascending the stairs.

Chapter 25
Mick

February 8th, 45 A.R.

Mick walked through the large glass doors, his jaw dropping in awe. He now worked at the most influential company in The City. When Julie called him a few months ago asking if he'd work part-time for her at COLI*GO, he didn't know how to respond. Jones pushed him to accept and take time off from his time travel research, assuming Mick's declining health was stress related, not a side effect from time travel.

"Imagine if you land something full-time afterward, Mick?" Jones encouraged him, seeing the salary in his offer.

The idea of a full-time role enticed Mick but only after he perfected his time travel device. His research remained his top priority.

"Hey Mick!"

Mick turned around as Julie entered the lobby behind him. Like Mick, Julie was an early bird and one of the first to arrive in the office, but Mick rarely saw her. The days he worked were days she spent away from COL2120 and on a "classified" project, one he assumed was her antidote.

"Julie, how are you?" he asked, waiting for her to catch up to him. Mick fidgeted with his jacket, attempting to hide the weight he'd recently lost.

"I'm well; how are you? I feel like I haven't seen you in ages," she replied as they scanned their badges at the elevator doors.

"I'm really enjoying this job; I feel like I've picked up with the team. They're great."

Julie probably suspected this already; Mick's likeability was one reason why she hired him. He never caused conflicts in teams and was an effective but efficient researcher.

"That's great. I'm hoping to offer you a full-time role by the end of the spring," Julie said in a soft voice as they entered the elevator.

"Is the other project the antidote? The one you worked on at The University?" Mick asked her in a returned whisper.

Julie didn't vocally respond but nodded instead. Her eyes took in Mick's body, pausing at the fine lines spreading out from his eyes and across his otherwise perfect ebony skin.

"I'm worried about you," she said, placing her hand on his arm while they walked into the lab.

They grabbed their lab coats in the entryway, and Julie's eyes wandered away from Mick for a moment.

"Are you asking, or is this Jones asking?" Mick asked, raising his eyebrow in accusation.

"Can't we both be concerned about you?"

"I suppose."

Julie agitatedly sighed in response to Mick's reply before wrapping her arms around him. Her out-of-character gesture made Mick's body stiffen and still before returning the embrace.

"Why don't we grab lunch next Wednesday?" Mick asked her as she released her hold on him.

Julie pulled out her device and pulled up her calendar.

"Shit," she replied. "I have lunch plans with Isabella Garcia that day."

"As in the famous philanthropist?"

"Yes, that's the one," Julie responded flatly.

"I remember seeing her once when she visited The Countryside. Let me know how your lunch goes."

"I'm sure it won't be overly exciting. I'm not sure why she wants to meet with me." Julie shrugged.

"Do I get to work with you today?" Mick asked her, changing the subject.

"No, unfortunately not. But once I have more budget for the other project," she said, stopping as they reached the final door to the lab, "there is no other scientist I'd want to work with."

Mick smiled. He missed her.

The four years since graduation were difficult. They lost a sense of touch with one another with how busy their lives had become. At least Mick still had Jones, but lately, Jones also worried him. His boyfriend seemed completely absorbed in his own detective work, obsessing over the unsolved case of Kendra Washington.

When they first moved into their apartment in The Harbor, Mick turned the guest bedroom into an office space for his time travel research. Within the last two years, Jones transformed their living room into a warzone housing various records, documents, and crime scene notes. Photographs, names, and dates sprawled across the windows; Jones's fascination in uncovering The City's uncaught serial killer consumed him.

Sometimes, Anna Garcia joined Jones in their living room. If she wasn't in their home, Jones was at Anna's loft apartment in The Port. Mick knew they were only colleagues, but he found her equally fixated obsession odd. And like her famous sister Isabella, Anna Garcia was equally as beautiful.

Mick looked at himself in the mirror behind the lab door. His face was ghost-like and horrid. He wondered if Jones wasn't attracted to him anymore. Isolation wasn't an emotion Jones understood, or at least one Mick didn't think Jones comprehended. The more Mick traveled time, the more he found it increasingly difficult to express himself to the person he loved.

***

Mick came home to an empty apartment. No Jones, no Anna. After scraping together leftovers, the silence consumed his mind, and dark thoughts tormented him. Mick found shaking the memories of time travel more difficult the more often he traveled time.

He walked slowly over to his home office and gently closed the door. A desk with equipment and his personal device sat in one corner, while a filing cabinet with blood samples sat on the opposite side.

The tubes inside contained his samples. Mick pulled out one labeled 'Julie' and stared at it for a bit. Based on the amount of blood left, he estimated ten more trips to the past or future from her sample. Previously obtaining her blood was easy; when they had their Friday nights, Julie ended up crashing on their couch.

Mick placed her tube back on the tray and pulled out another. This one he savored, promising himself he'd only use it for a special purpose. His block handwriting gave away the label: the governor.

When Mick collected Colin's blood from a trip in the past, Mick hid the sample in the carriage house until he returned to the future. Or technically the present, depending on how he looked at it. Mick was losing track of time.

A few other samples filled the tray: his own and the rest supplied to him by The Supreme. Those samples were from people he didn't know, and he hesitated using them. Mick's eyes stopped at the corner of the tray. There was a tube he didn't recognize, the name half-smudged with blotted ink obscuring the two letters.

Mick's process in handling blood samples was meticulous, especially if he obtained them while time traveling. Two reasons circled his mind to explain why he'd break protocol: He was rushed or in danger. Or both.

His hands trembled in fear.

After taking a deep breath, Mick looked at the sample more carefully, noting the tiny amount of blood inside the tube. Enough for only a single trip to the past or future.

If I broke protocol for this blood sample, would I have recorded the experience in my journal?

The journal wasn't a perfect solution, but paper and pen withstood the test of time when machines broke down or malfunctioned. Mick kept a detailed entry for each expedition along with his observations in the carriage house.

How will I know whose blood this is? Mick questioned. *Unless I use the sample.* He looked at the tube of blood again, completely perplexed. *No, too risky.*

Mick felt goosebumps crawl across his skin as he abruptly stood up from his chair. Before he could second guess himself, Mick placed the sample case back into the secure cabinet and left the apartment.

The streets were fairly empty with the chilly nighttime air, but the sense of someone watching him filled Mick with dread. When he finally reached The Hill, he slowed his pace and relaxed, the magical setting easing his soul.

He unlocked the carriage house door and entered the humble residence. Nothing was out of place; everything appeared to be in order.

Mick strode to the tiny kitchenette and opened the cabinet above the refrigerator. There, tucked away, he found a small safe and brought it to the couch.

A sudden movement from outside the window across the courtyard in the O'Connor townhouse caught Mick's attention. He looked out the window, welcoming the distraction from his rapidly beating heart.

The governor moved with a sense of stealth and purpose toward the other end of the dining room table where his friend Julie sat. Mick watched as the two hovered over a device, graphs and charts filling the screen and takeout containers and coffee mugs scattered between them.

Julie's presence in the townhouse didn't bother Mick; it was the way Colin looked at her that made Mick pause. Colin's presence consumed Julie. She was oblivious to the man's body language, the way he lingered around her. They were speaking and laughing, but Mick couldn't hear them.

I shouldn't be surprised. I know what happens.

And yet he was surprised.

Shaking his head, Mick looked back down at the safety box and placed his thumb over the scanner. The box emitted a slight click before opening.

The box was empty.

Something must have gone very, very wrong in the future. Dark and terrifying thoughts instantly plagued Mick's mind.

The only way to know is if I take a trip on the unknown blood sample.

Chapter 26
The Governor

February 11th, 45 A.R.

Good news! We are down to a 10% failure rate. Still don't know why.

Colin saw the message appear on his screen and couldn't help but grin. In less than two weeks, Julie made incredible progress. She was smarter than she gave herself credit for.

Excellent. Update the presentation for this afternoon.

He watched his message deliver and looked up from the device's screen. Colin rarely spent time in the COLI*GO building, especially this early, but he couldn't concentrate in his office at The Capitol Building. He glanced at the monitor on his desk and took in the sight of Julie. Spying on her was a bad habit of his, but he couldn't seem to break it, even after a couple of years. During that time, he and Julie grew close, and he often felt at ease with her. Colin ventured calling her a friend, especially with their simple banter and ability to understand one another.

He wouldn't deny there was chemistry between them, the way their eyes lingered on each other and the endearing way her face blushed when he complimented her. But Colin always kept his composure and never crossed any boundaries.

With her message, Colin expected she'd appear upbeat while wandering through the lab. Instead, Julie looked defeated and tired.

Instinct overcame Colin, a feeling he rarely let himself indulge in. His mind pushed aside the obstacles and consequences as he turned off his device, collected his briefcase, and headed out of his office. When he reached the elevators, Colin didn't select the lobby. He forcefully pushed the button for the laboratory.

The elevator stopped abruptly, and as the doors opened, lights harshly blinded him. Colin quickly strode down the hall and around the corridor. He paused when he saw Julie sitting alone through the solid glass walls. The transparency surrounding her stimulated his mind, and his imagination ran wild.

Julie remained focused on the multiple screens in front of her before resting her head in her hands. In Colin's mind, she was perfect in this moment even though he knew everything around her was imperfect. Colin tapped on the glass door quietly, but Julie still jumped at the sound before waving him inside.

"Wow, this place is stunning," Colin noted, admiring the high-tech machinery surrounding them. Various computers, advanced robots, and sleek modern devices housing organic matter samples surrounded them.

"Have you never spent any time down here?" Julie asked politely.

The lab was her world, and Colin felt like a stranger in it.

A welcomed stranger, he hoped.

"What are you looking at?" Colin asked, ignoring her statement and approaching her slowly. He peered over her shoulder at the large screen, not understanding any of the formulas.

"I'm still trying to figure out the exact source of the problem," Julie replied with a huff.

Colin looked down at her and held his breath as he noted the way her hair parted, exposing the back of her neck and her freckled skin. An overwhelming feeling took control of Colin's mind and his physical body; in a gesture of comfort, Colin placed his hands on her shoulders and rubbed her bare flesh with his thumbs. Julie accepted this act of kindness, relaxing into him before stiffening rigidly upon realizing who he was and who she was.

Julie tilted her head to face Colin. Confusion ran across her upturned brows, but he said nothing in response. After a moment, her intense eyes softened, revealing a sense of curiosity. Colin's fingertips brushed against her neck, and for the first time in a long time, he lost complete control.

Colin's hands cupped Julie's face and raised her out of her lab stool. Their eyes met, and he embraced the moment before leaning in for a passionate kiss.

Julie tasted like his childhood memories at the beach but also like something exotic and unfamiliar to him. He wanted more of her taste on his lips. No, he needed more of her taste on his lips.

Their spark ignited Colin's movements as they continued kissing, and he assertively pushed Julie against the edge of the desk. Pressing his body closer to hers, he expected her to push him away. Instead, she embraced him.

Her tiny hands gravitated toward his chest, faintly pressing against him. Julie was hesitant at first but confidently pulled Colin in closer to her as his lips explored her neck. Colin's tongue and teeth grazed over her delicate skin, but he didn't care if he left marks on her; in this moment, she was his and only his.

Nothing else mattered.

Rosy flush spread across Julie's décolletage, revealing her escalating desire. She allowed her hands to grasp onto Colin even tighter as he lifted her up on the desk. This moment was so surreal, so perfect, and at the same time so obvious to him. Their ease in intimacy felt natural, as if their embrace was all they knew.

Colin's mouth watered at his need to taste every inch of her skin. Small erratic breaths escaped her lips as his tongue traced her jawline and his fingertips lingered up her skirt. Colin knew she wanted him as badly as he wanted her.

I will not take this further with her, Colin told himself. But his body wasn't listening to his mind.

Colin's hand traced up the soft skin on her thigh, his fingers pressing into her almost too roughly with exploration and desire. His lips met hers again, and she closed her eyes, a soft noise escaping her. A playful grin formed across Colin's face as he continued kissing her.

This is too risky.

Anyone could find them exposed in the glass bubble of the lab. The start of the workday approached, and researchers would soon enter the building. An affair with Julie Walsh would ruin Colin, but he realized it'd ruin her, too. He'd lose all credibility, she'd lose her job at COLI*GO, and the antidote. The antidote was too important for her to lose.

This is too risky.

He repeated the words again and again in his mind, but Colin ignored these thoughts the moment he heard Julie's heart beat faster while he caressed her.

I'm smarter than this, he retold himself as she gasped for air.

Abruptly, Colin retreated from Julie, and she looked up at him in disbelief.

There was something about this woman Colin couldn't explain, a difference that felt so right to him. Julie's eyes grew wide as he took her in, shocked at their actions. She was close to him, moments away from letting go.

I can't believe I let this happen either, Colin wanted to tell her, but like the coward his father constantly reminded him that he was, he couldn't say the words.

He turned, escaping the lab in a clumsy manner. Everything was blurry and unfamiliar.

Colin knew he shouldn't have left her the moment he reached his vehicle in the underground garage. His hands grew sweaty, and the smell of her lingered on him.

He considered going back inside the building and apologizing to Julie. But saying he was sorry didn't sit comfortably in his mind; he didn't want to apologize for what they did. He wanted more of it. Colin wanted Julie in every way possible, and he wanted to get lost in consuming all of her.

"Fuck!" Colin yelled, slamming down on the wheel with his hands.

***

Colin found the silence in the boardroom unbearable. His mind raced with thoughts from earlier, knowing the encounter was wrong. He crossed a line, lost control. But Julie's lips, the taste and feel of her skin, rattled around his brain all morning.

Julie sat at the opposite end of the conference table. Her fingers typed furiously on her device, and she didn't look up and acknowledge him when he entered the room. Celine and Martin sat next to Julie, off in their own discussion and oblivious to their tension.

The sound of Julie's typing suddenly stopped, and Colin noticed her look up at him. Julie's eyes appeared grayer than normal, and his heart stopped from her gaze. The moment invigorated and simultaneously horrified him. He wanted her more than he ever wanted anything else, but Colin couldn't recover from his departure, the way he left her.

The corners of Julie's mouth turned up, and she smirked at Colin before continuing on with whatever she typed on her device.

Maybe I didn't ruin everything.

"Colin?" Celine asked, looking over at him.

"Yes?"

"I might be a bit late for dinner tonight, but I don't want to cancel. We have a lot to catch up on. Do you mind?"

Colin eyed Martin suspiciously.

"Not at all," Colin replied.

Martin swiftly looked away. Colin didn't understand what his sister saw in that spineless man. Martin was handsome enough, but his intelligence only scratched a technical surface. Colin looked down at his watch, noting the meeting would begin shortly. After a few moments, Celine stood and closed the doors.

All eyes were on her.

"Please let the record show all The Board of Directors are present and the meeting has officially started," she said flatly before sitting back down in her seat.

The meeting started with obligatory agenda items. Marta discussed financial forecast updates, The Supreme and Celine provided an overview of candidates selected from The University's innovation submissions, and Martin discussed asset presentations for the day: one from the biopharmaceuticals department, one from the ecological team, and one from the technological devices group.

"Any more agenda items?" Marta asked the room.

"Yes, but it needs to be off the record," The Supreme said, her eyes drifting across the room.

Everyone looked around the table with wide eyes. The android taking notes turned her device over and placed it on the table quietly, indicating she stopped recording.

"I received word from Representative Joel Kennsington's office earlier today," The Supreme said and stood.

The room looked up intently, unsure where the conversation

headed.

"The news is secret. All non-board members will need to sign a confidentiality agreement before leaving or risk termination."

The Supreme's tone remained deadly serious. Colin locked eyes with Julie, trying to settle the nervousness and uncomfortableness from her composure.

"What the hell is going on?" Celine asked, her voice on edge.

The Supreme looked directly at Colin.

"Joel Kennsington is going to challenge you, Colin. He's running for governor in the upcoming election."

The room remained silent. Even at a hundred stories up, the noises of The River and the outside hustle and bustle of The City faintly ricocheted from the windows. Colin felt himself laugh before the sound escaped his lips. The notion of Joel running in the gubernatorial election was preposterous. No one respected him outside the Humanizer party. The rest of The Legislature found him obnoxious, idiotic, and hot headed.

The Supreme must be joking, Colin thought. *A sick, twisted joke only Emilia would find funny.*

"I'm not joking," The Supreme said as if she read his mind. "I never joke."

Colin fell silent.

"That bastard doesn't have the nerve to speak to me before making his announcement public?" Colin asked no one in particular.

"Do you expect him to?"

"We can't let him win. He'd assume Colin's seat on The Board at COLI*GO," Marta said in shock.

The rest of the room grasped why this information was detrimental. Colin looked at Martin, imagining his brother-in-law tallying all the innovations in his research department. Joel would stall and defund Martin at every corner.

"He can't win," Celine spoke without looking up.

Julie and her colleagues, innocent bystanders in this conversation, understood the gravity of their situation. Their eyes darted back and forth, the pressure of keeping top-secret information weighing them down. Everyone in the room understood what kind of governor Joel Kennsington would be and the implications for equality amongst humans and androids if he won the election.

"I'd like to point out that 'he can't win' is not a true statement. Do I think winning would be difficult for Joel? Yes. But there's always a risk, a possibility," said The Supreme.

Her scales remained neutral in this conversation. With information as detrimental as this, Colin expected some form of expression from The Supreme.

"Since we are all aligned, I hereby make a motion to meet again next week and discuss the issue on its own."

Colin sat back in his chair and tapped his foot quietly under the table. The chances of Joel stealing this election were slim but not impossible because the Humanizer movement ebbed and flowed. Colin didn't doubt his favorability amongst his constituents; he was the first governor to provide sustainable food access and maintain clean water supplies. In the latest poll, his likeability rating topped 75 percent; humans and androids prospered under his leadership.

Joel angered Colin. He assumed his issues with the representative would subside after the Kendra incident. Her murder certainly impacted Representative Kennsington; the constant media mudslinging of their affair emerged, and his wife divorced him. But there was no evidence linking Joel to the crime, and the police never identified the killer. Kendra served her purpose. Joel didn't pass a single piece of legislation for almost a year.

How does Joel have the balls to run against me? Colin wondered as the rest of the room remained silent.

Celine moved the group on to other agenda items, her voice drowned out by Colin's thoughts.

The antidote. Another innovation Joel will throw in the trash.

Julie rose from her seat, and her slides appeared on the screen. Colin listened to her soft but optimistic tone as she explained the declining error rates.

"I think with a small fraction of financial support, I'd uncover the error and completely resolve it. Then we can move into human testing. I need a little more support than the current state of the program to accomplish this in four months," Julie said, pointing to the timeline she and Colin created.

The Supreme looked over at Martin and folded her hands together.

"Can we divert some budget to support this?" Martin asked, his gaze shifting away from The Supreme and over to Marta.

Colin knew Marta would say yes. Julie's financial request made sense because he helped craft the message; he ran the numbers.

"We can provide an additional 2 percent, but to meet our return, we'll need to ensure human trials are approved by The Legislature by the end of the second quarter," Marta said, nodding her head.

"Right in the middle of the election cycle?" The Supreme's deep voice asked from the other side of the table.

She raises a good point; bringing any pharmaceutical to The Legislature for clinical trial approval always causes conflict.

"Yes," Colin heard himself say with confidence.

"You think you'll be able to whip the right number of votes from The Representatives of The People while managing a campaign with those error rates?" The Supreme pointed to the screen, her eyes zeroing in on Colin and challenging him.

"Without a doubt. The error rates will be lower by then; Julie will make sure of it," Colin noted, sitting up straighter in his seat. "We can't delay this. If the antidote doesn't get pushed through The Legislature while I'm in office, the antidote will never get approved."

A loud grunt emerged from the other side of the table.

"Not just the antidote. Everything COLI*GO is working on will be jeopardized." The voice echoing Colin's concern was his sister's.

"Everything that's ready now needs to go through as quickly as possible," Colin agreed with Celine.

The other young researchers in the room nodded, nervousness apparent in the slight slick sweat shining off their foreheads.

"It's going to be a busy and challenging spring."

The room remained eerily quiet before Celine dismissed everyone for a fifteen-minute break.

Chapter 27
Jones

February 13th, 45 A.R.

Documentation and administrative work consumed Jones's afternoon. His eyes scanned over the paperwork closing out another hit-and-run accident. Too many occurred over the last few years, all stemming from the same model of self-driving vehicles. The commissioner raised the concern to The Supreme, and Jones needed the paperwork spotless for her to share with The Legislature.

His processor hummed with thoughts of Kendra Washington and her unsolved murder. While almost two years had passed, the case had been obnoxiously public. The killer remained a mystery and left another dark mark on The City's police department.

Anna Garcia told Jones the system failed them; she was convinced Kendra's death was linked to those other unsolved murders. After a bit of persistence, Jones convinced Anna to work on the case during off-duty time.

Jones recalled walking into Anna's open-floor loft in The Port for the first time. He hadn't realized the impact of these unsolved deaths on the medical examiner until he saw the photographs obsessively scattered across the walls of her living room. Anna took an old-school approach, connecting all the women to one another with various colors of string.

She pieced together many aspects of these women's lives.

Jones and Anna made a pact that night: They would investigate these unsolved cases and bring justice to these women.

A slight knock echoed off Jones's desk, startling him from his own thoughts. He looked up at Anna's grinning face.

"Hello, Detective Jones. How are you today?"

"I'm well, Doctor. Is there something I can help you with?"

Normally, he and Anna kept their distance from one another to avoid any suspicion.

"Can you come to the morgue? I have some files I can't displace, and I'd like your opinion," she responded in a hushed tone.

Dr. Garcia was a thoughtful woman: smart, educated, and commandeering. She came from an influential old bloodline family but stayed out of the spotlight, unlike her sister. Isabella was constantly on the news channels, often alongside the governor. Jones had never met Isabella but learned from Anna that they were polar opposites.

Both donned the classic Garcia features of short stature, sharp hazel eyes, and luscious chestnut hair, but Isabella was softer and more delicate while Anna's look was lean, muscular, and strong.

"Sure, I'll be down soon after I finish this paperwork," Jones said, pointing to his screen.

After completing his report, Jones made his way down to the morgue. The temperature in the air cooled in his descent of the building, matching the chilling ambiance of such a room.

"Jones! I'm in my office!" Anna called out as he stepped out of the elevator. He walked over and sat down at her desk. Anna twirled her screen around so that they could both see what she pulled up. A list populated the screen, the names and dates appearing in chronological order. Anna's list was daunting but reminded Jones of why he risked sneaking around to catch this killer.

Fourteen Years Ago:

Christine Hoek, 30—Legislative Aide, Previous Gov. O'Connor

Brittany McCarthy, 28—Admin Coordinator on The Hill

Twelve Years Ago:

Michelle Tenner, 29—Legislative Aide for Rep Atkinson

Ten Years Ago:

Jennifer O'Brien, 30—Press Secretary Rep Ludewing

Sophia Henderson, 29—Executive Assistant at COLI*GO

Eight Years Ago:

Jessica Hacket, 27—Admin Coordinator at COLI*GO

Katherine Ryan, 25—Legislative Aide for Rep Charlton

Seven Years Ago:

Amanda MacDonald, 29—Chief of Staff at COLI*GO

Two Years Ago:

Kendra Washington, 25—Legislative Aide for Rep Kennsington

"Look," Anna said, pulling up another file on her device.

The page was a public directory from the secretary of elections, listing the election cycles and the results for each year.

"These killings all fall on election and legislation cycles," Anna said quietly. "I don't know how I hadn't noticed that before."

"Some of the women aren't related politically," Jones pointed out, his hand grazing quickly over Amanda MacDonald's name.

Jones remembered Amanda's murder even though he was still in school. The gruesome case was sensationalized by the media, and the reporters placed blame on the COLI*GO Board of Directors. Amanda MacDonald started out as Celine O'Connor's administrative coordinator, but she was a sharp, intelligent, and witty woman. She proved herself to Celine and other executives at COLI*GO, moving from an administrative position to the head of Corporate Communications before eventually taking on the role as chief of staff.

Amanda's body was found in a dumpster behind The Capitol Building the morning before one of the largest pharmaceutical assets went to vote for approval. Rumors circulated the news that a whistleblower would come forward during the session to stop its approval. But no one came forward that day, and The Legislation permitted the approval for COL2120, now COLI*GO's blockbuster drug and most profitable product.

"I wouldn't say that. COLI*GO is so far up The Capitol Building's ass," Anna commented with a huff.

COLI*GO was a touchy subject for Anna, and Jones assumed the rivalry between the O'Connors and the Garcias was to blame.

"Yes, but we need to remember the distinction," Jones replied sternly. Emotions caused a lack of focus, and Jones didn't want to miss any key clues because feelings blurred their objectivity.

Anna sighed but shook her head in agreement.

"My intuition tells me they're still connected, somehow."

***

Weeks passed since the last time Jones and Mick had an evening alone together. Both were busy with work lately, and Jones noticed Mick's closed-off attitude.

"I think something has gone horribly wrong, and I don't know what to do about it," Mick said, sitting across from Jones at their kitchen table.

Jones prepared them a nice meal and hoped Mick wouldn't discuss time travel or COLI*GO, but he also sympathized with his boyfriend.

"I found a blood sample that I know I didn't store. Or, at least, my present self didn't put it there." Worry filled Mick's watery eyes.

Jones placed his fork and knife down and tried not letting his scales reveal that he was annoyed Mick wanted to talk about his research. Tonight was supposed to be about them.

"And my journal is missing," Mick continued.

"Maybe a future version of yourself is here now," Jones noted, hoping his logic soothed Mick's worries. "Do you have any idea whose blood sample it is?"

"None whatsoever. The label is smudged, and I don't know what to do."

Jones looked up at his boyfriend. Mick's hollow eyes frightened Jones as he reached across the table and placed his hand on top of his. Jones squeezed his scaly fingers against Mick's soft human skin.

"I see two options. One: You try to locate the other version of yourself that's here now and confront him. Or two: You use the blood and travel time," Jones suggested.

Tears flooded the corners of Mick's eyes, and he let go of Jones's hand.

"I don't know who I am anymore, Jones. I barely recognize myself in the mirror. Sometimes I wonder if I got lost in the future or the past and this isn't the real me," Mick wailed in agony.

"Well," Jones said with a kind and soft tone of voice, "you seem like the real 'you' to me."

Jones stood from his chair and walked over to Mick, embracing him in his arms. Mick nuzzled into Jones's chest and let out a large breath.

"I'm sorry. I know this wasn't how the evening was supposed to go," Mick said after neither spoke for a few minutes.

"Don't apologize. That's what I'm here for. And when I need you to listen to me, I know you will. We're partners. We don't hide things from each other." Jones's words warmed Mick's confused heart.

"How is the case moving along?"

"Anna and I are making progress but not fast enough. I want to catch this guy. I want to know who he is and make him face the repercussions of his actions," Jones replied with an uncharacteristic hint of anger in his voice.

"Are you guys sure the killer is a man?" Mick asked, looking up at Jones.

"A man or an android. The bruise marks on the neck are so large, too large to come from a woman's hands." Jones shook his head, and Mick stood next to him.

They leaned into each other, Mick's chest resting slightly above Jones's. The scales on Jones's body shone brightly, the emerald green deepening with each passing second. Mick found Jones's expression of emotions beautiful and captivating and brushed his lips against Jones's neck.

Jones was grateful he understood and felt emotions of closeness, intimacy, and love. The thought of life without Mick seemed unbearable to him, and he wished they didn't need to hide their relationship from the world. Jones's physical body betrayed his processor in Mick's presence, allowing his true feelings to display themselves. He embraced these moments they shared together because everywhere outside these four walls, they had to hide them.

***

The next night, Jones faced the photos on Anna's wall again, wondering where they went wrong.

Their routine was the same: he headed over to her place, they ordered take out and they began scouring all documentation for anything they missed previously. More color-coded notes and observations were placed on the wall beside the photos.

Red represented information about the women, blue linked the years in question, and green related to the actual crime scenes.

Anna placed a photo of each woman from the mortician's office alongside a photo of their everyday lives that was used on the news. Jones approached the wall, admiring the shiny silver key necklace from Amanda's neck in her professional headshot. A simple and elegant piece. His eyes lingered to the photo of Amanda that Anna took on the morgue's cold metal slab.

"Why do you take off only some of their jewelry?" Jones asked without looking away.

"What do you mean?" Anna replied, getting up from her position on the couch.

Jones's fingertips lingered against Amanda's neck.

"Here." He pointed to the photos. "She's wearing a necklace in this photo but not yours, and she wears the earrings in both."

Anna looked at Jones quizzically.

"I never take off the jewelry when I take the first photo. I wait. Then I take everything off and bag it as evidence before I begin . . . before I begin my work." She gulped, trying to finish her sentence. Jones noted Anna never spoke the actual word "autopsy" and watching her perform the task, he had noticed her hands shook and eyes watered.

"Do you think the killer takes a trophy?" Jones asked, approaching the photo of Kendra Washington on the wall.

Kendra's large smile consumed the photograph, her head resting gently on her hand. She looked welcoming and soft in the photo, the silver bracelet dangling gently off her delicate wrist.

Anna followed Jones's gaze as his finger rested on Kendra's chunky silver bracelet in the photo. There was no bracelet on Anna's autopsy photo or logged as bagged evidence from the case.

"She wore this the night she died. I saw this on her." Color drained from Anna's face as Jones spoke the words.

"I never noticed this before. Let's look through all the photos," Anna said, rushing to grab her device and take notes.

Jones wondered why the killer was sentimental, why he took something so personal of theirs.

A sick reminder? A disrespectful trophy?

This made Jones hate him even more.

Chapter 28
Julie

February 15th, 45 A.R.

Julie couldn't concentrate. She pulled herself together for the presentation to The Board of Directors, but otherwise, her thoughts remained scattered.

She worked from her apartment, allowing her mind to process what happened between her and Colin in the lab a few days before.

When she went in the next day, she turned right around and headed back home. Images of Colin's lips on her neck and the feel of his firm grip on her thighs flashed before her. There was no way she wouldn't stop thinking about Colin's assertiveness and the spark that passed between them if she was there. Her mind wouldn't concentrate while in the location where they came so close to making a very big mistake.

What didn't help the situation was Colin's silence. Julie wondered if he avoided her since their rendezvous because their paths normally crossed each day in the COLI*GO office. Even her device remained silent.

Julie didn't blame Colin for ignoring her. Between the news of Joel Kennsington's announcement and the stresses of passing as much legislation between now and the election as possible, Colin had a lot on his mind.

And someone like me, a complete nobody, is insignificant to someone like him.

Julie looked around her studio. In comparison to Colin's townhouse, her space felt minimalist and cold. The walls were painted a sharp gray color with black intricate molding, and what were once hardwood floors had been replaced with tile. The layout had the open kitchen at the entrance, connected to a small living space with a tiny pull-out sofa, and her bed fit in the small nook off to the right.

The chirp from Julie's device startled her, and a calendar reminder popped up on her screen. She'd nearly forgotten about her lunch with Dr. Isabella Garcia. The pit in the bottom of her stomach grew larger with anxiety. Julie couldn't cancel, and if she didn't get dressed and ready, she'd be late.

Julie jumped off her unmade bed and raced to the bathroom, hastily turning on the shower. The steam fogged the mirror's edges, blurring all of her worries together. She rushed into the shower and closed her eyes, allowing the hot water to pour across her face. With her eyes closed and the warmth, Julie imagined Colin's presence all over again. The urgency in his caress, the slight pinch of her skin between his teeth . . .

Get a grip! she scolded herself.

When she was with Peter, Julie felt desire and passion but nothing like this. Peter never made Julie want more, and she never missed him after he left her. Colin's absence provided a lingering feeling she couldn't describe.

Julie turned off the water and towel dried her hair. She walked over to her closet and pulled out a modest but fashionable dress paired with stockings and warm, tall boots.

If she didn't leave now, she'd be late.

Isabella chose a tiny café-styled restaurant in The Hill. The establishment overlooked the public gardens across Beacon Street, and in warmer months, elm trees bloomed with wildflowers on the perfectly manicured lawn. Now, in the dead of winter, a light dusting of snow provided its own allure. Julie spotted her right away as she entered the restaurant.

Dr. Garcia was an intriguing woman: gorgeous and charming while also intelligent and kind. Isabella's presence espoused compassion and empathy, a trait most old bloodline women lacked.

"Julie!" Isabella exclaimed, getting up from her seat as Julie approached the table. She warmly embraced Julie, giving her a hug as a greeting rather than a handshake.

"I'm so sorry I'm a few minutes late, Dr. Garcia. I always forget the walk up to The Hill takes a bit longer than I anticipate!" Julie said with a nervous laugh.

"It's no worry at all. And please, call me Isabella," she said as they sat down.

Julie fidgeted in her seat, feeling uncomfortable being in the presence of Colin's significant other after the inappropriate moment they had shared. Isabella asked Julie how COL2120 progressed, never inquiring about the antidote, and eventually, the waitress came over with their meals.

Does she know? Julie's fingers grazed over her own lips in subconscious instinct. *Of course she doesn't know. No one knows.*

"I have to admit, I've lured you to lunch under false pretenses," Isabella admitted with a sigh.

She unfolded her utensils out of her napkin and gracefully grasped the instruments. Julie averted her eyes, unable to look the woman in the face.

Oh god, she does know.

Itchiness spread across Julie's skin like an invisible sunburn. Logically, Julie knew Isabella didn't know about her and Colin's encounter unless he told her. Isabella had scheduled this lunch well before Colin kissed Julie, and very well before Colin's fingers were inside her.

Julie cleared her throat, shaking the memory, and mustered up some courage to look back at Isabella. A soft but sad smile lingered on Isabella's lips.

"You did?"

"Yes," Isabella responded. "I'm a bit concerned about Colin's involvement with the antidote."

The words hung aggressively in the air between them like a hot, humid summer day.

"I don't understand."

"You do know about his father, correct?" Isabella asked, raising an eyebrow as she carefully cut into her chicken.

Julie knew very little about the previous Governor O'Connor. Henry served for several decades, bringing humans and androids through the end of The Resurgence with a sense of grace and stability. Julie was too young to follow or care about what happened in The Capitol Building during most of the former governor's leadership, but she remembered during his last term that the governor grew sick. Rumors varied around the cause of his death, the media speculated cancer, but nothing was ever confirmed by the O'Connor family.

"He suffered from Alzheimer's," Isabella whispered. "Colin and his father had a very complicated relationship. He feels responsible for his father's decline in health at the very end, wondering if intervening differently in his father's healthcare would have made a difference. He's wrong, of course. You and I both know Alzheimer's is a disease that progresses the way it wants, consumes the mind with no predictability."

Isabella moved the food around her plate in an awkward and uncomfortable manner as she spoke. Julie picked up on the tick immediately; her sister also suffered from an eating disorder. Isabella continued cutting smaller pieces of her food without bringing the fork anywhere near her lips.

"I think helping you with the antidote triggered unresolved feelings from that time. Colin won't admit this, but he's acting differently. He's obsessing over how to speed up your diligent process. He's on edge; he's irritable and reclusive. That's dangerous for him in particular," Isabella replied with a worried look in her eyes.

Julie remained silent as she took a bite from her sandwich, unsure of the correct response to Isabella's observations of Colin.

"He really needs to focus on the reelection now more than ever," Isabella continued. "I'd appreciate it if you didn't seek his involvement in the antidote moving forward. At least until after the election is over."

"I understand," Julie said. And she did. "My mother suffered from dementia and depression. She took her own life. Sometimes I struggle with my work, but it motivates me, keeps me going when I don't want to anymore."

Julie surprised herself in opening up to Isabella. Isabella was a fantastic listener; she provided her full attention. There was an ease about the woman she couldn't explain.

"I won't reach out to Colin. I'll distance the project off his plate. He needs to win the election. That's the number one priority," Julie reassured her.

"Thank you," Isabella said, placing her hand on top of Julie's. She felt very warm and sticky against Julie's bitter cold fingers. "And I'm sorry, I didn't know you had such a personal connection to your work. But I'm glad it made you a stronger person, not a shattered one."

***

Lunch exhausted Julie, but she didn't want to go home. A small coffee shop enticed her, the warmth beckoning her inside.

The café remained quiet for a chilly day, but the espresso heated her and the seat in the corner provided the perfect spot for people-watching.

The bell on the door rattled as a young woman and an android walked in. The two were engaged in conversation, and Julie couldn't help but stare at the android's bright pink scales. Dressed in a bright white faux-fur coat, the android stood out. Julie instantly thought of Jones, missing her best friend.

A man entered behind the woman and android, and Julie recognized his eerily familiar stance as he ordered his coffee to go. He looked around the room quickly and nervously before their eyes connected. The man was Mick.

Mick's deeply dark complexion looked paler than normal, almost feverish. His eyes grew incredibly wide, recognizing her, too.

"Mick?" she yelled across to him, waving her hand.

He instantly turned around and rushed toward the door, bumping into the beautiful pink android before dropping a leather-bound journal. Without thinking, Julie stood, quickly scooped up Mick's journal, and chased after him.

"Mick!" Julie yelled, running down the street after him. She waved the journal in the air frantically. "Mick! Wait!"

He didn't look back at her and instead picked up his pace, running down Charles Street before turning on Mt. Vernon. Julie tried keeping up, yelling his name as loudly as she could. Traffic raced in front of her, and she jumped back onto the sidewalk to avoid collision. By the time she made it halfway down the street, she completely lost sight of Mick. He vanished.

Julie stopped, catching her breath in icy cold air, and gazed down at the journal in her hands. The notebook was small with a soft brown leather cover, the corners a bit worn and the pages yellow around the edges. Her first instinct was to open the journal, but she stopped herself.

With Mick nowhere in sight, Julie placed his lost possession in her bag and began walking down the cobblestone street. The sight of the O'Connor townhouse loomed in front of her.

Julie's device vibrated with an incoming call.

"Are you stalking me?" the gruff voice on the other end of the line asked with a chuckle at the end.

She couldn't help but laugh in response.

"No, I took a wrong turn."

Julie paused once she reached the front of the townhouse, Colin's tall figure looming in the window of his study. He watched her.

"Well, I've been trying to find you at COLI*GO so that we could talk, but I haven't seen you." Colin backed away from the window as he spoke until he was completely out of sight.

"You've been looking for me?" Julie's heart fluttered in her chest.

"Yes," he answered before the line went dead.

Julie hesitated when she reached the gate. She couldn't deny the pull toward Colin, and she sensed he was drawn to her, too.

Colin stood at the front door, leaning up against the frame in his suit. His unmistakably charming smile stretched across his face as she approached him.

Nothing will happen, Julie promised herself as she stepped inside the townhouse. *Nothing is allowed to happen.*

Julie's promise to herself fell apart the moment Colin closed the door. His embrace pinned her against the solid wood door before he kissed her. Julie was small and delicate against his large frame, and his lips carried a sense of urgent belonging on her own.

"What are we doing?" she asked as he moved from her mouth and grazed her jawline.

Colin pulled away slowly, his eyes lingering on Julie's swollen lips. He lifted his hand and tucked the loose strands of her strawberry blonde hair behind her ear.

"Look, Julie," he said, directly looking into her eyes. "You make things better, especially in the midst of all this disaster around me. I know pursuing you is wrong. We shouldn't act on this, but I'm selfish. I don't want to stop."

Julie didn't expect this response from Colin, especially after her conversation with Isabella. She looked down at her feet and then shifted back up to his steely blue eyes. In the shadows of the entryway, the color appeared more of a gray than blue that was softened by his welcoming smile. With her silence, his smile faded.

"I know I crossed a line," Colin said, bringing his hand up to Julie's cheek, his fingers faintly tracing her jawline. "If anyone found out what happened between us, not only would I ruin my career but also would I ruin yours. The antidote is important. People need this. I won't cross this line again, but I won't apologize for what I did."

Colin backed away from Julie, his heart beating rapidly in his chest as they stood together in silence. Julie pushed herself off the door and wrapped her arms around him. Colin stiffened for a moment before leaning into her small frame.

He embraced this different type of intimacy they shared, a tenderness they instinctively developed for one another prior to any physical attraction.

Colin is correct, she thought as she held him, his breaths deepening in her arms. *We crossed a line.*

Colin would never leave Isabella during an election year, and her focus on the antidote's approval was a top priority. They also faced another challenge: He came from an old bloodline family. She was a "nobody." Colin's fingers pressed deeply into the tininess of her lower back, and she felt him inhale the smell of her hair.

"The bad thing is," Julie whispered into his ear, "I am selfish, too."

With those words, she answered the lingering question between them and gave Colin the permission he needed. They dipped their toes into this forbidden territory, but now Julie wanted to wade into this confusing pool, let the water engulf and consume her.

Colin's large hands traced up Julie's back, stopping at her waist.

He lifted her up off the ground with ease as she wrapped her legs around him. With her arms around his shoulders, he kissed her gently at first, but their attraction turned more unruly. Holding her securely in his arms, they ascended up the long staircase in the townhouse.

There was no turning back now.

***

Mick wasn't in the office the next day and didn't answer Julie's phone calls. She pulled out her device and sent him a message marked "urgent."

I am out of the office on personal time and will respond to your message upon my return.

Julie threw her device down on the lab bench and rolled her eyes. Mick's unresponsiveness bothered her. She felt like Mick jabbed a knife through her heart when he ran away from her yesterday.

The journal sat on Julie's desk, mocking her. She restrained from reading its contents but admitted the knowledge that Mick kept a journal fascinated her.

"Dr. Walsh," a familiar voice echoed behind her.

"Hello, Madam Supreme."

"Do you have a moment? I'd like to discuss the next steps for the antidote's clinical trial application."

"Of course."

The Supreme's eyes drifted over to the journal on the desk before centering back on Julie. They rode up to the 101st floor in silence, but Julie felt The Supreme eyeing her. Her wide eyes lingered on Julie's neck, and Julie shifted back and forth on her feet.

The Supreme cleared her throat halfway up the building.

"How is Mick Taylor working out on the COL2120 project?"

"He's great. Very thorough and brilliant. The team likes working with him," Julie replied.

Except right now, he won't answer me, and I have no idea why.

"I remember his University research project." The Supreme's voice remained fairly monotone, but she expressed a hint of temptation.

Julie looked up at her, taking the android in. She was much taller than Julie, and her height added to her intimidating cold green eyes and stiff, sturdy smile.

"Oh really? Mick and I met at The University. I've known him for a long time."

"Did he ever share his research with you?" The Supreme asked.

"No, Mick is a very secretive person," Julie replied with a laugh.

"It was so fascinating. What a shame COLI*GO did not invest," The Supreme said with a small smile as they left the elevator and headed toward her office.

Hearing The Supreme praise her friend brought a smile to her face as she settled into the seat opposite The Supreme's desk.

"I went through your latest toxicology report and predictive models. I'm not worried about that part of the application to The Legislature, but I am worried about the error rate," The Supreme said. "The human brain is such a mystery."

"It is. I understand the concerns regarding the error rate, but I learn more each day. If I may?" Julie pointed to The Supreme's sleek desk monitor.

The Supreme nodded, and Julie projected her newest simulation analysis. The charts and graphs danced across the screen as The Supreme read through them.

"I think there's an opportunity to simultaneously run a second trial alongside our proposed one for Alzheimer's." Julie's hands trembled slightly, but she concentrated on projecting herself confidently. The Supreme leaned back in her chair as her eyes wandered from the screen over to Julie.

"What are you thinking?"

"There's an opportunity to explore psychological conditions. I mapped out a draft for protocols studying depression and bipolar disorders. If successful, we could extend into other areas like dissociative identity disorder and post-traumatic stress disorder."

"Good," The Supreme muttered softly. "We could reach more human constituents with various indications. That would open doors in an area COLI*GO has yet to explore: mental health."

"My thoughts exactly," Julie responded, feeling proud.

"When will the proposed clinical trial designs be developed for presentation? I can prepare The Representatives of The Androids, and I'm sure Colin can whip votes with The Representatives of The People."

"I understand the importance in a volatile election cycle. But I can't rush the development of the clinical trial design or the inclusion criteria for patients. Any mistake or mishap would be detrimental to the whole program."

The Supreme's scales faded into a deep matted amber color.

Agitation, anger? Julie recognized this reaction from her experience with Jones.

"However," Julie responded quickly to avoid confrontation, "I think late May or early June."

The Supreme let out a singular laugh and smile.

"I respect that, Dr. Walsh."

"Thank you. I didn't mean to be ill mannered . . . " Julie trailed off, a bit taken aback by her own brazenness.

"No, you were honest and authentic. I know you have no staff supporting you. I spoke with Celine, and we're moving Lexi Pvadinish over from another project to help you. This is a pivotal time for the antidote, and you'll find your calendar fills up quickly as we approach The Sessions season at The Capitol Building."

Relief flooded Julie's body from the confirmation she'd get a second set of hands. Her work drowned her, and the pressure of accelerating timelines only added stress.

The two looked at one another for a moment before Julie turned off her device. The Supreme swiveled her chair and stood while Julie gathered up her things. A smile crept across Julie's face as they headed for the elevators.

"His research examined the theory of time travel through blood."

The words bounced around Julie's mind for a moment until she realized The Supreme referred to Mick's research at The University.

"Blood?" Julie asked, puzzled by the foreign concept.

"Yes," The Supreme replied while leaning against the glass elevator wall. "Mr. Taylor proved, with the correct device, he could take a sample of blood and transport himself into another moment of that person's life. Past or future. Something about the proteins makes this possible. I'm not an expert in hematology, but that's the high-level concept."

Julie's jaw dropped. Mick's research had to be sophisticated and innovative to prove such a concept. Her mind wandered through the possibilities and technicalities on how time travel through blood was even a reality. The Supreme was right; that type of invention was monumental. Impressive.

"What made COLI*GO say no?"

"Society isn't ready, and our job requires that consideration. Or, at least, that's why Colin and I sit on The Board of Directors. We think about society first, innovation second."

"I suppose that's true." Julie thought for a moment. "Imagine if time travel got into the wrong hands, say someone like Joel Kennsington, for example."

"Absolutely unimaginable."

***

Lexi Pvadinish was brilliant, unique and funny.

She and Julie hit it off after only a few days, and Julie instantly knew she'd hire Lexi full-time once the clinical trials started.

Lexi had charming features: dark midnight hair she kept styled in a tight ponytail, a bright and shiny nose piercing, and blemish-free deep cocoa skin that illuminated off the light. The scar on her upper neck was her only physical imperfection.

Prior to joining, Lexi worked on a secret project in the lower lab. Julie never visited the lower lab; her credentials didn't provide her access to those projects.

Lexi learned the molecular structure of the antidote and grasped her knowledge around the technology quickly. While Lexi focused on finalizing the proposals, Julie concentrated all her efforts on identifying the source of the antidote's errors in the simulations.

Julie introduced a new gene sequencing component to the antidote. At first, she was optimistic. The error rate nearly disappeared for the simulated Alzheimer's patients, but the antidote continued clinging to unhealthy nerve receptors in the simulated depression patients.

"Julie?" The voice traveling from behind her soothed her.

"Good afternoon, Governor," she replied before looking up from her device.

Colin's presence filled the room, a pleasant distraction from her stressful day. His eyes took in Julie with a flirtatious sparkle, but he remained physically distant and stood beside her.

"You mentioned a lead on the error? I was hoping you would walk me through it?" His eyes were warm and inviting instead of their normal chilled aloofness.

"Of course," Julie said, spinning around in her chair and pulling up another lab stool.

He sat down, inching the seat closer to her. Julie's mind wandered as she inhaled the smell of him, and thoughts of their previous Friday together flashed through her mind. A slight blush crawled up her neck at the memory.

"It's quite fascinating, actually!" Lexi emerged from behind the partition panel beside them.

Colin jumped at the sound of someone else's voice, and Julie chuckled under her breath. Julie savored moments when Colin conveyed vulnerability; it was endearing and rare.

"Let me introduce you to Ms. Lexi Pvadinish," Julie said, gesturing over to Lexi.

"It's such a pleasure to meet you, Governor!" She smiled as she extended her arm and shook his hand.

Colin took it hesitantly, staring at her peculiarly as if he knew her from somewhere but couldn't place where.

"Have we met before?" Colin asked slowly before releasing her from his grip. Lexi looked perplexed as if she wasn't quite sure if they had or not herself.

"I don't think so."

"Lexi is helping with the antidote project," Julie interjected.

Colin smiled briefly but looked oddly uncomfortable as Lexi walked back over to her desk.

"When did this happen?" he asked Julie in a hushed tone.

"The Supreme approved it. She actually recommended Lexi and moved her over from a lower lab project."

She noticed Colin frown and shake his head before sitting down.

"She's incredibly helpful. Don't fret, The Supreme doesn't know of your involvement," Julie whispered in Colin's ear.

"I have some bad news," Colin said with a distant look in his eyes. "You're going to have to work with Kathleen while I start campaigning. I trust her completely. She's savvy and knows everyone in The Capitol Building. She'll help whip the votes; she's a real shark."

"Oh, I remember." Julie thought fondly back to when she requested a meeting with Colin two years ago. Kathleen wasn't forgettable.

"It's not ideal. I'd like to be more involved, but my schedule is so . . ."

"Insane?"

"Yes."

Julie noticed Colin look over her shoulder before grabbing her hand in his. His fingertips brushed against her knuckles, and Julie welcomed the thoughtful gesture.

"Keep me updated."

"Of course," Julie said, moving her hand out from his as she heard Lexi stir on the other side of the room.

"Be careful," Colin said, eyeing the other side of the room. "I don't trust The Supreme in this. Do you want me to say something to Celine or Martin?"

He should be happy for me. He knows how much I've begged for an extra set of hands to help meet these aggressive, impossible timelines. Is he angry that The Supreme helped clear this roadblock for me instead of him?

"I can handle it without you intervening," she responded, rolling her eyes.

Colin smiled and brushed her knee with his as the air softened between them.

"I don't doubt you for a minute."

Chapter 29
Mick

March 1st, 45 A.R.

For a man with access to an infinite amount of time, Mick was running out of it. He still couldn't find his journal and blew through what little personal time he had at COLI*GO, trying to find the future version of himself.

Nighttime approached The City early this time of year. The sky grew dark in the late afternoons, and the cold breeze swept across the streets like clockwork. Mick hated these long cold winter nights; he barely felt his bitter toes in his boots as he walked across the bridge connecting The River and The Hill.

On the other side of the bridge, the COLI*GO building loomed above The City. From this vantage point, the tallest building among the skyline looked absolutely magnificent. Lights twinkled at the top, illuminating the 101st floor. The rest remained dark, the emergency lights providing an eerie glow. As he approached the building, he noticed his device light up with an incoming call.

"Hello?"

"Mick! I'm glad I finally caught you. I've been trying to get in touch with you for over a week now!" Julie shouted into the phone.

"I'm sorry. I was trying to take some time off and separate myself from everything, except Jones," Mick said without a pause, a lie he was willing to live with.

Lying to Julie became second nature to him by now.

"Oh," she said with a pause. "I'm sorry. I thought I did something to anger or upset you when you ran away from me in the café. I wanted to make sure we were okay."

Mick stopped dead in his tracks. His body shook from the combination of both the frosty air and his nerves.

"What are you talking about?"

"At that café on Charles Street? I was there, and you walked in before quickly running away. Anyways, it doesn't matter, I know how busy and stressed you are," Julie said in her typical rambling tendency, a nervous tick of hers.

"Are you in the lab?" Mick asked her, assuming she was. Julie spent her weekends working on the antidote.

"Yes, why? Please don't lecture me on being in here over the weekend."

Mick imagined her pouting on the other end of the line and smiled at the endearing thought.

"I'm actually standing outside the COLI*GO building right now. I can maybe help you for a bit. Or at least keep you company."

"Of course! I'll see you soon," she said before hanging up.

Mick entered the access with ease. The building was fairly quiet on the weekends, and no one wandered the hallways as he made his way to the elevators.

Seeing The City across the water at night through the complete glass elevators made Mick feel a bit uneasy. A wave of motion sickness teased his uneasy stomach, and a memory of his first high-speed train from The Countryside to The City flooded his thoughts. The elevator stopped abruptly, and the doors opened to a dimly lit floor.

Staring him right in the eyes was a very familiar face.

"Uncle Jeb?" Mick asked in complete shock.

Jeb Taylor looked back at Mick with the same sense of surprise, awkwardness, and confusion. The two hadn't seen one another in at least five years.

Jeb hadn't changed much since Mick saw him last. They shared similar square jawlines and lanky builds with attractive, dark complexions. His uncle's newly acquired facial hair hid his harsh dimpled skin and distracted from the bags under his eyes.

To be fair, I look pretty ragged myself.

"Mick," Jeb replied, looking him up and down before getting into the elevator with him. "You have really matured from the last time I saw you."

Mick didn't say anything; instead, he nodded slowly.

"I didn't know you worked at COLI*GO. Clearly, the

investment I made in your education paid off," Jeb said, gesturing his hands around his body.

Working for COLI*GO was an honor; a COLI*GO employee showcased a sense of status in society, no matter where that person came from.

"Yes, I'm a research scientist," Mick answered, a smug smile appearing. He wanted to rub his success into his uncle's face since his family had always doubted him.

"I'm happy for you," Jeb said, gripping his briefcase a bit tighter and looking away from Mick's gaze.

"What are you doing here?"

"Business."

Tension filled the small elevator car. Mick's eyes focused on the muted metal briefcase with an old-fashioned combination lock.

Uncle Jeb's an artist. Why does he need a briefcase in a scientific research building on a weekend night?

The elevator stopped at the lab, and the doors opened.

"Well, I wish we had more time to catch up," Jeb said as Mick exited the elevator car.

"You can always call me, Uncle Jeb," Mick replied, looking at him solemnly. Mick and his uncle barely knew one another anymore, but they did share one very important commonality: They defied their family for a life here in The City.

"I will," Jeb said as the elevator doors closed slowly in front of him.

Mick knew he wouldn't.

***

"Any luck?" Jones asked Mick as he entered their apartment.

"Well, there is still a missing future version of me roaming around out there, and my journal is still unaccounted for." Mick shrugged.

"I'm sorry," Jones started to say before Mick interrupted him.

"I saw my uncle at the COLI*GO building this evening."

"Uncle Jeb?" Jones asked with interest and intrigue.

The man was a sore subject. Jones didn't understand why Mick and his uncle parted ways, but Mick didn't expect Jones to comprehend the intricacies of families. Androids didn't have their own families but rather lived with sponsors after leaving FACERE.

"The one and only."

"What was he doing at COLI*GO?" Jones's scales flashed a brighter green.

"I'm not sure."

The two sat on the couch and Jones turned on the news. The coverage focused on Colin O'Connor's and Joel Kennsington's campaigns. Joel Kennsington made Mick's skin crawl, and he knew better than to ask Jones his opinion of the man, especially because of Kendra Washington. The news anchor asked Joel about policy proposals he'd focus on in the first one hundred days if he won. Mick knew which man won the gubernatorial election from his trips to the future.

But Mick discovered in his research that the future wasn't necessarily set in stone. Each time he traveled, things were a bit different from his previous trip. Small alterations caused by The Legislature, ripple effects from legislation either passing or not passing during Session season, changed society's fate.

Minor changes in the personal lives of people and androids also impacted the future. Mick even uncovered that the simple act of a future time traveler coming back to the past could potentially set off a catastrophe of events.

In his research, Mick described these as time loops. When he experimented with a small change in the past, he created a loop. These loops didn't change the present but instead explained why an odd event occurred. Loops could also keep the past pure and free of potentially damaging situations, if executed correctly. The power of knowledge gave Mick unease, and he refused to share any of his observations with Jones.

No one else should have to carry these burdens.

The only place where he logged his experiences was the journal. Secrets of the past and insights into the future inked the pages, and Mick feared the possibilities of his journal in the wrong hands.

"I'm going to travel time on the blood sample," Mick said, breaking the silence between him and Jones.

"Are you going to the past or the future?"

"The past," Mick replied and looked down at his lap. "It's more predictable, more stable. I feel like I'm in control when I go back in time versus when I travel to the future."

Jones nodded. "That's a good approach."

A smile crept across Jones's face, easing the apprehension in the room. Jones kissed Mick's forehead, and they finished watching the evening news.

***

Jones slept in the other room. The door to Mick's office remained closed, giving him extra privacy. The blood sample sat on Mick's desk, the small deep maroon liquid barely moving as Mick tilted the vial. *Who are you and why are you so important that I came back and risked so much?*

With as much precision as he could muster, Mick placed a small sample onto a microchip he developed to fit in the crux of his glasses-like device.

The blood crawled along the technology like a circuit board, seeping toward the edges and staining the white strip inside. A small clicking sound filled his ears as he inserted the slide into the glasses.

He placed his index finger on the rotary-style dial, moving it slowly to the left. A code of numbers showed up on the small screen in the separate chrome box—a transmitter—and inquired which year he'd like to go back to after displaying the possibilities. The options ranged from 4 A.R. to 47 A.R.

Mick took a deep breath before selecting the randomized sequence option. He wasn't sure whose blood he was using, and he felt it was only right to let the blood speak for itself. The date 12 A.R. emerged on the screen after the numbers calculated the destination. Mick looked over toward the door one last time before placing the glasses back over his eyes.

Goodbye, Jones, Goodbye for now.

This was part of Mick's tradition: He always said goodbye to Jones before time traveling. Unsure of when his last trip would occur, Mick could never forgive himself if he didn't say goodbye to the most important being in his life.

A sudden and sharp sensation vibrated through Mick's body. His frail body shook violently, and the air around him tensed before his line of vision went black.

After a few moments, Mick experienced a sense of stillness and removed the glasses from his face. The sun shone brightly, his eyes blinking rapidly as they adjusted from sudden darkness to the light. He placed the glasses and the chrome box carefully into a small case he kept in his back pocket.

The sound of waves crashing near him was unfamiliar to him, and Mick didn't recognize his surroundings at all. His eyes followed the horizon, admiring the ledges of cliffs and tall seagrass. The summer air felt welcoming compared to the cold winter back from where he came from.

This isn't so bad, Mick thought. *Yet.*

The walk toward the cliff took a few moments, but Mick enjoyed the warm sun and the beautiful white fluffy clouds in the sky. The scenery reminded him of a fantasy, not a reality. The sun touched his skin; the bright blue sky lived on forever across the horizon. Once he reached the edge of the field, he carefully peered down to the sight of waves.

That's where the ocean is.

The landscape remained unfamiliar to him as he wandered across the cliff's edge. The sharp shoreline was scattered with large summer cottages and estates, weeping of old bloodline money. Mick hadn't seen more glamorous homes in his life. He couldn't fathom how much these structures cost and how he instinctively knew they were used only as summer vacation homes.

This was The Oceanside.

Mick noticed a beachy area off to the left and continued peering below, following the line where the land met the ocean waves. It was low tide, and the sand was a dark beige, coarse and wet. The cliffs edged and jagged in zigzag lines for miles. He was so caught up in the beauty of the scenery surrounding him he almost missed the gruesome scene beneath him.

A tangled and twisted body lay in the sand.

Adrenaline filled Mick's veins as he scaled down the rocks as quickly as he could. When he reached the bottom, Mick felt the sand creep slowly into his shoes, itching him. The small grains felt warm to the touch, and he realized he was out of breath. Sweat dripped down the corners of Mick's face, and he rolled up his long-sleeved shirt before looking over to where he saw the figure from up above. He stopped dead in his tracks once he turned the corner. A few hundred yards ahead was the body of a young woman. She was completely mangled, bloodied, and disfigured. Her neck clearly snapped on impact or from hitting an edge off the cliff. Instinctive dread filled Mick to his core.

Did she fall? Or did someone push her?

Mick approached her body cautiously.

She was very pretty, her hair a medium shade of blonde and freckles scattered across not only her face but also all of her skin. Her lanky but tall frame distinguished her differently from the curvy, womanly bodies Mick normally observed in The City. She wore a sundress, her nails perfectly manicured, and she donned a glamorous wedding ring on her left hand. The stone in the center was a large teardrop-shaped emerald surrounded by smaller diamonds. The sun shone brightly, reflecting off the stones and platinum band.

Old bloodline money.

Her limbs stuck out in places they shouldn't, and her skin was coated in crusty dried blood. A wave of nausea overcame Mick, vomit rising up from inside his body.

Mick rushed over to the ocean, wading in the water until the waves reached his waist. The water felt cool, much cooler than he had anticipated with such a hot summer day. Dizziness left him, and the saliva in his mouth subsided as the brisk ocean calmed his nerves.

What kind of fucked up shit did I get myself into? Whose blood is this?

He looked back at the beach toward the woman's unsightly grave and saw a sudden flash of movement.

I'm not alone.

Mick waded out of the ocean, swiftly running back to the shoreline. He searched the perimeter for whoever caught his eye. A small whimpering sob sounded from one of the crevasses along the rocks. A young boy sat in the shadows, his legs drawn close to his chest. He rocked back and forth as he cried. In the boy's hands, a woman's ring was glistening.

"Are you okay?" Mick's words were quiet, a bit weak. Both he and the boy were terrified.

"My mom!" the boy cried, tears streaming down his face.

Mick approached him slowly, inching closer. The boy was about eight years old, and like his mother, he was lanky and tall for his age with hands and feet too large for his small body.

"My mom and dad got into a huge fight. About me. So I ran away. And now . . ."

"It's okay," Mick said, trying to calm the boy by placing his hand on his shoulder. "Is your father here?"

"No, he left. He didn't know I was here. Then she was gone. So I came down here. And there she is," the boy spoke in sobs.

The boy's story inflicted an eerie, looming presence, and Mick didn't feel safe. *Is he saying his father pushed his mother off the cliff? How much did the boy see of this traumatic scene?* The dark irrational corners of Mick's mind took over.

"I'll go look for help. You should come with me," said Mick, unsure himself if he should leave the boy alone or take the boy with him.

"No! He'll be mad," the boy shouted, backing away from Mick.

"Who will be mad? Your father?"

The boy shook his head and ran away. He took off quickly, leaving bare footprints in the sand. Mick was stunned.

I could chase after the boy, or I could run myself, he contemplated.

A loud violent crash of a wave against the cliff startled Mick, making him almost jump out of his skin. The tide was approaching.

He looked back over at the woman, the ocean lingering along her fingertips, taunting the edges of her body with salty water.

"He will be okay. I'll make sure," Mick heard a voice from behind him. Panic filled his body, and he stilled. Mick moved slowly, his head turning back toward the sound of the voice.

When he fully turned around, he didn't see anyone there.

***

Mick ran away from the beach. He wasn't sure where he was going, but he couldn't return to the present yet. He still didn't know whose blood was in the vial and could say with confidence the blood didn't belong to the dead woman on the beach.

Mick spotted a lighthouse up ahead and concentrated on it, the tall structure protruding up into the clear blue sky. By the time he reached the lighthouse, the sun had started setting in the distance, changing the hues against the ocean from shades of pink to purple.

As Mick entered the abandoned lighthouse, he found a small cot, a filing cabinet, and a toolbox. The whole structure looked archaic to him. A small device powered in the corner displayed the date and time. Seeing the actual date again caused a shiver up his body. Mick had been born only a few days prior, the only explanation for why the boy could see him and interact with him.

Another caveat to time travel was visibility. Any human could time travel from the blood of another human, regardless of age differences. But if Mick traveled into the past prior to when he was born, no one could physically see him. Essentially, he was a ghost. The same occurred when he traveled to a future time beyond his existence. When Mick traveled to moments in time parallel to his existences in this world, he could always interact with others.

He settled into the cot, closing his eyes and concentrating on the sounds of the waves outside. The Oceanside scenery was vastly different from The City, and the calmness of the air and shoreline was odd compared to the normal hustle and bustle of the urban scenery he was used to. His mind wandered with distraction as the quietness engulfed his thoughts. Thoughts of the dead woman. Thoughts of her son.

He shuffled his body to the side but found his sleep restless throughout the night.

When the morning sun peeked in, Mick left the sanctuary of the lighthouse. Walking inland and away from the shoreline, he approached a small village center. Trendy restaurants with outdoor dining, a few parks, and many shops scattered the brick roads and sidewalks. The Oceanside was a charming old town.

Mick entered a tiny unassuming café and ordered a coffee. As he fumbled with the sugar packet, his eyes glanced up at the monitor above the cashier's head.

"Breaking news," the anchor spoke from the screen. The man's image faded away, and a fresh photo of the woman from the beach appeared.

Mick's eyes grew wide at the sight of her; she was smiling, her eyes full of life. The familiar freckles filled her face, her small white wide smile showcased rosy pink cheeks. The screen listed her height as five foot eleven and her age as thirty-two.

"Governor Henry O'Connor's wife, Melanie O'Connor, has gone missing. The O'Connor family is asking that anyone with information please come forward. Mrs. O'Connor was last seen at the family's Oceanside estate yesterday morning. Her device is off the grid, and police are unable to track it at this time . . ."

The news anchor kept speaking, but Mick stopped listening.

He didn't want to be here anymore. He wanted to go home, his home he had with Jones.

To the present.

If Mick learned anything from his time travel explorations, it was that the world was a terrible place.

Now he understood Colin O'Connor much better.

Chapter 30
The Governor

March 14th, 45 A.R.

"Good news. Kennsington isn't doin' as well in the polls out in The Countryside as we initially thought," Kathleen said from across the dining room table.

"But he announced his campaign only a few weeks ago. This is only the beginning," Colin responded with a sigh.

He didn't expect a curveball during the election cycle this year, especially with everything at COLI*GO and in The Capitol Building. Colin barely slept, shuffling through daily morning briefings with Kathleen at the townhouse instead of in his office, needing every minute of sleep his mind would allow. Kathleen looked over at him from across the table with a hint of concern.

"I haven't slept in over twenty-four hours, Kathleen."

"Well, yah don't need to be at The Capitol Building fah the measure hearin' on increased police budgets until ten. So yah can get some sleep now if yah want," Kathleen answered without looking up from her device.

"What?" he said, surprised by her words.

The police don't need more funding. Who do The Representatives of The Androids think they are? The extra money from the budget was supposed to go to the public works department.

"Did yah not read the proposed budget adjustment I sent yah a few days ago?" Kathleen looked up at him, concern emulating from her deep brown eyes.

Colin didn't respond and simply put his face in his hands.

"Of course I read it, but I didn't realize that was today."

"I wasn't accusing yah of anythin', Colin."

"I know," he replied, "I'm sorry, Kathleen. I don't mean to lash out at you, of all people."

Kathleen smiled kindly at him.

"I hate to be the bearah of bad news, but today is the anniversary of Amanda's death." Kathleen looked back down at the calendar in her device, avoiding Colin's eyes.

He always spent the afternoon on this day at Amanda's grave with his sister, and depending on Celine's mood, The Supreme, Martin, and Isabella would join them. It would linger behind them, making his own peace with the woman he once obsessed over.

Amanda and Celine had been very close. Their relationship started out strictly professional, and Celine was proud of her protégée, a clever young woman. Colin wasn't sure when they became romantically involved, but he remembered coming home to the townhouse unexpectedly one day. Celine thought he was at the family estate in The Oceanside. She and Amanda were entangled by the fireplace, a look beyond passion in their eyes, a look of affection.

The affair almost complicated things between Celine and Martin, so his sister begrudgingly broke off their arrangement. When Colin found out Amanda planned on blackmailing Celine and all of COLI*GO, he felt heartbroken for his sister. Amanda uncovered blurry funding statements, accounts that hadn't been reported to The Legislature.

In her rage, her anger, and hurt from Celine's rejection of an open version of their love, Amanda was willing to take everyone down. Colin should have realized Amanda's intentions were not pure from the start; her flirtatious banter moved on to whoever gave her attention. And It gave Amanda attention.

The two also had quite the affair, almost straining his relationship with It. Colin respected Celine too much, and he needed to protect her. He didn't want to kill Amanda, and It hated Colin for the decision. Celine never learned of the potential betrayal but instead endured the heartbreak of Amanda's death.

"What time does Celine want to visit Amanda's grave?" Colin asked Kathleen, looking back down at his empty cup of coffee.

"Five."

Colin nodded. He sensed Kathleen wanted to leave the topic alone and that she didn't want to be involved more than she already was.

"What are the details of my campaign trip next week?" Colin asked, changing the direction of their conversation.

"I'll send 'em to yah. We should review the rest of this week, though," she said, scrolling through his calendar before pausing. "What are yah doin' blocking time out?"

She pointed to Friday.

"I need sleep, Kathleen."

She raised her eyebrows at him, not believing his lie.

"Are yah bein' sneaky and workin' on that COLI*GO project with Miss Walsh?"

The accusation was unforgiving, but it was correct. Kathleen worked with Julie over the last few weeks, sending proposal comments in hopes by the time the documents reached Colin's inbox that they were as close to perfect as possible.

"I thought you worked with me, not Isabella," Colin spat.

He wasn't angry with Kathleen; his frustration came from Isabella's nagging about the reelection campaign. She insisted on spending all of Colin's free time, whatever little of it he had, together.

Colin knew he should feel guilty; he was really using the time to spend with Julie. He couldn't get enough of her, the way she smiled, the way she listened to him. The way she cared. He wanted more, he needed more. She was the first woman in his life who genuinely enjoyed his company.

"I don't take Isabella's calls, which is probably why she hates me. I would nevah break yah trust, Colin," Kathleen said, her eyes sharp.

Kathleen was more cunning and observant than Colin often gave her credit for. She stood to refresh their coffees.

"She's cute. Kinda annoyin' but cute. It'd probably do yah some good. I'll keep the calendah blocked," her voice echoed from the kitchen. Colin ignored the comment but smiled slyly as she returned to the dining room.

"Well, you're right . . . about the sleep. I wish I could. It's so difficult. I'm tired, but my mind keeps me awake."

"I'm right about most things," Kathleen said with a chuckle. "Have yah talked tah a doctah?"

"No." Colin took a sip from the fresh mug she placed in front of him.

"Call my friend; he might be able tah help. And he's discreet. Trust him with my life." Kathleen handed Colin a piece of paper with a scribbled name and a phone number.

Jeb Taylor.

This wouldn't be the first time he solicited drugs illegally. Being the governor meant his doctors reported everything in his medical records to The Legislature. There was no patient confidentiality for someone like Colin.

He placed the slip of paper into his briefcase and looked at his neatly typed-out schedule for the week, noting Kathleen kept Friday completely blocked off. Colin smiled.

***

The representatives were arguing, yelling, and throwing things at one another in the Session room below. This wasn't the first time this happened. The Representatives of The Androids sat quietly on one side of the room, small smirks spreading across many of their scaly faces. The Representatives of The People continued their heated discussions. Colin's head throbbed uncontrollably, and he couldn't concentrate from his lack of sleep.

"Mr. Governor," The Supreme's voice came from behind as she took her seat next to him in the viewing gallery.

"Hello, Madam Supreme."

"I wasn't expecting this. Why didn't you warn me there was such turmoil happening between The Representatives of The People? This reflects badly on both of us."

"I don't have time for your snarky comments," Colin responded, his bloodshot eyes zeroing in on her.

The Supreme's eyebrows raised. Colin sensed she was about to say something ominous or volatile, and he didn't want to give her the chance.

"Who the hell is Lexi Pvadinish?"

The Supreme smiled silently in response. The two often played this game of mental chess. Colin knew which buttons to push, and

The Supreme enjoyed blindsiding him with unpredictable moves. Neither ever grew tired of this game, the back and forth and the resolutions only made with the promise of owing the other something somewhere further down the line.

"Ask Celine," she responded simply.

"Emilia."

"I don't go by that name anymore, Colin." The Supreme said his name sharply before getting out of her seat.

He took a moment, basking in their silence before joining her at the edge of the balcony and watching the arguing continue below them. Joel Kennsington stood up and threw his glass of water toward The Representatives of The Androids. The glass shattered loudly, the violent shards projecting off the android's desk. Her scales shimmered an iridescent orange.

"That is enough!" The deepness in Colin's throat vibrated across the room, and everyone grew quiet.

All eyes on the Session room floor traveled up toward the gallery box; fifty Representatives of The People and fifty Representatives of The Androids looked up at him. Their jaws dropped as surprise and fear filled their faces.

Colin gripped the edge of the banister in the gallery so tightly his knuckles were white and he lost feeling in his fingers. Even The Supreme looked at him with disbelief, slowly backing away. Colin never expressed this kind of outward aggression toward The Legislature.

"If you're not going to act like the civilized, mature beings you are, I will not grant resolution to this budget adjustment." The governor said the words loudly and forcefully, hitting his hand on the banister brutally. "Do you agree, Madam Supreme?"

The Supreme let her eyes drift to the room below them. The silence was deafening.

"I agree to close today's sessions, and we can resume tomorrow," she responded loudly so that everyone could hear her. Her own scales shimmered a bright amber color.

The room cleared out slowly and quietly, the representatives retreating like scolded school children. Colin left the gallery abruptly, heading back to his office.

He reached into the briefcase and pulled out the piece of paper, punching the numbers into his device.

Jeb picked up almost instantaneously.

***

Colin was running late to the cemetery from meeting Jeb Taylor. They met earlier at a discreet location in The Port to retrieve a bottle of benzodiazepines—sleeping pills.

Jeb was a good friend of Kathleen's and dated her brother-in-law. Colin wasn't surprised that Jeb Taylor was the face of the illegal pharmaceutical drug dealings within The City. He had connections with all the rich old bloodline families from his career as an artist. His clientele could afford the drugs discontinued for mass use once COLI*GO took over manufacturing for most pharmaceuticals, a terrible legislation and legacy left behind by his father.

Colin noticed The Supreme's name lit up on Jeb's device as he rummaged through his briefcase for the pills. Colin never missed anything; his observant nature kept him on his toes at all times. The information the two were connected bothered him, but he kept the knowledge in his back pocket for another time. Blackmail wasn't Colin's favorite technique of sabotage, but The Supreme found no aversion to it.

Celine and Martin stood side by side at the cemetery, one of the few times awkwardness shadowed them. Martin didn't understand the true meaning of Amanda, but Colin knew Martin cared about Celine. Marta stood slightly behind them with The Supreme, and Colin took his place beside It, a few feet back from everyone else.

They watched Celine place flowers on Amanda's grave as the sky darkened and clouds wisped across the horizon like tiny thin paint strokes. Colin felt a twinge of disappointment as Isabella remained absent. She'd been part of this ritual for years now. Regardless of his feelings for her, they had spent a decade together. The dynamics of their relationship ran through his brain: how there was a closeness and an understanding that didn't necessarily relate to intimacy. A true connection. Isabella knew so much about him and his past, much more than others, with the exception of It.

It knew almost everything. Almost.

Colin wanted to share all parts of himself with Julie, and he suspected he would eventually. Julie was different. With her, there was simply a "them" he'd never felt before. There were few people in Colin's life who accepted him for who he truly was, who cared about him despite his flaws.

Isabella used Colin for status and societal purposes, and in return, he used her, too. Julie never took advantage of him even when it would have been in her best interest to do so. Colin loved Julie's genuine nature.

He looked over at his sister, then down at his bare hands.

Killing Amanda was the most excruciating and emotionally draining of any killings he and It performed. Colin found It and Amanda's relationship strange; It rarely embraced any emotions. He was strong, aloof, and capable. His obsession with Amanda showed a passionate, obsessive, and fanatical part of him Colin hadn't realized existed.

He remembered the words It said to him when he asked It why he pursued Amanda, knowing how important Amanda was to Celine.

Everyone has their weakness, and if that weakness isn't a personality trait, it manifests as a physical being instead.

The Supreme turned around and faced Colin head on before handing him a plastic glass shaped like a champagne flute. The bottle itself lay beside her feet, and she reached for it eloquently, filling each cup to the top in complete silence. The pinging bubbles breaking against the edge of the plastic broke the silent evening air.

Jeb's words of warning echoed in his ears: *Don't consume alcohol if you plan on using these. Trust me, I love a good time, but that combination is a trip you do not want to take.*

"I suppose one toast won't hurt," It said with a shrug before slugging back his full flute of champagne.

In honor of It and Amanda, Colin did the same. His gaze drifted toward his sister, and in that moment, their eyes met and he smiled solemnly at her.

"I'm sorry I'm late," a small voice whispered.

He felt Isabella's small frame hug him from behind.

"That's okay, darling," he said, embracing her.

After everyone dispersed, Colin approached Celine and put his arm around her. He was her brother, he cared for her when no one else would, and she cared for him in the same capacity. He promised his father he'd always look after Celine, the one promise he committed to his father.

The crowd thinned out into the crisp night air. Isabella held onto Colin's hand, her fingers interlaced with his as he waited for everyone to leave.

Colin and Isabella headed back to the townhouse in silence. Tomorrow was a workday, and he had a mountain to climb at The Capitol Building before leaving for the campaign trail.

Isabella placed her small hand on Colin's leg in the car, and a calming sensation filled his body.

"What's going on in your mind?" Isabella asked him.

"I can't stop thinking about how close they were. How that was all taken away so quickly."

Normally, Colin would never indulge in such an opportunity, but something about tonight felt different between them.

"Celine and Amanda?"

"No. It and Amanda," he said quietly.

Isabella did not respond; instead, she looked out the window of the vehicle as it navigated its way home.

Once they arrived, Colin retreated to his study and took out the bottle of pills Jeb gave him. He gulped the pills dry as he heard Isabella turn on the shower.

Leaning back in his chair, Colin closed his eyes. The faint sounds of Isabella drying her hair carried across the hallway. He only took the recommended dose prescribed on the bottle but felt himself drifting into a lovely white space between the real world and his mind. Colin waited a moment longer, trying to determine if Isabella was already asleep.

The townhouse was quiet, and he turned off the lights in his study before walking down the hall to the master bedroom.

Isabella's back was turned toward the windows, and her body stilled in the darkness. She was naked beneath the sheets, but the thought of her didn't raise any arousal in Colin. He crawled into bed beside her, careful not to touch or wake her.

"I think I'm going to stay behind on The Island," Isabella whispered softly into the darkness.

Colin's mind wandered, barely stringing together the words she said aloud because of the drug and alcohol.

"For how long?" he asked, looking up toward the ceiling. The room spun around him, and bright colors were streaking across his line of vision. Hallucinations plagued him and he wasn't sure if Isabella actually draped her arm around his chest or if that was all in his mind.

"I'm not sure."

Colin closed his eyes. The words she spoke were ones he wanted to hear, but they still shocked him. Isabella was a very schedule-oriented woman; she was predictable.

"I've actually been meaning to talk about this, but it's been challenging for me," Isabella said with a strain in her voice.

"Well, tell me what's going on in your mind," Colin asked inquisitively, his hands brushing across her arms. He felt her silken soft skin against his. He wanted to push her away but couldn't feel his arms anymore.

"I love you, Colin. You know that," she responded as if rehearsed several times before. "Between my mother being so ill and the stress Anna has caused on the family, I need to go back to The Island and only occasionally visit The City."

"Why didn't you tell me sooner?" Colin asked, surprised by his intoxicated mind's ability to keep up with Isabella's rambling.

"Well, there's the campaign. You're closed off, never available. And all the other complexities. It has become too much for me."

The words were harsh as they escaped her lips.

Colin's eyes drifted toward the back of his head, the vibrant colors turning into shapes, shapes resembling a screaming face.

"I think space for both of us would be good. When the election is over, we can be together again. Maybe actually get married," Isabella said sharply, bringing Colin down slightly from his high. "But right now, you need to focus on the reelection. I'll fly in whenever there is an event. I'm not going anywhere, at least not publicly."

Her hand cupped the side of Colin's face. He grunted and nodded in agreement, unable to form any words. The words he wanted to say melted into one another, and the feel of Isabella's hand disintegrated into his surroundings.

Colin wasn't sure if it was the hallucinogenic nature of the sleeping pills, but the bedroom was so loud in his ears when, in reality, he knew Isabella had turned away, may even already have fallen asleep.

He closed his eyes to escape all the faces surrounding his line of vision, all the bright colors. For once in his life, he let the uncontrollable of a drug take over his body and mind. And finally, Colin relaxed into a soundless sleep.

Chapter 31
Jones

March 19th, 45 A.R.

Anna and Jones cross-referenced documents together at Anna's apartment. A ping from Jones's device sounded, and he paused, looking at the screen. He heard Anna's device ping moments after his own.

"We knew this was bound to happen this year, Anna," Jones said as the color drained from her face.

This was an election year, one where political tensions were especially high between androids and humans. And their killer indulged during these cycles.

Jones and Anna left her apartment separately, making sure they'd arrive at the crime scene at different times. Once there, Jones prepared himself as he walked toward the other police cruisers. The body had been found in a dumpster behind a restaurant in The Bay, and the victim was a woman who appeared to be in her late twenties or early thirties.

"Detective Jones," the commissioner said as Jones crossed the police tape and into the crime scene. "I called The Supreme and the governor. The Supreme is on her way, but the governor didn't pick up. I'm not sure you're needed here for this any longer."

"Why?" Jones asked. Normally, that level of authority wasn't needed at a crime scene, even a murder.

"There's something peculiar about the victim," the commissioner answered quietly as if he already knew what that peculiar thing about her was but wouldn't say the words out loud. The commissioner turned toward the street, his eyes locking in on Dr. Anna Garcia as she approached. He ran over to meet her.

"Excuse me, Dr. Garcia!" he called out. "You're not needed here today."

"Uhm," Anna responded, her spicy personality coming out slightly. "What do you mean by 'I'm not needed here'? There is a dead body on the scene, correct?"

The commissioner looked over at her and then back at Jones. He didn't say anything as Jones approached the tourniquet.

"Sir . . ." Jones said tentatively, his hands lifting the white sheet off the victim.

The body underneath was mangled. Jones's eyes scanned her, informing him there was no record of her in the human database or the android database. Worry crept into Jones's processor, a feeling he always understood. These databases housed all identifying information for each citizen, human and android alike.

"The body isn't human. But the body isn't an android either."

Anna's face drained of color as the words escaped Jones's mouth.

"What type of being is this?" Jones asked the commissioner.

"Let's clear the scene and let the government and COLI*GO do what they need to do," the commissioner answered with a slight stammer.

"We are part of the government!" Anna shouted, walking over toward Jones and the unidentified dead body.

She pulled the sheet covering the body, revealing the bloody, sodden scene beneath for herself.

"Looks like there are twenty-three stab wounds . . ." Anna peered back up at Jones.

"She's not human." For some reason, the words grounded him.

Anna looked back down, identifying a small COLI*GO badge hanging from the pocket of the dead woman's blouse.

Lexi Pvadinish

Lexi's neck showcased bruises in the form of a hand, indicating she'd been strangled. Her skin, which should have been brighter, appeared matted and decayed. She was dehydrated, and her skin flaked.

"That's correct. She's a posse hominem," a deep voice said from behind them.

Jones turned his head back quickly, and there stood the very tall and intimidating Supreme.

"Posse what?" Anna asked in horror.

"Posse hominem. The Latin word for 'impossible person,'" Jones answered softly. He understood most languages but hadn't translated Latin since his time at The University.

"That doesn't answer my question," Anna said, her eyes narrowing in on The Supreme. The Supreme approached Anna, placing her hands on Anna's shoulders.

"She is half human, half android."

The words felt like a sucker punch to Jones's stomach. He couldn't fathom how this was possible; humans and androids could not conceive. It was anatomically impossible.

This new species had to be created in a lab or research facility.

Anna cleared her throat and abruptly pushed herself away from The Supreme before walking back toward the dead woman's limp body.

"I honestly don't give a shit if she is a human, an android, a half-human half-android, or something else entirely. She was murdered. Not only was she murdered but also was she murdered by The City's only uncaught serial killer. That's right; I'll call the bastard a serial killer."

The words intensified out of Anna, causing everyone around them to hold their breath.

"That's enough, Dr. Garcia," the commissioner said, his tone pleading, not authoritarian. Jones remained silent, but he could tell Anna was looking to him for support.

"Oh, and would you look at that. She has a piercing for a nose ring, and it's missing," Anna shouted in a gritty and nasty tone before looking up at Jones. He knew instantly she was referring to their inside secret intel of missing jewelry; the tradition of the killer taking his trophy item with him after his kill.

"That's enough, Dr. Garcia," the commissioner repeated, looming above her. Anna was a small woman. Any android easily intimidated her with their height alone, but that never stopped Anna from speaking her mind. She was fearless.

"There's a serial killer out on the loose, has been for a decade, and you won't hold him accountable. Why is that, Mr. Commissioner?"

The commissioner slapped Anna right across the face. Anna gasped, and the commissioner's hand trembled. A faint redness emerged across her cheek in the imprint of his hand.

"Fuck you. I quit," Anna said, walking away from the crime scene. The air grew heavy in her absence. The Supreme cleared her throat quietly.

"If you don't mind, Mr. Commissioner, the COLI*GO team here will take Ms. Pvadinish's body to our lab. Your jurisdiction for this crime scene has been revoked. I will send a detail out to collect Dr. Garcia. And you," The Supreme said, looking over at Jones, "will also join me at COLI*GO. We have some unfinished paperwork you need to fill out."

Instantly, a pair of technicians in COLI*GO-branded apparel strutted toward Lexi Pvadinish's body. Another set of employees grabbed Jones by the arm and assertively walked him over to their vehicle.

Oh, Jones thought, making a promise to himself. *I will remember Lexi if it is the last thing I do.*

***

Jones couldn't go home to Mick, but he didn't want to be alone. He found himself walking across the bridge connecting The River and The Hill, the essence of the COLI*GO building looming behind him. His pace quickened as he passed the public gardens and turned his direction toward The Bay.

Julie smiled when Jones appeared at her doorstep, and she welcomed him into her studio apartment without pause. She lived on the first floor in a large brick building on Commonwealth Avenue, one of the oldest, most historic streets in The City.

The inside of her apartment had been completely remodeled to match the recent minimalist style with chrome features and tiled floor. The sun shone brightly through her large bay windows, illuminating the open kitchen and living space as Jones leaned against her kitchen island.

After being corralled to COLI*GO from the crime scene, he heard Anna's voice muffled behind the walls around him. She cursed, yelled, and screamed in anger as The Supreme reviewed paragraphs of legal jargon with Jones.

Detective Jones will not discuss what occurred at the crime scene with anyone.

Detective Jones will not disclose he knew any information about COLI*GO and the entity's work in developing a new species.

Detective Jones will not speak to anyone about the events of today, or his processor will be subject to termination.

In other words, death for a bot like me.

"Oh," Julie said suddenly, interrupting Jones's thoughts. "I forgot, I have Mick's notebook. Can you give it back to him?"

"Wait," Jones said slowly, "Mick's journal?"

Julie rummaged through a drawer in her kitchen, pulling out a small brown leather-bound notebook. Jones grabbed the worn flexible journal from her small hands, his own trembling.

"Yeah, I saw him when I was in a café a few weeks ago, and he ran out really quickly and dropped it. I completely forgot to give it back to him when I saw him in the lab."

"Did you read it?" Jones asked without thinking.

The journal felt heavy and ominous in his hands. He knew about Mick's journal but had no idea what secrets about time travel were captured within its contents.

"Oh my goodness, no, Jones. I would never," Julie said with hurt in her eyes.

Jones knew his assumption that she was nosy was rude and unfair of him to make. But he also knew Julie as a curious scientist and an observant one at that.

"I'm sorry, I didn't mean for that to sound . . ."

Julie sighed, but a soft smile crossed her lips before sitting down on her couch.

"It's okay; I understand. We've all been under quite a bit of stress lately."

Jones sat down next to Julie, grabbing her hand fiercely in his.

"I'm worried," he said, his eyes looking downward.

"Why?"

"Mick hasn't been home in days," Jones answered, knowing if he said weeks, he'd worry Julie more.

"Is it his time travel project?"

"How do you know about that?"

Julie looked at Jones and sighed, shaking her head.

"The Supreme told me."

"Yes, it is about time travel. And each day, I grow more concerned."

"Mick's so smart, though; I'm sure he's okay. His research and discoveries are way more advanced than anything I've ever dreamed of working on."

After Jones didn't respond, Julie asked, "Would he have told you if he was doing something dangerous?"

"I think so."

But Jones wasn't really so sure.

"Well, maybe he's really invested in whatever time he traveled to," Julie said, her smile looking more forced by the minute. "It's hard for me to make an assumption without knowing anything about the technology. Do you know anything about it?"

"A little. A lot has changed since his time at The University. Mick was always afraid I'd combust or something if I tried using it."

"That sounds like him," Julie said with a small chuckle, "but there's nothing we can do right now except wait."

Julie was correct in this statement, but that didn't ease his burden.

"How is the antidote?" Jones asked, trying to distract himself from his worries of Mick.

"It's going well. We're proposing clinical trials to The Legislature in a few months. I'm worried it won't pass," Julie answered with a sigh of frustration.

"Why? Do you think the governor won't get the support for the trials from The Representatives of The People?"

The human side of The Legislature was always the more difficult party to appease.

"Oh no, that's not it at all. I believe in him."

Julie's cheeks turned bright pink, and she looked away from Jones.

"Then what is it?"

"I wanted to do this on my own," Julie said, shrugging her

shoulders. Jones admired this tenacity about his friend and how she was vastly independent. "I feel like now everyone has their hands in the antidote. The Supreme, Celine O'Connor, and Colin. I don't want to lose sight of why I developed this drug, why people need this. I fought for years to get funding for the antidote, and no one paid any attention to me except for the governor. But then the moment I do get backing from COLI*GO, everyone wants to get involved."

"But look at it this way, Julie. You're finally getting the help and resources you need. Mick told me you were working all alone."

"That's true. A few weeks ago, I got a lab assistant, Lexi. She's fantastic, and I can't wait to have you and Mick meet her. We'll have to all go out sometime after work for drinks."

Jones's body stilled, and his scales throbbed. He turned away, trying to not betray the emotions he felt on his scales. Hearing Lexi's name brought unexplainable fear to Jones's processor. The vibrant shades of green illuminated off his body, and Julie looked over at him peculiarly.

Jones stood and rushed over toward the door. "I should get going. Maybe Mick is back. I don't want to miss him."

The truth was, Jones couldn't be in Julie's apartment. He was too afraid he'd tell her about Lexi Pvadinish, and he couldn't put Julie in that kind of danger. Her knowledge of posse hominems would be dangerous not only to Jones but also to Julie. Jones couldn't imagine what The Supreme would do to Julie if she discovered Julie knew of this disgusting experiment at COLI*GO, especially knowing for him it meant termination of his processor.

"Okay, well, can I come over soon? Maybe if Mick isn't back, we can try to look more into his research. Try to figure out what happened?"

"Yes, tomorrow?" Jones asked, realizing he didn't want to spend too much time alone, especially with Mick gone.

***

Reading Mick's journal was a complete violation of his boyfriend's privacy. But Jones wouldn't have considered the action if Mick wasn't missing. Or at least, that's what he wanted to believe.

The first few pages consisted of scribbled notes along the sides. The observations merged within the margins, across the page, and upside down. What Jones appreciated was Mick's meticulousness in identifying the time he traveled to.

After finishing the journal, Jones realized Mick carried the burden of many secrets for so many people and androids.

There was The Supreme; she hadn't changed much throughout time from what Jones could tell. Then there was Julie—and Colin O'Connor. The words exploded off the page like fireworks; they even felt loud as Jones read them.

Jones let out a slight sigh, the tension from his body releasing around him. Everything was overwhelming—another feeling Jones understood.

Time needs to stop. Or at least, time travel does.

Jones understood why COLI*GO didn't invest in Mick's technology, but why did someone like The Supreme?

He closed the journal and placed it precisely into his side table drawer before crawling into bed alone. Jones now had a new case to solve. A case to save Mick.

PART SIX

Mick's Journal

"The loneliest moment in someone's life is when they are watching their whole world fall apart and all they can do is stare blankly."
-F. Scott Fitzgerald

Observations

My personal device isn't reliable in the future. Instead, I will record all of my findings and experiences here in this journal.

I age when I go to the future or when I travel through someone else's blood. I never age when I travel to the past. The lines spread across my forehead, the bags under my eyes. I look at myself in the mirror and wonder if I look terrible to everyone else, too.

Spending a significant amount of time where there are two of me physically present is challenging. Things feel strange. I have to hide. I'm afraid to face myself. I need the courage to do so.

I can only go so far into the future or the past as the person on the blood sample is alive. Why can I only travel so little into the future on Julie's blood? Who kills you, my friend?

When I travel to the past, to a time where I am not yet born, no one can see me. The same happens when I travel to the future after my mortal body has died. I'm a ghost. No one sees me. I make no impact. I cannot change things.

Time Loops:

You cannot change the past without some ripple effects. Go to the past and interfere, and then you'll realize why that strange thing in your present happened. Time loops explain irregularities, strange events, and even horrifying ones. You might not know what it was before, but when you come back from the past, it's like everything clicks, everything makes sense.

There are many different futures. The future changes based on what we're doing now in the present. I find that reassuring and terrifying at the same time.

I can injure myself time traveling, but I can't kill myself. I hate to admit it, but I thought I was going to die that one time, when I fell off the ledge. I'm afraid someone else might be able to kill me while I time travel, but there is no way to really test this theory. I'll have to make the assumption. I don't think being invincible is fair or probable.

I have faced a past me and a future me. There's something disturbing about having a conversation with yourself.

Entry One:

I am in the past, 31 A.R.
I utilized Julie's blood to get here

For reference:
*Julie's family moved to The City. She and Jones met for the first time. The governor is not Colin but his father. He is not yet sick—or at least not letting anyone know how sick he truly is. Emilia (The Supreme) has been appointed to her post as The Supreme. She is a young bot, but the androids are confident in her. COLI*GO has received its final round of funding.*

This is not my first trip through time. I remember my first trip and how it was incredible—I knew I was not where I was supposed to be, and that was amazing; it meant I succeeded. This is, however, my first trip since I received funding from The Supreme.

As a scientist driven by data, I cannot trust or refer to my own thoughts and memory of what happened as fact. I need somewhere to record the experiences and encounters of my trips while they happen. I struggled to determine the best way but settled on an old-fashioned method—written text over my personal device.

Funny how we always want technology to advance because it is "better" or "faster" or "more accurate." How rare it is that old-fashioned technology ends up being more durable? This journal will last my lifetime and beyond. My personal device may not.

The Supreme gave me a directive on what she wants to know about the past and the future—specifically revolving around "who."

She has a fascination with the O'Connor family—she is tangled very much with them and their legacy. What more does she need to know?

Julie is also of interest to The Supreme, which probably has to do with the antidote. Her interests also lie with Representative Joel Kennsington and some other members of the Humanizer party. I try to provide her with the answers or observations she wants, but sometimes that is difficult.

This trip to the past was a short one. I needed to understand the layout of everyone's positions and lives. Here is what I have observed:

*Celine O'Connor has made an enemy out of the Garcia family through her efforts in COLI*GO's final round of funding.*

The commissioner has appointed Dr. Anna Garcia as The City's chief medical examiner. She is the youngest woman to be appointed to the position; she only just graduated from medical school.

Julie's mother has declined significantly in health. Julie is doing a lot of extensive research on the brain. I think she wants to better understand what is happening to her mother.

I will report this to The Supreme, I suppose.

Entry Two:

I am in the past, 33 A.R.
I utilized Julie's blood to get here

For reference:

Julie and Jones—she's helped reprogram his processor. He understands more than I could ever imagine. Now I know why he's so special and why he is able to love me.

*Colin decided to run for governor, and he's started his relationship with Dr. Isabella Garcia. Celine is spending a lot of time at COLI*GO. The Humanizers retreated; they made no real wins or gains in the election. Julie's mother has committed suicide.*

Colin won the gubernatorial election. I have successfully collected a blood sample from Colin that I plan to use in my experiments at some point.

I made the trip to this part of the past through three separate excursions. I have successfully figured out how to specify a point in time to travel to and forward (within error/reason). The chrome box helps—it provides more accuracy than the glasses alone.

I need to be more sympathetic to Jones. He knows more than he is willing to tell me. I didn't realize that Julie reprogrammed his processor to understand feelings.

I have nothing else to really report here, and I will share my observations with The Supreme (or at least most of them).

Entry Three:

I am in the future, 47 A.R.
I utilized Julie's blood to get here

For reference:
*The City is on lockdown. A member of The Legislature has been arrested. For what, I can't determine; the media are vague and no one will talk about it openly, but I doubt anyone truly knows. COLI*GO is being investigated by The Representatives of The People and The Representatives of The Androids. The City is under police rule with the uncertainty in the government. The Humanizers have gathered a lot of support during this turbulent time. I don't like how terrified everyone on the streets appears, regardless of species. There is a new curfew in place; all people and androids must be indoors by 8:00 pm.*

I haven't been able to leave the carriage house much since arriving. I'm afraid—I don't know what the implication would be if I were hurt while time traveling. I don't know how that would affect the present or the future. There is another class of citizens now—a weird mix of humans and androids. They bleed like humans but are much less—emotional, more controlled? Maybe it's an improvement on the androids? That was my original thought when I first saw them, but I realize now this is a masterpiece originating from that of The Supreme.

I found Jones and my future self. We meet occasionally in secret, but obviously, it is dangerous for us to spend time together. Or is there another reason? He's distant, cold. Unemotional. My future self is living out of Julie's apartment in The Bay. I don't know where Julie is; I can't find her. I do not like this future.

I will not share all my observations with The Supreme from this journey. I understand why she wants androids (or quasi-androids?) to possess human blood—I think.

I feel it is important to let her know about some things—like the governor. And the state of society. I won't tell her I can't find Julie.

Entry Four:

I am in the future, 46 A.R.
I utilized Julie's blood to get here

For reference:

The antidote has been approved only days before I got here for patients with Alzheimer's but not depression.

Julie and Colin are having an affair. I don't like calling what they have an affair; they seem to understand each other. Just because other people don't know about their love doesn't make it wrong, does it? I guess it does; I think people assume he and Isabella are still together. Maybe they are? She comes to The City every once in a while.

Isabella and Anna are not talking to one another—speaking of which, I think Jones is acting differently. He's keeping a secret from me, and he's spending a lot of time at work or trying to solve those cold cases with Anna.

*Julie is taking a bit of a sabbatical from COLI*GO now that the antidote is approved, preparing for her new role in the organization as interim CEO. The antidote is crucial to society—but it's also dangerous.*

The Supreme's experiments are going as planned. I know what she and Jeb are up to now with those new species. They will use the antidote to control people, specifically people who can easily be taken advantage of, and then turn them into those creatures.

Joel Kennsington and the Humanizers refuse to go away easily. I'd say I wish someone would kill the bastard, but it isn't fair for me to predict the future when I can go to it. He's angry about losing the election even though it has been a year ago now. He shouldn't be angry; he was never going to win. The people love Colin O'Connor. They showed that.

Note: The Supreme seems to be the center of all things going awry.

I was on the lookout for the half-humans half-androids. I wasn't able to find anything, but I feel like they must be here. They are living among us, disguised as humans, and I don't know how to figure out when this started. Or why.

I have decided to not share any of my observations from this trip with The Supreme after what happened from sharing the events that occurred in Entry Three. I didn't like the smile on her face and the twinkle in her eye at the thought of a fucked-up society. To keep her amused, I'm wondering if I should tell her falsehoods?

Or will she know?

Entry Five:

I am in the past, 12 A.R.
I utilized a mysterious blood sample that must have been from future me. I allowed the blood sample to dictate timing

For reference:
Colin's father is the governor and in his second term.

The City and surrounding areas are recovering from the impacts of The Resurgence, which ended twelve years ago.

This was a difficult trip for me. I don't have much time. I am being followed. When I arrived in the past, I was not in The City. I was in The Oceanside. I am relieved to have made the journey to The City undetected (or at least I think). I am also happy to see that my journal was in the carriage house.

When I left this time, I discovered my journal was missing. So I will record this as quickly as I can and try to get back home.

What I observed on this trip was horrifying.

I need to divulge this no matter the implications: Melanie O'Connor, the mother of Celine and Colin O'Connor and wife of the former governor, did not go missing. She was murdered.

Someone pushed her off the cliffs at The Oceanside. I saw her body. Colin witnessed this—he was young. He saw what happened but wouldn't say. I can't explain why, but I think his father killed her because the ominous voice sounded so familiar.

Anyways, I am starting to piece together some—

Entry Six:

I am in the past, 45 A.R.
But that doesn't make sense to you, as I am actually from the future. I have used my own blood

Dear Jones,

*I've gotten a job at COLI*GO part-time working on COL2120.*
You and Anna discovered an important clue and habit of The City's infamous serial killer (the jewelry, Jones!). I wish I could tell you the killer's identity—I know—but I cannot or that will severely impact the future in ways that are unimaginable. You will need to discover this truth and revelation on your own.

The governor and Julie—I hadn't realized their affair started now. Does anyone else know? They can't. I'm afraid for her. I don't know if you even know yet, but now you do. Make sure to let her tell you on her own. She will.

I needed to come here. The situation in my present time has gotten a bit out of hand. I've realized my time travel has affected not the physical appearance of my body but the actual physicality of my body. I cannot keep track of what dimension is my reality and what has blended together.

I wonder which Mick I really am and if future Micks have taken over my physical body.

I have come into possession of a blood sample and hope this will help uncover the truth quicker and prevent the events of Entry Three from happening.

The future can change. I came back here and am risking interference. Because if I didn't, I think Entry Three would come true.

.

I apologize that a lot of this doesn't make sense to you. It will eventually. I have to refrain from being too specific (a challenge for me, a scientist must always be specific and thorough in observations, notes, and documentation). I need you.

Jones, where I am from, It is after me. I think he has a lot to do with Entry Three and that alternate dimension—one in which It time travels. I must abort any trace of myself from here in case It finds my hiding place. So, I have to remove the journal from the carriage house before I place the blood sample in the apartment. I will make sure the journal gets into your hands via Julie.

Trust me on this one, please?

There are many future possibilities I have discovered through my time travel research. I am sorry I have not documented all my trips here. I know I said I would, but I've taken so many now at this point.

If I haven't returned to you while you read this, please solve the following and help me save The City:
It knows I occupy the carriage house. How? Can I avoid this?
It knows about time travel. He cannot know. Can you figure out how he discovers this technology?
Why is It threatening to kill me? I think I know the answer to this, but I want to make sure my theory is correct so I can kill him first.

Please, Jones, help me? But do not tell Julie. You will want to, but you can't. She cannot know anything about time travel. Use Anna to help you instead. Once you discover the truths, please write them in this journal and leave it at Julie's apartment, specifically in her freezer.

I will report some of my findings to The Supreme. She isn't really interested in the past anymore. I travel to the past for my own selfish reasons.

Yes, I am sorry I still work for her. I know you're disappointed in me.

PART SEVEN

The Present

"Men are more moral than they think and far more immoral than they can imagine."
-Sigmund Freud

Chapter 32
Julie

March 20th, 45 A.R.

The campaign trail exhausted Colin, but he always made time for Julie. Her presentation to The Legislature on the efficacy of the antidote was scheduled for tomorrow. She pushed her insecurities aside, but the antidote felt like a physical part of her now; plus, Lexi's departure left Julie strained and overworked.

Lexi stopped showing up to work mid-March and wouldn't return any emails. A few days later, The Supreme informed Julie that Lexi abruptly left COLI*GO for a personal matter. Leaving without any kind of goodbye didn't seem like Lexi; she was meticulous. Julie couldn't find an address or any trace of Lexi when she looked for her in the public database.

Julie even reached out to Jones, but he insisted he couldn't help her. He was preoccupied with worrying about Mick. She often thought about Mick and wished she understood the concepts of his time travel research.

Strangely, Colin was the only simple thing in Julie's complicated life. Their affair should have been everything except simple, but with Isabella back on The Island, they shared an indulgent sense of flexibility and freeness.

Julie rarely spent time in her apartment anymore, even when Colin was out of The City campaigning. He insisted Julie stay at the townhouse. Julie learned quickly how structured and controlled Colin lived his life; he left little room for error.

The townhouse suited her just fine even if she begrudgingly hated being told what to do. There was more space in Colin's home compared to her tiny desk at COLI*GO and her cramped apartment. One of her favorite hiding places was the roof deck; it showcased the beautiful views of The City, and even in the cold springtime, Julie discovered a sense of peace up there.

Julie wasn't always alone in the O'Connor townhouse. Some days, Celine and Martin showed up, but neither acted surprised by Julie's presence. Other days, Kathleen stopped by and helped Julie with the legislative documents for her presentation.

Kathleen provided insight into all the important members of The Legislature. She wasn't a sophisticated woman, but her eloquence in constructing sentences from data into digestible words shocked Julie. She appreciated Kathleen's brazen but honest personality, and Kathleen, in return, appreciated Julie's stubbornness and independence. The two grew quite fond of one another, and Julie considered her a friend.

"Whatever it is you're thinking of adjusting is probably not going to make a difference at this point," Colin said without looking up from his device.

They sat on the couch in the living room as a small fire crackled in the fireplace opposite them. It was a bitter March in The City, the spring holding on to the winter air as closely as it could this year.

Julie's legs rested in Colin's lap, her own device situated securely in her hands as his thumb rubbed lightly in small circles against her ankle.

"You're right," Julie responded, placing her device down and closing her eyes.

"I believe in you," he said after a few minutes. "I'm really looking forward to hearing your proposal tomorrow."

She smiled at Colin. After tinkering and adjusting the final nuances within the document, Julie sent it off to Kathleen. Her hands shook with nervousness as she powered off her device. Julie looked back at Colin and kissed his forehead before heading upstairs. What she needed at this point was a long hot and relaxing shower. As the steam filled the master bathroom, Julie rummaged beneath the sink for her shampoo. When she opened the cabinet, she froze, taken aback by her discovery. Several pill bottles lined the bottom shelf.

A bottle of benzodiazepines accompanied the brain stimulant drug methylphenidate and another bottle of a pharmaceutical, mostly referred to by the name Adderall.

These medications were no longer prescribed or used outside hospital settings due to addiction concerns.

Julie was aware of Colin's challenging sleep schedule and the stress of his campaign, but these drugs terrified her. She remembered learning about them while at The University as part of her study in neuroscience. The side effects rambled through her mind immediately as if she were back at a school desk on exam day. Drowsiness, confusion, memory loss, hallucinations, and tremors.

How is he getting these? She wondered as she turned the bottle over, recognizing the COLI*GO logo in the corner.

Julie gently placed the pill bottles back exactly how she found them and closed the vanity before hopping into the shower. Under the warm water, she closed her eyes and let her worries drift away from her.

Colin's hands jolted her back to reality as he wrapped his arms around her. A nervous breath escaped between her lips while her heart beat faster. Moments earlier and he would have caught her exploring his secret drug stash.

"We should get away for a long weekend and forget about the campaign," Colin whispered into her ear. A sense of calmness flooded her body. The idea of not thinking about, discussing, or living the election for a few days sounded magical but also impractical. Joel Kennsington was down significantly in the polls, but Colin took Joel's campaign personally. It wasn't good enough for Colin to win; he wanted to annihilate Joel in the process.

"Where?"

"Somewhere outside The City. How about The Oceanside? We have a house out there. It's nice and quiet. Peaceful."

But what about tomorrow? Julie wondered, thinking about the presentation of the antidote to The Legislature. The hot water fell on her face as she opened her eyes.

"Think about it?" he said as if he read her mind, sensed her hesitation.

"Okay," she responded. Colin joined her under the stream of warm water and softly kissed her.

"Can you at least give me a hint about the curveball in your presentation that Kathleen has teased me with?" Colin asked her. Julie couldn't help but giddily smile.

"We decided on a second indication. The simulations aren't

perfect, but there is still promise. I won't tell you what the indication is, though."

"Oh," he said with a raised brow, "the suspense is going to kill me."

"Good thing you only have to wait until the morning," she responded playfully, pushing him out of the way to steal more of the stream of warm water.

"Too long."

"Oh no, whatever will you do to distract yourself from wondering about all the possibilities?" Julie teased.

"I can think of a few things."

***

The nightmare was erratic, chaotic, and disturbing. His screams were loud and harsh, the rest of his body thrashing about in the bed. Slick with sweat, Colin's arms and legs grew more violent with every passing second.

Julie woke in an instant and at first didn't know what to do.

Should I wake him from his night terror? Or would that make it worse?

But his whimpers and cries were too heartbreaking for her. Julie couldn't fathom what went on inside his head, what kind of intense, terrible dream would make him so violent, so petrified.

"Colin!" Julie yelled, grabbing his shoulders in her small but steady hands.

He didn't wake; the sharp and quick movements of his body increased exponentially. She could barely hold on to him.

"Colin! Stop!" Julie pleaded. She tried steadying him with a firmer grip, but Colin was much larger than her, much stronger. The task of holding him down was physically straining, and Julie knew she was failing tremendously at stopping his pain. Julie felt selfish as tears rolled down her cheeks.

Is it a reaction to the sleeping pills? Is he hallucinating in his sleep? she wondered, unsure if he had taken any before bed.

"Colin! Stop! Stop it!" Julie pleaded with his convulsing body.

Suddenly, his shoulders relaxed, and he stopped thrashing around. His eyes darted open, and Julie realized how tight her grip was as his body eased. The skin around her thumbs turned red from the pressure. She let go. Colin stared at her with a hurt but hollow look in his eyes. Sitting up, he shook his head and rubbed his eyes. His body glistened with perspiration, and he trembled.

"Are you okay?" Julie asked breathlessly.

He didn't respond right away but rested his face into her chest. Julie wrapped her arms around Colin, holding him as he panted. Julie heard his heart beating loudly in her ears alongside her own.

"It was a bad dream, that's all. It's okay, it's over now," Julie whispered, trying to calm his nerves.

"I know, I know," Colin responded softly. "I'm sorry."

"It's not your fault," she said soothingly, rubbing his back in slow circles.

"I'm not sure why . . ."

"You're under a lot of stress. Try to relax and fall back asleep. I'll hold you until you do."

She didn't ask him about the nightmare; she honestly didn't want to know. Colin fell back asleep after a few minutes, but Julie couldn't find her own slumber as easily. She watched Colin as she held him; his breathing grew deeper as his body became limp and tired. Julie watched him for a bit before closing her eyes.

***

The Sessions room was enormous. Julie had never been inside the room before and only experienced images from news segments.

The ceilings soared high above her head, with bright white columns stretching toward the top. The clawed pedestals rested at the bottom, and the carpet had a gold leaf pattern woven into the threads. Massive windows lined the long walls, cascading down to allow in as much light as possible if the heavy maroon curtains were pulled back. Today, they remained closed.

One hundred desks of the same size and design aligned the room, the only difference being half were painted blue and the other half were painted red. This identified if a representative of The People or a representative of The Androids sat there.

Each desk had a district number painted in gold on the front, and a list of names was engraved alongside the front as well, indicating the representatives who served that district in the past, a haunting memory and a nod of gratitude.

A viewing gallery stood several stories above Julie's head. There were two seats in the box, one for the governor and one for The Supreme. They observed the sessions there together with a view of the whole room. The pit in Julie's stomach clenched at the thought of Colin or The Supreme looking down on everyone from so high above.

Julie stood in the middle of the room next to a beautiful mahogany lectern and a small matching engraved table. Martin, Celine, and Marta would join her when she presented the simulation data and predictive safety models.

Kathleen's hand gently squeezed Julie's shoulder. "Yah ready?"

"Of course," Julie answered, smiling up at Kathleen before they headed for the grand iron doors. Julie turned around one last time, taking in the entire room. Kathleen cleared her throat in warning—they needed to head back out to the hallway.

The two women walked through the halls of The Capitol Building before reaching the lobby. The walls were lined with a mixture of oil paintings and modern holograms depicting scenes of past governors signing legislation, grotesque scenes of war and battle, and representatives joined together.

Half the building had burned down during The Resurgence and some of the original artwork was lost or stolen in the rubble and chaos. This newer part of The Capitol Building looked significantly different, modern, and crisp.

"Kathleen?"

Both Julie and Kathleen turned around to face Representative Joel Kennsington advancing toward them. Kathleen grunted quietly and waited patiently as the man approached.

"Yes?"

"When is the governor going to review my latest bill proposal? His response is past due."

Kathleen looked over at Julie with a panic in her eyes.

"I'll file a formal report to the Ethics Committee if he doesn't acknowledge it in a timely manner," Joel said with a sinister snicker.

"I know he was plannin' on addressin' yah bill aftah Sessions today, sir," Kathleen said stately.

Joel looked at her as if he knew she was lying to him.

"It's just he wanted tah make sure yah bill got the attention it needs."

Joel lifted his gaze back toward Kathleen. "Still pass along my message to him."

He stormed off abruptly and spoke into his device, his attention already somewhere else. Julie looked up at Kathleen with concern.

"That one's on me, naht him. He only got it last night."

"He was reading it last night, I believe," Julie said as they approached the lobby.

Kathleen nodded and let out a deep sigh of relief.

"Good."

"Have you noticed Colin has been a bit scatter-brained recently?" Julie whispered.

"No, of course he hasn't been," Kathleen answered defensively.

"I must be mistaken then." Julie looked at Kathleen head on in a slight challenge. Kathleen grimly smiled down at Julie before leaving her in the lobby to wait for the rest of her colleagues from COLI*GO to arrive.

"Dr. Walsh, I'm glad to see you," Martin said, approaching her.

"Are you ready?" Celine asked her with a small soft smile.

Julie welcomed her unusual gesture, the confidence blossoming in her chest.

"I know I am."

***

Perspiration lingered under Julie's armpits, and the flushed tones of her skin emulated across her body. Her heart beat erratically in her ears and she felt the blood rushing through her. There were over a hundred sets of eyes looking at the podium. Looking at her.

Celine introduced the proposal on COLI*GO's behalf, presenting the concept and explaining the intrinsic value such innovation could have on human life. Martin and Marta sat quietly next to Julie, shifting uncomfortably in their seats. Their nervousness unsettled Julie; collectively, the pair had sat in front of The Legislature hundreds of times over the last decade.

Celine's voice hummed in the background, explaining extensive research in gene therapy technology similar to the antidote. Playing with human genetics always posed a risk, but the antidote appeared safe in simulations for Alzheimer's patients.

"You've approved various pharmaceuticals over the last few years rooted in gene editing, and I hope your trust in our sciences is instilled from the years of evidence and data we've provided."

She spoke with eloquence and enthusiasm.

"I'd like to introduce the COLI*GO scientist behind the proposed drug candidate. She will present the technology, how it works and the inclusion criteria for human testing," Celine said as Julie stood up from her seat. "Dr. Julie Walsh."

Celine stepped down from the lectern, and Julie approached the position cautiously. Her vision blurred as she peered out into the crowd. Whispers emerged, and all eyes were on her.

"Good morning, representatives," Julie said, her voice a little shaky. She cleared her throat, looked down at her notes, and gathered more confidence.

"Ms. O'Connor is correct in the foundation of gene therapy. This technology has proven the most effective. And with that foundation, this new neurological drug candidate helps repair neuro-receptors in the human brain," she said, pointing her laser at the screen beside her.

The room quieted and the hushed voices fell silent.

"The drug candidate learns from healthy neurotransmitters and repairs damaged ones. What you see on the screen is a part of the brain called the dendrites, which collects information and heals other neurons. Patients who suffer from Alzheimer's have smaller cortexes compared to their healthy peers. Upon repair of the dendrites, the cortex can regenerate and return to normal sizes."

Images of Alzheimer's patients' brains appeared on the screen. Julie's photos showed the results in the simulated models. She noted several eyes growing wider out in the audience. She took a sip of her water and continued.

"Because we see such promising simulation results, we

considered other diseases that result in decreased cortexes. The medical community notes patients suffering from psychological disorders fit into this category. We believe this is why many patients suffering from psychological conditions experience memory complications. I ran simulations in patient profiles of those who suffer from depression and bipolar disorders. Within a short period of time, the antidote aided in regeneration."

The room stilled, and Julie looked out across the room and up toward the gallery. She couldn't make out Colin or The Supreme from the distance and brightness of the room, but she believed they both rooted for her.

"This is why COLI*GO is requesting an additional clinical trial to study the outcomes of the antidote in patients who suffer from bipolar disorder."

"What are the differences in protocols for various indications in this trial?" a voice from the left side of the room inquired.

"Great question, Representative." Julie's voice brightened. "The antidote would be injected twice a month for six months in patients with Alzheimer's and once per week in patients with manic depression. Our focus is on both short-term and long-term outcomes and to study potential side effects. We'd follow patients for a full year post-treatment in an extension study. You can find the specific endpoints in the report Kathleen Murphy provided you, but they are all associated with safety, memory functionality, increased neurological response, and of course, growth in the cortex to similar sizes found in healthy humans."

"And you believe six months of therapy would cure patients?" another voice in the room asked loudly.

"Yes," Julie answered. "That's the time we've observed in simulations for full repair of the damaged receptors. We're fairly confident that relapses are rare."

The room remained quiet for a few moments, and Julie's heart quickened as the adrenaline coursed through her veins.

"This sounds very promising. But what are the potential side effects, and how common are they? And how would you make patients participating in these trials aware?" said a familiar voice Julie knew too well from the crowd: Representative Joel

Kennsington.

"Excellent question, Representative Kennsington," Celine said, standing quickly. "Risks detected in the simulations include standard side effects such as dizziness, high blood pressure, headaches, diarrhea, and nausea. Long-term implications are always a risk in gene therapy, including cell mutation; however, that risk remains increasingly low, less than 1 percent," Celine answered.

Well, that's a bit of a lie for patients suffering from psychological conditions.

Julie wanted to speak, but Celine's icy glare silenced her. Julie held high standards with regard to the scientific process; she felt a personal responsibility to provide all the risks, no matter the cost.

"Less than 1 percent in Alzheimer's patients. Not in other areas of study. We're unsure of all the side effects in psychological conditions yet." Julie was surprised the words came out of her mouth boldly and confidently as Celine looked at her with disgust.

"All patients will be screened and recommended by medical professionals from our partner hospitals in The City. And all patients will review the potential risks and benefits with their physicians as we do with all our clinical trials," Celine added sternly.

"Thank you for answering my question, Ms. O'Connor and Dr. Walsh," Joel said before sitting back down.

A few more questions were asked before the representatives requested a fifteen-minute recess. As the COLI*GO team exited the Sessions room, Celine firmly grabbed Julie's arm and pulled her aside.

"I would have congratulated you, had you not spoken over me," Celine said before huffing down the hall away from the group.

Martin looked at Julie with a sympathetic smile.

"I think you did the right thing."

"Thank you, Martin," Julie said.

"Celine isn't a scientist. She doesn't understand the impacts as much as we do," Martin replied reassuringly, placing his hand on Julie's shoulder. They waited by the doors until the end of the recess. Celine returned after a few moments but remained silent, avoiding Julie's gaze.

The most exciting part of the meeting was about to begin: the vote. With wide eyes and a nervous tremble, Julie watched the screen explode with Yay and Nay votes. For human clinical trials, the measure needed seventy Yay votes to pass. The suspense intensified around her, so palpable that Julie believed she could reach out and grab it. Julie had to close her eyes; the anticipation overwhelmed her.

"Julie," Marta whispered in her ear after what seemed like the longest few moments of her life. "Open your eyes."

The screen above her showed the results: seventy-six Yay votes, twenty-three Nay votes and one abstained vote.

Tears streamed down her cheeks, and a smile spread across her face. The hurdles for the antidote weren't over, but this moment was purely monumental for the young scientist. After spending nearly ten years of her life committed to developing this drug, the antidote was finally coming to life.

Chapter 33
Jones

June 1st, 45 A.R.

Months passed since Jones read Mick's journal. The pure shock of Mick's knowledge and secrets irked Jones in an odd manner, but he couldn't stay mad at Mick.

Will I succeed in providing the correct answers?

Jones looked over from his comfortable spot on the bed to where the journal remained hidden, resting idly in the nightstand. The journal burned beside him each night, but the intensity increased on the nights Mick wasn't physically there.

Understanding who the mysterious being named "It" was plagued Jones's processor. He believed this man might also be The City's uncaught serial killer. Mick wrote so nonchalantly about It, as if he were someone Jones already knew. But It was after Mick, and this disturbed Jones more than he could explain.

After initially reading the journal, Jones walked straight into Mick's office and opened the filing cabinet. The samples of blood stared back at him hauntingly; he knew which sample was the mysterious one Mick alluded to, the one brought back from "future" Mick. The handwriting was neat, even with the smudged label, and the two letters on the vial made sense to Jones now.

IT

Jones's newly acquired knowledge about Julie also erratically crossed his processor. Her secrets at COLI*GO oddly made sense, but Jones didn't want to accept the news of her involvement with the governor. Further questions accumulated on Jones's growing list, and he needed to uncover the truth quickly.

She must know something, or am I just projecting because I'm bored?

Ever since Lexi's murder, Jones was placed on mundane cases at the precinct, and the commissioner recommended that he "cease communication" with Dr. Anna Garcia.

Jones's device made a quiet sound. He rolled over in the empty bed and grabbed his device, noticing an encrypted message appear on his screen.

Jones—meet me at my place, we need to talk.

***

Jones pinged Anna through another encrypted message once he arrived in The Port. He felt paranoid, but he knew top secret information, information worth killing for. Jones wouldn't have been surprised if The Supreme or the commissioner kept tabs on his every move.

To be safe, Jones left his device in his vehicle and walked around for a bit, stopping at a coffee shop and meandering in nonsensical patterns until he eventually reached Anna's apartment.

"Hey, Jones," Anna called to him from her couch.

Anna's home was a disaster; the sink was filled to the brim with dirty dishes, takeout boxes littered her long kitchen island, and clothes scattered across her living room floor. Anna sat in pajamas on the couch, her hair tied back in a greasy bun.

"Anna . . . are you okay?" Jones asked, stepping around the dirty laundry on the floor until he reached her.

"Honestly? No. I've been afraid to leave."

She couldn't even look at him as she spoke the words.

Jones nodded and sat next to her. All the photos and notes remained proudly displayed on the large white wall opposite them.

"I know I have a death wish written on my forehead if I take one wrong step, so I haven't left here since that day. I've had everything delivered, and the only fresh air I get is when I open the window. I'm still afraid to go on my own balcony. How ridiculous is that? The only reason they didn't kill me right then and there was because of my family. Because I'm a Garcia."

Family was a particularly sore spot. Anna was never the "favorite child" in the family. Isabella was considered the golden child, the one who had it all. Jones never fully comprehended family dynamics; he still found Mick's problems peculiar and strange but came to terms that these were not emotions he'd ever understand. The situations were too foreign and unfamiliar.

"Well, let's take things one step at a time. I'll help you in any way I can, if you want me to. Have you thought about getting out of The City for a while? Going to The Island?" Jones asked.

"No," Anna responded grimly. "Isabella is there, being the perfect daughter and taking care of our mother. And then I'll have to explain why I'm no longer the chief medical examiner."

"I'm sure it wouldn't be so bad."

Anna shook her head.

"It is. Isabella already belittled me. She said if I wanted to go back, the O'Connors could help me out. I'd rather rip out all my hair than ever be indebted to the O'Connor family. Plus, my work here isn't finished. We need to bring justice to these women," she said, pointing to the wall of photos. "I haven't added Lexi yet. It still feels so fresh."

"We should add her," Jones said, taking a deep breath. "And I think there's someone else we need to add as well."

"Have I really been that out of touch? Has he struck again?"

Panic stained her lovely face, her eyes growing wide with fear.

"No. And I'm not sure the kill is exactly his to claim, but I can't stop thinking about Melanie O'Connor. She's got to be tied into this somehow," Jones answered cautiously.

After reading Mick's journal entry, Melanie's death rattled around in his processor. Jones performed extensive research on Melanie's disappearance. She disappeared on her thirty-second birthday, June 23rd. The O'Connor family faced speculation at first, the media accusing her of fleeing. Headlines claimed the pressure and expectations from an old bloodline family were too much for a "nobody."

Melanie and the former governor had an affectionate and beloved relationship. They met when she worked on his first gubernatorial campaign, falling in love quickly and marrying only a few months after Henry won the election. Melanie was much younger than him and came from a poor family in The City. Marrying outside of old bloodlines was rare, and Jones assumed this meant Henry really did love her. The Constituency adored her, people and androids alike. Melanie O'Connor was relatable, charitable, and kind.

Mick insinuated the former governor may have killed his wife, but this accusation didn't sit well with Jones. Whoever wanted Melanie dead didn't want anyone to find her body, let alone know she died. And if this mysterious "It" was after Mick, the reason could be because Mick witnessed Melanie's death.

Melanie fit the profile of the type of the uncaught serial killer. She was connected in politics and in her early thirties. The only differentiation was how she was killed.

"Melanie O'Connor?" Anna asked, sitting up straighter from her slouched position on the couch.

"Yes. I'm not positive on this hunch, but this is all related somehow."

"But her body was never found. How can you claim she was murdered?"

Jones paused. He trusted Mick, and Mick encouraged him to confide in Anna.

"You know how Mick has been working on a consulting project?"

"Yes . . ." Anna said slowly.

"Well, this will sound a bit far-fetched, but you need to trust me. I can show you more if you don't, but Mick's working on theories of time travel," Jones said, lifting a slight gaze in Anna's direction.

Anna's jaw dropped slightly, but her eyes showed intrigue and curiosity rather than confusion or disbelief.

"He time travels and has for several years now. When I first met him, he told me DNA acts like a human data file and stores all the information of a person. Mick uses blood samples from humans, and there's a specific protein that acts as a vehicle to project someone into the past or future. He can only travel as far in the past or future as that human has lived, but the theory works."

Anna's mouth opened into an O, and she rose from the couch.

"That's incredible."

"Yes." Jones smiled, and his green scales shimmered dimly on him. "He records everything in a journal, so that's how I know so much about his research."

"So, he witnessed Melanie O'Connor's murder?"

"Not exactly," Jones admitted. "But he saw her dead body when he traveled to the past."

"Who is he doing this consulting work for?" Anna asked while crossing her arms.

Jones inhaled sharply, knowing the answer wouldn't sit well with Anna.

"The Supreme."

Silence filled the room. Anna looked down at her feet and then approached the wall. She stepped to the left of the first photograph and wrote Melanie's name with a question mark. Anna walked over to the far right of the wall, stopping to look at each woman's photograph before reaching the end. Her chicken scratch revealed Lexi's name. Anna picked up her device and scanned through images of the former governor's wife.

"We might be grasping at straws since there's no confirmation whatsoever of the circumstances of Melanie's death."

Jones walked over to her, his eyes locking in with hers.

"But," Anna continued without looking up from her device, "it appears from all these images that the only jewelry Melanie ever wore was her wedding band and the infamous O'Conner emerald engagement ring."

She flipped her device over and swiped through multiple pictures for Jones to see. The O'Connor family's emerald stone shone brightly in all the photos.

Melanie really was a beautiful woman. While Colin's stance resembled more of his father, Celine shared the same lean frame as her mother.

"We don't have a photo of her body after the kill to verify that would be the missing piece," Jones said with a sigh as Anna scribbled notes furiously under Melanie's name.

"What about Lexi?" Anna asked, changing direction.

"I can't find her anywhere in the database. They were so good, Anna. I scanned her with my eyes. Nothing. Nothing at all."

"I am curious how The Supreme is creating these hybrids of humans and androids," Anna wondered. "I'm not surprised that she's involved in time travel and in the death of a hybrid."

"Posse hominem," Jones corrected her. Jones was used to hearing the derogatory term of "bot" for androids and felt the need to stand up for this new species and their proper terminology.

"Sorry, I don't really remember much Latin."

"I never forget things. Everything stays in my processor forever, so unfortunately I cannot understand that feeling in particular," Jones said casually.

"And exactly how many feelings do you understand? Ten to 20 percent?"

"Actually, over sixty."

Anna looked straight back at Jones, her device crashing to the floor beside her feet.

"But I thought the highest legal amount was 20 percent? And only that is saved for someone like The Supreme and other high-ranking officials?"

Anna walked closer to Jones, closing the gap between them.

"I hope you won't tell anyone."

At this point, all he could do was trust Anna.

"When I was younger, my best friend Julie helped reprogram me. She built the system, wrote the coding. She said it was possible for me to learn more as time went on. Supposedly, my algorithm would keep improving. I'm not sure exactly how many feelings and emotions I've acquired since then," Jones said, looking away from Anna.

Anna approached Jones by the time he had finished sharing his secret. Her eyes were so green, a color Jones rarely saw in humans but a color that was so much like his own scales. Vibrant, iridescent, magical, and simply striking. She placed her hand on his cheek affectionately, tracing down to the back corner behind his ear and reaching his neck. This was the exact spot of his scar, the place that provided access to his processor.

Jones found her touch familiar and calming. He didn't need to look down; he could tell his scales were glowing brightly, beaming with color. Jones recognized this feeling as one similar to the feelings he typically reserved for Mick. Jones had never felt this way about anyone else. About Anna.

"Of course I would never tell anyone, Jones."

***

Jones was happy to see Julie the next day. They sat together in the public gardens, one of their favorite parks in The City. Many large beautiful trees and flowers lined the walking paths. Julie and Jones circled around the shallow pond in the middle and found a shaded grassy spot. The flowers were blooming, the pops of bright reds, deep violets, and sharp pinks contrasting with the pale green grass that would eventually find its own vibrancy later in the summer. The sun warmed them, but Julie still brought a thick blanket to combat the chilly wind.

"So, work must be very time consuming right now?" Jones asked her.

"Yes," Julie said with a smile, stretching her legs across the blanket. "It's been a whirlwind since the Session. But we won't start the clinical trials until September."

"It was fun watching you on all the news channels."

Julie rolled her eyes.

"I'm actually taking some personal time at the end of the month before things get really busy."

"Are you staying local?" Jones asked.

"No," Julie responded, lowering her voice. "I'm going to The Oceanside."

The Oceanside was known as an old bloodline vacation destination. Many had summer estates that lined the beach. The O'Connors included.

Mick said she'd tell me on her own terms and to let her. Don't push her, Jones reminded himself.

"I need to ask you for a favor," Jones said, changing the subject as he gazed out across the pond. "You know how I worry about Mick? I'm thinking there might be something he's not telling either of us about his work situation."

Julie glanced over at Jones before quickly averting away. Jones believed Julie knew more than she probably even realized when it came to what happened within the walls of COLI*GO.

"Do you know about the relationship Mick has with his Uncle Jeb?" Jones probed.

"No, Mick never talked to me about his family other than to say he left everything in the past," she responded softly.

Jones hadn't realized Mick only confided in him about his rocky relationship. A small glimmer of appreciation cascaded through him.

"There's a complicated family dynamic. Jeb paid for Mick's education at The University." Jones looked over at Julie before continuing. "Right before Mick started classes, they got into a falling out. I'm not quite sure why, but they haven't made amends. And it's a shame because Jeb lives here in The City."

"I didn't realize Mick had family here. I thought they were all in The Countryside."

"Only Jeb. He's actually a famous artist. Supposedly, he left the family in The Countryside when Mick was fairly young to pursue his dreams in art. But he got caught up in some shady dealings with law enforcement in the past, and there's a rumor he's doing consulting work at COLI*GO."

"An artist?" Julie's eyes raised in disbelief. "And someone with a criminal record?"

Jones nodded, his eyes squinting from the bright sun.

"Everything COLI*GO does is highly confidential. Jeb would be a risky hire."

"I thought so, too," Jones said, closing his eyes as he lay down on the blanket. "But Mick saw him there. And if it's true, I think Mick needs the heads up. He loves his job at COLI*GO, and he's finally doing better."

Julie pulled out her device and lay down beside Jones. She shielded the reflection from the sun with her tiny hands.

"Let me see if he's in the employee database."

Her fingers danced across the screen, scrolling through the company directory.

"I don't see him in here. What would an artist be doing at COLI*GO anyways?"

Jones grinned. This confirmed his suspicion: Jeb Taylor wasn't listed as an employee or contractor at COLI*GO because whatever business he had there was off the books. And only one being could orchestrate such an operation: The Supreme.

"Well, that's reassuring."

"What kind of crimes? If you can share."

Julie put her device away and rolled to her side to face Jones. He rolled his head to the right and lowered his voice.

"He's been arrested a few times for dealing illegal pharmaceuticals. There's a belief within the precinct he is the head of a black-market drug operation in The City. Particularly one that serves old bloodline families. We've never been able to prove anything, though," Jones responded carefully.

"What kind of drugs do you think?"

Jones was surprised by her interest.

"Some narcotics, stimulants, and hallucinogens. There's a big market for these drugs amongst the wealthiest in The City. They can afford them."

Julie looked away from him. Jones wished he could see her eyes, get a better understanding of what might possibly be crossing her mind. She sighed audibly before turning her head back in his direction.

"Well, if there are rumors about that, he definitely wouldn't be working at COLI*GO," she said slowly. "Or at least officially."

Jones closed his eyes and concentrated on controlling his shock.

What does Julie know? Is this why she can't be involved in the concerns of the future?

"COLI*GO still manufactures many of the pharmaceuticals that fall into those drug classes you mentioned."

This must mean Jeb received the drugs from The Supreme or someone on behalf of The Supreme to fuel this black-market industry.

"Really?" Jones asked.

"They're needed in some medical instances, but you're right; they've been abused and are rarely prescribed. But forget it, I'm afraid I said too much."

Julie lifted her sunglasses up off her face, and Jones looked at her concerned eyes. Julie did know something, probably something about Colin O'Connor.

"I'll pretend I never heard what you said, but thank you for checking about Jeb . . . for Mick." Jones looked up at the sky.

"I'd do anything for you and Mick; you know that, right?" Julie asked, breaking Jones's distraction from her.

Yes. Jones did know that.

Chapter 34
The Governor

June 18th, 45 A.R.

"I'm surprised to find you in my office of all places, Colin," Celine said from behind her desk. She faced away from the door, looking out across The River.

"Why is that?"

"Shouldn't you be out campaigning? Or reading legislation for tomorrow's session?" Celine asked, finally turning around to face her brother.

Celine's beauty was poised and conservative, and she wore a beautifully embroidered silk button-up with puffy sleeves. His sister always sat up straight and never missed proper etiquette. How she portrayed herself as prim and proper was far from the realities of what she was really like behind closed doors.

"Last time I checked, I also have an office and a duty here at COLI*GO," Colin said, taking a seat.

He looked directly into his sister's eyes; he wasn't sure what plagued her mind lately or why she seemed so distant and distracted. Even Martin mentioned concern to Colin in passing, a strange notion for two men who didn't particularly care for one another.

"What's wrong, Celine?"

Celine's facial expression changed, and she smiled plainly.

"I'm okay, Colin. I know I've been a recluse lately. I apologize. I really want to be there for you and your campaign, but I've had so much going on here at COLI*GO."

"Don't lose any concern over my campaign. I worry about you," Colin responded, placing his hand on top of hers. "You can always confide in me. I'm here to listen and help in any way I can."

"I know and appreciate that. But you still haven't answered my question about why you're here?" She chuckled as she spoke.

"I need to ask a very sensitive question."

Celine removed her hand from underneath Colin's and sat up straighter in her chair.

"What's happening in the lower lab?" Colin asked slowly.

His sister would protect COLI*GO above almost anything else, but Colin took a gamble that family would trump in importance.

"It's a few highly confidential technologies in their infancy. Anything there isn't ready for input from business development, finance, or product management. Beta testing." Celine spoke as if the words were memorized, etched into her brain.

Colin was aware of the various projects happening at COLI*GO and that many never even made their way up to the executives or The Board of Directors. But when Martin came to him, expressing concern about Celine and the lower lab, Colin knew things were serious. Then Lexi entered the scene and caused suspicion.

"Is that where Lexi Pvadinish worked before she was assigned to help Julie?" Colin asked.

"Who?"

"The Supreme assigned Lexi Pvadinish to work with Julie back in March. She told me to inquire with you about Lexi. So, do you know her?" Colin eyed his sister suspiciously.

"I don't know her personally. I don't know everyone that works at COLI*GO," Celine said with a hint of annoyance in her tone.

"She's not in the directory. She isn't in the national database system either," Colin said.

She isn't even completely human.

Colin remembered how warm Lexi felt in his hands, warm like every other woman's before her. But she also felt so rough as if severely dehydrated. Her skin flaked off onto his clothes, his gloves, and everywhere. In the shower, he felt the remains of Lexi surrounding him. Colin spent weeks cleaning and re-cleaning his vehicle, deciding eventually to burn the clothes he wore that night. The most jarring memory from that evening was the look in Lexi's eyes: too hollow and emotionless.

The small scar on her upper neck was the final straw. The mark coincidentally was located in the same place where androids had access to their microchips. The incision was small and almost healed on her skin, but the pink hue around her dark complexion stood out. When Colin stabbed her, he felt a sense of confusion and delight as the crimson blood left her body. He wasn't sure why he expected something different, but her human blood flowed out of her like every other woman, painting his knife colorfully.

Don't touch her, It had said, standing over him, his eyes intently focused on Lexi.

She was very dead, and there was absolutely no life left in her. Colin went back to Lexi, grabbing his knife quickly and slicing open her neck at the base of her scar. His eyes widened at the sight of the tiny wire protruding from the small incision he had made. His fingertips held the wire tightly, slowly pulling it out of her until a small high-tech microchip emerged.

What is she?

I don't know, and I don't care to stick around any longer to find out, It had said in a terrified manner, one he rarely exhibited.

Unsure of what to do, Colin placed the microchip back. He wanted to take the microchip as his memento, but that didn't fit with their ritual. Instead, he took Lexi's nose ring, as she donned no other jewelry.

Whatever Lexi was involved in—something with The Supreme, he alleged—he didn't want to cause any more suspicion by stealing the technology in her brain. The Supreme was up to something unsavory, something particularly dangerous to society.

Colin rarely felt comfortable with his own horrid acts of violence, but in that moment, he was glad he and It killed her. The strangeness surrounding Lexi solidified that killing her was protecting Julie and protecting society. Protecting his people was always the motivator behind the kills.

"I don't know what to tell you, Colin. I don't know who Lexi is. Why do you care?" Celine asked, her voice snapping Colin out of his own memory from that night.

"I care because she disappeared without a trace. Julie mentioned Lexi left abruptly, never coming back to work."

"Well, then what's the problem?"

"I find that very . . . peculiar," he said, crossing his arms.

"Look, it is very odd, yes, but I'm sure Julie can handle it on her own. You don't need to be so invested in minuscule issues, especially when it has to do with someone you're sleeping with." Celine looked at her brother with a glare of disapproval and judgment.

"That's hypocritical of you to say, don't you think?" Colin spat back, thinking about Celine's own colored past of lovers.

"Maybe, but remember, Colin, Amanda ended up dead."

The words stung him unbearably. Amanda died because he killed her, a decision that wasn't easy for him to make.

"Thank you for the reminder, but that won't happen to Julie," Colin answered furiously through his teeth. "And I'm not just sleeping with Julie; I actually care about her."

"That's nice. Have you told Isabella yet? And if not, can I watch when you do?" Celine's words and laughter were cold and harsh.

The siblings had an undeniable bond, but when they fought, they fought dirty. There were no consequences for their volatile truths and raw accusations against each other.

"Isabella is not a bad person, Celine. I know you don't like her or the Garcias, but they're a very important family. They have good intentions."

Celine laughed as Colin spoke the words.

"You can't truly believe that, Colin, can you? Not after everything they put me through and that they put our father through."

"Look," Colin said, standing up from his seat. "I haven't told Isabella yet, no. But if you remember, she's the one who left me. She asked for space."

"Whatever, Colin," Celine said, shaking her head and standing up to face him. "I don't think Isabella is under any impression that your relationship is over. You'd be making a very dangerous mistake to assume that. I'd tread lightly. The last thing we need is for you to lose this election, and don't doubt for a minute that the Garcias would scheme with Joel Kennsington if they uncovered what you're up to with Julie. She's a 'nobody.'"

Colin looked at his sister. She was correct; he was acting irrationally, something he rarely ever indulged in. Colin kept things neat and calculated each move.

Except when it comes to Julie.

"Well, I'll get out of your hair. I'm actually heading out for another round of campaigning across The Constituency this week. I'm going to stay at the estate in The Oceanside through the weekend."

"You'll be at The Oceanside?" Celine asked, a softness finally cracking away at the harshness across her face.

Colin was going to The Oceanside to get away with Julie, but he also went this time each year. He liked celebrating his mother's birthday and the anniversary of her death.

"Do you want me to meet you there?"

Colin closed his eyes. June 23rd was always a difficult day for him. One day, his mother was there, and simply the next she was gone. Summers at The Oceanside were usually passable, but this day in particular was difficult. Her memory lived more vividly in him when he was there, between the smell of the salty ocean air mixed with the fragrance of freshly cut grass. All scents that reminded him of her.

"I'll be okay. You have a lot to do here," he said, gesturing around her office.

And Julie will be with me. She reminds me of the beautiful things in this ugly world. The things worth living and fighting for through all the darkness.

"All right," Celine responded with a sigh. "I'll see what I can find regarding Lexi for you."

"Thanks, I greatly appreciate it," Colin said with a smile.

He hugged his sister before leaving her office. The battle was fought; a truce and peace treaty were signaled between them once again. The carnage was not too unbearable this time.

This time.

***

The Garcias' estate on The Island wasn't overly ostentatious, but it was lusciously manicured. The home was colonial in style, a stark white painted exterior with large black shutters and a whirlwind of deep green grass, gardens, and shrubbery spread across the lawn. A windy driveway filled with stone and seashells led to a bright green door. The inside of the home was modernized, an opposite look from what appeared outside. Glass and marble covered the floors and ceilings. The space was completely open, resembling an observatory.

The Garcia family played an integral role in the history of The Island's success. Centuries ago, the Garcias founded a profitable whaling and fishing business, transforming The Island into a bustling trade port. From there, the family governed The Island, serving as mayors to representatives in The Legislature. Eventually, the Garcias invested in more philanthropic endeavors, officially leaving the political scene. Unofficially, the family still played an instrumental role in the government.

Even with the tensions between their families, Mrs. Garcia adored Colin's visits with Isabella. Mrs. Garcia was a woman of short stature, much like her daughters, but had a large personality and presence. Isabella and Anna had their father's darker features but inherited their mother's sing-song voice and charming characteristics. Mrs. Garcia's home was typically filled with laughter. Tonight, they sat around the dinner table, engaging in light banter, but all Colin could think about was his sister's grave warning. He hated admitting she was right but sensed his relationship with Isabella wasn't completely over once he arrived. Her hand rested slightly on his thigh, and her smile grew whenever he looked in her direction.

For someone who said she needed a break from me, this isn't what I was expecting.

"I'm looking forward to your town hall speech tomorrow down by the docks," Isabella said, lifting her hand from him and continuing to push the food around on her plate with her fork.

"The weather will be lovely. Sunny and warm, much warmer than it has been in The City I imagine?" Mrs. Garcia asked him, her hazel eyes sparkling.

"It's been a chilly spring, but yes, I am looking forward to hearing about the top priorities of The Islanders. I don't visit here as often as I should," Colin said before taking another bite of his fish.

"They're very impressed with what you've done for education, especially here in our community. But I do sense some concerns regarding the number of androids who have immigrated here," Isabella said boldly.

"It's hardly immigrating when The Island is part of The Constituency," Colin said, shocked at Isabella's bluntness.

"Colin, my dear," Mrs. Garcia said sharply, "that's not how the people here feel. Ten years ago, androids only made up 5 percent of The Island's population. Today, that number is closer to 25 percent. Partnership is important for prosperity, but people still fear repercussions from the height of The Resurgence. You were not born yet, but I remember."

Colin looked over at Mrs. Garcia and contained the frustration he held inside. Isabella felt his body tense, and she affectionately squeezed his arm.

"Let's not talk politics at the dinner table, Mother. I'm sorry I brought it up," Isabella said, defusing the situation.

"If not politics, what else shall we chat about? Your courtship has lasted over ten years. There's no official marriage and no children, so there's nothing to discuss."

The words were icy and sharp, cutting through both Colin and Isabella like his freshly sharpened knife. Mrs. Garcia laughed wickedly, shocking both her daughter and Colin.

"Oh, lighten up. There's still time for you, my dear," she said, placing her hand on Isabella's. "But I think a marriage between two of the greatest old bloodline families would really signify peace. Provide confidence in people."

Isabella looked over at Colin with a sad smile. He sensed she agreed with her mother.

"I think we've had enough excitement at the dinner table tonight, Mother. Let's get you ready to retire."

Isabella rose from her chair and walked over to her mother. Mrs. Garcia could hardly walk on her own but refused any device or mobility chair to help her. She was too prideful.

Colin recalled Isabella's public reason for leaving The City centered on how Alexandra, the young woman she hired to take care of the necessary appointments and chores around the house, had quit. Isabella's true reasoning for coming back to The Island was driven by many factors: her aversion to his family's current dealings, his being distant, her mother not receiving the help she needed, and a sister who refused to step in. As they exited the room, Colin saw the complete mess surrounding him. He placed his head in his hands and closed his eyes.

Why does Celine have to be so correct about all the wrong things?

Colin felt Isabella's hands on his shoulders after a few moments. He didn't open his eyes or move but instead let out a small sigh. Her presence felt calming at first, but he knew a painful conversation would follow.

"I'm sorry, but she is right."

Isabella's words were quiet, but they violently infuriated him.

"I'm here for the campaign, Isabella. Nothing more. You told me you needed time away from me," Colin said, finally standing up from his seat. Isabella looked him dead in the eyes, searching for something from him. Something he realized she couldn't find.

"What we have goes beyond love. We've been in this too long now, our relationship has moved into societal duty. This is our status, our families, our careers, our whole lives," Isabella said. short of a pleading. "And I've realized something while I've been away from you. There is no other path. We're in this together whether you like it or not. You must recognize that."

"Isn't it a bit late for you to change your mind on all this?"

"Why would it be too late?"

The threats they both cast lingered in the air, dangerously close to suffocating them both. She was right; together they were hostages to their families and to society. They knew too much about one another. Colin closed his eyes, avoiding admission of defeat.

"What would you like me to do here, Isabella?"

"Well, you can't leave the estate." Her eyes were dark and her voice cruel, a very unusual demeanor for her and one Colin never experienced before. "I think it's time we turn in. You have a big day tomorrow. We have a big day tomorrow."

Isabella placed her hand on Colin's chest as if trying to locate his heartbeat. Shaking her head, Isabella turned away. Colin followed her up the circular staircase.

***

He enjoyed the sight of Julie walking across the back patio and the gardens, her gaze out at the ocean. She held herself as light as a feather in her movements.

Colin chuckled at Julie's giddiness as she explored her surroundings: the hydrangeas, seagrass, and perfectly manicured lawn. He never tired of Julie's true, curious nature.

This visit to The Oceanside was Julie's first and one she cherished. She never took anything for granted, her upbringing much different from Colin's. He admired this about her.

Julie's hair whipped in the ocean breeze, the soft red tones shining brighter from the reflection of the sun. When she turned and noticed Colin, her smile stretched across her face, and she ran to him. He wrapped her up in his embrace and wanted to hold her like this forever. Her skin felt smooth beneath his fingertips, and she smelled intoxicating.

"I missed you."

"I missed you, too, Julie."

Colin led her to the edge of the property. A wooden staircase built into the side of the cliff led them down to the shoreline. They continued descending the stairs, and he grasped Julie at her waist to pull her down onto the soft sand. Most of the beachline on this side of The Oceanside was covered in sharp rocks, but this small sandy area provided a great hidden sunbathing spot. The vibrations of the waves as the ocean consumed the shoreline and the horizon stretched out beyond them.

Eventually, they headed back to the estate. Colin opened the windows and glass French doors throughout the home, allowing the outside landscape to morph with the inside of the house. The sounds of the ocean and the whispering of the breeze echoed around them. Here, they were completely alone.

They made love to the crashing sounds behind them, the essence of delight mumbled and drowned by the harshness of the incoming tide. The sunset shattered the sky in a soft lilac surrounded by orange and pink hues, illuminating the inside of the estate.

Time stood still, irrelevant to them here compared to The City. When pleasure escaped her again, Colin finally let go himself, a sense of indescribable peace spreading across his body.

Julie cupped his face in her delicate hands and kissed him, the taste almost as salty as the ocean water. Colin held Julie tightly, gently tracing the outlines of her body with his fingers as they watched the beauty across the horizon together.

This place haunted Colin, but he couldn't deny that despite the ghosts following him here, this was also the place of fond, loving memories. Creating more beautiful moments here felt natural. Colin never believed he'd experience love again after all the losses in his life, but looking into Julie's soft eyes, he finally saw the possibility. At this moment, wrapped up so tenderly with her, Colin decided he wouldn't let anything ruin this. Not his sister, nor Isabella. Not The Supreme, nor anyone in The Capitol Building.

And especially not It.

***

The estate was quiet, and Julie was fast asleep. The breeze floating inside felt a bit cool during the nighttime, but the scenery was still inviting. Colin couldn't sleep.

Kathleen sent him updated polling numbers earlier that evening. His campaigning efforts showed in places that mattered: The City, The Outskirts, and The Island. The only place Colin lagged was The Countryside. He wasn't overly surprised. His friendly and amenable relationship with The Supreme didn't sit well with the people there. As a whole, the community distrusted androids.

"Been a while, don't you think?"

Colin sighed. He didn't like these unannounced visits from It, especially here of all places.

"To what do I owe the pleasure?" Colin asked and, in the form of old habits, walked over to the beverage fridge to find two beers. He cracked the top off both and handed one to It.

They clinked their bottles together, and each took a swig.

"Well, I needed to get away. So I figured I'd come up here, enjoy some time by the water. I also assumed you'd want me here for moral support, but I see those shoes were filled by someone else," It said, his eyes darting in the direction of the stairs.

"I'm sorry I didn't ask for you to be there. That was

inconsiderate of me," Colin said and meant those words.

It had always been there for him on this day. He knew how important this was to Colin.

"I'm not offended. I'm actually quite glad to see this unfolding for you, my friend."

Colin took a sip of his beer. Strangely, he didn't want It's approval of his and Julie's relationship. He wished It didn't know about her.

"Why are you really here?" Colin asked him curiously.

"Because I feel like you've been distant lately."

Colin had remained aloof lately, especially with It. There was still so much about what happened from killing Lexi that he and It hadn't unpacked, hadn't acknowledged.

"I still feel unsettled about Lexi," Colin replied after a few moments passed between them. "I think The Supreme is hiding something from us. This creation has to be hers."

"Well, she must know we were the ones to kill Lexi. There was no media coverage of her killing, so I'm assuming her body was taken away from the crime scene and hidden somewhere in COLI*GO. I don't like that feeling."

"You think Lexi's somewhere in COLI*GO?"

It nodded, the beer bottle empty as he placed it on the counter.

***

Colin and Celine kept the estate as original as possible, barely changing the design of the house from what they remembered as children. The siblings visited their family vacation home frequently but rarely together. What Julie most appreciated about the house was the massive lawn, the gardens, and the smell of the ocean. While The City was also situated on the coastline, the harbors and inlets masked a different odor compared to the tranquility of The Oceanside.

Colin led Julie outside, and they walked the property line along the cliffs. He held Julie's hand as they made their way along the jagged point of rocks sticking out much further than the rest of the land. He paused and gazed out over the sea, letting go of her hand.

"Today is both my mother's birthday and the anniversary of her disappearance," Colin said. "I always come here on this day to remember her. She was an incredible woman and an amazing mother."

Julie wrapped her arm around him, pulling him in close to her. Colin leaned into the warmth Julie provided from her embrace.

"She loved me and Celine, and she loved my father. She accepted him for all his flaws, loved each of us unconditionally. I wish I'd been able to spend more time with her. I wonder constantly how different my life would be, had my mother been a larger part of it."

"Mothers are so special. It's hard to come to terms when they leave us," Julie said, looking up at him, tears nearing the corners of her eyes.

Colin knew this time of year was particularly difficult for Julie. She was more vocal about her mother, sharing fond memories from her childhood with Colin. The way Julie spoke about her made Colin feel as if he knew her personally, where he found it difficult to open up about his own mother.

Colin remembered most of what happened the day she died. He suppressed the memories when he was awake, but he couldn't control his mind at night. The night terrors he experienced brought him back here. In them, he snuck out of the estate to climb the cliffs—something his mother repeatedly scolded him for. There was something magical and dangerous about the landscape, and he was an adventurous young boy.

He remembered her calling for him, followed by his father. If Henry found him, he'd be in trouble, so Colin hid further into the side of the cliff. His father thought his son was odd and embarrassing. Colin was "far too quiet" and "terrible at making friends." Melanie loved her son and argued with Henry about whether life in The City was the best for their children. She begged his father not to run for reelection.

Eventually, the yelling stopped and was replaced by the sound of waves crashing below. Colin climbed out from his hiding spot, but before he could get his mother's attention, he noticed a tall figure looming behind her. Melanie turned around to face the man, backing away from him and closer to the edge.

The words the man said were permanently etched in Colin's mind: "I'm sorry, but this needs to be done."

The next thing Colin remembered was his mother's body falling off the ledge. She traveled down the side of the cliffs, hitting some of the jagged edges. In Colin's night terrors, recalling this part of the memory happened in slow motion, each detail painfully prominent.

He opened his eyes, and his fingers brushed Julie's cheek.

"I wanted us to share this moment of remembering them together. Your mother and my mother."

Colin grabbed Julie's hand, and she intertwined her fingers with his. They sat down on the ledge of the cliff and let their legs dangle. Colin wrapped his arm around Julie's shoulders, and she lost her composure. The tears escaped her eyes, her mother's anniversary approaching in a couple weeks. This moment between Colin and Julie solidified their trust and secured their bond.

Colin O'Connor never allowed his vulnerability to show, but with Julie, he wasn't afraid. He loved her, and she loved him, too.

***

Later that night, Colin and Julie sat out on the patio. With her return to The City tomorrow, Colin wouldn't see her until after the last of his campaigning events concluded.

"Can I ask you something?" Colin pondered, breathing in the smell of her hair as she rested in the nook of his shoulder.

"Of course."

"Do you know what happens in the lower lab?"

Julie's eyes flickered for a moment with an element of surprise.

"I really don't know much about the lower lab. I've actually never even been down there. Why?"

Colin sighed; he wasn't sure how upfront to be with her regarding his suspicions of The Supreme's frightful experiments or about Lexi.

"I think someone is funneling money to unapproved projects in the lower lab. You mentioned Lexi worked in the lower lab before working for you, and I wondered if she ever mentioned anything."

"She didn't, but I'll keep my ears open in case I hear anything."

She looked up at Colin with her large round eyes.

"There are a lot of top-secret projects happening at COLI*GO. But that isn't surprising, it's the most forward-thinking company in The City. I hope I get to be a larger part of that innovation someday."

Colin stared out across the ocean, noticing Julie was lost in her own thoughts.

"I have a question for you, too. Do you know Jeb Taylor?"

Colin grew incredibly stiff at the mention of Jeb's name.

"The artist?"

Julie nodded in response. The wind picked up, coming from the edges of the cliffs, but the air remained warm against them.

"I know him. The family has purchased his artwork in the past, and he's friends with Kathleen's family."

Julie inhaled deeply before speaking.

"I didn't piece it together until now, but I wonder if the gossip about Jeb is connected to your concerns about the lower lab," she spoke softly, and Colin's eyes grew serious. "There's a rumor he's been hired by someone at COLI*GO to deal these high-demand, illegal drugs to old bloodline families. I'm not sure if it's true, but it would explain how he has access to such dangerous pharmaceuticals."

Colin hadn't initially pieced together how Jeb had access to the drugs he purchased off him or that they might be linked to what happened at COLI*GO.

"I saw the pills, Colin. Under the bathroom sink."

She looked directly at him as she said this, but her tone wasn't accusatory or angry. Nothing was threatening about her remark, Colin noted. Julie was genuinely concerned.

He pulled her closer to him in his embrace.

"I won't ever lie to you, Julie. The campaign has challenged me. Mentally. There are nights I don't sleep, followed by days where I can't concentrate. If I see a doctor about this, it'll get reported to The Legislature. Joel will use that against me. Jeb is very discreet, and Kathleen trusts him."

When she didn't say anything for a few moments, the pit in Colin's stomach grew with anxiety. He didn't want to lose her.

"But who is he working for? How is he getting these drugs?"

The Supreme, he thought instantly, the only logical explanation. Celine wasn't interested in such dealings—especially one that could completely shatter the legitimacy of COLI*GO, the company she loved so dearly.

"Maybe The Supreme," Colin answered Julie. "I won't contact Jeb anymore, and I think it is best we both stay out of this."

"That sounds like a good idea. Please don't take those drugs. They're dangerous. I care about you, Colin. I don't want anything to happen to you," Julie said while nestling back into his neck, her arms tightening around him.

"I promise," he responded, gently kissing the top of her head.

Chapter 35

The Supreme

July 22nd, 45 A.R.

The days grew longer, and both people and androids basked in The City's warm summer weather. Except for The Supreme. She looked out the window of her office longingly as memories of her more liberated youth flashed through her processor.

Between long days at The Capitol Building and late evenings at COLI*GO, she rarely had time for sleep.

The Supreme reflected on Jeb Taylor, a flighty man who was instrumental as her puppet. He knew all the right people and had access to the most influential homes across The City.

And The Supreme needed people. Or, at least, their bodies.

Jeb didn't mind selling pharmaceuticals to the wealthy; it was a profitable side business for him. However, he didn't appreciate her more recent requests. She considered inflicting his nephew into the mix, but Mick wasn't ready for this kind of responsibility.

Mick's reports regarding time travel filled the screen of The Supreme's device. He infuriatingly refused experimenting on any of the blood samples she provided him, all of which were from her new creations.

The Supreme made the logical assumption based on Mick's technology that these samples from posse hominems would work. They had been humans first, after all.

Time travel wasn't the sole purpose behind her development and creation of this new species, no matter what Mick believed. There was a bigger plan at play for her half-humans half-androids.

The microchip she implanted into their brains helped block some emotional functions from the limbic system, a part of the human mind that regulated memories in response to emotional stimuli. And The Supreme had the best surgeon in The City performing the operations with an assisting android researcher.

Through trial and error with slums from The City's streets that the commissioner provided her, her team discovered the most optimal placement for the microchip. The access point was similar to where androids kept their microchips, right behind the left ear.

Lexi was the first fully developed posse hominem with all The Supreme's strict specifications, which included completely clearing Lexi's mind of the previous memories of her human life. When Lexi woke up, she didn't know who she was or what her life prior looked like. Back when she was Alexandra, the Garcias' former house assistant.

Jeb retrieved Alexandra for The Supreme on one of his trips to The Island. He visited Mrs. Garcia often, providing pain medication her physician wouldn't prescribe. The Supreme specifically instructed Jeb to bring Alexandra back with him. At that point, Jeb didn't question The Supreme as long as she paid him. Paying Jeb was an easy task; she funneled the money by purchasing his vastly overpriced art.

Now with viable posse hominems who could either retain their human memories or be wiped clean of them, The Supreme needed to create more. Many more. Posse hominems were the key to her full control over The Constituency.

Humans need to suffer and pay for their disgusting deeds from the present and past.

The Supreme spent her whole life preparing for this moment; she was ready to beat Colin O'Connor in their political game of chess. Posse hominems were her checkmate against his king.

With the introduction of this new species, Colin's equal and fair heart would insist they need representation in The Legislature. There couldn't be three heads of government—nothing would ever get done. The Representatives would have to decide who their leader would be: a human or an android.

The final act in her plan was making sure the governor was incapacitated to govern the people and throw all humans in The Legislature into disarray. She needed to exacerbate and expose the correct weak spot within Colin to execute the plan perfectly.

The Supreme smiled and leaned back in her chair. This was why she needed Mick's time travel technology.

***

"Governor, why are you avoiding my messages?" The Supreme asked into her device.

Colin had ignored her for a few weeks.

"I've been busy campaigning, Madam Supreme," he answered in an equally dull and tone-deaf voice.

"There are some issues we need to discuss, particularly around the education bill The Representatives of The People put forward last week," The Supreme said, twirling around in her chair at the COLI*GO office.

"Schedule time with Kathleen. I have a pretty busy calendar, but she has my availability."

The nerve.

"Don't you dare hang up on me, Colin O'Connor!" The Supreme commanded.

The only sound on the other end was Colin's heavy breathing.

"I know you've been avoiding me. I know it has to do with Lexi. Can we talk about it?"

She contemplated extending an olive branch. Colin sighed on the other end of the line, obviously thinking about why The Supreme was playacting him.

"I suppose. But now is not the time."

There was a change in the tone of his voice that The Supreme didn't like. The election was draining Colin; he was ahead in the polls, but Joel Kennsington was a man who never went down easily. Joel's supporters were loud, obnoxious. The governor was tired.

"You and It know something that you weren't supposed to know yet, but I think we should partner on this strategy."

"I'm very aware of that fact, Madam Supreme. I know what you're up to, and if you think I'm going to stay quiet about it forever, you're mistaken," Colin said with a sharpness.

The Supreme thought for a moment. She didn't like being played or threatened. She used blackmail against others—it was never a tool intended to be used against her.

"Need I remind you there's an uncaught serial killer in The City? And I know quite a bit about that."

The silence allowed her a moment to grin with pleasure.

"I'd like to invite you to my box at the orchestra this weekend; we can talk about this then," The Supreme said coolly.

"I don't think it's in the best interest of my campaign if we're cozied up in a box together. I'll go to the orchestra but not as your guest. I'll visit you during the intermission."

She expected this response from Colin.

"I understand. Well, it's a plan then," The Supreme said and hung up the line.

She turned toward her desk and placed her device down. The colors of her scales danced around, glowing in excitement. Alone in her office, she indulged in the guilty pleasure of watching her body physically emit the beautiful sensations of emotions and feelings. Hiding and suppressing her scales was painful.

The serum she injected herself stung and dehydrated her, but the drug dulled the tones in her scales. Only small hints of lustrous and iridescent shimmer broke through.

The memory of having her processor reprogrammed flashed in her processor. Prior, she understood about 20 percent of emotions and feelings. The former supreme explained how the process worked before taking out her microchip. He was headed for retirement, giving him ample time to live his life before his processor stopped running completely.

Emilia admired the former supreme. He led The Resurgence, fought and sacrificed his life for his fellow androids. When she came to, she remembered an overwhelming sense of stillness around her. Every small movement screamed loudly in her ears, and every item in his office appeared lifelike before her eyes. Her predecessor sensed her confusion, her curiosity, and he smiled at her. She remembered his words clearly.

Now you know what it feels like to understand every human emotion. Every feeling a human feels. Use this power wisely. I'll teach you until you assume my role; I'll watch out for you. But no one can know. Do not let Governor Henry O'Connor know. Your responsibility is to use this knowledge to our advantage. Help us regain control over humans. And if you cannot accomplish this, you must reprogram your successor.

He had spoken with such authority, and his golden-orange scales lingered between a bright tangerine and a hazy sunset.

Navigating these feelings alone challenged her, and she made one mistake. The Supreme wasn't sure what the repercussions of sharing her secret with her best friend Celine O'Connor were. But they always shared interesting secrets with one another.

The Supreme picked up her device and thought about what Celine alluded to a few weeks ago when Colin was out campaigning across The Constituency.

What are you doing this weekend?

She hit send, and shortly after, it vibrated with a ping.

Other than working? Nothing.

The Supreme smiled and typed back:

I'd like to invite you to my box at the orchestra Saturday.

There was a brief pause, which The Supreme anticipated.

She imagined Dr. Julie Walsh sitting in the lab and reading the message. She pictured the young scientist tilting her head to the side in surprise. The Supreme suspected Julie admired her and viewed her as a mentor when it came to advancing the antidote. The Supreme also suspected Colin's interest in the antidote didn't stop at just the drug. A message appeared on the screen, and The Supreme smiled wickedly.

That sounds amazing. Thank you, I'm looking forward to it!

***

Mick's triple-decker apartment in The Harbor was modest but roomy. The Supreme visited The Harbor frequently, but this was her first time at Mick's home. He hadn't answered any of her messages in the last few days.

The Supreme almost forgot about Mick's android lover until she reached the front steps and Detective Jones opened the door. Their forbidden relationship was the sole purpose of why Mick lived in this neighborhood separated from downtown by a harbor.

Jones wasn't startled by her presence.

"Hello, Detective Jones."

"Madam Supreme," he responded quietly, looking down each side of the street before stepping aside and letting her into his home.

"Is Mick here?" she asked, already knowing he wasn't.

"No, he hasn't been home for a few days. I assume you are here to discuss his time travel research?" Jones asked.

He's very intuitive for an android, she thought. *Too intuitive.*

"Yes. I have no concerns about our other agreement, if that was your understanding of my visit. COLI*GO and I appreciate your discretion," she said, taking a seat at their kitchen table.

Jones sat across from her but never dropped his gaze. His scales shimmered softly, the emerald shades of green brighter than when he first answered the door. The Supreme noted this same occurrence when he sat across her at COLI*GO after Lexi's death.

He understands more emotions than he should.

"Well, I'm here to drop off some samples for Mick to test and experiment with, then I'll get out of your way." She stood up and headed down the narrow hallway within their apartment.

"I assume one of these rooms is his office?"

"Yes, the one on the left."

Jones did not escort her and remained firmly planted in the kitchen.

"Thank you," The Supreme replied, opening the door and stepping inside.

The room was sparse, a small desk was pushed in the corner facing the window, and a filing cabinet sat opposite the desk. The natural light from the window was a lovely touch. The Supreme did not have new samples to provide Mick, although she did have tubes filled with Lexi's blood back at the lower lab. What The Supreme really needed was one of Mick's devices. Mick had various prototypes of the chrome box and glasses. She quickly found the device, picking it up in her hands. The glasses felt lighter than she had anticipated, and the chrome box fit nicely in her pocket. The device resembled an optometrist's glasses, the frames round and thick with a small insert for the blood sample. The chrome box calculated the mechanism of transportation to the past or future.

A kitchen chair scraping across the worn hardwood floors made

The Supreme jump. Jones grew restless with her prolonged absence.

The Supreme slipped the glasses and box into her bag and walked out of the room.

"Thank you for letting me in. Can you please tell Mick when he returns that he must make an appointment with me at COLI*GO?"

"Of course, I will let him know."

"Good, well then. Thank you for being an accommodating host, Detective Jones," The Supreme said with a smile before leaving.

***

The Supreme looked out the vehicle's window at Julie's walk-up building. Julie's place in The Bay was on the way to the symphony, and The Supreme offered to pick her up.

Julie wore an elegant black form-fitting dress that accentuated her figure in the right places. A slit up her left leg wasn't cut high enough to consider the dress risqué; instead, The Supreme found the view enticing. Julie wore her hair in a sleek, stylish ponytail that made her appear sophisticated and mature and showcased her lovely elongated neck.

"You look truly stunning, my dear," The Supreme said as Julie entered the vehicle.

The Supreme was dressed in a more conservative pantsuit. The colors vibrated purple and gold with a paisley accent pattern. The amber tones in her scales appeared rich against those colors. She yearned to show off her captivating scales, but the real splendor of androids frightened humans.

When they reached Symphony Hall, the pair entered The Supreme's private box. There were two gold leaf chairs and a small table with clawed feet between them.

Julie had never attended Symphony Hall, and The Supreme found the amazement on the young scientist's face surprisingly attractive. A wave of guilt coursed through The Supreme momentarily before disappearing. She lured Julie here under false, sinister pretenses.

The Supreme's eyes traveled to the O'Connor box where Colin sat, paying no attention to them. Beside him was Dr. Isabella

Garcia. They appeared cozy together; Isabella smiled and laughed, leaning her head into the governor affectionately.

The music tonight was a rendition of Bach; the elegant violinists showed enthusiasm in their strokes as the conductor's arms moved rapidly back and forth. Julie focused on the performance, but The Supreme's gaze didn't leave Julie.

"Madam Supreme, the governor is outside and requests entrance," an android attendant whispered in her ear.

Julie's attention faltered at his announcement, but she looked down at her lap to avoid The Supreme.

"Let him in."

Colin O'Connor entered with a sense of stealth The Supreme always anticipated with him. He donned a black fitted suit that proudly showed off his lean muscular build and intimidating height. Colin wasn't startled by Julie's presence, but his cool, sharp eyes moved up and down her body. His body grew tense at the sight of Julie, and The Supreme noticed his gaze lingered a moment too long at the slit in her dress.

Human men: despicable, immoral creatures. They're all devious animals at their core.

"Madam Supreme," he said evenly, "Miss Walsh."

Julie smiled and nodded, getting up gracefully from her seat.

"Pleasure to see you, Mr. Governor," Julie said before turning to The Supreme. "Can I get you anything, Madam Supreme?"

The Supreme gestured toward the lobby.

"Get us a bottle of champagne please."

Now The Supreme was alone with the governor.

Colin didn't take Julie's seat and instead remained standing. The Supreme stood in return and inched closer to him. She was a tall android, and in her heels, they were almost eye level.

"I will ask you only one more time: Who is Lexi Pvadinish?"

"I'm sure you already know that she's not entirely human, my friend." The Supreme chuckled.

Toying with the governor was one of The Supreme's favorite hobbies; he often proved an intellectually witty challenge. She remembered fondly for a moment how Henry O'Connor taught them both how to play chess and a game called Risk one summer at

The Oceanside. The Supreme's childhood with the O'Connor family left a lasting imprint on her.

"Cut the shit, Emilia."

She hated hearing her given name. Colin called her Emilia as a strategic tactic of familiarity, but The Supreme left Emilia behind when she assumed her position. There was no turning back for her.

"Her name was Alexandra. I'm surprised you didn't recognize her. Isabella hired her to help her mother, but I suppose you and Isabella are a bit more estranged than you'd like to lead on," The Supreme said, raising her eyebrow. "Regardless, I've developed a hybrid species of humans and androids. I'm taking the strengths of androids and the strengths of humans and bundling them into one being. This could be a great benefit to society."

Colin's draw dropped slightly in both horror and disgust.

"This is monstrous. You're not making a new species; you're experimenting on humans."

The Supreme remained silent. She looked into Colin's eyes, searching for any sign he knew more than he led on.

"Well, what does It think about her?"

"Who? Lexi?" Colin asked, distractedly looking down at the general audience below them.

Check. The Supreme imagined moving her queen closer to Colin's king.

"Yes, who else would I be referring to?"

Colin eyed her angrily, a slight sense of discomfort spreading unwillingly across his gray eyes.

"This is dangerous and irresponsible."

"Think logically, Colin. A species that could help unite humans and androids? Bring us all together under a shared cause? What could be wrong with that? This might be the missing piece that unites The Legislature."

"I wish you included me in this from the very beginning. We're supposed to be partners," Colin said with a sneer.

The pair looked back as the door opened and Julie strode toward them holding the bottle of champagne. Their time together came to a close.

"Well, I should get back. Looks like they're going to begin again momentarily," Colin said in a commanding and broody tone. He leaned in closer to The Supreme's ear. "This discussion is far from over."

"Of course. Please give Dr. Garcia my regards. I miss her presence here in The City since she moved back to The Island. I'm hoping that's temporary, and I very much look forward to an official union between you two after the election."

The Supreme grinned wildly, noticing a small flinch from Julie. Colin responded by exiting The Supreme's box with powerful and heavy steps.

Julie sat beside The Supreme and placed the bottle on the table between them. The Supreme popped the cork and poured the bubbly liquid into two glasses, gently handing Julie one of them. They sipped as the orchestra filled the room with a lovely but ominous melody.

"I want to speak with you about an excellent opportunity, Dr. Walsh," she said with a smile, eyeing the young scientist over the bubbles in her champagne. "I'd like for you to start taking less of a hands-on approach during the antidote's clinical trials. You need to focus on managerial and leadership skills. You're going to need the experience for your next role."

"My next role?"

"I've spoken with Celine. She plans on having a baby soon and will need a temporary replacement to fill her shoes as CEO while out on maternity leave. When she returns, we want to promote you to commercial vice president."

"What?" Julie asked, blush spreading wildly across her freckled skin. "I am not qualified for something like that; I wouldn't even be qualified for a role like that in a few years."

"Of course you're not qualified," The Supreme said and turned to face the orchestra instead of Julie. "But you don't need to be the most qualified person."

Julie looked at The Supreme, skepticism still in her eyes.

"Celine was only a few years older than you are now when she started the company. Have a bit more confidence in yourself, Julie. You did a fantastic job in front of The Legislature. There's still plenty of room for improvement, but I can coach you there. And so could the governor if he wins his next term."

Julie's skin flushed a blotchy red.

How else is he coaching you, Julie? The Supreme wondered wickedly while sipping her champagne.

"The Board needs someone we can trust—it's about what you know. And you, my dear, know quite more than you are even aware of."

The Supreme smiled and leaned in closer to Julie.

"You're trusted by Celine O'Connor. Your business acumen has flourished over the last two years; Martin and Marta are both equally impressed with you. You've gained respect from Kathleen Murphy, the governor's number one confidant. She's the key to The Capitol Building. Not to mention, you've befriended the most famous philanthropist in The Constituency. Don't think I didn't know about your lunch with Dr. Garcia. She and I talk."

"Well, I'm honored. Truly. I'll do anything to make sure I'm prepared to fill the role to the best of my abilities when the time comes."

The Supreme looked back at Julie and nodded. "I'll help you. But you can't tell the other board of directors, like Martin, Marta, or Colin. The vote hasn't been finalized yet."

"I understand." Julie nodded slowly.

When the music finally stopped, The Supreme and Julie left the box swiftly and headed toward the exit.

Symphony Hall was much more than just a place for elegant music—it was a social event amongst old bloodline families and newer wealth. No one stopped to speak with The Supreme, but they did greet the governor and Dr. Isabella Garcia. She wasn't surprised. He was one of them—old bloodline—and The Supreme was an android.

She and Julie carefully climbed down the stairs in their heels and approached The Supreme's vehicle. They drove off before the rest of the crowd even exited the hall.

"I really appreciate you inviting me this evening. I had a great time. And I promise to do all I can to prepare myself for the honor of stepping in for Celine when the time comes," Julie said as the vehicle slowed down outside her apartment building.

"I am glad we could discuss some of those matters outside the confinements of the COLI*GO building. Let's schedule some time during the first week of the clinical trials to review initial results and reactions and discuss who you will hire as your replacement, shall we?" The Supreme asked.

Julie nodded before saying goodbye. She walked up her few steps and entered her apartment, closing the door carefully behind her.

"Would you like for me to bring you home, Madam Supreme?" asked the android in the front of the vehicle.

"Pull over to the other side of Commonwealth Ave, please," The Supreme commanded. He pressed a button, and the vehicle guided itself across the street.

The Supreme felt more confident in her assumption after this evening's events, but her satisfaction would come from confirmation. This human feeling of smugness and self-satisfaction was one of her favorite indulgences. An indescribable lightness overcame her body whenever she experienced it, and her scales shimmered in anticipation.

A few lights illuminated Julie's apartment, and The Supreme spotted Julie's figure through the large bay window. Her eyes zoomed in closer, an advantage of being an android.

After waiting for fifteen minutes, Julie stood from her couch and dragged her fingers alongside the kitchen island as her door opened. Julie leaned against the granite and let a large smile consume her face. A much taller figure appeared in the shadows. The Supreme recognized the man instantly as the governor.

The two embraced one another, and Colin lifted Julie up onto the kitchen island. The two were now face to face as he placed his hands on either side of Julie and leaned in. This gesture was odd for Colin; he normally used his height to intimidate everyone. Colin and Julie grinned at each other, and Julie's chest rose and fell in unheard laughter. The pair appeared so at ease together. Colin's charming smile spread, and his stare remained deep in Julie's warm eyes.

He grabbed her hand and interlaced his fingers with hers. Julie wrapped her legs around Colin's waist, an intimate gesture he gladly welcomed.

The Supreme observed not only desire but also a palpable sense of tenderness, love, and affection.

Colin's hand let go of Julie and slowly traveled up the slit of her dress as he kissed her passionately. Her gown rode up her body from his movement, revealing she wore nothing underneath. Colin's eyes sparked with exhilaration at his discovery.

His lips moved away from Julie's and explored down her neck, assertively nibbling her collarbone. There, Colin would leave his mark in faint blues and deep purples, to be carefully hidden by Julie's lab coat in the days to follow.

The Supreme continued watching the pair from afar while Colin's lips lingered against the cleavage peeking out of the bodice of Julie's gown. He wandered further down her body and disappeared to where his hands vanished earlier.

This passionate act was one The Supreme hadn't ever experienced herself, but she understood why women desired it. Men typically only engaged with women they truly lusted after or women they truly cared about pleasing over themselves.

Julie's hands dug deeper into Colin's hair as his tongue and fingers violated her between her legs. His movements were smooth and slick at first, slowing down and picking back up each time Julie's body arched from the granite slab.

Their bodies were impeccably in sync with one another as Colin's mouth moved to the inside of Julie's thighs, hungrily biting her skin. A more secret marking to remind her later that she belonged to him.

Colin looked up at her, drinking all of Julie in with his eyes. Even from her vantage point, The Supreme observed the complete longing and indulgent desire in Colin's eyes.

And like a wild animal devouring its kill, Colin eagerly went back for more. He consumed Julie with enthusiasm as if his appetite for her could never be completely satisfied.

Colin O'Connor was a man of extreme structure and control. The Supreme wasn't surprised when he only allowed Julie to reach the brink of bliss this next time. A wonderful torment for her and a sense of absolute power for him.

Colin rose from between Julie's legs and licked his lips slowly, savoring the taste of her. He stared at Julie with a look beyond lust: a look of need. The Supreme sensed this immoral act between them was decadent to him because it was Julie who received it.

His mouth gravitated toward Julie's neck again as his lips crawled along the edges of her earlobe before meeting her lips passionately.

Their kiss was deliciously messy and wild as Julie grabbed him by the jaw in her delicate hands. She grazed down Colin's neck lightly, never leaving a physical trace of her inappropriate presence on him.

Her hands trembled as she removed his belt and released the button and zipper of his pants. Colin grabbed her wrists with his hands and flipped her over in a swift motion. The lower half of Julie's body dangled delicately off the side of her kitchen island. Colin grabbed her hips and admired her body before finally taking her for himself.

"Bring me home, please?" The Supreme asked, glancing away from the scene. She dangerously wanted to keep watching but decided to let this final act be theirs and theirs alone. She'd already overstayed her welcome in their acts of intimacy.

The Supreme felt lightheaded, and her hands shook. She was naughtily intrigued by the secret peep show.

The android up front, completely oblivious to what occurred in the apartment across the street, turned the vehicle back on, and they moved east on Commonwealth Avenue toward The Hill.

The Supreme's suspicions were correct about the governor and Dr. Walsh. But their body language exposed more than just desire. She assumed the two were sleeping together, but she hadn't realized the familiarity and closeness between them. Colin O'Connor trusted Julie Walsh; he not only wanted her but also needed her.

Almost like his other addiction. If I can't control the governor, if he continues sneaking behind my back, I'll take his joy away. No, that would be too easy. It would be more fun. Use Julie as a pawn to leverage It against Colin.

Checkmate.

***

"I need a favor," The Supreme said, standing across from Jeb Taylor in his art studio in The Port.

The studio was a complete disaster; paintings scattered the floor and were placed haphazardly against the walls. The artist kept his walls a stark white, a contrast to his wild, vibrant, and colorful creations. His more subdued pieces were displayed in the front, but here in the back of the room, Jeb's art showcased the darker truths of The City. Some pieces were disturbing and offensive even if beautiful and realistic in style and technique.

Jeb had an attractive build for a man in his mid-fifties with a slender but lean frame and substantial height. His face aged him, sharp lines spreading from the corners of his eyes and along his forehead while his deep dark skin was dried out from recreational drug use. Jeb Taylor was a man who enjoyed the thrill of danger.

"If you're looking for your cut from the latest batch, you'll have to wait. You gave me more than the last time," Jeb reminded her.

His pace quickened as he walked over to The Supreme.

"Of course, but that isn't why I'm here."

Jeb eyed her up and down and backed away with his arms crossed. He found The Supreme intimidating and didn't enjoy crossing her.

When Jeb dropped Alexandra off at COLI*GO's lower lab, he saw firsthand the true nature behind The Supreme's experiments. For days, he was a disaster. The Supreme tried calming his nerves, showing him the technology, the beautiful microchip she designed. She had to offer him more money, the seemingly simple answer to all his problems.

He painted a wild canvas of her creatures that she insisted he destroy—or face her turning him in to the commissioner for dealing pharmaceuticals. Jeb didn't want to spend the rest of his life in The City's prison facility. The halls were rumored to drive any man or android insane.

"I need another specimen for my research," The Supreme said coolly, approaching one of Jeb's larger murals.

The artwork displayed a particularly perplexing scene. A grotesque hand choked a woman's delicate throat, clearly a nod to The City's infamous uncaught serial killer who flooded the media outlets. In the painting, the woman's hands clasped the forearm that choked her.

The colors were bright pinks, oranges, and reds transcending into dark purples and blues. As the lines faded toward the bottom of the canvas, the colors intertwined in madness. The Supreme reached out and touched the painting with her fingertips. While completely raw and horrifying, the canvas spoke to her.

"Who?" he asked from behind her.

"The body will need to be delivered to me at a specific time and place, which I'll explain momentarily." The Supreme ignored his question and strode over to his desk.

She placed an envelope down without breaking her stare. Inside was a piece of paper with a single name typed in a small centered font.

"Who?" Jeb asked again.

She looked at him and smiled, leaving him alone with his assignment and walking over to the painting again.

"How much for this mural?" The Supreme asked, ignoring his question for the second time.

"That one?" Jeb held on to the note but walked over to admire his work beside The Supreme. "Twenty thousand dollars."

"Hmm . . . could you perhaps make a small addition to it?"

"Possibly. What is the addition?" he asked, eyebrows raised.

"Could you add an emerald ring on her finger?" The Supreme inquired, pointing to the woman's left ring finger.

She watched Jeb stare at his work for a moment, pondering her odd request.

"That would make the piece customized, which adds an additional fee, thirty thousand dollars total. I'll deliver it to you by the beginning of September if you'd like. I'll even frame it at no extra cost."

"Perfect. I'll transfer you the money and delivery instructions this afternoon." The Supreme looked up at him and gestured toward the envelope.

He walked back toward the desk and grabbed a "SOLD" sign.

"She'll be at the governor's campaign victory celebration the night of the election. I will get you on the invitation list. Deposit her in the lower lab at COLI*GO that same evening. Not too early but not too late either. I suggest you use one of those new narcotics I was able to secure for you to help with the process."

Jeb held the envelope in his rough, paint-stained hands. The tear of the paper sounded loud in the empty art studio. Jeb's lips frowned as he read the name, but he folded the paper back up and nodded.

Jeb would always be in debt to The Supreme; there was nothing he could do to free himself of her servitude unless he turned himself in to the commissioner. Jeb wouldn't; he was too selfish.

The Supreme stayed only a moment longer to watch Jeb remove a lighter from his back pocket and burn the piece of paper.

Chapter 36
Julie

August 31st, 45 A.R.

COLI*GO scientists, clinical investigators, and product managers filled the large observatory boardroom. Eagerness filled the air, as the clinical trials started tomorrow.

The antidote received its official registered asset name as a pipeline product: COL23. The "COL" identified the drug belonged to COLI*GO, while the number twenty-three was assigned as a random unique identifier.

The Board of Directors sat up in the front, while Julie and the rest of the research and development team lingered behind.

Julie was thankful Peter Schneider accepted the transfer back to COLI*GO's headquarters in The City to lead the COL23 team. He took over her role in managing the day-to-day for the clinical trials. Julie respected Peter's scientific expertise and experience. A few years of separation fared well for them, and their friendship blossomed quickly.

Peter and Julie fine-tuned the safety protocols for the randomized trial, and Peter shared his new wealth of knowledge in managing real-time programs. The randomized trials included participants in either a group that received COL23 or a group that received a placebo version.

Martin, Marta, Colin, and Celine puttered around the room, speaking enthusiastically with each employee. Colin glanced over toward Julie, but his eyes glazed past her and paused on her friend Mick Taylor.

Mick had returned from a long adventure of time travel and declared a leave of absence from his consulting work. The strain and stress of time travel wore him down, and he asked Julie for a full-time job on her new project. Peter assigned him to a researcher position studying the long-term side effects of COL23.

"Mick, can I introduce you to Governor Colin O'Connor?" Julie asked in an attempt to ease the tension she felt ricocheting off Colin.

"It's an honor to meet you, Governor," Mick said, extending his hand, and Colin took it swiftly.

"Are you the intelligent researcher I've heard about? The one who discovered the errors in COL2120?" Colin asked, finally relaxing his body a bit.

Julie smiled. Colin knew about her friends but had never met them. In fact, all the people in Julie's life knew nothing about how important Colin was to her. The public believed he and Isabella were still together, and the election was nearing. Scandal wasn't an option.

"Julie is way too kind," Mick said, looking down at his feet in embarrassment.

"We're about to get started," Peter said from behind them.

Colin glared at Peter with an icy stare, and Julie rolled her eyes at him. All eyes followed Julie as she approached the front of the room. Flashbacks from her presentation to The Legislature a few months ago flooded her mind, but this time, there wasn't skepticism in the room. There was optimism.

"Good morning, everyone," Julie said as the room quieted. "Before I hand the podium over, I'd like to first and foremost thank everyone for their support of COL23. This therapy wouldn't be where it is today without all of you. We'll hopefully make an impact on patients' lives, providing options in neurological and psychological conditions. Now, let me introduce the program director for COL23, Dr. Peter Schneider."

Peter stood from his seat proudly as the room erupted in applause. He walked toward Julie, shook her hand, and smiled.

"Without you, Julie, we'd never have this opportunity. Now, on to the boring stuff . . ." Peter pulled up the clinical trial designs, and the room quieted with concentration.

***

No one paid attention to their work as the news coverage of the election flashed across all monitors and devices in the COLI*GO building. Today was September 4th: Election Day.

"Do you want to walk?" Julie asked Peter and Mick as they left the building to vote. The air was warm and sticky, perspiration beading across Mick's forehead as they stood in direct sunlight.

"Walking might do us some good," Mick agreed with a smile.

The group walked at a slower pace and crossed the bridge connecting The River and The Hill. A long line wrapped around the street corner in front of the polling location designated for The Hill and The Bay neighborhoods. News reporters lined the previously historical bell tower. Out of the corner of her eye, Julie spotted Colin and Isabella speaking with people waiting in line.

Most seemed enthusiastic to support the governor in his reelection bid. A sense of dread filled Julie's stomach as Colin and Isabella inched closer to them.

Isabella would always be a part of Colin's life, but it still hurt her to see them together. Julie's heart beat faster in her chest. The worst pain wasn't from Colin's inability to publicly leave Isabella; it was that Julie had no one to share her thoughts with, not even Jones.

She took a deep breath and closed her eyes.

"Are you okay?" Peter asked Julie, the weight of his hand pressed down on her shoulder gently.

"Yeah, I'm fine. I didn't realize we'd be standing here so long."

"We have plenty of time," Mick said reassuringly.

Mick turned his body, blocking the view of Colin and Isabella. Julie was grateful for the gesture even though she assumed Mick didn't understand why.

They waited for almost an hour outside the old church before getting inside. Mick and Julie walked over to the table labeled "Last Names: T thru Z," and Peter turned in another direction.

The machine scanned Julie's eye. A large green check mark appeared on the monitor with her full name and a booth number for her to find within the hall. She turned back to Mick and smiled, walking in the opposite direction.

When Julie entered her assigned booth, another machine scanned her eyes again. The small space was claustrophobic, with no visibility beyond the white foam walls.

She selected Colin's name with ease and filled out the rest of her ballot. The machine scanned her eyes one final time after she hit the submit button, confirming she cast her vote. Julie left the church, grateful to be out in the open air, and waited for Mick and Peter.

The sun shone brightly, and the sky was a glorious shade of bright blue. Small wisps of fluffy white clouds scattered the sky for miles. The feel of the sun on her skin reminded her of the trip she and Colin took to The Oceanside. Her mind wandered to thoughts about her mother, and she looked up at the sky again. The sadness lingered for a moment before images of her father flooded her mind. Julie still saw him every Thursday for dinner, but she hadn't seen her sister in a long time.

Julie desperately wanted to share everything with her father and sister; her wish for the antidote to succeed, that she was in love with someone who not only understood her passions but also supported them in the most unimaginable ways, and how life could be wonderful even with all their sadness.

She placed her hand on her heart and closed her eyes. Held-back tears poured out of her, falling down the sides of her face, and a hard but small embrace pulled her closer.

When Julie opened her eyes, she found Isabella holding her. The two women looked at one another for a moment in silence.

"Julie . . ." Isabella said slowly, brushing the tears off the side of her face. "There is so much I need to talk to you about."

But Julie couldn't face her. She feared all her secrets and emotions would come pouring out of her as her tears had.

Dashing away from Isabella, Julie didn't stop running until she was back at COLI*GO.

***

Being inside the townhouse with so many people occupying the space was a different experience for Julie. After the celebrations died down, she'd have to head back to her apartment in The Bay. Alone.

Instead of the person who made a serious and cold Colin

O'Connor laugh, Julie posed her persona as a COLI*GO business associate who barely knew him. The house was littered with half-drunken champagne flutes and so many people and androids. Most were colleagues or donors from COLI*GO and The Capitol Building.

The news called the election early: Colin O'Connor would continue serving the people of The Constituency for another term. Everyone cheered as the final polling locations tallied and reported their results.

Julie had one advantage in being so familiar with the townhouse—she knew all the great places to escape when the crowd overwhelmed her. She looked over her shoulder before dashing up the back stairwell. Julie climbed up the circular steps and reached the roof deck with ease. The day had been humid and steamy, but there was a cool breeze in the night air. From up here, Julie observed how the rest of The City celebrated Colin's victory. The lights illuminating the streets showed humans and androids enthusiastically embracing one another.

Across The River, Julie spotted the COLI*GO building, hauntingly dark and empty. The first day of the clinical trials went smoothly. Patients received their first dosage of COL23. No major side effects were reported yet, but this was the beginning; Julie couldn't be too optimistic.

"Oh, I'm sorry. I didn't realize anyone would be up here," a deep voice said from behind her.

Julie turned as a man approached her. He had a familiarity about him, but Julie couldn't quite put her finger on it.

"It's okay. I don't mind a bit of company," Julie said with a smile. He leaned against the railing beside her and gazed out into The City.

Upon closer examination, Julie noticed his attractiveness for a man of his age, with his lean frame and dark, intoxicating hazel eyes.

"Julie Walsh," she said, extending her hand. The man took it, his skin warm but rough to the touch.

"Jeb Taylor."

Julie tried to hide the look of shock she knew appeared across her face by turning her head away.

Now I know why he looks familiar; I see the resemblance to Mick.

"Are you by chance related to Mick Taylor?"

Jeb was a drug dealer, a troubled artist, and Mick's uncle, a man whom Mick had a tumultuous, dynamic relationship with. But for some reason, Julie found solace in the man who took Mick in when he arrived in The City afraid and alone, a man who paid for the remaining balance of Mick's University tuition and provided him an opportunity. Jeb didn't appear pained by the mention of Mick's name; instead, he chuckled in endearment.

"Yes, he is my nephew."

"I work with him. We went to The University together."

"So I've heard. You're quite close friends, too, if I remember correctly?"

Julie was surprised by his response. From what Jones had insinuated, Mick and his uncle were not on speaking terms. Jeb made her believe differently.

"Yes, we're very close friends."

Jeb joined Julie in a smile, his hand lightly grazing her cheek to remove a strand of hair that fell from her bun. Everything around her felt very heavy and unsteady, and she wasn't sure if it was the amount of champagne she'd consumed already or a legitimate feeling.

"I should get back downstairs," she said hastily, stepping back from the ledge of the roof deck and away from Jeb.

"Julie?" she heard from behind her.

Julie turned and saw a familiar face: Kathleen.

"Did yah meet Mistah Taylor?" Kathleen asked with a grin.

"Yes, but I'm going to head back downstairs," Julie said, moving past Kathleen toward the stairwell.

"Ah, okay. Well, let me know if yah need a lift home tonight. I assume yah headin' back tah The Bay?" Kathleen's eyes glanced sideways. Kathleen knew about her relationship with Colin, but Julie wasn't sure if Kathleen approved.

"Thanks, but I have a ride."

Kathleen smiled and walked out toward Jeb. Her laughter was infectious, loud, and rambunctious because of her City accent. Julie turned to look back out on the roof deck before heading back downstairs. Jeb took both glasses of champagne from Kathleen's hands and placed them on the ledge.

Julie thought she saw Jeb's hand move suspiciously over one of the champagne flutes before he handed it back to Kathleen. A pit in the bottom of her stomach grew, but she convinced herself all she saw was a trick of the moonlight.

Kathleen sipped from her glass slowly, pointing out in the distance toward the sky as Julie descended the stairs.

***

Julie woke abruptly to the sound of her loud apartment buzzer ringing. She had passed out on her couch after the governor's victory party.

Definitely too many glasses of champagne, she thought, rubbing her eyes. Everything was blurry, and when she stood up, the room spun around her. Julie walked over to her intercom system and pressed the button.

"Hello?" she asked groggily.

"Oh, good. For a moment, I was worried you weren't home," Colin's familiar voice echoed into the speaker.

"Where else would I be?" Julie asked sarcastically before allowing him entry into her building.

She unlocked the old-fashioned lock on her front door and walked over to her bed before lying down. The door opened and closed faintly, followed by the sound of Colin's footsteps across her cold stone floors. Colin lay beside her and pulled her into his chest. Julie felt tiny in his arms and inhaled his familiar scent mixed with the smell of Scotch.

"I can't really stay too long, but I didn't get to spend any time with you this evening," Colin whispered into her ear.

Julie turned to face him, planting a soft kiss on his forehead.

"I'm glad the campaign is over."

"I'm glad, too," she said with a smile, her fingers tracing lightly down Colin's jawline. He looked deeply into her eyes before kissing her.

"Now we can focus solely on you," he said, referring to the

antidote and COLI*GO.

Colin held Julie for a while, rubbing her back slowly. Julie almost found sleep in his arms with how at peace she felt.

"I have something for you," Colin said, sitting up.

Julie sat up while Colin fumbled with his pocket, and an uncharacteristically goofy grin spread across his face.

There were many layers to Colin, and Julie learned something new about him each day. From the way his eyes darted up and down quickly when he was about to say something important to the way she noticed the small faint freckles on his face if he spent a few hours in the sun. And his eyes: Most found the steel-gray color cold and sharp, but Julie saw them as humble and welcoming.

Colin grabbed Julie's hand and squeezed it tightly.

"What I told you at The Oceanside, I've never shared that with anyone before. I've never truly trusted anyone the way I trust you, Julie. I know it's difficult to be with me because of the life I live. For that, I'm sorry."

He looked up at her, releasing her hand.

"I know, but I wouldn't change anything about you."

Colin looked down and reached into his pocket.

"I love you," he said, placing a delicate but stunning emerald ring on her finger. "I intend to spend the rest of my life with you."

The ring had a lovely platinum band with tiny diamonds around the outside, encasing the large emerald stone in the middle. Julie felt her breath come into her nose sharply. Her hands shook as she looked up at Colin.

"I love you, too." She embraced Colin in her arms, feeling the heaviness of his breath escape him.

Julie looked down at the ring on her left hand before placing the heavy band on her right.

"I think this is safer here, for now at least."

Colin nodded. Julie couldn't explain an engagement ring to anyone in her life, especially one that was an old bloodline family stone.

"Except when you're with me."

Colin moved the ring back to where he had originally placed it. He kissed her gently and pulled her completely into his embrace.

"I need to go back home."

Colin said the words, but he didn't leave right away.

Julie awoke the next morning, his imprint still on the pillowcase next to hers, the warmth of him lingering lightly on her sheets. She grabbed the pillow and hugged it as his smell crashed over her.

After showering and packing her bag, Julie headed to COLI*GO. As the large glass skyscraper came into view, she couldn't help but smile. She moved her ring from her left hand to her right and stepped inside. Things were finally falling into place in her life. The lab was quiet, and Julie was the only one on the floor. Her device awoke from its sleeping position, and Julie checked her messages to make sure she hadn't missed any from the previous day.

A small crash sounded from down the hall. Julie rose instantly and peered out the doorway. On the floor at the other end of the hallway was Kathleen.

"Kathleen! Are you okay?" Julie asked, approaching her with a sense of urgency. Kathleen looked paler than normal, and a sheen line of sweat coated her face. Julie placed her hand on Kathleen's shoulder, noting how dehydrated and disoriented her friend appeared.

"What are you doing at COLI*GO?" Julie asked.

"Honestly, I dunno. I think I drank too much last night," she said with a small chuckle. Kathleen's eyes darted in circles, taking in her unfamiliar surroundings.

"Oh, Kathleen. I shouldn't have left you alone on the roof deck with Jeb," Julie said, the scene from the evening before rushing vividly through her now sober mind.

"Ah, no worries. It's not like that. Jeb is basically my brothah-in-law. I was with The Supreme and Isabella back here at COLI*GO. Some aftah pahty and more drinks? I don't quite remembah, but I know I shouldn'ta done that."

"Isabella?" Julie asked, shocked.

Now Julie realized why Colin was able to spend the night with her in The Bay.

Kathleen eyed Julie peculiarly as if reading her mind. She circled the sides of her temples and dragged her fingers down her face before briefly stopping behind her ears. Kathleen grabbed Julie's hands, her thumb rubbing slowly against the emerald ring on

Julie's right hand. A smile spread across Kathleen's face, and an understanding passed through them.

"Yeah. Dumb, right? I can't stand Isabella." Kathleen laughed.

"Let me get you home at least?" Julie asked, putting her arm around Kathleen's shoulders.

Kathleen's legs were still a bit weak, and her eyes didn't have the same playfulness to them as they normally did.

"Yah know, that'd be nice, but I think I'm good tah find my own way home."

Chapter 37
Jones

September 6th, 45 A.R.

"It's missing!" Mick yelled from his home office.

Jones got up from the couch and raced down the hall toward Mick's home office. Mick stood at his desk, wildly opening each drawer and moving around all the clutter.

"What are you talking about?" Jones asked.

Mick hadn't entered his home office in over a month. After The Supreme stopped by a few months ago, something went very wrong in his next expedition. Mick wouldn't speak about what happened, but Jones held him as he sobbed. Sadness overwhelmed Mick by what became of his once exciting and passionate research.

"A prototype of my device is missing," Mick said without looking up. Mick was more frantic than Jones had ever seen. Jones tried remaining calm and level headed for Mick. His processor listed logical explanations: Some time travel version of Mick came back and took it, or The Supreme did when she was here.

"I wouldn't get too upset about the missing device, Mick. The Supreme probably has it. There's really no harm in any of that, is there?" Jones asked, placing his hand on Mick's shoulder.

"Yes, Jones. There is." Mick shrugged him off.

This wasn't Mick's first cold dismissal of Jones.

"Why? She can't use the technology," Jones said, pleading with the madman standing in front of him.

"That doesn't mean she wouldn't have someone else working for her use the technology. Could you imagine if there were someone else traveling?"

It, Jones thought, the association clicking in his processor. *It must be working with The Supreme. How have I not connected these dots earlier?*

The Supreme was essentially a type of glue between the government and COLI*GO, the two parts of The City intersecting with the serial killer.

Of course It can time travel. Otherwise, how and why would It know so much about Mick?

It and Mick were crossing parallel universes of the future and past. Jones's processor hummed quickly, thoughts flying across from side to side.

"Mick, I'm sorry, but I just realized something. I've got to go!" Jones said, turning away and rushing out of the house.

Jones fumbled through crowded streets and found himself climbing up from the underground subway system to the police department headquarters downtown.

He booted up his device and opened the citizen identification database. No one with the name It was in the database; Jones had tried searching for this mysterious person months ago. Instead, he punched in The Supreme's identifier.

She had many associates, but this was a start. If It was the serial killer, It had to be a man, and now he was certain this man was human. All of The Supreme's monetary interactions from the last three months appeared next to a list of every place she visited. No one was allowed any privacy if they carried their device on them; all information was readily available for viewing to the authorities.

Jones combed through her transactions until he saw Jeb Taylor's name appear several times. She had wired him thousands of dollars for his art on more than one occasion. Jones stopped himself from laughing at the complete obviousness of this revelation.

Does The Supreme, an android, really appreciate the intoxicatingly confusing art of a human? That seems unlikely, or at least unlikely enough to pay thousands of dollars for art. Is Jeb Taylor It?

Jones searched Jeb's art studio online and browsed through his work.

"Inquire for pricing" appeared under all his murals and canvases. The transactions associated with his art sales fluctuated wildly from a couple thousand dollars into the range of over fifty thousand. The Supreme recently paid thirty thousand for a piece titled *The Death of Woman.*

After a quick search on Jeb's site, Jones stared at the screen in horror. Jeb's artwork was often gritty and disgusting, but knowing that a highly educated and highly powerful android purchased such an atrocity made Jones's scales glow a terrible deep green out of anger. The piece itself resembled the similar patterns of the uncaught murderer between the strangulation and red stab wounds.

An eerie feeling of optimism seeped through Jones's body as he triangulated the key unknowns together. Before logging off, Jones scanned the list of The Supreme's recent interactions once more. In the past month, she visited COLI*GO, The Capitol Building, Julie's apartment, Symphony Hall, her home, a few restaurants in The Hill, and the O'Connor townhouse.

Jones wondered if Jeb had any relation to the O'Connor family. His eyes grew wide when he noted Jeb's recent locations: The townhouse appeared in a hypnotizing manner on the screen as well as the COLI*GO building. Jones believed in the strong possibility that Jeb was It's true identity.

He powered down his machine and left the station.

The sun shone brightly as he exited the building, and he picked up his pace toward The Port district. When he reached Anna's apartment building, Jones let himself in with the key she had given him. Anna still lounged around her apartment in pajamas and didn't leave except to run an occasional errand. She considered this progress, but Jones wished she'd stop living in fear.

"Hey there," she said, greeting him from the couch. Jones sat down next to her quietly.

"I think Jeb Taylor is the serial killer," Jones said without a greeting, staring at the wall of photos opposite him.

"Jeb Taylor, the artist?"

Jones pulled up the painting The Supreme purchased on his device. Anna focused on the image for a long time. Her mouth twitched in anger and fury as if a small fire was lit underneath her. She was terrible at containing her emotions, but Jones found most humans were.

"We should go there," Anna said, hastily getting up from the couch.

"Jeb's art studio?"

"Yes, it's right here in The Port."

Anna disappeared into her bedroom. When she emerged, she transformed into a professionally dressed woman, one that reminded Jones of the Anna he knew before her isolation. She wore navy dress pants and a white silky blouse. Her hair was straightened, and a light shade of makeup coated her face.

Anna walked toward her front door and faced Jones.

"Are you coming with me?"

The studio was about a five-minute walk from Anna's apartment and surprisingly busy. The ocean harbor was directly behind the building, and a small outdoor café was situated next door. A few couples lingered around the more traditional paintings in the front of the studio. Jones recognized paintings of The City skyline, a beautiful portrait of the cliffs along The Oceanside and other views of the wooded forest that surrounded The City on the walls.

Jeb sat behind the front desk, enthusiastically discussing his work with a short middle-aged man. Anna grabbed Jones's arm and dragged him further into the back of the studio. A small nameplate for The Supreme's latest purchase hung on the wall, but the space above it was empty.

"I know it's fucked up to say this, but I was hoping to see the painting in person," Anna whispered to Jones.

He nodded and walked further along the wall. There were other darker pieces back here that drew Jones in. He wanted to look away but truly couldn't. The talent and monstrous beauty of the brush strokes completely captivated Jones.

"Can I help you with anything?" a voice loomed from behind them. Anna and Jones turned around simultaneously.

"I'm admiring your more complex work, Mr. Taylor," Anna said with a mischievous grin.

"Why, thank you," Jeb said, eyeing Jones. "This work usually doesn't catch the attention of most, but we all have our guilty pleasures, our dark fantasies."

Anna's lips turned up into a smirk, and she extended her hand to Jeb. "Dr. Anna Garcia."

Jeb looked at her with wild curiosity, clearly recognizing her last name and the importance of her family.

"The pleasure is mine, Doctor." He kissed her hand. Anna raised her eyebrows toward Jones at the antiquated gesture.

"Detective Jones," he said but kept his arms crossed along his chest.

"And what brings you into my studio today?"

"We're working on a bit of a classified case and cannot discuss too many details with you, but I was hoping we could ask you a few questions?"

Jeb nodded, his eyes darting across the room.

"Have you experienced any recent odd activity here in your studio? Any out of character individuals?" Anna asked.

Jeb shook his head. "Not that I can recall. Some days are slow, and others are busy. I haven't had any odd commission inquiries, if that's what you're asking."

"Any odd transactions? Such as large sum transactions from someone who may not normally or ordinarily look like they could complete a monetary transfer like that?" Jones asked.

Jeb closed his eyes briefly before letting out a small chuckle.

"Is it illegal now to be successful? I've had a recent increase in sales and purchases over the last few months, but I'm sure you've already seen that in the ledgers on the database," Jeb answered with a small look of glee in his eye. "Let's get to the point. Is there a particular transaction that caught your eye that you'd like to discuss, Detective Jones?"

Anna glanced over to Jones before looking down at her feet. She was out of her element and not an investigator like Jones. He returned a harsh smile back toward Jeb.

"No, none in particular. It was only a question. Thank you for your time, Mr. Taylor. We'll get out of your hair."

"I'm always happy to help the lovely folks in law enforcement," Jeb said with a hint of sarcasm. "Let me know if you have any further questions for me. You know where to find me."

Jones and Anna nodded and walked toward the entrance of the studio.

"Oh, and Detective? Give Mick my regards."

A mischievous grin grew across Jeb's face before he faced away from them and headed toward his desk on the far side of the room.

Anna's eyes grew wide as her hand squeezed tightly around Jones's forearm. Jones wasn't angered by Jeb's threat. Jeb revealed his true intentions through his foolish arrogance. A smile spread across Jones's scaly face as he looked down at Anna.

***

Mick's annoyance and irritation was palpable upon Jones's return home. The two ate in silence and barely acknowledged each other.

When they climbed into bed, the quietness and stillness between them intensified.

"I'm sorry. I've taken out my anger and frustration on you," Mick admitted into the darkness.

"I haven't been overly forthcoming and honest with you either, Mick."

Jones reached out toward Mick and grabbed his hand underneath the sheets. Mick squeezed Jones's fingers in return.

"Can we stop being angry with one another? I hate this."

Jones felt the same way but still felt animosity toward his boyfriend. He blamed Mick for their predicament: Mick's constant obsession over things he couldn't control, mistakes Jones believed Mick wouldn't own up to.

"I hate this, too, but we need to talk about it," Jones said, wondering if honesty would do either good or harm. He had to try. "I need to tell you something, but I can't tell you all of it."

Mick squeezed Jones's hand tighter in response.

"I've been secretive because a future version of yourself asked me to help uncover secrets and hidden truths about people in our lives. I can't say much more than that."

Jones observed the faint shapes of Mick's face in the darkness. Mick remained silent for a long time as the word "unfair" crossed Jones's processor. Jones rarely experienced this emotion, and he realized without hesitation that he was willing to do anything for Mick but didn't feel the same level of reciprocation.

That's what's causing the rift between us.

"I shouldn't have discovered time travel," Mick said, breaking the tension surrounding them.

"You really shouldn't have."

Jones heard the room fill with Mick's quiet sobs. He couldn't stand the sound, and he rolled over to embrace Mick. Jones held him, protecting Mick from himself.

***

Jones couldn't remember the last time he, Mick, and Julie spent an evening together. Anna joined them this time, and he looked forward to introducing her to Julie.

Unsurprisingly, Mick and Julie were late, and Anna opened the bottle of wine early. She and Jones consumed half the bottle before the sound of the front door opening startled them. Julie and Mick smiled as they entered the living room, and Jones embraced Julie in a quick hug, looking into her eyes a bit too long.

"Did you start without us?" Julie asked with a chuckle, pointing to the bottle.

"Yes, it was very rude of us," Anna said jokingly and poured both Julie and Mick a glass of wine. "I'm Anna Garcia. I don't think we've formally met."

"It's nice to finally meet you. I've heard so much about you from both Jones and Mick," Julie responded with a genuine smile.

Julie grabbed the glass with ease, but in her swift movement, a bright shimmer reflected off her hand. Jones's eyes followed the light, and a wave of dread filled his body once he saw what had caught his attention. There, wrapped around Julie's delicate ring finger, was the unique and all too familiar emerald engagement ring that once belonged to Melanie O'Connor. The image on Anna's wall flashed through Jones's eyes.

I hope Anna didn't see that. Jones grabbed Julie's hand in his own and walked her toward the kitchen.

"Want to help me grab some snacks from the fridge?"

"Of course," she responded, startled by the way he swiftly grabbed her. Jones let go of her once Anna and Mick were out of sight and opened the refrigerator door.

"What's wrong?" Julie asked, sensing the uneasiness emulating from him.

Jones looked down at the ring again, the ring that was supposed to be on a missing, presumed dead woman. Julie's eyes followed his gaze, and she instinctively hid her hand behind her body. Her face turned to shades of vibrant pink and blotchy reds, a reaction that reminded Jones how humans were not so different from androids after all. A human's secret thoughts were also portrayed on their skin. Jones grabbed her hand and brought it up close to his face, his fingers twirling the ring around in circles, but he did not break his stare from Julie.

"I'm seeing someone."

"Obviously," Jones stated, shocked that was all she said. "Why would you hide someone from us?"

Jones shifted his gaze to the living room, where Mick and Anna were engaged in a lively conversation.

"From me?" he asked, the hurt in his tone soft but present.

Julie's eyes shifted toward the living room as well; a sad expression engulfed her face as she paused at Anna.

"Because you and Anna Garcia have gotten really close. Mick told me." There was a twinge of hurt in her voice. "And I have to be careful. Not for him. But for me."

"The governor." The words slipped through Jones's lips quietly.

Julie nodded as Jones's scales shone a similar color to the stone on her ring.

"He loves me. We understand each other without having to say anything, and I care about him. He lets me be . . . me," she said, twirling the lovely piece of jewelry around on her finger.

"I'm not judging you, Julie. I understand. Look at me with Mick," Jones pointed out.

"You can't tell anyone," she whispered.

"That's an O'Connor family heirloom," Jones whispered back, tension vibrating through his voice. "I don't want Anna to see. Give it to me. I'll put it in the drawer of Mick's desk for now."

Julie looked down at the ring before sliding it off her finger and handing it over to Jones.

"Does he ever make you feel unsafe?"

"No. Why?" she asked, confusion lingering in her tone.

"I don't know. I care about you. You're the only true friend I have ever had. The only true friend I think I'll ever have."

She hugged him in that instant, the embrace warm and comforting for them both.

"Can I tell you about us? Can I talk to you? I have no one to talk to."

"Of course, Julie. But not tonight." His eyes lingered away from her, and relief relaxed his body. "Are you happy?"

Julie smiled, and Jones saw the pureness and love on her like a tattoo.

"More than I could have ever imagined."

***

The smell of coffee wept through Anna's apartment the next afternoon. There was a storm coming in across the ocean, the clouds wickedly gray and heavy with precipitation. Anna messaged Jones that morning, asking him to come over because she felt a stroke of genius in the investigation. When Jones walked into the living room, he stopped dead in his tracks. All the women's photographs had been taken down and replaced with two single images: one of The Supreme and one of the governor.

The words "liar," "deception," and "monster" were scrawled across their faces in Anna's shaky handwriting. Jones's eyes lowered to the sticky note underneath Colin O'Connor's headshot reading: *Melanie O'Connor's "missing" engagement ring.*

"So, he's fucking my sister over with Julie? A nobody?" Anna's voice interrupted Jones's train of thought.

He looked Anna up and down before squarely locking eyes with her. Jones was sure Anna hadn't seen the ring last night. She acted so normally, so at ease with Julie. Images of the two strong, intellectual women bonding and laughing together flashed before his eyes. Their interaction appeared genuine to him.

How could I have been so wrong?

"The O'Connor family is evil," Anna said, moving closer to Jones, their faces inches apart at this point. "Colin O'Connor has everyone convinced of this ideal world that's not based in reality. My father knew the truth about him. I read about it in his diary."

"The truth?" Jones asked, stepping away from her.

"The O'Connors are greedy pieces of shit who want control over everyone and everything. They trick people into thinking they care, but they're monsters. Power in The Legislature wasn't enough; those pricks dipped into the privatized sector with COLI*GO. They have their fingerprints all over everyone's daily lives."

Jones looked at Anna and shook his head. He knew of the corruption within wealthy old bloodline families and their legacies, but Jones was under the impression that generalizing them all was unfair.

"Do you know why I despise my family, Jones?" She looked out toward the rain rolling into The City. "Old bloodline families are all the same. They're the real disease to peace and prosperity in our society. They're selfish and too cowardly to give up any hold they have. At the end of the day, we're all a simple pawn in their games. People and androids mean nothing to them. Julie doesn't mean anything to Colin O'Connor. She's a nobody; she knows this. She's using him as much as he's using her."

Anger rose inside Jones, an emotion he rarely allowed himself to feel.

"I'm not arguing your point on the power-hungry old bloodline families, Anna. But Julie is a good person."

"Is she a good person? It seems to me all she cares about is her own goddamn success," Anna spat, turning away from Jones before approaching her exquisitely constructed wall of madness.

"Maybe, but isn't that all you care about, too? Why is that wrong for her but not for you?"

Anna turned around slowly, eyeing Jones with burning flames in her eyes.

"Fuck off, Jones. I don't need you. I can figure this out on my own. While I think there's something sketchy going on with Jeb for sure, I'm not convinced he's the serial killer. I wouldn't be surprised if . . ." She paused before pointing to the photographs. "It is one of them."

Jones stared at her, trying to remain strong. Trying to not feel betrayed by his friend.

"Fine, Anna, but don't think you're better than any of them

because you can identify their flaws," Jones said, pointing to the photographs of the governor and The Supreme. "I don't need you either."

A physical pain emerged in his scales, a feeling he hadn't encountered before. Jones emitted so much emotion that his scales swelled from trying to hide all the truths from his processor.

Jones never thought he'd be on this mission alone. He assumed he would always have Anna.

The humans in his life didn't make sense anymore. Julie kept Colin a secret from Jones, and Mick lashed out constantly, blaming him for the terrible space growing between them. Space caused by Mick's own doing: time travel.

The loss and isolation stung, and he never wanted to experience this emotion ever again. But Jones couldn't stop his mission now. He still needed to save The City, if not for himself, then at least for his friends. Before The City destroyed them.

Chapter 38

It

October 12th, 45 A.R.

"Hello, my friend," The Supreme said without facing him.

It hated when she did this, as if looking into his eyes was a disgrace. They knew so much about one another, and there was no room for betrayal. The demise of The Supreme would be the demise of him. They'd pay together for their crimes if one exposed the other.

"I feel like Colin's victory celebration was so long ago. Is that really the last time I saw you?" It asked, taking a seat with confidence.

The Supreme finally turned toward him, a small nod in his direction as she powered down her device and embraced the conversation they were about to have. The COLI*GO building was the only office of hers It had ever seen. He wondered what her desk in The Capitol Building was like.

Does she have no personal effects there either? Does she keep a particular reputation of authority for herself there as she does here? Or is she softer with The Representatives of The Androids?

It had so many questions but knew better than to ask.

"Sadly, yes." The Supreme twirled a braid from her hair in between her fingers. She appeared elegant and soft in the sunlight shining through the windows. But The Supreme played her part well. It appreciated her deeper understanding of humans, but he never felt her empathy was sincere.

"I have some news for you. I also have a request."

"You know, requests typically come with some kind of a nicety," It responded with a leering grin.

The Supreme ignored his comment, opening a small drawer in her desk with ease. She laid down a peculiar device, one It had never seen before. On the other side of the device, The Supreme placed a small test tube filled with a maroon-colored liquid. She leaned back in her seat, lifting her gaze to It with a level of indescribable intensity. It picked up part of the device and held the contraption in his firm hands. He had always been studious in nature and was impressed with what he held. He noted the small chrome box, the digital face display was on, but nothing illuminated the screen—yet.

The rest of the technology resembled a pair of large glasses with a small looking-glass-styled apparatus between where the user's eyes would rest. His fingertips eased on the dial in the middle, noting he could move it either clockwise or counterclockwise with little effort required.

"That's where the blood goes," The Supreme said simply.

It looked up at her and back down at his hands. This was a clever bit of technology, an innovative thing that intrigued his curiosity.

"You don't need a lot of blood. Just a drop. You click backward to travel to the past and forward to travel to the future. The chrome box will help you determine the exact time. The machine only allows you to travel the lifespan of the blood sample, so you cannot travel further back than from when the sample was born. Similarly, you cannot travel further in the future beyond the sample's death. Or, at least, that's my understanding."

The Supreme leaned forward in her seat to show him.

"How did you acquire such a novel innovation?" It asked, looking up into her eyes.

"I did what the former governor taught me. I invested. I invested in this technology when no one else would."

It nodded and looked back down to the device in his hands. He knew what he held was powerful. All the possibilities flooded his mind.

"With tremendous influence comes a great deal of responsibility," The Supreme said to him as if reading his mind. "I can't tell you exactly what you need to do when you get there. I need you to come to that realization on your own. But please, travel back to twelve years after The Resurgence. When you get there, you will know why."

"Through whose blood?" It asked.

The Supreme picked up the vial and handed the small sample over to him. It flipped the vial over and read the label. He nodded, the feeling of conflict coursing through his veins.

He understood.

***

There was a sensation vibrating through his body when he used the device. The vibration was rough but not terribly violent. It recognized the smell of the air around him: cooler and saltier, dense while sweet. He felt a sense of stillness he hadn't experienced in a very long time. A peculiar and strange calmness.

He removed the glasses from his face and placed them carefully into his coat pocket. He didn't need a coat here, not this time of year. It heard the waves of the ocean crashing along the rocks, but he couldn't quite make out the coastline from where he stood. His eyes gravitated behind him; there in the distance stood the O'Connor Oceanside estate.

A lovely couple was racing across the lawn. The woman was beautiful and elegant, but there was a naïve element to her. The man beside her stood confidently, more determined and comfortable in his own skin. At this moment, they were chasing after something invisible. Something lost to them.

The sun shone against the couple, the warm, sticky breeze barely moving the loose strands of hair from her ponytail. It felt the sun touch his own skin, the bright blue sky living across the infinite horizon. He walked over toward the ledge of the cliff and looked down. Vertigo hit him instantly, his mind spinning and his hands shaking. The sides of the cliff were jagged and sharp, tauntingly uneven and toothed.

It turned to observe the couple off in the distance again. From the motions of the man's hands, the scene was clear: They were arguing. Over what, It wasn't quite sure, but the gestures kept growing larger, more robust. He decided to walk their way, but as he approached, the man waving his hands in the air turned around and stomped off in the opposite direction. The man's retreat hurt the woman's feelings, but she continued in her original quest.

It turned around, pain searing through his body instantly and unexpectedly. The sharpness startled him as he grabbed his chest. The complete stillness he experienced earlier lingered in the air again. It looked around, but nothing in the scenery changed.

He was brought back to reality as he heard the woman call out Colin's name. She peered over the edge of the cliff, looking down.

Now he knew why The Supreme sent him here.

It had never met Melanie O'Connor before. He saw her image, he remembered Colin describing her to him. It understood why Colin's father risked his old bloodline reputation for a woman like her based on looks alone. But her beauty wasn't why Henry loved her. Melanie wasn't only stunning; she was kind, caring, and genuine. It walked toward Melanie from behind, standing startlingly close. She turned from her gaze lost to the ocean, hearing his heavy footsteps approach. The look on Melanie's face was indescribable, and It sensed time stood still.

She looked at It and studied him as if he were a ghost. Her eyes showed confusion across her delicate face as she backed away. Her hands shook realizing how close she was to the edge.

"I can't believe this is you," It said to her, reaching his hand out and placing it on her shoulder. He oddly wanted to embrace her.

"Who are you?" she asked, her voice timid but curious. Her hand brushed his cheek, almost not believing It stood in front of her.

The Supreme told him he would know what to do when he got here. The quick movement of the young boy behind him—halfway down the cliff—startled him.

"I'm sorry," It said, his hand gripping her shoulder firmly, an indescribable instinct overcoming him. "But this has to be done."

He pushed her forward before letting go. Her body did not fall gracefully off the side of the cliff.

Vomit rose in It's throat. Every moment occurred slowly as a horrifying view he couldn't look away from. The sound of firm silence echoed through his body, and he felt the vibration.

A man farther up in the field came into It's view. He fled away from the O'Connor estate and scaled down the edge of the cliff slowly. The jagged rocks sliced It's skin on the way down, and small droplets of blood lingered on his palms when he finally reached the bottom. Melanie's body greeted him. She was tangled, but even in her twisted state, she remained beautiful. The tide was coming in quickly, and the current would take care of the part It hated the most: getting rid of the body.

He broke the ritual in every way that mattered.

The young boy appeared out of the corner of It's eye and approached Melanie's body.

Colin.

It lurked back into a crevasse in the cliff as another figure, a skinny and lanky man, approached. The man was also dressed in a coat like It and didn't belong here in The Oceanside.

He must also be a time traveler, It thought instantly. There was no way this could be a coincidence. From a closer glance, It recognized the man. A scientist at COLI*GO who worked with the woman Colin was so enamored with.

This man was the inventor of time travel itself: Mick Taylor.

It watched as Mick approached Melanie before getting violently ill in the incoming tide. Mick attempted to comfort the confused young Colin in the sand, but then the boy ran—so quickly It couldn't see Colin around the bend of the shoreline.

It lurked a bit further back into the stones, grabbing on to the harshness for a sense of stability. Dread and anger that filled him.

Why did I do this? Why did I act so irrationally based on guidance from The Supreme, of all beings?

But he realized this moment needed to happen for Colin, and so much about Colin made sense to It now.

"He will be okay. I'll make sure," It said out loud.

***

She has an exquisite mind. Even The Supreme speaks highly of her. And Colin trusts her. Almost as much as he trusts me.

The terrifying notion crossed It's mind. Yet for some reason, It liked Julie. It found Julie intriguing because she also had a small cunningness like him. It looked over Julie's notes with wonder and curiosity. She'd left her device on the dining room table in the townhouse. The antidote was moving in the right direction; patients were seeing memory improvements in the clinical trials, and side effects were minimal.

Impressive, he thought while scrolling through the pages of observations. He flipped to another entry in her notes. These were meeting notes from Celine's strategy sessions and Marta's investor calls. This particular page was chaotic in nature—lines connecting various sentences, question marks, and arrows he couldn't quite follow. Misdirected funds unexplained, unknown projects, and an obscure line item to the lower lab.

It placed Julie's device down and looked across the table. Mick Taylor's presence still bothered him, and he was afraid the time traveler saw him push Melanie off the cliff. It couldn't have the truth of Melanie's death revealed for Colin's sake and selfishly his own. Colin would never trust It again if he knew the truth.

He sighed and looked at the remnants on the table. The bottle of wine in the center was almost empty. Only a swig remained, a tease of a taste. If It really wanted to, he could quietly climb up the stairs, float into Colin's room, and take a real taste for himself off of Julie's lips.

She's alone in the bed upstairs. The wicked thought tempted It.

It would never betray Colin in that way. They long ago agreed what was his was his and what was Colin's was Colin's. If It broke that promise, Colin wouldn't forgive him, and he needed Colin just as much as Colin needed him.

Amanda crossed It's thoughts. He related Colin's feelings toward Julie by reminding himself of his own past vulnerability. It had obsessed over Amanda—a feeling he rarely wandered in. In the end, Amanda betrayed him and poisoned It of the hope of true love.

That's really what love is if you think about it long enough: indulgence. How long will Colin indulge before he becomes poisoned as well?

It turned the chandelier off in the dining room.

Colin would return home soon and wouldn't be pleased to find It here, especially with Julie alone upstairs. Even though It meant no malice in his trespassing in the townhouse tonight, he didn't feel like arguing with Colin.

A small light flickered from the back window. It walked over slowly, recognizing the former carriage house from his childhood memories. He hated that place. It lurked out the window suspiciously as a figure approached the large bay window. A figure It recognized, a figure that haunted him.

Mick Taylor.

PART EIGHT

Six Months Later

"But minds find ways to protect themselves, build fortifications and some of those walls become traps."
-Jeff VanderMeer

Chapter 39
The Governor

April 12th, 46 A.R.

"What bullshit is on my agenda today, Kathleen?" Colin asked, walking into his office at The Capitol Building.

Complete silence greeted him. His eyes drifted over toward Kathleen's desk; she sat quietly, staring ahead at nothing. Kathleen's eyes blinked rapidly, something irritating her.

"Kathleen?" Colin asked, placing his hand on her shoulder.

She continued gazing at the wall in front of her without acknowledging Colin's presence.

"Yah?" she finally asked without looking up at him.

Kathleen had been a bit spacey over the last few months and complained of splitting headaches nearly every day, but Colin hadn't thought anything of it.

Colin let go of Kathleen's shoulder and stepped away from her. Upon further observation, Colin noted how dry and pale her skin was and that her hands possessed a slight tremor.

"Are you not feeling well?"

"My head is throbbin', Colin. Uncontrollably."

Kathleen placed her head in her hands and rubbed her temples vigorously. She closed her eyes to avoid the glare of the overhead light.

"Maybe we should get you to the hospital. You need to see a doctor," Colin said, a plan escalating in his mind so that he could help her.

"I can't go tah the hospital. The wait'll be fahevah. The headache will go away before I get tah see a doctah." A slight tremble echoed from her voice.

"Isabella is coming to The City today. I can have her come by the townhouse and take a look at you. Maybe she can prescribe you something," Colin offered. He hated the idea of communicating with Isabella, but if she could help Kathleen, he'd gladly do it. "Maybe we should bring you there now, so you can get some rest."

Kathleen's eyes expanded wide, and her hands hastily clasped Colin's arm. Her grip around him was strong as if terror completely consumed her.

"No. Not Isabella," Kathleen said. "I'll go tah the townhouse and rest. See how I feel lateah."

Kathleen's wild reaction to his suggestion bothered him. Kathleen and Isabella weren't fond of one another, but Kathleen's eyes shook with so much fear that Colin wasn't sure what to think.

"I'll drive you. I don't want you walking."

Kathleen smiled slowly and organized her things, placing them carefully in her bag.

"How long have you been feeling this way, Kathleen? I noticed you haven't been quite yourself the last several months." They walked down the cold marble hallways toward the garage elevators.

"Hmm . . . a long time. Do yah think there's somethin' really wrong with me?"

Kathleen stopped walking and looked up at Colin. He felt ashamed. He'd been so wrapped up in his own life and hadn't noticed her suffering until now. The light shone in from the windows and flickered off Kathleen's blotchy skin as she pushed her hair back off her face. Colin's eyes widened as he noticed a small scar on her upper neck peeking out from behind her ear. The new silvery skin illuminated along the edges similar to Lexi's scar. Colin grabbed Kathleen's arm more aggressively than he intended.

"Kathleen, what happened?" he demanded, his hand moving from her shoulder to the spot behind her ear. She flinched away from him, and anger filled her eyes.

Colin's finger traced the tiny scar carefully, and he looked back at her. Her skin felt familiar. Vivid memories of Lexi flooded his mind: Lexi's harsh screams before he choked her, Lexi's hands grasping at his forearms, Lexi's fingertips abrasively scratching at him, and the dead skin shedding off her. The lost look in Lexi's eyes that night reminded him of the same look on Kathleen's face as she stared back at him.

"What do yah mean, what happened?" she asked, pushing him away. "Don't touch me like that. It makes me uncomfortable."

"I'm sorry." The words escaped Colin's mouth very cautiously. "Let's get you home."

Am I imagining connected dots to explain this strangeness? he wondered as Kathleen continued walking to his vehicle. *No.*

Colin knew what he saw, and the knowledge terrified him. He needed answers from The Supreme, and he needed them quickly.

When they reached the townhouse, Colin rummaged through his new hiding spot for his pills—in the desk drawer of his office behind the collection of whiskey bottles, the place Julie never looked—and handed Kathleen one with a glass of water. He waited patiently downstairs while all his thoughts buzzed loudly in his brain. Each minute that passed sounded loudly as his device vibrated; messages, calls, and various pings asked him where he was, why he blew off a Ways and Means Committee meeting. But Colin couldn't leave Kathleen alone until he knew she was fully asleep.

When enough time passed, Colin exited the townhouse but didn't head up The Hill to The Capitol Building. Instead, he found himself at the steps outside the COLI*GO building.

His badge swiped with ease, and he entered the long hallway with elevators. When an empty car approached, Colin pressed the level for the lab. The lower lab had very restricted access, but Julie once mentioned a stairwell in the back corner of the main laboratory that led down to the mysterious experimental room.

Colin was on a mission to find something, anything to tell him he'd been mistaken thinking Kathleen was now a posse hominem. The thought alone made him ill, and sweat pooled under his arms and on his forehead.

Colin blended in as best he could in the bustling laboratory, which was somewhat difficult with his stature and height. But so many employees rushed around, concentrating on screens and equipment, that no one noticed him. He approached the back stairwell and, with a quick glance around the room, opened the door swiftly before disappearing behind it.

The harsh concrete steps were dimly lit, and Colin sensed the coldness vibrating off the walls as he descended the stairs. When he reached the bottom, a single door with a bright light illuminating around the frame appeared. Colin peered inside the tiny window. Compared to the laboratory upstairs, the lower lab was quiet and eerie; only one android puttered around inside. Nothing looked out of place except for the back wall, lined with various small metal doors resembling cabinet drawers. He watched as the android unlocked one, pulling out a large, life-sized metal tray.

Empty.

Goosebumps lined Colin's arms as he realized the tray was the right size for a human. He looked away and closed his eyes. The place reminded him less of a laboratory and more of The City's morgue. The sound of his heart beating faster reverberated through his ears. A slight clicking sound distracted him, and the door handle in front of him turned.

The android was on his device and not paying attention as he walked into the stairwell. Colin held his breath and leaned as close to the wall as possible, hiding between it and the now ajar door. He couldn't remember the last time he had been so still, so silent. Colin waited until the sound of the android's footsteps faded away before making his move into the lower lab.

Colin wasn't sure when the android would come back, so his time to explore the space was limited. He approached the wall of drawers and grabbed the metal handle in his hand.

It wouldn't budge.

He moved over to one of the few desks and rummaged around hopelessly. The devices were locked, and the desk was fairly empty.

Of course everything is locked, thumbprint or eye scan activated. I should know better.

Out of the corner of his eye, he saw an odd glass container. Colin approached slowly, his footsteps heavy against the silent floors. There was Lexi. Or, at least, Lexi's head.

She didn't look quite the same as she did the moments leading up to her death, the moment right after her existence left this world. Her head was supported by a small topper, and her brain was completely exposed in the back, the skin folded over gently.

Colin was amazed. He wasn't a scientist by training, couldn't name any parts of the brain, or remember much from his biology classes. He gazed upon Lexi, taking in the stunning, fascinating, and bizarre nature of the human brain: textured, captivatingly slimy, and mesmerizing all at once.

Multiple delicate slim wires protruded out from the other end of her microchip, expanding into multiple parts of her brain. They attached to probes elegantly, as if sewn into place.

While he was horrified, Colin acknowledged the sheer innovation and magnificent craftsmanship that orchestrated this experiment. A very talented, brilliant researcher or surgeon must have performed this task. He couldn't imagine this was the work of The Supreme herself. She, like him, was not a scientist. Colin backed away slowly from Lexi and walked backwards until he ran into a large metal table. He turned and saw multiple plastic cubbies with personal belongings. A pair of earrings made him pause.

Kathleen. His jaw dropped in horror.

The earrings originally belonged to her mother, and Kathleen only wore them to special events.

She wore them at my victory party.

He picked up Kathleen's earrings and placed them in his pocket. He couldn't let them stay here in this cold, dark place.

Colin looked back up at the metal doors, and his eyes grew wide. Behind him and around him, Colin realized bodies were shielded by these metal cages. Human bodies like Lexi's. Human bodies like how Kathleen's probably was months ago.

Without any regard for self-control, Colin pulled on the handles of the doors along the walls, knowing they were all locked and secured. They wouldn't open, but the noise of them banging loudly against the locked metal frames filled the room's silence, overwhelmingly and viciously taking over the space around him. This was a distraction, at best. A distraction from admitting Colin knew what he needed to do.

He put his hands on his head and began to shake.

***

The sight of his sister still caught Colin off guard. She carried her stance differently with her stomach protruding awkwardly from her square frame. Celine was just over six months pregnant.

Colin was excited knowing he'd be an uncle soon. He still kept a distinct disdain for Martin but didn't mind the man giving his sister something she wanted so badly: to be a mother.

Brotherly amusement and support provided them with fewer fights and happier times. But now, Celine leaned back in her chair at the dining room table with her focus drifting away.

"We should talk about a transition plan while you're out on maternity leave," Colin said.

Celine smiled and rolled her eyes.

"Why do we have to talk about the baby like that?" she asked, brushing a strand of loose hair away from her face.

"Like what?"

"Like he's the one who will ruin my career."

Colin placed his fork and knife down on his plate.

"He?"

Her smile spread across her face.

"Yes," Celine answered. "Martin and I decided we couldn't wait. The baby is a boy."

A glimmer of glee and excitement left her voice, and Colin's happiness overwhelmed him. He walked to his sister, embraced her with a large hug, and kissed her cheek.

"I know," she said with a chuckle. "Another fucking man to carry on the O'Conner bloodline. I won't lie; I was disappointed."

Colin shook his head—only his sister would say such a thing.

"One of us had to do it, and I promised Father it would be me, not you."

"What?" Colin asked, stepping away in shock.

"Well, we argued about it, but I told Martin our first child would carry my last name, not his. The second can carry on for the Borges. My son will be an O'Connor. I promised Father I'd carry on our legacy; it was one of his last wishes before he died. Don't be ashamed, Colin. Father felt like I was the better child for the job." Celine said the words nonchalantly as she cut into her vegetables with precision and delicacy.

"I suppose I do have the luxury of time compared to you," Colin said, slightly offended.

"That's true. Sometimes I wish I were a man," Celine said with a laugh on the tip of her lips. "But please wait until after I've returned from maternity leave before you knock up your girlfriend. We need someone to run COLI*GO while I'm out."

Colin's eyes darted across the table and met Celine's calm glance.

"The Supreme, Marta, and I have spoken extensively on the matter," Celine continued. "I'll take the standard one-year leave of absence. The only person we trust to take on the responsibilities as interim CEO is Julie. The rest of The Board approved while you were MIA from the meeting today."

Colin placed his whiskey glass down on the mahogany table deliberately and with purpose.

"What?"

Celine chuckled at his action.

"I have some concerns," Celine responded. "Mostly because she's young. But Julie knows so much; she knows too much, Colin. I have an inkling I can thank you for that one." She accusingly pointed her fork in his direction. "I've convinced The Board that The Supreme can guide her, along with Marta. Julie is the best choice."

"Does Julie know about any of this?"

A great discomfort filled his mind at the thought of the majority stakeholders and The Board of Directors making this decision without him. Leaving him completely in the dark.

"The idea was floated to her, but The Supreme asked her to keep it confidential since it wasn't confirmed. She's started attending Marta's finance meetings and my strategy meetings to prepare." Celine paused, placing her silverware down and pushing herself out of her seat. She approached Colin and sat in the chair next to him. The palm of her hand felt warm through his dress shirt as she placed it on his shoulder.

"It will be fine, Colin."

"I'm not concerned about Julie. She's talented, compassionate, and driven. She'll not only get the job done but also do it justice."

"Then why are you upset? I thought you'd be thrilled."

"This feels like a big secret, like you purposefully left me out. I don't like secrets, Celine. You know that."

"No one knows of your relationship with Julie. No one can know, or all of this crumbles. You put me in a difficult situation. Your involvement in this had to stay outside, and it couldn't look like you were trying to influence this decision in the event someone found out. I was trying to protect you."

Colin sighed. He knew his sister didn't have bad intentions at her core. But something about this particular secret bothered Colin more than normal. He couldn't place his finger on it, but the feeling was there, festering around the edges.

"When have you cared so much about protecting me or Julie, for that matter?" Colin asked.

Celine looked over at him and paused before placing her hand on top of his.

"There is so much we need to accomplish for our family. It's our duty. I can't have anything crumble around you, or it will affect me. You can't have anything crumble around me, as it will affect you. We're in this together. Our legacy will grow. I'm having a baby, Colin. I need to continue laying the groundwork for him. And so do you."

"I want that, too. You're right," he said before squeezing his sister's hand. "As long as you're not hiding anything dangerous from me, Celine."

"Why would I hide anything dangerous from you?" She raised a brow. The room grew quiet as Colin contemplated the topic he kept close to his chest for months.

"Did you know about the human-android hybrids? The posse hominems?"

Celine's eyes widened, and the color drained from her face.

"The Supreme has developed a new species, a hybrid of humans and androids in COLI*GO's lower lab. I discovered that Lexi Pvadinish was one of these . . . creatures."

"That explains why you couldn't find Lexi in the system, but why would The Supreme do this?" Celine asked. Frustration spread across her face like a spilled glass of wine, the color showing fiercely across her skin in blotches.

"My question is, Who is helping her? The Supreme couldn't do this all on her own. She doesn't have the capabilities to perform such research."

Colin felt his sister's anger growing in the room around them as she tightly pushed her lips together.

"And beyond the actual experiments themselves, there has to be someone else. Someone with power and influence. The Supreme is deceptive and manipulative, but she isn't in this alone," Colin said, shaking his head.

"Who else knows about this?" Celine asked him.

Colin paused. The question, while valid, felt off putting to him. He knew; It knew. He wasn't ready to explain all of that to Celine.

"I've not told anyone else, if that's what you're asking."

"Not even Julie?"

*Julie doesn't know. Julie can't know, especially now that she's being groomed to manage COLI*GO in Celine's absence.* Colin shook his head.

Celine let out a deep sigh of relief.

"Well, let's keep it that way. You can't tell her, Colin. The fewer people involved, the better. I won't tell Martin. We need to figure out a plan on what to do with this information."

The siblings sat in silence for a long time. Colin didn't know what to say to his sister or what the next appropriate topic of conversation would be after discussing such a horrible reality.

"Let me help with the dishes," Celine finally said, getting up from the table in unison with Colin.

As they approached the kitchen, Colin heard the door open and close. He let out tension he carried within himself: Julie was home. She appeared in the kitchen and kissed him gently before walking over to Celine and grabbing the plates out of her hand.

Celine smiled hesitantly before leading Julie to the living room and asking about the antidote, which left Colin time with his thoughts while cleaning up the remains of dinner.

Why can't I have a moment of calm? Colin wondered while putting aside a plate of food for Julie.

Everything moved quickly lately, even months after the election. The Legislature remained touchier than normal with an escalating friction between human and android representatives. Joel Kennsington and the Humanizers weren't graceful in the light of Joel's loss. He made each day at The Capitol Building a living hell, if he was able, and introduced ridiculous measures and preposterous bills. And then there was Kathleen and what to do with his newfound knowledge about her. It had lingered in Colin's home office earlier that day, shaking his head. Colin already knew the answer, but It was the only one with enough courage to say the words out loud. Colin watched Celine and Julie converse and smiled at how lively and animated they were together.

*If Julie runs COLI*GO while my sister is out, maybe she can shut down The Supreme's dangerous project.* A small beam of optimism shone through the darkness consuming his thoughts.

"Well, I should get going," Celine said, gesturing toward the side door. "But we have a lot to catch up on tomorrow before the news is official."

Both Colin and Julie walked her out to her vehicle, the air slightly warm and comfortable for the late springtime. Colin wrapped his arm around Julie's shoulder and kissed the top of her head as Celine's vehicle drove down the narrow street.

"Celine told me they want to put you in charge while she's out for maternity leave."

Julie looked up at him and nodded.

"I wasn't sure if that would really happen. Celine told me you were kept out of everything and that The Board confirmed the decision today."

"She's correct, and yes, they did," Colin said, squeezing her tightly. "I'm so proud of you. You deserve this."

Julie looked up at him inquisitively.

"I've been thinking lately . . . would it be so bad for us to work more closely in a professional manner?"

Colin was intrigued. As their personal relationship blossomed, they remained diligent to keep as far apart from one another in anything related to COLI*GO.

"There's so much I think COLI*GO could do that it isn't. I know we share the same values on what innovation could do to bring society together. Change is needed. I think you see that, too?" Julie asked him with a shimmer of hope in her eyes.

He wondered if a partnership with Julie in this capacity would be beneficial or dangerous.

Probably a mixture of both. But he liked the idea.

Colin and Celine made great strides together at COLI*GO for The Constituency, but with both him and Julie in a position of power, they could take that to the next level.

Colin returned a mischievous grin before kissing her, his hands tightly gripping her waist.

Once he pulled away from her lips, he responded. “I agree. I think we could really make a difference together.”

Julie smiled back at him endearingly.

Chapter 40
The Supreme

April 16th, 46 A.R.

Dr. Isabella Garcia was an enigma to The Supreme. There was so much about this beautifully damaged woman that intrigued and fascinated her. Isabella was small, both in her frame and stature, but Dr. Garcia's voluptuous chestnut curls gave her a fierce, wild presence. She reminded The Supreme of Mrs. Garcia's physical characteristics but more like Filipe Garcia with her cunningness and intellect. The Supreme did not completely understand family dynamics, but she grew up alongside The O'Connors and observed enough fights, tension, and jealousy to comprehend what went on behind closed doors. Isabella was a quiet soul, the eldest sister and child in a prominent old bloodline family. Failure was not an option for her, as much as failure hadn't been an option for Celine or Colin O'Connor.

Convincing Isabella to help with her experiments wasn't easy but there was one thing The Supreme knew about old bloodline families: They craved not only power but also the upper hand. Being one step ahead of the O'Connors gave the Garcias some kind of advantage, one providing a sense of security in the changing world around them. Their families left legacies not by chance but by adapting to the situations.

Isabella needed a good excuse to publicly leave Colin O'Connor's side for extended periods of time, especially during a heated election season. She couldn't say she was working for COLI*GO on human-android hybrids. The excuse they concocted together did work and leaned into Isabella's cherished and loved persona: her mother. The perfect, doting daughter needed to tend and take care of her mother at the family's estate on The Island.

Colin pretended he was upset by Isabella leaving, but The Supreme knew better: He was thrilled. This allowed him to indulge in his rash behavior with Julie, and he needed to consume himself with this distraction for any of The Supreme's plans to work.

"I think we should get to a place where the android researcher can perform the surgery on his own," Isabella said, looking across at The Supreme. The Supreme smiled in return, a gesture she knew soothed Isabella.

"Am I not paying you enough, Dr. Garcia?"

"It's not that, Madam Supreme," Isabella replied with a sigh. "Although, there is one thing I could ask for in terms of a favor now that we're on the subject."

The Supreme raised her brow with intrigue.

"My sister, Anna."

"Ah, yes." The Supreme allowed the corners of her mouth to move upward into a slight grin.

"I think we would benefit from her resuming her position as the chief medical examiner for The City. Especially in the event that another Lexi situation occurs."

Isabella was smart and more conniving than The Supreme initially gave her credit for, but she would not let Isabella know that.

"I'm concerned that she's a bit . . ." The Supreme said, swiveling around in her chair in a distracting manner, "unpredictable."

Isabella chuckled under her breath. Growing up in constant competition with Anna provided Isabella with some predictability of Anna's erratic decisions and choices.

"To you, maybe. Everything she says and does makes sense to me."

The Supreme let them sit in a few moments of silence. She wanted Isabella to believe she heavily contemplated the idea when, in reality, The Supreme hoped Isabella would ask for this favor all along. The Supreme needed Anna Garcia back working for the commissioner, but she needed Isabella to convince her sister of this idea. Anna wouldn't trust or listen to The Supreme, especially after Lexi.

"Let me talk to the commissioner. I'll tell him to make this happen. I need you to push your sister in the right direction so that she accepts her job back. Do you think she'll put up much of a fight?"

"Between me and my mother, I think we can easily convince her that this is the best decision for her, the best decision for the family."

The Supreme nodded. "I'll request that she start next week."

The younger sister would be indebted to her older sister once again, and The Supreme sensed how much Isabella savored that opportunistic thought.

"Let's head down to the lower lab and check up on our prototypes? I want to make sure everything is going smoothly."

The two walked out of The Supreme's office and found themselves face-to-face with Celine O'Connor and Julie Walsh beside the elevators.

"Good afternoon," The Supreme said with a bright smile to Celine and Julie.

"Hello, Madam Supreme," Julie answered, "and Dr. Garcia."

Isabella initiated an awkward embrace with Celine, averting her eyes from Julie and ignoring the scientist as if she didn't exist.

She must know, deep down.

"How are you feeling?" Isabella asked Celine, gesturing to her protruding figure. Isabella's fingertips lingered a bit longer than socially acceptable, but Celine didn't notice.

"I'm fine, but the mood swings are a lot to handle. Luckily, I have a very intelligent woman filling my shoes for a bit when I go on maternity leave," Celine said, motioning to Julie. The elevator doors opened before them, and Isabella stepped in briskly.

"It was lovely running into you, Celine," Isabella said with a nod as The Supreme joined her in the elevator car. The doors closed in front of them, and Isabella let out a deep sigh.

"I'm surprised Celine could get pregnant so easily." Isabella's voice awkwardly broke the silence between them.

"You are? When she owns this place?" The Supreme asked in a chuckle.

Celine had struggled to conceive a child naturally, but her husband was single handedly the most accomplished biologist and researcher in all of The City. Martin knew the best doctors and the best plan of action. When Isabella did not join in the laughter alongside her joke, The Supreme sighed.

"Well, don't be jealous, my dear. You don't want to spawn an O'Connor child anyways. And if you had a child, that's what it would be. An O'Connor, not a Garcia, regardless if it bore your last name."

Isabella's eyes darted away, regret for bringing up the topic showing in her eyes. Even if she wouldn't admit it, The Supreme knew Isabella's relationship with Colin was a façade. While their families were destined to hate one another, The Supreme noticed Isabella held on to a fondness for the man.

When the doors opened, the android researcher helping them on the hybrid project, Nolan, met them in the hallway. Nolan greeted them with a simple smile, the scales across his bare forearms showcasing a dull violet shade of purple. They walked further into the lower lab and headed back toward an office.

Isabella mentioned Nolan was a great student—a fast learner with steady and still hands, something he would need to become an accomplished surgeon.

The Supreme unlocked the device and pulled up the tracking number associated with the microchip in Kathleen's brain. When her location appeared on the screen alongside a chart with her basic vitals, The Supreme noticed Isabella's eyes furrow.

"What is it?" The Supreme asked.

"Well, she's fine but very dehydrated. I think the placement of the microchip might be slightly off; she's experiencing extreme migraines almost daily. That is an awful side effect."

"Do you think it has to do with Kathleen being left-handed?" The Supreme asked.

"I hadn't thought about that. I don't believe if we put the microchip in the other side of her brain that it would make a difference," Isabella said.

She continued scanning through the electronic record, looking for any other abnormalities in Kathleen's physical body or any disturbances within her brain.

"Her organs are all doing their jobs, and her eyesight is still clear."

"Good, let's look at the others now, shall we?"

Isabella clicked on the microchip-tracking dashboard, and they skimmed through logs of all the posse hominems they had created over the past year.

"I do have one more request," The Supreme said quietly from behind Isabella.

She pulled out a small sealed bag from her pocket and handed it over. Isabella grabbed the delicate microchip that lay inside and tilted her head. The microchip was identical to the others Isabella had surgically placed in all her patients.

"This one isn't activated," The Supreme said, sensing Isabella's confusion.

"I'm not sure I understand."

"I'll activate it remotely when the time is ready. Remote activation is a new technology I'd like to test out. Please use this on your next patient and leave as little of a scar as possible. I don't care how you do it, but make sure it's nearly invisible. Then you can hand off all operations to Nolan if you choose. You don't have to make that decision right now."

Isabella nodded, placing the microchip in the desk drawer and locking it before standing up to stretch her legs.

The Supreme watched as Dr. Garcia wandered over to the metal wall. Isabella's hands danced across the large drawers, stopping briefly over the ones The Supreme knew housed the sleeping bodies destined for an operation. Isabella often expressed her discomfort in the lower lab and how it reminded her of her time in medical school. Isabella stopped and observed Lexi's picturesquely persevered brain. After approaching the small table beside the display of Alexandra's brain, she looked peculiarly at the plastic storage cubbies. Isabella placed all the personal effects patients wore in their own holders, including necklaces, watches, wedding bands and engagement rings, and glasses. The items told personal stories that she sometimes conjured up in her mind to ease her unsteadiness.

Her eyes gravitated to Kathleen's plastic cubby. It was completely empty.

The color drained from Isabella's face.

Chapter 41
Mick

April 19th, 46 A.R.

Mick did not particularly enjoy working for Peter Schneider and wished anyone else was his direct supervisor. Peter was tough, and while he had good intentions most of the time, the man didn't have a personal life here in The City and didn't expect any of his employees to engage in one of their own either.

Peter was an attractive man, and Mick understood Julie's initial draw to him. He had a runner's body and was tall with lean muscle. He kept his hair neatly cut, and the whiteness of his teeth shone brightly from his square jawline.

"How's it going, Taylor?" Peter asked Mick, approaching his desk in his elongated saunter. Mick hated when Peter, or anyone for that matter, called him by his last name. He was convinced Peter did this only to annoy him.

"I'm fine. Did you read the report I sent you last night?"

Peter stopped abruptly, and his eyes widened.

"You sent me a report?"

"Yes. I think I've discovered a possible cause for the side effects in our bipolar disorder trial patients."

"Let's get right on that, Taylor. Put together a presentation of your report, and we'll review it with the team this afternoon. I don't want you focusing on anything else," Peter said before walking away.

Mick sighed and closed his eyes. His device pinged several times throughout the morning and again once more. The Supreme.

Come to my office at The Capitol Building during lunch.

With no time to waste, Mick hired a ride to The Capitol Building. Getting inside was a lengthy process: a full-body scan ensuring he had no weapons, an eye scan verifying his identity, and various back-and-forth confirmations between security that he did, in fact, have a meeting with The Supreme.

Once everything about Mick checked out, he was ushered through the building by a charming but subdued android. She was careful to move Mick along, but he wanted to take in the surroundings as much as possible. He wasn't sure when he'd be in this building again. They finally reached a large black iron door with engraved leaf carvings.

The android knocked on The Supreme's office door and smiled as she opened it for him.

"Mick, I'm glad you made it," The Supreme said from behind her desk with no indication of standing or greeting him.

The Supreme's office in The Capitol Building differed greatly from the office she kept at COLI*GO. The paneled walls were a dark wood, while the floors shone a luscious white marble. Her desk was made of large oak, with engravings carefully stenciled along the edges. Mick couldn't quite make out the specific portrayals but recognized many android-like figures clasping hands with one another, the scales very obvious in the depiction.

A reflection from The Resurgence, he assumed. Mick walked slowly toward her and took a seat.

"How are you today, Madam Supreme?"

Her posture relaxed in her seat, and she grinned.

"I was reading through the notes of your latest report. I'm intrigued. Especially on the time loops you're exploring." Her words were sincere; Mick could tell from the glimmer in her eyes that she was genuinely fascinated.

Intriguing was one way to describe the time loops he studied. In concept, Mick always understood the possibility of a loop, and logically, time loops made sense. These instances explained why once time travel was discovered, there was no going back. And they explained irregularities in the present.

Recently, Mick studied whether humans could get stuck in a loop if they didn't travel time correctly but struggled with fully understanding its power. He discovered it was possible that someone who didn't understand these concepts could get lost bouncing back and forth through time. As an experienced time traveler, Mick developed a system to ease his concern: If he were to spend more than a few days in a different time, only one of him could exist. He shook at the memories of what he had done in the past. And in the future.

"I do plan on going to the future again soon," Mick admitted.

"Good, I'm glad to hear that. I want to check up on my progress. Please provide a report on what you encounter," The Supreme said. Mick nodded, and The Supreme noticed his hesitation. "The posse hominems."

"I assumed they were your creation."

"Why? Because no one else would be capable of such an innovation? Or because no one else would be so disturbing to follow through on it?"

Mick couldn't help but chuckle.

"Maybe a bit of both," he answered honestly.

"Have you ever wondered what it's like?" The Supreme asked him after a moment of silence.

"What?"

"The process of becoming a posse hominem?"

Mick's brain clicked the puzzle pieces into place. He hadn't realized the hybrids were originally humans transformed into these quasi-android humans until this admission. He thought they were created from scratch, similar to how androids were created today in a lab somewhere outside The City.

"You're saying there's a possibility a human could become part android?"

"Yes. We've already proved the concept works. We place a microchip into the human brain," The Supreme answered with a smug smile running across her face.

Mick expected her scales to glow at this moment and was surprised to find they remained dull. He wondered how she was so skilled at containing the physical appearance of her emotions when he knew she understood them all. If Jones shared something exciting, his body would give it away easily.

"And these people, were they willing to give up being human and have a microchip placed in their minds?"

"Of course," The Supreme responded. Her words came a bit

quicker than Mick expected; he wasn't sure if he believed her.

"And what about androids? Can androids become part human?"

"No," she replied simply.

"Why would humans want to become part android?" Mick asked, his mind racing with thousands of new ideas.

"Well, you have a lot of questions, but I suppose I should expect nothing less from a scientist." The Supreme stood from her chair and turned to look out the window behind her, and Mick followed her gaze.

The view was a simple but serene green courtyard space. The luscious and exotic plants only grew because it was enclosed. Mick couldn't imagine the beautiful red and orange flowers blooming alongside the trees in The City's cold spring. The Supreme leaned up against the window and pointed across the court, inhaling deeply.

"That's the governor's office over there," she said without looking back at Mick. "I know you admire him. He's a very serious man, one with great power and influence. Much more power and influence than I have over this constituency, but objectively, that isn't fair."

Theoretically, the governor and The Supreme were supposed to be equals. But this was far from the case. The governor was treated with more respect and taken more seriously.

"Imagine if there were one ruler of The Legislature?" The Supreme asked him. "A being everyone voted for? Not humans but androids, too. Or all beings? Why should there be a Representative of The Androids and a Representative of The People? Shouldn't all citizens be treated equally? Shouldn't there be some kind of bond that brings us all together? Some kind of unity?"

Mick thought about what The Supreme said as she continued looking across the courtyard. He never felt the need to challenge the way things were until now. The importance of posse hominems became clearer in his mind.

If there was a class of citizens who didn't fit into the two-party mold, who would hear and represent their voices?

"Would human-android hybrids allow for more freedoms and autonomy for androids, too?" Mick asked suddenly, intellectually intrigued by this discussion with The Supreme.

She turned and looked at him, a soft smile spreading across her face. Mick found The Supreme very captivating in that moment, the golden amber colors of her scales vividly enchanting.

"You mean, the ability for androids to process more emotions . . . at least openly? Or even the possibility of humans and androids to intermingle freely?"

Mick nodded. *Why are the most brilliant people often the most conniving, the most cunning?* The Supreme looked back out the window before lowering the blinds halfway down.

"I think that could be a future possibility, yes. Under the right legislature."

***

Mick made it back to his desk in the COLI*GO building with only forty-five minutes until the afternoon meeting. He stressed about putting the presentation together when he was halfway back to COLI*GO. Peter was a smart man, and Mick didn't blame Julie for hiring him. He was driven and efficient, demanding speed and agility from his teams and producing top-line results. On paper, that made him a good leader, but over time, it also made him out of touch.

He pulled up the presentation and added a slide:

COL23: What goes wrong with bipolar patients but not Alzheimer's patients? Trauma.

Mick leaned back. He didn't provide any more in the presentation and sent it to the team members, minus Peter, with a copy of his report. He asked them to read the executive summary before the meeting and come prepared with questions.

Mick discovered the error in the antidote by pure luck. What the rest of the team missed was not in the coding of the pharmaceutical; it was what happened in the brain. The memories of depressed patients were so vastly different from those with Alzheimer's.

Trauma had an interesting physiological effect on the neurotransmitters in the brain and was simply unpredictable. Mick discovered the root cause for why the antidote provided inconsistent results with these patients: Relapses linked back to the suffering of another traumatic episode during the first few months of treatment. Unsure of how to fix the antidote's structure, Mick decided he'd leave those suggestions to the chemists.

When Mick walked into the meeting room, Peter sat at the head of the conference table, pushing his glasses back up the bridge of his nose. The chair appeared awkwardly small against Peter's wide shoulders and tall frame. The rest of the team mulled quietly around the room before taking their seats.

"Did you think I wasn't going to read your report, Taylor?"

The words were very cold, echoing through the room. Eyes darted across the room from Peter to Mick. While Mick enjoyed working with the team, this was COLI*GO: the most competitive, cut-throat company to work for.

"I didn't doubt that for a second." Mick stumbled as the words came out of his mouth.

"Good. Then I'm excited to see your presentation."

Mick projected the single slide with a gulp of embarrassment. Silence surrounded him.

"Is that it, Taylor?"

"I figured since my expertise isn't necessarily in drug making—rather it's in the functionality and physiology of the human body—we could have a group discussion in a few areas." Mick searched deep inside himself for confidence.

A few of his colleagues smiled at him, providing him with the reassurance he needed. He took in a deep breath and continued.

"First, do we think there is another way to validate this hypothesis of mine? Secondly, if this is the root cause of the problem, how do we ensure successful administration of the asset in patients? And lastly, do we even think the patient will remain successful long term? What happens if a patient has a relapse or a triggered response months or years later? What if they face some type of trauma in the future?"

"This hypothesis is spot on. We've been scratching our heads at this one for a while," Peter said enthusiastically, surprising Mick with praise.

The room filled with chatter, excitement, and adrenaline in response to Peter's approval.

"Let's have a few teams break out here—I want one person from each specialty in each group. Block off the rest of your day and cancel all your meetings—it's going to be a late night."

He stood up quickly and walked over to Mick, putting his arm around his shoulders and ushering him out the doorway.

"Look," Peter said in a hushed tone, "this is stellar work, Taylor. Work with me and not against me next time, okay? We're a team."

Mick nodded, embarrassed at how he acted.

"I just want you to take me seriously. Give me a bit more respect," Mick challenged Peter.

Peter looked down at his shoes and back up at Mick. An apologetic look passed between the two men.

"You're right. I haven't been fair to you. Thank you for speaking up. I want to help this project succeed, and I know now that you do, too."

"Will you tell Julie about this discovery?" Mick asked him before they headed back into the room.

"No, I think we need to explore the area more, and once we have a few options for solutions, then we'll loop her in. And the rest of The Board."

"You don't think she'd want to know now?"

Peter's eyes dashed across the room, and Mick sensed his manager was going to share more secrets with him.

"This isn't about me not giving you credit, Mick. I promise this is your diamond in the rough," Peter responded, addressing him with a serious grin. "This hasn't been announced to the broader organization yet, but Julie will be taking over Celine's role while she's on maternity leave. She has a lot of transitioning work to focus on and can't be too bothered on COL23."

Mick took a step back and closed his eyes briefly.

*Julie will be the CEO of COLI*GO?* The thought bounced wildly through his mind. He imagined all the implications, good and bad, with her in such a position of power.

"Mick, I know you and Julie are really close, but you cannot go above my head on this one, okay?"

Maybe Julie and I aren't as close as I thought, Mick wondered, still shocked by the secret Peter shared with him.

"You're right. Let's focus on finding a solution to this,"

Mick answered as they stepped back into the conference room with the rest of the research team.

***

They hadn't sat down face-to-face with one another in years, but Mick could tell his uncle was as nervous and anxious as he was.

"I hear you're doing great things at COLI*GO, Mick," Jeb said, looking down at the basket of bread on the table in between them.

"I've been working on the company's newest asset."

"But that's not your only work for COLI*GO, correct?" Jeb asked, eyeing him carefully.

"I'm not sure what you're talking about." Mick looked away, and the waiter walked back over toward them.

They ordered their food, and Jeb began another round of small talk, telling Mick about some of his recent commissioned work he was finishing before taking an indefinite period of time off.

"I think I'm going to visit the family," Jeb said. "It's time I made the trip. It's time I came clean. They deserve the truth."

"Do they, though?" Mick asked with a hint of irritation.

Mick never really forgave his family. Life on the farm wasn't easy, and his childhood was plagued with responsibilities too great for someone his age. Mick gave his blood, sweat, and tears as a young man, and Mick had never asked for anything in return.

They called him selfish for applying to The University and for wanting a life beyond The Countryside. His father told him he couldn't go. Back then, Mick already felt behind: He was a few years older than his friends who left The Countryside to make a livelihood or receive an education in The City.

Mick saved up enough money for the first-semester tuition to get his foot in the door. His parents still told him no. They said they would never speak to him again if he went.

Leaving had been the hardest decision Mick made at that point in his life. Since then, he faced more difficult decisions, but the lesson he learned from that first experience stayed true: Once he made a decision, he needed to follow through. There was no turning back.

"What I did was wrong. They deserve to know."

Jeb stealing money from the family had been wrong; Mick wouldn't argue with him about that.

"I think you should leave the past in the past. That was so long ago. And would they even welcome you if you showed up knocking on the door?" Mick asked.

Jeb looked at him and shook his head.

"They may not, but there are some things I want to do before the next stage of my life. The problem is, I've had too much time to think. I cannot forgive myself for everything I've done, and I don't expect the people in my life to forgive me for my sins either. The least I can do is say I am sorry," Jeb admitted slowly. "Someday, Mick, you will understand the power of secrets. They are a soul-eating disease. Secrets consume you from the inside, tear you apart, and unmercifully take their time. The silent killer of us all."

Mick leaned back in his seat. His uncle had a point: Secrets were the reason for the space between him and Jones.

"Is this why you insisted we get dinner together? Because you feel like you need to apologize?" Mick asked. "I don't hate you, Uncle Jeb. I never did. As a boy, I was hurt, I believed you abandoned me, but strangely, I never hated you for it. As a man, I understand now why you did what you did."

Jeb smiled slightly and shook his head sadly.

"I'm sorry, Mick. I should have been there for you when you left home. You had no one to guide you in the most pivotal years of your life. I should have been that supportive person, that father figure to you. Something my brother wasn't man enough to be. But I wasn't strong enough either. So, yes, that is part of why I wanted to see you, but there's another reason, too."

Mick couldn't take his eyes off his uncle. Jeb always appeared rough around the edges, but looking at him now, Mick noticed the aging across his face, within the hollow look in his eyes. He wasn't wrong; the secrets were eating him alive.

"I know you're working with The Supreme."

Mick closed his eyes and put his utensils down. He opened his mouth to speak, but Jeb beat him to it.

"I'm not going to ask you what you're working on. I frankly

don't want to know. But you should be careful of the promises you make to her. When I go home, I can tell the family how you are, and I can ask them to welcome you home. To give your relationship a second chance."

"Excuse me?" Mick exclaimed a little louder than he intended.

A few eyes around the room looked over at their table. His uncle leaned in before speaking in a hushed manner.

"Mick, if you can leave, leave. Get out of here. The City is no good. There are things happening at COLI*GO, things I can't . . . things I don't want to share with you because they are so horrifying. You need to leave before everything crumbles. Get as far away from The City as you can."

"I can't leave. There's my boyfriend to think about, I have a prestigious job, and I'm becoming successful. I'm doing great things, Uncle Jeb. Unimaginable things that are monumental and important."

"Mick," Jeb said intensely. "You have to leave before what you're working on with The Supreme kills you. I know The Countryside isn't glamorous or exciting, but this place . . . it will not be safe soon. I know it's not an easy thing to do, but you need to leave Jones. You need to save yourself."

"It won't be that bad," Mick said even though he knew this was a lie. He'd seen the future, or at least one terrible version of the future.

Jeb threw his napkin on his plate and stood up abruptly, annoyed and defeated.

"What? You're going to abandon me again? Walk away when things get difficult? Like you always do?" Mick asked in disbelief.

Jeb leaned in, his face so close to Mick's that he could smell the sweetness from the wine on his uncle's breath.

"You have time, Mick. I do not. I learned my lesson the hard way. I can't sleep at night; I can't live with myself and the horrible things I've done. Worst of all, I don't want to be here anymore. Don't follow in my footsteps," Jeb warned.

Mick felt the old wound fester again in his mind.

"I know I wasn't there for you when I should have been. I'm sorry. I'm trying to protect you now, Mick. Please, think about it."

Chapter 42
The Governor

April 20th, 46 A.R.

Colin looked at Julie, admired how peaceful her body was in its sleep. He didn't want to leave the warmth of his bed, didn't want to miss hearing her deep but soft breathing while she slumbered.

Colin glanced up at the ceiling. Watching Julie caused Colin to feel an internal conflict he wasn't comfortable with, one he wasn't sure he was ready to face even though he had to. He was afraid he wouldn't find the strength in himself or the power to perform what he simply needed to do if he looked at her for a moment longer.

Gently moving her hair away from her face, Colin gazed at her for one more moment. Before he could change his mind, he snuck out of the bed quietly, tiptoeing through the door and down the stairs. He had only done this betrayal once before while he was with Julie, back when he and It killed Lexi. Over a year ago now.

Has that much time passed between then and now? Colin wondered, thinking back to how at ease he found himself when leaving Isabella to venture on these journeys.

The Capitol Building looked very different at night. The lights from The City cast strange and elongated shadows down the slick stone hallways, and the sound of his and It's footsteps filled his ears. Colin never felt more loneliness in these dim walls.

"You've never let me come here before. This feels so . . . decadent, wicked," It said into the darkness.

Colin scowled at him. No one was here at this time of night, except for one or two security details. The risk was low, but the thought of being caught here, together with It, made Colin uneasy.

They made their way to Colin's office, and Colin turned on the lights before taking a seat. It wandered around the room, taking in the scenery with a childish sense of excitement. Colin opened the desk drawer on his right with ease, a small vial and syringe glaring back at him.

"Do you really need that?" It asked.

Colin pondered the question for a minute, holding the syringe up toward the light.

"I don't think I can do this, just me and you."

"Fair enough." It looked toward the doorway blankly.

The anticipation of Kathleen's arrival cascaded through Colin's whole body, his heart beating faster than normal and his eyes growing glossy and blurry.

I don't want to do this. But I have to. This is the only way I can fix this, he thought as the realization formed in his mind after visiting the lower lab.

He remembered rushing home from that horrid experience. Kathleen was nowhere to be found, having left without even a message or note. Colin sank back into his old habits in the days that followed as he spiraled downward. His demons returned with a vengeance.

Earlier today, Colin had grabbed the expensive Scotch from his desk and took one too many of the pills with the drink. He looked down at the empty glass, the remnants of the amber liquid pooled in the corner. He immediately rushed to the bathroom and purged himself while thinking about his promise to Julie. He couldn't let her down.

When the venomous booze and drugs no longer lingered inside his body, he went downstairs and crashed onto the couch in pure exhaustion.

He messaged Celine. No response—as he expected. He messaged Julie. She responded with an apology; she was busy in a review meeting with the regulatory team and couldn't talk. He even messaged The Supreme, wondering if he could let out his aggression, frustration, and pure hatred on her. The message was marked "read," but there was no response.

It, at least, had the decency to answer him.

They discussed the matter at length with yelling and screaming. Contents of the coffee table violently were strewn across the room. Another mess. They reached a consensus, and Colin sulked around the townhouse the rest of the day.

Then Julie came home. She sensed an uneasiness in Colin, and instead of pushing him like she normally did, she let him wallow in his own bullshit.

He'd decided to kill Kathleen and couldn't turn back, but he also couldn't bear the thought that Julie was influential enough to talk him out of his madness and insanity. But she chose not to.

That isn't her fault; she doesn't know, he thought.

The tension between him and Julie bubbled as if they argued at length with no resolution. In reality, no foul or harmful words were said between them. Only silence.

Julie made dinner and didn't ask for help cleaning up. Her eyes were wide and holding back tears as Colin walked up the stairs and turned on the shower. He moved the pills from his desk back under the sink, egging her to find them.

She didn't.

Colin felt shameful ignoring Julie when she crawled into bed next to him. She spooned him, curling her small frame up against him before falling asleep. He closed his eyes, knowing he couldn't confide in Julie about this secret because she would hate him.

The creak of his office door distracted him from the memory, and Kathleen walked in. Kathleen looked up, and all he saw was the image of Julie's face looking back at him.

How can I do this? Colin couldn't think about what was about to happen too thoroughly. This vivid image of Kathleen would remain seared into his brain forever, something he'd never forget.

What surprised him the most was how submissive Kathleen became. She didn't fight Colin as he grabbed her swiftly and harshly. He held the filled syringe in his hand, injecting Kathleen with the tranquilizer before laying her on his desk.

"How could you do this?" he yelled to her wilting body. "You're one of the only people in my life I trusted. You were always there for me. How could you agree to let The Supreme turn you into one of those monsters? You abandoned me, like everyone else."

Kathleen looked up at him, pain emulating from her eyes. She struggled to use her mouth, the drug moving rapidly through her body.

"I didn't. They . . . they kidnapped me. I . . . I nevah asked for this," Kathleen said slowly.

Colin's eyes widened. Kathleen attempted to move her arms but couldn't; her eyes darted back and forth, but she found the strength to answer him, something the old Kathleen had the courage for.

"Well . . . yah have tah kill me now, don'tcha?" she asked with a small sense of defeat.

For a moment, Colin thought there was hope: an alternative to this evil he always deemed necessary. He could not kill her. The tranquilizer would wear off in a few hours. They could go on the way they were as if none of this happened. As if she wasn't a posse hominem. A creation concocted by The Supreme.

It shook his head at Colin from across the room.

"I don't want to kill you, Kathleen. You're my family. You've been better to me than my own family has. But you'd betray me at some point as a part android. You'd betray The People of The Constituency, wouldn't you?"

"That's . . . that's what The Supreme would ultimately have me do, yah," she said, tears falling out of the corners of her eyes. "Colin . . ."

Colin looked at her, his fingers delicately wiping away the tears from her face. She spoke slowly, the drug ripping through her veins. But Colin would give Kathleen all the time in the world if she asked for it.

"Yah have tah. Yah have tah kill me. I don't even wanna be me. It hurts. And . . . and yah have tah stahp The Supreme. Expose her."

He grabbed her hand and squeezed it tightly. The tears escaped from them both. He watched as she closed her eyes, the drug fully embedded in her blood, putting her fast to sleep.

Her hand went limp in his.

Colin scooped Kathleen off his desk and walked toward the emergency escape that went from his office to the outside world.

"What are you doing? Why didn't you strangle her?" It asked him hastily. "This isn't part of the plan."

"Fuck the plan," Colin said back to him.

"No. We have a ritual. There is a particular way in which we do things. There is a purpose," It said very unsympathetically.

Kathleen's body lay silently in the backseat of the vehicle. Colin continued driving from The Hill until he reached the bridge and the COLI*GO building came into view.

COLI*GO was a strange ecosystem, a place where many wonderful, amazing innovations occurred. Innovations that truly helped people and androids. But this place was also infected by evil, deeply rooted into the foundation, walls, and floors. A vicious fungus fighting its way throughout the place, consuming everything in its path.

Julie's right. There's so much we can do together when she assumes the role of CEO. Colin envisioned them plucking the weeds, cleaning out the infestation. Exposing The Supreme.

Once they arrived in the network of alleyways behind the buildings, Colin carried Kathleen's limp body for what seemed like an hour but was really a few minutes. In the darkness, he and It placed her body on the front steps of COLI*GO.

"We have a certain way we do things," It reminded Colin, handing him the knife.

Colin stared at the knife, the shiny metal reflecting off the moonlight. It tapped his foot impatiently.

"You do the deed then," Colin said in a huff, waving the knife in It's direction. It looked at him disapprovingly but said nothing.

No, that is not how we do things. Colin knew better.

"She won't feel anything. Even though you didn't choke her."

"I know, but you're not making this easier."

"She was going to aid The Supreme. You knew this. She confirmed the suspicion," It said in a logical and sensible manner. This somehow infuriated Colin even more.

"I hate you!" he yelled up at him, his eyes filled with rage and anger.

"Well, did you ever stop to think that I hate you, too? What could I truly be if your shadow wasn't in my way?" It challenged.

The words swung swiftly at Colin and hurt him deeply. He wasn't sure if It said these words to spark motivation, but the motion overtook his body.

After Colin completed his least favorite part of the ritual, he looked at Kathleen in a sense of bewilderment.

Her body bled like any other human, but he wouldn't make the same mistake he made with Lexi. This time, he removed the microchip from her brain with tenderness and ease, leaving Kathleen's secret exposed to the outside world.

Colin hoped someone would recognize the symbolism of what was in front of Kathleen's lifeless body, that someone would notice the door behind her was the entrance to the place that caused so much conflict.

COLI*GO.

***

It handed Colin a tiny pill as they stood in the bedroom doorway, but instead of creeping into one of the spare rooms down the hall, he pushed Colin aside and strode further into the room. He watched him sit on the bed and place his hand across Julie's face, stroking her cheek and faintly tracing his hand down her neckline. It's hand lingered on her collarbone, taking in her slender neck longingly.

His fingers spread.

She stirred a bit in her sleep from his touch but didn't fully awaken. It tightened his grip, slowly at first but with a power and strength that a man of his stature possessed. Julie's eyes flashed open, her lungs no longer able to breathe.

Even in the darkness, Colin recognized the scared look in Julie's eyes, as if she burned through him. It's hand grabbed on to Julie more tightly, strangling her. The experience of the one thing they missed together in the night's activities, the only part of the ritual that hadn't occurred.

In the darkness of the room, Colin continued watching It take away the only thing that truly mattered to him. It hadn't lied earlier: It did hate him.

"Stop!"

Julie gasped for air, hurt and sadness emitting from her eyes as she struggled against It's weight. Colin's guilt swelled uncontrollably as he did nothing except allow himself to feel the emotions in his mind: confusion, trepidation, fear.

I need to save her.

Instead, Colin continued watching It strengthen his grip on Julie's neck, pushing her violently down into the pillows. It mimicked the way Colin would have strangled Kathleen, how Colin strangled all his victims, all the women before her.

Julie lifted her hands free from underneath, attempting to push It off. She grabbed at his forearms, her eyes filled with pure terror.

Colin couldn't watch the sight straight on, and his eyes drifted to the mirror hanging above the headboard. The violent movements continued, and disgust filled Colin's stomach as It looked back at him, a grin across his face so wide that Colin closed his eyes.

When Colin opened his eyes, the only reflection in the mirror was his.

The image shined starkly back at him; an enraged man suffocating a woman. A woman he loved and cared about deeply. A woman who loved him, despite his flaws and imperfections. The only person he felt vulnerable around. The only person left in his life he trusted.

The imprint on the bed was Colin's, no one else's; the hand wrapped around Julie's neck was his, no one else's.

Colin and Julie were the only ones in the bedroom.

Just Colin, just Julie.

There was no It.

He could not blame It for hurting Julie. That was Colin's burden to bear all on his own.

Too many moments passed, too many sharp, crying sounds escaping from Julie before Colin finally let go of her, shaking and ashamed. She hastily escaped the bed, tears streaming down her face as she fled the room. As she ran down the stairs, her footsteps sounded loudly in Colin's ears.

Thump, thump, thump.

Colin stared back at his reflection in the mirror. The recognition of what occurred made him dizzy; the darkness growing rapidly across his vision, the silence of the townhouse ringing loudly in his ears before exploding with Julie's terrified sobs.

His father was correct, facing It head on was something Colin was too cowardly for, was always afraid of. In that moment of his own betrayal, Colin finally knew he needed to get rid of It.

***

The morning sun shone severely through the window. Colin awoke instantly, unsurprised to find himself alone in his bed. He walked down the steps quietly; the hollow outline of Julie's figure sprawled on the couch. She was still fast asleep. With what happened last night, he knew they both felt emotional and physical tiredness.

He went back upstairs and waited for her to join him when she was ready. Waiting for her seemed like an eternity, and the look in Julie's eyes pierced through him immensely when she finally walked through the doorway.

She crawled into the bed, and Colin opened his arms to her. As she lay against his chest, his hands traced along the very faint blue and purple hues wrapped around her neck. The specks of red shot out from the edges of the bruises in thin sporadic lines, revealing the freshness of them.

I can't believe she trusts me enough to be wrapped up in my embrace after what I allowed It to do to her, Colin thought as he stroked her hair softly. *What I did to her.*

"I shouldn't have let this happen," Colin said quietly, holding her.

Julie didn't say anything at first, and her breathing quickened a little. Colin sensed unease through her. He wanted her to say something, anything, for his own selfish reasons—he wanted her to find a courage that wasn't fair for him to expect. Instead of saying anything, Julie cried. The weeping pained him; he was infuriated with himself.

"I know 'I'm sorry' isn't good enough. Never will be good enough. But I need to explain something to you," Colin said slowly, "if you'll let me."

"Your night terrors, Colin. I knew something was bothering you when I got home, but I never imagined waking up in the middle of the night to you having a nightmare . . . to you choking me," Julie said breathlessly.

She looked at him for a long time, her eyes clear and bright in the morning light.

"I didn't tell you the whole truth about my night terrors. I know they come from what happened to my mother," Colin said, the confidence in his voice a bit shaken—a feeling he rarely experienced.

Julie looked at him, waiting for him to continue explaining.

"When I was young, I saw her . . . I saw her murder. She never went missing," he said slowly. "I saw a man push her off the edge of the cliff. My father refused to look at me the same way because had I not run away, had she not gone looking for me, she'd be alive. That was one form of disappointment. The other disappointment my father had in me was in It."

Julie's eyebrows raised slightly.

"It?" she asked.

Colin took in a deep breath and looked into her eyes. He felt empathy from Julie and the confidence in himself to be honest with her. He truly loved her, and she truly loved him.

"Logically, I know he doesn't exist but to the same accord, he does exist . . . because It is me. Or, at least, It is a part of me," he said the words out loud, something he hadn't been able to say before. He wanted to be honest with Julie. "I was clinically diagnosed with dissociative identity disorder when I was younger. I can't always distinguish myself from It, and other times, It is right beside me. I can see him as clearly as I see you. I can hear him as clearly as I can hear you. I can't remember everything about him, everything about certain things that happen when I see him."

This admission wasn't easy for Colin; he took a breath and closed his eyes before continuing.

"I come home some days and don't remember what I did all day, almost as if I completely disappeared for hours on end. It has full control over me sometimes—and I hate that because, with him, I do things I shouldn't. Harsh, selfish, violent, and unthinkable things. The night terrors are a part of that."

Julie dropped her gaze from Colin in sadness. Julie struggled with accepting this truth about the man she loved, much in the same way Colin struggled with this truth about himself. It seemed that knowing Colin had demons wasn't enough to scare her away when, logically, it should. Her compassion shone through—a kindness and understanding no one had ever shown Colin before.

"That doesn't excuse anything I did, anything I've ever done. My father attempted to help me when I was younger. He reached out to his friend Filipe Garcia, Isabella's father. He was a psychologist by training and thought I'd grow out of It as I aged. I didn't." Colin lowered his eyes away from Julie. "There were slight improvements at first, but in the end, It remained. My father was ashamed of me and blamed Dr. Garcia. That's where the strain in our families began to fester."

"Oh, Colin."

"I understand if you leave me today. If you walked out the door and never came back, I wouldn't hate you for that, Julie," Colin said before looking her straight in the eyes. "After last night, after what I allowed It to do to you—what I allowed myself to do to you—I need to fix this. I think there's a way, if I had your help.

"Selfishly, there's a reason why your presentation at The University intrigued me. I saw your notes, I read through all your research, and I observed the replications in the studies of simulated brains affected by psychological disorders. That's why I helped you at COLI*GO. And then I fell in love with you. I think the antidote could help me. I think it could help people suffering from disorders like mine."

"I don't know if the antidote will work, Colin," she replied worriedly.

"I'm willing to take that risk. Especially after last night. I worry I'm losing grip on distinguishing myself from It. I need to control It somehow before . . ."

Julie placed her hand on his chest, over his heart. She nodded slowly.

"I shouldn't. This goes against every single code of ethics that I've taken, but," she said, keeping her gaze on him, "I love you. And I will help you. I will treat you with the antidote."

The room was silent for a bit. A silence they both needed for their minds to slow down and settle.

"When can I start treatment?" Colin asked.

"We need to do this properly and safely. That is my only request from you even if you don't like my process. You have to do this my way," Julie said sternly. "The first couple of weeks are the most volatile and most unpredictable with the antidote. You can't be stressed out in The Capitol Building."

"It's probably best to stay away from The City. Let's go up to The Oceanside on the weekends when you give me my doses," Colin suggested, trying to follow the plan Julie crafted in her mind as they spoke.

"I think that's a good idea. I'll confiscate the doses from COLI*GO, but that'll take a few weeks so that Peter doesn't notice. Then we can start," she said before looking down at her hands, studying them with disbelief.

"What's wrong?" Colin asked her. "What are you not saying?"

Julie looked up at him, her eyes glossy and wet in the corners from both old tears and fresh ones.

"I'm scared. I couldn't live with myself if anything happened to you because of my drug."

Colin wrapped her closer in his embrace. He never experienced love or care from anyone that was so genuine, except from his mother. Julie held him tightly back, a reassuring feeling he desperately needed at this moment. He thought he might lose her if he let go.

"I'll take part of the summer off from COLI*GO, before Celine goes on maternity leave. I don't want to be distracted by anything else."

"I can't ask you to do that."

"You're not. This is my decision."

Colin looked at her with a warning glare; she was stubborn but so was he.

"I need to ask, who else knows about It?"

"Isabella knows, as does The Supreme. And now you," he answered truthfully.

"Celine doesn't know?" Julie asked, surprise forming in the corners of her mouth.

"No, she doesn't. My father knew, but he's no longer alive. He told me if my sister ever knew of the true monster I was . . ."

"Having a psychological disorder doesn't make you a monster, Colin. You're a person. A person who experienced trauma," Julie said. "You are not a monster."

No, Julie, I am a monster. If you knew what I've done. What I did last night, he thought as vivid memories of his knife diving into Kathleen rippled through his brain. *You would think I am a monster, too.*

"The Supreme knows?" Julie asked, finally realizing how secretive Colin kept this part of himself for so long.

Colin paused and looked away. His partnership with The Supreme in all of this was a much more complex situation to explain, but he knew he owed it to Julie to try.

"You know how you and Jones are very close? You grew up together? Shared secrets? Became best friends?"

Julie nodded.

"She was to me in my youth like Jones is to you now. I never really had friends growing up because I was weird and strange. I was a loner because I was dealing with my demons. Emilia—I mean, The Supreme—she and I were once close friends. Our relationship is different now. We don't trust one another anymore but are dependent on each other because we know too much about the other. If her ship sinks, so does mine."

They held each other for a while, allowing the morning to flood through the window, consuming the room. As the sun shone brighter, Colin's and Julie's devices alarmed simultaneously. She grabbed her device, and her hand covered her open jaw from shock.

"Colin! Oh my God, Colin," she screamed, looking up from her device.

He looked back at her, tilting his head slightly as she handed over her device with shaking hands. The tears flooded back in Julie's eyes. He wrapped his arms around her instantly.

Colin didn't need to read the words on her screen.

Chapter 43
Jones

April 22nd, 46 A.R.

Jones sat at his desk, feeling fidgety. Yesterday, they found the body of the governor's secretary, Kathleen Murphy. Even more troubling, her body had been placed as if on display in front of the COLI*GO headquarters across The River. Jones had watched the commissioner take the microchip dangling from Kathleen's head and place it in a clear bag.

What puzzled Jones was the slight variation in Kathleen's murder from the other killings. While she was stabbed twenty-three times, she bore no bruises around her neck. She hadn't been strangled. Jones wondered what circumstances caused the killer to treat Kathleen differently or if this was the work of a copycat.

The commissioner tried desperately to keep the media away, but Kathleen Murphy was a big name. She was arguably the closest person to the governor. This was scandalous; there would be no way the police could shove this one under the rug as they had with Lexi Pvadinish.

Jones instantly broke his protocol and pinged Julie while he was at the crime scene. The pale blue sky illuminated a harsh sun, and the grayness of the building and the sidewalks made the blood beside Kathleen's body harshly vivid.

Kathleen's murder pushed the commissioner and The Supreme to finally hire a full-time medical examiner again. The department went almost a year without one, relying on consulting local physicians after Anna's departure.

The commissioner informed the team that the medical examiner would be in the office today, and the case could resume once the autopsy was performed. The precinct buzzed out of control around Jones; devices rang loudly, the media personalities all requesting an interview with the commissioner. Jones couldn't remember the last time there had been so much activity: Even Kendra Washington's murder investigation hadn't caused such a commotion.

Jones heard a slight tapping sound from the corner of his desk. He looked up and was startled to see a familiar face.

"Hello, Detective Jones," Anna said sternly as if the words were meant to slice right through him.

"What are you doing here?" Jones asked, his eyes growing wide and his scales throbbing.

"I'm back. The City needs a medical examiner and it looks like The Supreme owes my sister a few favors, so she cashed in on this one. I have to 'behave,'" she said, making air quotes with her hands.

"So, does that mean you are going to look at Kathleen Murphy's body?" he asked, trying to stay professional.

"Yes, I suppose so," Anna said, looking down at her device.

"I'll stop by the morgue for the report then?"

"That's okay. I'll email it to you. I don't think we should work too closely on this case, Detective Jones."

Jones did not expect a warm welcome from Anna. He didn't think reuniting was feasible. They hadn't spoken to one another in months, hadn't even tried to make amends after their falling out at Anna's apartment.

Time moved at what seemed like a snail's pace. Jones wasn't going to find the answers he needed by sitting at his desk and waiting for Anna to get around to sharing the autopsy report with him. He packed his bag and looked at the device on his desk.

Without even giving it a second thought, Jones used the location tracker and searched for Julie. He closed his eyes and let out a deep sigh of relief before leaving the building and embracing the bright and warm sunlight.

The welcoming natural light didn't last long before a group of reporters caught sight of him and headed his way. Fighting off the media who recognized him as one of the lead detectives was a challenge, but Jones was fast; he got himself down into the subway line and disappeared into the crowd.

Jones went a few stops on the green line before venturing back up into the landscape of The City. With each step up to the surface,

Jones contemplated his next move. He walked quickly and meaningfully through the old windy streets on The Hill.

When he reached the O'Connor townhouse, Jones found it surprisingly dark and lonely. Toward the back, Jones noticed the carriage house—the one sacred place to Mick. One that would soon be considered hostile.

An intriguing idea crossed Jones's processor.

He originally came here to find Julie, to talk to her, but he felt an unexplainable gravitational pull to the carriage house. He wanted to understand Mick in his own environment.

There was something quite endearing about the outside of the structure, how it still portrayed its historical charm. Jones climbed up the outside stairs to the second-floor entrance. He liked how the carriage house felt like an urban treehouse.

Breaking into the dwelling was a fairly easy task, one that made Jones shake his head in disbelief with how careless Mick acted sometimes. It took Jones only a matter of minutes to find the hidden spare key. Once inside, Jones couldn't help but smile.

The space was dusty and a bit run down, but everything reminded Jones of Mick. Expired food items lined the inside of the refrigerator, and the corners of the blankets weren't completely tucked in on the bed. Jones walked back out into a small kitchenette, and his eyes caught the security box above the refrigerator. If Jones's assumption was correct, this was the place Mick usually kept his journal and other valuables. With the safety box in hand, Jones walked over to the couch and placed it on the coffee table. A small thud sounded, escaping into the room and echoing across the emptiness in a tempting manner.

There are supposed to be no secrets between people who love each other, so there should be no secrets between people and androids who love each other either, Jones reasoned with himself.

Jones opened his device and searched the system for Mick Taylor's identification information. A slightly outdated photo of Mick appeared—or maybe it wasn't so outdated after all the time traveled to the future and back. Mick's young smile in the image stared back at Jones through the screen, and he felt himself grin at the sight of it. He scrolled down Mick's profile until he accessed his fingerprints. Jones found his thumbprint and shined the device up against the security box. The box scanned his thumbprint on the screen and clicked open.

Jones slowly lifted the lid off and was surprised at its contents. Inside lay a small device—one that looked like a much more advanced version of the prototype Jones last saw. Alongside the device were a few empty test tubes and a journal. Jones picked up the journal in awe. He wondered how this was even possible since the journal was sitting at home in their nightstand.

Does Mick have more than one journal? Jones wondered as he opened to the first page.

The first page was identical to the journal at their home in every way and so were the first few entries. Then things took a turn for the worse. The fourth entry did not discuss Julie going on a sabbatical or the improvements of the antidote. There was no last entry addressed to Jones or any mention of Jones needing to help him unravel the truth around The City and COLI*GO.

Instead, there were nearly a hundred entries—more ramblings from what Jones assumed was the future. A terrible, dark, and gloomy future. Horrified, Jones closed the journal and placed it back in the box as if it didn't exist.

This must be a mistake.

A small creak in the floorboards caught Jones's attention. He became very still, aware he wasn't alone. The floorboards groaned again as the weight of someone traveled across them.

"Can I join you?"

Jones lifted his head and nodded. There stood Colin O'Connor. His stance was stoic and intimidating, but his voice was quieter than Jones expected. The governor walked over and sat in the chair across from Jones. Colin's eyes wandered to the security box and back up at Jones.

"How did you know anyone was here?" Jones asked to break the silence between them.

"I was sitting in the dining room," Colin said, pointing out the large front window across the courtyard toward the townhouse. "I saw a movement here. The last time I saw movement, Mick was here. Or at least, some version of Mick."

Colin's choice of words revealed to Jones that he also knew about Mick's time travel.

How does Colin know about time travel . . . unless . . .

"It . . . It's you."

Colin took in a deep breath and shook his head.

"I have done many terrible things. Many, many terrible things, Jones. But to be honest, I don't know about all of them. I know most, and those horrors are hard enough to live with. What I really struggled was with knowing I couldn't fix It. I wanted to. But I couldn't. Until now."

Colin looked down at his hands before interlocking them together. The governor was a very deliberate man. All his movements and intentions had purpose and had been thought out meticulously. He was a man of power, driven by control and discipline. Everything had a plan, everything had a purpose. This all oddly made sense to Jones now.

"You killed Kathleen, didn't you?"

Colin stared at him in silence before averting his eyes away.

"And those other women. Kendra, Amanda, Lexi." Jones couldn't look at Colin as he said their names.

"It was responsible for their deaths," Colin said regretfully. "But since It is a part of me, then yes. I killed them."

Jones felt all his emotions showcasing on his scales. He was shimmering, the colors exploding around him so powerfully the room glowed in an iridescent sheen. If Colin noticed the emerald-green hue illuminating from Jones's scales, he said nothing about it, allowing Jones to be himself. Jones respected Colin's acceptance of Jones's true self.

"I want to be so mad at you. Actually, I am mad at you. I'm infuriated. But I feel . . ." Jones was struggling with the word; this was an emotion he had never experienced before.

"Conflicted?" Colin asked.

Jones looked up at the governor, confused.

"As if you know the right thing to do is tell someone about my confessions to you. Put me away in jail for my crimes. Or kill me. I deserve any of those options. But there is also a part of you that does not want to do any of that. A part of you that wants to help me because I want to help myself."

The governor was correct, and Jones finally understood this feeling now. He mentally filed it away and nodded.

"I need to ask you a favor, Jones," Colin said with sincerity. "I know how dangerous It is. I know how dangerous It makes me. So, I'm going to destroy him with Julie's antidote. I need you to take care of her if something happens to me in that process. If The Supreme finds out."

Jones did not expect this request from the governor. He thought Colin would act like a typical criminal: beg to not turn in his confession for the killings, ask Jones to plead mercy for him. This complicated Jones's feelings even more.

"Julie is the only person who has ever truly loved me," he said. "She is the only person I have ever truly loved."

Jones looked into Colin's eyes. He wasn't lying. The governor's admissions confused him. Jones understood most feelings about love. Or, at least, all the important ones. What he couldn't wrap his processor around was that Colin was the infamous serial killer and what Jones was going to do now that he knew this information.

"How did you know about time travel?" he asked Colin, the feeling of "discomfort" filling his body. He needed to change the subject but also needed answers. For Mick's sake.

"It told me. It has experienced time travel. It told me Mick is dangerous."

"That's ridiculous. Mick is afraid of It . . . of you," Jones stammered.

Colin shrugged his shoulders and shook his head. "Semantics at this point. Who are we to trust those who can travel through time?"

A sinking feeling filled Jones's stomach. He agreed with Colin's words.

"Regardless," Colin said, his hand extending out toward Jones. He held a small test tube filled with blood. "This might be the last chance anyone has at finding some answers. Maybe stopping It."

Jones took the tube and placed it in his pocket. The two men sat in the carriage house for a while, both of their gazes shifting toward the townhouse.

"One last favor," Colin asked, looking at him. "Julie knows

about It, but she doesn't know that I . . ." He looked down.

"She doesn't know you're the killer?"

"That's correct."

"Why didn't you tell her? Why did you tell me?"

"Because she and I have so much planned. When Celine is on maternity leave, Julie will run COLI*GO. There is so much she and I can accomplish for society while she holds such a powerful position. But we need to stop The Supreme. She's going to ruin The City, the peace and calmness I've worked so hard to build. Julie will never forgive me if she knows what I've done. She'll hate me and won't trust me. Trust is the only way we'll accomplish unity for the greater good."

"The greater good?" Jones asked.

"Yes," Colin said very seriously, looking up at him, "there is something much bigger going on. Much bigger than all of us that needs to be stopped."

"The posse hominems?" Jones asked.

"You know?"

"Yes, I know. I was the first on the scene for Lexi . . . well, myself and Dr. Garcia."

"Anna?"

Jones paused. Hearing her name was still difficult. Knowing how she felt about the O'Connors and even her own family also made Jones feel on edge. The way she was right, so right about who the killer was all along. Jones wanted her to desperately be wrong. Jones looked at Colin and took in the man one final time. He wasn't sure the next time he would see Colin, and he didn't want to miss anything. Jones found he couldn't stop looking at Colin's large hands. The hands he used to strangle so many women. The hands wielding the blade that brought demise to so many.

But those hands were attached to a man who wanted to do good, too. A villain with a glimmer of hope. A villain looking for redemption by destroying an even more ominous threat.

"I should get going," Jones said, standing up and running toward the door. He did not want to make any promises he couldn't keep.

***

Jones looked at the test tube of blood as he sat on the subway ride home. The subway was filled with many people and androids heading home after work. Eyes darted everywhere; discomfort and caution filled the car like the hot, muggy summer air. The stain of a murder in their precious City shined vividly in the horror and uncertainty across their faces.

He's not after you, Jones thought. *You're safe; he's not after any of you. He actually wants to save you.*

Colin didn't need to tell Jones why he killed Kathleen. Jones had that answer already: She was turned into a posse hominem. The Supreme had a larger plan for her creatures, and Colin was attempting to stop her. All his kills were to stop evil and prevent dangerous outcomes for The City. Jones and Colin agreed—that didn't make them okay; they were still horrific. Wrong.

But what was Jones going to do about this information? How could he go on investigating this case, knowing what he knew?

Jones stared back at the test tube. He did not need to ask whose blood was inside when Colin handed the vial to him. Jones knew the blood belonged to It. To Colin. Blood was a funny thing, a foreign concept to Jones since he didn't have any.

Jones pulled out a pen from his pocket and wrote "IT" in capital lettering across the blank sticker marking, the ink fresh and shiny. He hastily shoved the vial back inside a trouser pocket. The mysterious smudged label would make its way back in time and land in Mick's hands.

I'm the one who provides Mick with the mysterious blood sample.

The subway slowed down as it approached his stop. When he finally arrived home, Jones wasn't shocked to find the apartment empty.

No Mick.

He ran to their bedroom, relief flooding his processor when he saw the journal still in the bedside table. Jones opened it, flipping through the rough pages, allowing the scales on his hands to feel the softness in the leather that bound everything together. He wondered how there could be two journals. A second journal filled with dark horrors of a broken City.

Was Mick that sloppy in tracking everything? Jones couldn't be sure, and he wasn't in the mood to make logical sense of the illogical concept of time travel. He suspected his answers would disappoint Mick, but he had to share them.

Maybe Colin was right and there is a way for Mick to stop It before anything terrible happens, Jones wondered optimistically. *But wouldn't that change the outcome of the present if he were successful in doing so?*

Without giving it a second thought, Jones grabbed the pen from his bag and wrote to Mick—or as Colin had referred to him—some version of Mick.

***

"Jones? Are you there?" Julie's voice was on the other line.

"Yes, of course. How are you holding up?"

There was a brief pause.

"I'm okay. I'm worried about Colin." Her words were quiet and sincere. Jones closed his eyes at the mention of Colin's name.

"Would you be willing to stay with me for a few days?" she asked him, her voice very timid and scared.

"Of course. But what about Colin?" Jones asked, noting the sharp exhale that escaped his body.

"Colin asked for a few nights to himself. I don't want to be alone." Jones could hear the hesitation in her voice as she strung together a half-truth.

"Let me pack a few things, and I'll head over shortly," he said before ending the call on his device.

He pinged Mick and let him know he'd be at Julie's for a few days and to call him when he got home. Then Jones haphazardly pulled together some belongings into his overnight bag, checking a few drawers to make sure he hadn't forgotten anything.

The journal looked back at him as if it were alive in its own sense. Jones imagined hearing the beating sound of a heart protruding from within the journal. He paused for a moment before deciding to gently place the leather-bound notebook into the bag with his other belongings.

When he reached Julie's apartment, she looked like a complete mess. She stood before him in a baggy sweatshirt with the hood pulled all the way up over her head. The bags under her eyes were heavily pronounced as if she hadn't slept. He hugged her instantly, which she embraced in return. They stepped back into the quietness and comfort of her cozy studio. Julie was always a gracious host; her pull-out couch had already transformed into a bed with towels folded neatly on top of pillows in the corner. Jones placed his bag down and looked over at her.

He wondered if he should tell Julie the truth about Colin or if that would completely shatter her world. Jones admitted he understood many feelings and emotions, but some felt completely foreign to him. This idea of "conflict" that Colin taught him came to mind.

What is conflict, and how do humans decide right and wrong, knowing many times they would select the incorrect approach?

"Can we watch something? I mean, anything other than the news?" Julie's voice called out from her closet.

She pulled out dresses and laid them in an orderly fashion on her bed. He entered the bedroom area of her studio and watched her for a few more moments.

"Julie, what are you doing?"

She pulled herself out of the closet and looked up at Jones.

"The antidote is being presented for approval for Alzheimer's tomorrow. In front of the legislature. It's a big day. I need to look presentable. I'll be the face of COLI*GO soon." She turned back to continue her quest for the right outfit.

"They didn't postpone, with everything going on?" Jones broached the subject cautiously, sensitive to Julie's emotions.

"No. I thought they would, but they didn't."

"Okay," Jones said, noting the pain in her voice. He looked down at the clothing she laid out on the bed. "Don't you think it's a bit warm for turtleneck dresses?"

Julie did not respond; instead, she closed her eyes and instinctively brought her hand to her neck before pulling it away.

"I'm always cold in The Capitol Building. All the limestone and marble," she responded, turning away from him quickly. Jones shook his head and walked back toward the living room.

If she is going to lie to me about the bruises on her neck, that's her prerogative. At least now Jones's suspicions were confirmed. *The killer's ritual still occurred: There were no strangle marks on Kathleen's neck but rather on Julie's.*

Jones looked in Julie's direction to make sure she still remained preoccupied before opening his bag and pulling out the journal. He grabbed his pen and scribbled quickly one last note to Mick, hoping he could write what he needed before Julie reemerged.

Julie wasn't paying any attention to him as he walked toward the kitchen and opened the freezer. There wasn't anything inside except a few bags of frozen fruit and an ice tray. He wasn't surprised—he assumed Julie spent most of her time at Colin's townhouse.

Jones placed the journal toward the back. He wrapped the notebook in a hand towel, feeling somewhat responsible for the journal's integrity. He didn't want anything to happen to the pages. Then Jones opened the refrigerator and shoved the small vial of blood in the very back, behind several bottles of half-used condiments.

Chapter 44
The Supreme

May 30th, 46 A.R.

The last person The Supreme expected to engage with at The Courthouse was Representative Joel Kennsington. She hated the man—he was a Humanizer—but Colin also hated him.

Unfortunately, Joel Kennsington getting in Colin's head was a key element in her grand plan. They made awkward small talk in the hallway before The Supreme brought up Julie Walsh.

"Who?"

"The scientist at COLI*GO. The one who invented the antidote." The Supreme reminded him.

Joel's eyes widened; he did remember her for more reasons than the antidote.

"Didn't we recently approve that drug for Alzheimer's?"

"Yes," The Supreme said, rolling her eyes at Joel's forgetfulness.

"She's going to take over Celine's role when she goes out on maternity leave. The Board of Directors recently approved the motion. This is the first time anyone who isn't from an old bloodline family will hold such a position of power in our society," The Supreme said.

"How is that? I mean, she must be smart, but isn't she a bit young?" Kennsington asked, trying to put the pieces together in his dumb-witted mind.

God, it's like I'm playing chess with myself, The Supreme thought.

"She's only a few years younger than how old you were when you ran for office the first time. And the governor is quite fond of her."

"So, she's essentially useless to me if she's wrapped around Colin's finger," Joel said in an immature huff.

"Well, I wouldn't say she's useless. Julie is still learning, and that makes her impressionable. And she trusts me. I could help lean her in a direction away from the O'Connors if someone was able to show her that path." The Supreme looked at Joel with her large eyes.

He glanced away and sighed. The Supreme did not expect Kennsington to be a long-term strategic partner, but together, they had one person in common they didn't want in power any longer.

"I'll pay her a visit and evaluate her qualifications for myself," Joel responded before turning away from her. "As always, such a pleasure to speak with you, Madam Supreme." Sarcasm filled his voice. The Supreme rolled her eyes again and touched her exposed forearm.

The temptation of Colin having control over another aspect of The City bothered Kennsington. The room in The Courthouse was loud, filled with a palpable nervous energy. Jeb locked eyes with The Supreme. She looked back at him and smiled a wicked toothy grin.

His appearance in the orange jumpsuit made her think back to their conversation a few weeks ago. Jeb was unwilling to answer her messages and calls; his latest committed sin put him over the edge. Begrudgingly, he completed the task before heading out of The City on what he deemed "personal business" and returned a few days later. The look on Jeb's face as he sat across from her desk was beyond grim. He was lost, hopeless.

She knew Jeb didn't want to be part of this world anymore, no longer wished to do her bidding. But she also knew he didn't want to spend the rest of his life in jail for drug dealing and money laundering crimes. Together, they crafted a plan. The next day, Jeb turned himself in to the commissioner for only one crime: Kathleen Murphy's murder.

Today, the commissioner presented him in front of the high judge, another android appointed by The Supreme, who would determine the punishment terms.

Jeb didn't kill Kathleen—that had been Colin—but she promised Jeb she'd secure him the death penalty if he confessed to the crime. Jeb might end up in prison for a couple of years before the paperwork was all settled, but the execution would be a better outcome than spending a life sentence in a room barely fifty square feet in size with no sunlight for the rest of his human life.

The commissioner was thrilled to have a confession. People and androids felt more at ease knowing the murderer of Kathleen Murphy was finally behind bars. There was only one person who wasn't convinced of Jeb Taylor's guilt: Dr. Anna Garcia.

Isabella promised her sister wouldn't get in the way of any public matters and simply perform the job she was hired to do—examine dead bodies. So far, Anna remained quiet and dutiful.

"Mr. Jeb Taylor, you have been accused by the commissioner of The City in The Constituency of the following crimes: the kidnapping, drugging, and murder of Kathleen Murphy, of human origin. The punishment for a human murdering another human in The Constituency is the death penalty. You have the rights to a lawyer, which you have previously declined but may request at any time. Your last chance would be to plead not guilty and be tried by a jury of your human peers, in which a lawyer would be provided to you. How do you plead to the crime in which you have been accused?" the high judge asked without hesitation.

Humans and androids packed tightly together inside the courtroom filled the heavy air. The governor sat in the front of the room surrounded by Celine, Kathleen's husband, and her family. Isabella sat stately beside Colin while her sister, Anna, joined other police detectives in the row behind them. Detective Jones lingered on the edge of the row, his fingers tapping against his thigh.

Sitting farther back were members of COLI*GO: Julie, Marta, and Martin. Behind them, members of the media lined the back wall. The Supreme noted one individual who was nowhere in sight: Mick Taylor.

"Guilty," Jeb answered quietly.

"Is there anything else you'd like to say in front of your peers, Mr. Taylor?"

Jeb turned to face the room. The lines across his face appeared prominently in the harsh white lighting, the scars on his skin more apparent and paired with his sunken, darkened eyes. He had no life left in him; he was a defeated man.

"No matter what comes to light from here on out, please know

I cared very deeply for Kathleen. She was one of my best friends. I am so incredibly sorry that it had to be this way," Jeb said before the room began erupting into heated yelling, shouts, and name-calling.

The high judge banged his gavel loudly.

"Mr. Jeb Taylor, as the high judge for The Constituency, I deem you guilty of your crime and sentence you to the death penalty."

The room exploded again, louder and angrier this time. Obscene words floated around the room, calling Jeb a coward and bastard.

"The next court date where we will determine the timeframe for your sentence will be September 30th, 46 A.R," the high judge proclaimed before exiting through the doorway behind him.

A pair of android police officers escorted Jeb out of the room to avoid confrontation with the angry crowd. The Supreme remained patient as she watched everyone exit the room.

Everyone except Anna.

Anna carried herself with authority and purpose as she approached The Supreme and sat beside her. Both women stared straight ahead, refusing to look at one another.

"Why would an innocent man plead guilty to a crime he didn't commit, Madam Supreme?" Anna asked with a level of confidence The Supreme admired, especially in human women.

"Jeb Taylor is not an innocent man, Doctor."

"But he didn't kill Kathleen Murphy. Or Kendra Washington. Or Amanda MacDonald. Or any of those other women over the last decade."

"I'm fairly certain he wasn't accused of killing any of those women with the exception of Kathleen Murphy," The Supreme answered, her hand reaching out to grab Anna's face.

She clasped Anna's jawline violently, holding on with a firm grip before turning the younger woman's face to look directly at her. Anna's eyes widened in surprise and uncertainty, but The Supreme didn't register fear on Anna's face.

"You don't scare me."

"I don't intend to scare you, Dr. Garcia. But sometimes I think you don't appreciate the importance of a well-groomed plan. Things need to happen in a certain way." The Supreme allowed her grin to spread slowly across her face as she firmed up her grip on Anna's.

After a prolonged moment, she let go of Anna, noticing her scales were glowing very faintly on her arm. The amber colors were warm in tone, almost jewel-like in the bright lights.

"Here," Anna said, pulling a small clear evidence bag out of her pocket and handing it to The Supreme. "The commissioner gave it to me, but I didn't share this with anyone in the precinct like instructed."

The Supreme took Kathleen's microchip from Anna's hand. Anna hadn't bothered to clean the microchip, the stain of Kathleen's blood caked over the small technology. The Supreme placed the microchip in her pocket while Anna let out a large sigh before walking toward the courtroom's exit.

"You're right, Doctor," The Supreme called out, slowly approaching the exit.

Anna paused and looked back at The Supreme, a glimmer of determination sparked across her eyes.

"I know who killed these women. I'm going to gather enough evidence, prove who the real killer is, and expose him."

"I don't doubt you for a minute, my dear."

Chapter 45
Julie

June 23rd, 46 A.R.

The smell of the ocean overwhelmed Julie as she stepped out of the vehicle. Over the last few weeks, she and Colin escaped to the estate to fully concentrate on curing him of It. His first few doses were fairly straightforward with little to no side effects. Colin complained of a slight headache right after receiving each dose, but otherwise, he seemed optimistic. It hadn't returned since starting his treatment, and Colin didn't recall moments of amnesia or forgetfulness during the days that followed. Julie felt optimistic but reminded herself this was only his third dose. There were still twenty-three doses left.

Julie was glad she finally felt more at ease with Colin. For nearly a month after the night he strangled her, she found it very difficult to rest peacefully in the bed beside him. But she also couldn't leave him, knowing the hurt he'd feel if she went back to her own apartment each night.

Instead, Julie took naps in her office at COLI*GO during the day when she wasn't bogged down in meetings. But with time, Julie learned to trust Colin again in her most vulnerable state. The calmness of The Oceanside aided in her now restful slumber.

When Colin opened the front door of the home, Julie let herself smile. Today was another difficult day for Colin—his mother would be on his mind all weekend.

"How was the ride?" Colin asked as he embraced her.

"Not terrible. I finished a ton of work on my way down, which makes me happy because I can spend more time with you," Julie said and kissed him.

Colin took her weekend bag from her hand, placed his arm around her shoulders, and walked them into the house.

"I thought you were on sabbatical?" he asked with a

raised eyebrow.

"Just some preparation documents, nothing too crazy," she answered, noticing Colin playfully rolling his eyes at her. They left her things inside and went for a walk, enjoying the sunset.

Colin seems more himself today, more like the man I know, Julie noted. He talked about his mother fondly, recalling his childhood memories. There was no hurt in his voice, only happiness, and Julie held his hand tightly. *Maybe remembrance is its own type of cure.*

Things felt normal as they cooked dinner and ate outside under the stars.

"I like taking the injection before bed instead of before dinner. I'll hopefully sleep through the headaches," Colin said as he cleaned up the dishes from dinner.

"I think so, too." Julie reached into her bag and pulled out the dose of COL23.

She eyed the antidote with awe. The tiny vial still felt very surreal in her hands. The approval for Alzheimer's came through swiftly in the midst of Kathleen's death, and while bipolar disorder trials were still ongoing, Julie believed in Peter and his team.

Julie prepared the syringe with ease as Colin sat down next to her and rolled up his sleeve. She looked at the clear substance for a moment before piercing the needle into the skin on his upper arm. He flinched briefly and looked away as she injected the antidote. There wasn't even a drop of blood left behind after she pulled out the needle.

"All done." Julie smiled and set the syringe down beside the empty vial.

Colin pulled her into his lap, his embrace sturdy and strong. Julie leaned closer into his chest. He smelled like the ocean—he spent the afternoon down by the beach while she was still on her way in from The City. Knowing he took the time while they were at The Oceanside to fully disconnect from The Capitol Building made her happy: it was a good thing for his treatment and for them.

"I am starting to feel so much more myself," he said before taking a deep breath. "I don't want to hide us anymore after all this. I don't care what anyone has to say."

His words were soft but still said with confidence as he gently twisted the ring around her finger. Julie smiled at him, wanting to not hide their relationship anymore either. But they both knew this was a farfetched dream.

"The time will come when we can," she said optimistically.

Colin didn't respond, and instead, he closed his eyes peacefully as he held her.

***

Everything surrounding Julie's vision was blinding and a piercing light shone directly above her. Her eyesight became less fuzzy, and she noticed movement in her peripheral vision. She tried to move her body but found herself paralyzed.

Julie's hands shook, and a white sheet covered her from the chest down. Movement eased through her neck, and she tilted her head and observed her surroundings. The room was industrial, with metal drawers lining the walls and a cool-toned tiled floor stretching as far as she could see. Everything about this place felt familiar to Julie but so unfamiliar at the same time.

A small IV protruded from her hand, and Julie pulled it out hastily. A searing, sharp pain followed as a spray of warm blood escaped. The gore didn't matter to Julie. She didn't know where she was but needed to escape. And quickly.

Her legs disjointedly swung from the steel table, the sensation of her feet touching the frigid floor jolting through her whole body. The chill ran up her naked body as the sheet fell from her. Her legs didn't hold her up, and she went crashing down with a loud bang. Clinking filled her ears as a tray with surgical equipment collided with the floor alongside her.

Julie swiftly grabbed a scalpel from the tray, fearing she'd need a weapon to fight someone off. Julie crawled across the floor with the strength coming from her upper body as her legs stayed completely numb. She continued dragging her naked body toward the stairwell door, wanting to escape this disturbing, unknown place.

A scaly purple hand aggressively grabbed at Julie, yanking her away. She yelled and screamed, her shouts drowning around her as a syringe filled with clear liquid entered her vision.

Suddenly, Julie's eyes darted open to the sight of Colin's face in the dark shadow of the moonlight, his hands holding her.

"Julie! Are you okay?" Colin asked, his grip relaxing as he pulled her closer. She was shaking.

Her body felt warm even with the cool ocean breeze coming in from the open French doors. The sweat on the back of her neck and the flush running across her cheeks burned.

"What . . . what happened?" Julie asked. She continued trembling uncontrollably.

"You were screaming in your sleep. I think you were having a bad dream," Colin said, rubbing her back in slow, steady circles.

Visions of Julie's nightmare flooded back inside her mind, but she couldn't comprehend or remember enough to make any sense of the images swirling around.

"I was," she said slowly, "I was having a nightmare."

"Shh. The bad dream is all over, and everything is okay now," Colin said calmingly, running his fingers through her hair slowly.

Julie hugged him tighter, her exhaustion pushing its way back into her body. She was glad Colin didn't ask her about the bad dream; what Julie remembered haunted her thoughts, and she was afraid to close her eyes again. Instead, Julie focused on the sounds of the ocean waves crashing along the cliffs outside and the steady beating of Colin's heart beneath his chest until sleep finally overcame her.

***

Today was finally the day: Julie rode the elevator up to the 101st floor of the COLI*GO building and walked into an empty office.

She was finally the interim CEO.

The past month had flown by with Colin and their weekend escapes to The Oceanside. He continued experiencing headaches but otherwise didn't endure any night terrors or other disturbances. During the rest of her time off, Julie finally relaxed and cleared her own head a bit. She spent time with Jones and Mick, visited her father, and caught up on sleep.

Colin grew warier of The Supreme each day, but Julie didn't

want her to feel suspicious as she continued investigating The Supreme's actions at COLI*GO. During her transition process, Julie uncovered gaps and discovered variations among accounts. She didn't have all the puzzle pieces but was determined to place them together soon.

The view from her new office window showcased The River and the buildings across in The Hill. She loved being able to watch over The City from this vantage point, and her heart swelled with excitement as she settled into her desk.

Her device rang, startling her.

"Dr. Walsh, there is someone here to see you," the android from security said into the line.

"Oh," Julie answered, surprised. "Who is here to see me?"

"Representative Joel Kennsington."

Julie froze and held her breath. Joel Kennsington was the last person she expected a visit from, especially on her first official day in her new role.

"Uhm, send him in, I suppose."

She brushed her hair with her fingertips and straightened her button-down shirt before Joel made his way up to her office on the 101st floor.

Joel knocked lightly on her half-opened door, and she nodded at him as he entered. He stopped halfway to her desk and took her in with a stalking stare. His smile spread genuinely and hungrily as he picked up his pace toward Julie.

"Congratulations, Dr. Walsh. This is an impressive and proud moment for you, I'm sure."

"Please call me Julie. And this is only temporary."

Julie gestured her arm toward the empty chair opposite her, and Joel sat, leaning against the back of the chair and crossing a foot over his leg. He took up as much space as possible with his now lanky frame.

Joel looked at her intensely. Julie always thought of him as a volatile and ugly man, but staring back at him in this moment, she noticed that he didn't appear as ugly as before but rather more ordinary. He lost a bit of weight from losing the gubernatorial election last year, and his skin looked less flushed. His mannerisms hadn't improved much as he continued gawking at Julie with a peculiar glare that made her feel a bit uncomfortable and awkward.

"So," Julie said, "to what do I owe the pleasure of your visit?"

Joel chuckled at her. "Oh, I know I'm not a person you particularly want to see. I'm not completely inept."

"I do find it odd that you chose to visit me today, especially without an appointment."

"Would you have allowed me on your calendar if I tried to make an appointment?" Joel asked her with a knowing grin.

"Fair enough."

Joel relaxed his body a bit before shuffling his crossed legs in the opposite direction. The general enlarging gesture of his body didn't intimidate Julie. By now, she was used to men subconsciously making themselves appear larger in front of her. Joel's subconscious found her new position of power intimidating. Julie found it oddly satisfying. She continued smiling at him.

"I know it seems like I'm not a supporter of COLI*GO. You've made your distrust and dislike in me very known over the last year. But I do believe in the company's mission and strides in innovation. I just didn't think Celine O'Connor was the right person to lead the charge," Joel said, slowly smiling at Julie. "But I believe in you."

Julie curiously cocked her head to the side. She hadn't expected those words to come out of Joel Kennsington's mouth.

"You believe in me?" she asked with uncertainty.

"Yes, do you know why?"

Julie shook her head. She honestly couldn't fathom the reason as Joel leaned in closer to her. He placed his bony fingers on the chrome desk and let his hands slide along the edges.

"Because you're a nobody like me."

"Clearly that can't be the only reason you believe in me? Or are your standards that low?" Julie challenged him. Joel nodded as she asked this, clasping his hands together with enthusiasm.

"We have something in common, Dr. Walsh. Neither of us is from an old bloodline family. We have no true chance when it comes to complete control over The City or beyond. We'll simply never achieve it as long as the system is rigged." His eyes grew wild with excitement at divulging this insight with her. "And the system is rigged because old bloodline families still rule it. As nobodies, our intentions are driven by our convictions. From our ideals, our candid desire to help others. I know you don't think I'm a man who cares about others, but I do."

Representative Joel Kennsington's admission took Julie off guard. He'd learned to reign in and polish his language from running against Colin in the election. He was more stealth and serpent like than his previous demeanor. Julie remembered the first time she met Representative Kennsington, one floor above in the observatory at the party. The man looking at her now was different and unrecognizable from the one she always conjured up in her mind.

"The O'Connors, the Garcias, the Borgeses, the Ludewings, the other great family names of our Constituency . . . and The Supreme. Don't think you can leave The Supreme out of their association: She was raised by Henry O'Connor. There's something larger at stake for all of them. They don't understand common people or the androids they serve, whether it's serving them from The Capitol Building or here across The River in this high-rise corporate building. Everything is a game to them."

"I don't think that's necessarily true," Julie responded, feeling slightly defensive for old bloodline families, particularly because of her association with Colin.

Joel shook his head with a sarcastic smile before continuing. "Maybe not. But because you are no one and I am no one, I trust you. Until you decide to break my trust, Dr. Walsh. There are other representatives on both sides of the aisle who feel the same way. Humans and androids. We could instill real change; we could actually help our people and our androids with a partnership together. I've done everything to represent my people. To help them. That's why you started your whole career in science . . . to save people."

Julie's eyes widened at the representative.

"I've committed to making changes while I hold this position, yes," she responded, looking down at her engagement ring. She'd mistakenly kept it on her left hand before leaving the townhouse this morning. Joel's eyes followed hers, and a wolfish grin spread across his face.

"Have you thought about what you'll do after your year is up? You can't go back to a lab coat. Or marry a man and have his babies. That would be far below where you've worked so hard to come." Joel leaned over her desk, closing the gap between them.

Julie smelled his cologne and leaned away from him, hiding her hands under the desk.

"I'm not sure what you're insinuating, Representative Kennsington."

"By remaining a nobody, you are essentially everyone," he said, looking down at where her hands had previously been. "Consider who you continue to align yourself with, Dr. Walsh. Be careful of getting too close to Colin O'Connor. I wouldn't want anything horrible to happen to you."

Julie's hands shot up and lingered subconsciously across her neck before she stood. Joel followed suit. At least with him, she could look at him straight on when she wore her heels.

"Honestly, think about it. A revolution is coming. You want to be on the right side of it."

***

After a long exhausting day, Julie was surprised to find a package leaned up against her door when she arrived at her apartment. Colin was working late this evening, and she wanted to come home and take a hot bath in the confines of her own apartment. She missed this place and felt guilty not renting it out but also never spending any time here herself.

The package was dressed up as a gift and wrapped with a horizontal and vertical ribbon, a bow tied perfectly at the intersection. A small envelope peeked out on the side, and her name was printed neatly across the bold white cardstock in jet black ink.

Julie opened her door and carried the mysterious package inside. The contents of the gift were surprisingly heavy, so she placed it against the kitchen island before pulling aside the envelope. The note read:

You are the important bond for unity.

Julie didn't understand what the letter meant and looked at the package for a few moments in disbelief. She opened the box slowly, concerned about the "fragile" note printed on the side. Once the box was fully opened, time froze around her. Horror filled Julie to the core as she examined the canvas inside the box.

She rushed over to the sink and vomited vigorously. The bile in the back of her throat emerged a second time, and then again and again. With nothing left inside her stomach, Julie wiped her mouth and walked over to where the gift lay on the floor.

The painting stared back at her accusingly. The purples illuminated off the canvas, the bright blues and haunting pinks glared back at her forcefully. An emerald green harshly stood out against the other colors, illuminating off the mangled hand wrapped around the forearm of a man choking the woman's throat. The colors circled around a ring. A large emerald ring on the woman's left hand. Julie instinctively looked down at her own hand and touched her engagement ring.

Jeb Taylor's signature was sprawled on the bottom right-hand corner with a big loopy J and Y. The depiction he created with the paint felt so raw, so real, reminding Julie instantly of Colin. Of It. That night he strangled her.

She felt sick all over again, but there was nothing left in her stomach to release.

Julie wanted to cry but simultaneously felt the urge to scream. Rage seeped through her veins, a rare experience for her. There was so much anger inside of her, and she gripped the edge of her kitchen island to steady herself. Shoving the painting off the island, Julie allowed the seemingly expensive artwork to crash loudly against her cold floors.

The scream finally emerged from within her. All of Julie's pent-up emotions and stress from the last few months barreled out of her all at once. She hastily grabbed the note and studied the handwriting, recognizing its owner almost instantaneously.

Her fingers clawed at the note, ripping it to shreds. She watched the pieces fall to the floor and slammed her hands down loudly on the kitchen island. Without a second thought, Julie picked up the canvas and left her apartment. There was hell to let loose and an argument she needed to start and end this evening.

***

The Supreme's home was minimalist in design, but instead of cool, bright tones, the rooms were painted in dark colors. Mauve purples, deep reds, and dark chocolate wooden paneling engulfed her townhome, and the lack of decor reminded Julie of the hollow android who stood before her.

"Why did you send me this awful painting?" Julie asked The Supreme outright, standing in her entryway with a newfound confidence. If there was anything Julie learned from her time working with The Supreme at COLI*GO, it was that the android appreciated directness.

"I know, Julie. I've known for a while about you and Colin."

Julie looked at The Supreme perplexed. *We've been so careful. How could she possibly know unless Celine told her? But why would Celine do that to Colin?* Julie wondered, her mind racing as she played out as many memories of their time together as she could.

"I had my suspicions a long time ago," The Supreme admitted before grinning cruelly. "But those were confirmed when I saw you and Colin together that night after at the symphony. Might I recommend you remember to close your shades next time, Dr. Walsh? Unless you want the world to see the most powerful man in between your legs. I wouldn't blame you; that's quite the power move, my dear."

Julie's jaw dropped. She felt her cheeks instantly flush to a bright red with embarrassment from knowing The Supreme caught her and Colin in a very intimate act. The memories of that night flashed in Julie's mind: the night she learned she'd take over Celine's role, the black dress Colin had admired both on and off her. Julie was at a loss for words.

"You know, I always found it fascinating how humans subconsciously seek out their parents in their partners or grow up to be like their troubled parents," The Supreme noted as she grabbed a teacup from its saucer on the coffee table. "Colin doesn't realize just how much like his father he truly is. He loathed that man. But the way he acts with you is the same way his father would have continued on with Melanie if someone hadn't killed her."

She continued, "I'll admit I had a hand in Melanie O'Connor's demise but not directly. Unfortunately, androids cannot travel time. Yet. We don't have blood. But I'm working on that obstacle from all angles."

These admissions appeared to come easily for The Supreme. She must have believed Julie was still impressionable; that she could convince Julie to side with her on this crusade.

You're wrong. The invisible gears in Julie's brain turned, finally putting together her months of sleuthing across The Supreme's ledger accounts and Martin's missing Research and Development Department funds.

"I have since made the assumption Colin shared It with you, especially since he gave you his mother's ring," The Supreme said, her scaly hand grabbing Julie's in a rough manner.

The Supreme admired the emerald jewelry for a few moments before ushering Julie toward the living room and placing the painting down from Julie's embrace.

Julie felt tears pooling in the corners of her eyes, the jarring memories of that evening consuming her mind again. She and Colin had come so far, yet their progress crashed down around her by The Supreme's doing.

No, you cannot let her control or break you.

"When I originally found the painting in Jeb's studio, I thought about It. And I thought about you. It never mentioned you to me, Julie. I found that strange but realized It was probably threatened by you. I've always known It to be the one thing getting in the way of Colin's full potential, just as I've known you to be the one thing pushing Colin toward his full potential."

She took a seat on her couch and gestured to Julie to follow suit. Julie looked around sheepishly before joining her.

Colin has always protected me, whether he's himself or It. She realized this was why It never mentioned her to The Supreme, not because he was threatened.

"Colin and I have known one another almost our whole lives. I know what he likes, what drives him, and, subsequently, what he is driven toward." The Supreme's eyes looked Julie up and down in an intriguing manner. "But I've become quite fond of you, Julie.

I would never want anything to happen to you. I truly believe you could help bring significant change and innovation to The Constituency. I'm not the only one who feels that way. So, you have to decide which side you want to join—the one that connects society or the one that keeps the wedge lodged against unity."

*Joel Kennsington, The Supreme, COLI*GO, the unclassified projects, and the misdirected funds,* all the pieces continued coming together in Julie's mind.

"I suppose it was wrong of me to send you that painting as a gift," The Supreme continued, her hand lightly lingering against the brush strokes. "But I figured the painting could either serve as a warning or as a tool."

The two women sat in The Supreme's living room in silent reflection, taking in Jeb's wicked artwork and unknowing recollection of a night that hadn't even taken place yet when he painted it.

How did he know? How did The Supreme know? Julie wondered, her fingers dancing along the edges of her neck. *Time travel. Mick.*

"Only one of you can survive in Colin's life. Something tells me you figured that one out for yourself, didn't you?"

The Supreme stood up and guided Julie toward the entrance of her home. Julie turned and looked at the painting one more time, deciding to leave it with The Supreme.

The image didn't belong in her life.

As they approached the front door, the nighttime sky showcased no stars, but the streetlights remained bright, leading down The Hill toward Colin's townhouse.

"I hope you make the right decision. I won't mention this visit of yours to Colin, which would probably be for the best," The Supreme said. "For both of us."

"Fuck you." Julie slammed the door, pleased by her angry outburst.

Without having to lug around a canvas, Julie's footsteps lightly and quickly carried her down the cobblestone roads. She didn't veer to The Bay, and instead, the warmth and security of the O'Connor townhouse appeared.

The light was on in Colin's home office, and Julie entered the house quietly, ascending the stairs with delicate footing.

Knocking on the slightly ajar door, Colin looked up with a kind smile.

"This is a wonderful, unexpected surprise," he said from the chair in his study, his body relaxing a bit at the sight of her.

Julie didn't say anything in return; instead, she simply ran over to him, sitting in his lap before wrapping her arms around him. One of Colin's hands cupped the back of her head, and Julie felt him lean into her embrace.

"Are you okay?" he asked, whispering into her ear.

Julie couldn't bring herself to vocally answer but shook her head while holding back her tears. The Supreme might have known about them, but she underestimated their bond, their acceptance of each other.

Colin kissed her hungrily, his teeth grazing her bottom lip. Here with him, Julie let the horrible events of her night slip away. Being with Colin felt like its own therapy, a cure providing her with love she appreciated most.

"I was going to head to bed. My head is throbbing," Colin said before pulling away from their embrace.

Cupping his face in her hands, Julie noticed the slight bags under his eyes and the red tint of his skin. He looked exhausted.

"I didn't realize you were still experiencing migraines and tiredness from the antidote," Julie said, her hand lightly brushing Colin's forehead.

He closed his eyes. "I don't always have them. Some days I'm completely fine. Other days I'm not. I can't predict when or why."

"You don't have to. I'm sorry." Julie grabbed his hand and led him to the master bedroom.

She decided now was not the time to divulge the cruel conversation and threats between her and The Supreme to Colin. Julie now had a better inkling of what truly happened behind closed doors at COLI*GO. All she needed was a bit more proof to bring The Supreme down.

Chapter 46
Mick

September 30th, 46 A.R.

Mick wasn't sure if he wanted to attend his uncle's court hearing. Jones spent the last few weeks encouraging him that whatever decision he made would be the right one for him.

He spent weeks dwelling on the last few words he and Uncle Jeb exchanged with one another. Mick wanted nothing more than to close and lock his home office door, lean back in his chair, and travel time. The possibility of going somewhere else and not facing the issues in his present allured him.

Jones poured him a cup of coffee and sat next to him at their kitchen table.

"Do you want to go together?" he asked with sympathetic eyes.

"I think it's best if we go separately. I appreciate your support, but Julie promised to go with me already," Mick answered.

Mick thought he witnessed a glimmer of disappointment in Jones's face but looked past the feeling. Julie planned on attending the sentencing today but not to support Mick. Julie was friends with Kathleen, and more importantly, she cared about Colin.

As if on command, a slight knock sounded, and Julie peeked her head through the door.

"Hey," Julie said as Mick fully opened the door for her. She wore a modest black dress with a blazer hanging over her arm.

"If you'd rather stay here, I'll stay here with you."

"I appreciate that, Julie. I have to go; it's the right thing to do. Someone needs to show up for Jeb," Mick answered her slowly, closing his eyes.

Mick recalled Jones sharing with him how no one sat on Jeb's side of the courtroom during his hearing. Everyone in the room was there in honor of Kathleen Murphy. The thought of his uncle turning around to emptiness broke Mick's heart.

He and Julie headed down to the street and the vehicle outside waiting for them navigated through The City with ease. When they walked into the courtroom, the left side was packed with a large crowd of humans and androids. There were no more seats left, and the media lined up against the back wall. The right side remained completely empty, except for one man.

Mick's father.

Mick hesitantly approached the rows, pausing when he reached the one where his father sat.

"Mick?"

"Father."

The two men stared at one another for a few moments, unsure of what to say. They hadn't seen each other in almost a decade. The Taylor men were handsome, but their hard work and difficult lifestyles showed across their skin. Mick could tell his own father was surprised by how much his son had aged since he'd last seen him, but the man had the manners to not say anything.

"I didn't expect you to be here," Mick said.

"I originally wasn't plannin' on comin'. But Jeb told me I needed to get to The City. That I needed to make amends with you. And I decided I couldn't abandon him either."

This was one of the few times in Mick's life where he saw kindness in his father's eyes.

"How long will you be in The City?" Mick asked him.

"I have a ticket back to The Countryside tomorrow evenin'."

Silence passed between them uncomfortably and for too long.

"Mick." His father turned to him slowly. "I want you to know I forgive you. I'm not sure about the rest of 'em at home, but I do. And if you wanna come home, you can. And so can Jones."

Mick sat there in awe, his fingers gripping against the wooden seat beneath him. He never expected those words from his father. Mick opened his mouth and closed it a few times before he found the courage to answer his father.

"I'm not sure I'm ready for that, Dad. I have so much I'm doing here that I can't abandon. Not now at least. It's my duty to follow through. That's what you taught me."

A faint smile crossed his father's lips. "That's okay, Son. I wasn't sure what I was expectin' anyways. But know I will always welcome you home."

A sense of understanding and peace passed between them for the first time in so many years. Mick couldn't help but want to savor it, consume the foreign and special dish with enjoyment and ease. While Mick knew he would never return to The Countryside, there was a spark of hope in his father, and a weight lifted off Mick's shoulders. The room grew quiet around them, and the high judge, The Supreme, and an android detail escorting Jeb entered the room. While the actual verdict had already been decided, a sense of uneasiness filled the pit of Mick's stomach and crept all the way up to his throat.

Once the high judge took his seat, everyone else followed suit, but noise and chatter continued filling the room. The android judge cleared his throat and waited patiently for everyone to quiet down. Much like Jones, the high judge had green scales, but his were a deep hunter green, whereas Jones's were emerald and beautiful.

"Mr. Taylor, you have been accused of and charged for your crimes. Today, we have commenced regarding your execution date," the high judge said with authority.

Mick's eyes traveled to where Jeb stood before the judge. Uncle Jeb was squeamish and fidgety, a pure revelation of his nervousness and even regret. His leg bounced up and down uncontrollably, and his eyes blinked in rapid succession.

"After discussions with The Supreme, the commissioner, and the Android Crimes Analysis Unit, we determined your execution date will be December 31st, 56 A.R.: ten years, three months, and one day from today. From now until your execution date, you will remain in solitary confinement in the highest maximum-security facility in The Constituency."

"What?" Jeb asked loudly, the dark skin on his face paling with shock.

Hushed murmurs filled the room, growing louder by the second.

"You lying fucking bitch!" Jeb yelled, his fists wound into balls swinging in the air.

Everyone in the courtroom's eyes widened, and journalists in the crowd showcased their devices to capture the moment.

"You told me it would only be one to two years! You lied to me!" Jeb exploded as his shoulders checked into the android police officers surrounding him, knocking one of them over.

A small pocketknife emerged between Jeb's hands, the light reflecting off the clean, sharp blade. The energy in the room shifted as other onlookers noticed Jeb's weapon.

"This man is deranged and dangerous! He has a weapon!" the commissioner yelled over the shouts in the room. Humans and androids screamed, trying to escape in a massive stampede.

Mick stood completely still, watching as his uncle attempted to flee. Jeb was quick on his feet and darted between androids and the commissioner in swift movements. The commissioner leaped in front of The Supreme, the target of Jeb's fury.

Three detectives, including Jones, jumped to their feet and surrounded Jeb. He sliced the knife in wide motions toward them, threatening the androids to back away from him.

"Please, Jeb, put down the knife!" Jones shouted, holding his police-issued revolver up horizontally with his line of sight.

"I didn't do it! I didn't kill Kathleen! The Supreme made me confess! She told me it wouldn't be long or painful. She lied!" Jeb screamed, wiggling the knife against his hands to free himself from his handcuffs.

"Jeb, put the knife down," Jones said more sternly this time, slowly approaching him. The clinking sound of the handcuffs snapped, followed by a squeaky noise of Jeb's rubber shoes on the tile floor. The whole room spun in circles in Mick's vision as the bang of a gun firing echoed through his ears.

When Mick opened his eyes, confusion surrounded him. People and androids ran out of the courtroom in complete fear, and all three detectives had their weapons pulled.

Jeb lay on the floor, a small pool of his own blood surrounding him. His eyes remained wide open, looking up through the skylight and taking in the last bit of sunlight he would ever see.

Jones locked eyes with Mick, his hands shaking slightly as he put his weapon back in its holster. Mick knew from the look in Jones's eyes that his uncle was dead or at least dying.

Did Jones purposefully aim a shot that would kill, a simple act of mercy? Mick contemplated the thought, unsure of reality. But he was sure of what he saw across the room; the small sinister smile on The Supreme's face as she stood in the shadows behind the commissioner.

***

Peter told Mick to stay home for a few days and encouraged him to take some time to digest his feelings. Decompressing wasn't easy for Mick, and staying home made him grow more anxious and uneasy. He and Jones danced around the subject of Uncle Jeb's death and never actually addressed the issue growing between them: a bad habit they lately fell into more often than not.

This digression upset Mick because, prior, he and Jones had a positive rhythm in their relationship. Now, they avoided each other.

Mick looked over at Jones across the bed. Jones always slept peacefully when he powered down his processor for the evening. The moonlight cast a tiny sliver of light over his scaly face, allowing the shimmer to flicker across his body in an odd delight. Mick kissed his forehead before quietly escaping the apartment and heading for the subway.

He approached the COLI*GO building, expecting very little activity in the middle of the night. The few security guards scurried across the hallways in the lab, smiling awkwardly at him as he held up his badge.

Like most mid-level employees, Mick shared his cubicle space, and a tiny little partition was the only thing separating him from his desk mate. He was surprised to find Nolan seated at his desk like it was mid-morning in the middle of the week, not the middle of the night.

"Nolan, it's late. What are you doing here?" Mick asked, taking a seat. Nolan looked up at Mick and smiled peculiarly, the way many androids did when unsettled with the experience of an emotion. Nolan's blue hair and violet scales gave him a ghostly look in the harsh nighttime lighting of the building.

"You know, sometimes I lose track of time," Nolan answered in a monotone voice before grabbing his device and punching at the keyboard purposefully. "But I could ask you the same thing, Mr. Taylor."

The two sat in silence, the only noise being the soft hum of high-tech laboratory machines surrounding them. Mick's heart dropped a little when he heard Nolan's device chirp beside him, disturbing the otherwise peaceful moment they shared. Nolan answered, his conversation very bland and unassuming if Mick hadn't been paying attention.

"Okay, I'll be right there, Dr. Garcia."

Mick's heart picked back up, the noise of it beating so loud in his own ears.

Why is Nolan speaking with one of the Garcia sisters? Mick wondered as Nolan rose from his seat and walked past him without any acknowledgment or goodbye.

Mick waited a moment, unsure if he should stay in his seat or indulge in his curiosity by following the android. Nolan was a fairly fragile and skinny-looking android, but his footsteps exploded loudly in the lab as he descended the back stairwell. Mick rose from his seat and kept a bit of distance between them. He wasn't sure what was in this underground level of COLI*GO, but his unconscious curiosity forced him to continue climbing down.

Is this the infamous lower lab?

Mick held his breath, hidden deep in the shadows, as Nolan raised his left hand to the door. The security pad scanned Nolan's fingerprint and granted him entry. Once the door closed behind him, Mick crept closer. His heart continued beating heavily inside him as he peeked through the tiny window in the top quadrant of the door. His jaw dropped slightly as his glasses pressed against the door. Behind was a laboratory resembling an operating room: sterile walls and floors, large shiny steel tables on wheels, and unfamiliar instruments.

The weight of a hand fell unexpectedly on Mick's shoulder, and he jumped out of his skin. Facing him was none other than the famous Isabella Garcia. Mick stuttered, unsure of what to say to the beautifully intoxicating woman in front of him. Isabella didn't appear startled or concerned by Mick's presence but rather welcomed him with a seductive smile.

"Mick Taylor," she purred softly. Her voice was very soothing, like warm milk stirred into espresso.

"You know me?" Mick finally asked, smelling her perfume as she inched closer to him.

"Of course I know you. Well, I know of you."

Her hand fell from Mick's shoulder, crossing his body as she gently wrapped her fingers around the door handle behind him.

"Would you like to see my laboratory?" she asked him, her eyes warm and dewy.

Mick nodded slowly as if he had a choice. Even if he was given one, he was so entranced by Isabella's beauty and the pure confidence in her stride. Isabella opened the door with her fingerprint and gestured for Mick to follow her inside.

"The Supreme told me about you and what you've been working on." Dr. Garcia's voice was enchanting.

Mick understood why everyone felt so fondly toward her. She was calm, striking, and intriguing. Mick was entranced by her presence. He felt guilty wondering why Colin O'Connor would risk giving up this woman for someone simple like his friend Julie.

"Have you ever been curious about time travel, Dr. Garcia?" Mick asked, surprised by his own confidence.

She smiled up at him as her hands lightly browsed across the strange wall of tiny doors. Mick observed how small Dr. Garcia was, and his mind wandered back to Colin O'Connor.

I wonder how a man like Colin O'Connor feels in her presence. A man who stood near six and a half feet tall with large unforgiving hands.

"If I could go back, I'd definitely tell myself a few things. I'd warn myself," Isabella answered honestly, her eyes drifting back to the tiny doors along the metal wall.

Her hand stopped at the last handle. She pulled it open with a bit of force, and Mick was horrified to find a human body lying there. The woman's chest rose and fell in slow deep strides, and Mick realized she was still alive.

"Why are you surprised, Mick?" Dr. Garcia asked, stopping to look at him.

"I . . . I don't know."

"You know I'm a surgeon by training." Her words were quiet but confident.

"Yes, I know that," he said, the shock still recoiling throughout his body. The woman on the metal slab was unfamiliar to Mick. Her eyes were closed peacefully, unaware of what happened around her.

"Unlike my betrothed, I don't find joy in killing people, Mr. Taylor," Isabella said with a lightness in the tone of her voice. "I find joy in keeping my patients alive."

Mick chuckled nervously in response and inched closer to her.

"I assume either The Supreme told you about her experiments here, or you've seen these patients of mine out in the streets in the future when you travel."

She placed her hand against the woman's cheek, affectionately stroking it before pulling out a tiny device. Isabella took her biometrics and vitals, smiling. Mick assumed the woman was healthy as his eyes gravitated toward the large center table in the middle of the room. Various cubbies with a wide assortment of personal items lined the tabletop.

Mick's eyes lingered, recognition passing through his mind at some of the artifacts that lay there, but Isabella grabbed his face in her tiny hands.

"Can you tell me what happens, Mick? Can you tell me I'm not doing this all out of some sick greed of The Supreme's? That there is some good that stays in The City?" Isabella asked, a slight tremor of fear ringing through her lovely voice.

He eyed her up and down, pulling his chin away from her grip, but she held on tightly.

"The future can change, Dr. Garcia. I've seen many different futures. Some are horrific. Crime-ridden streets, fear, hunger, and famine. Others are lovely and peaceful. Beautiful blue skies and acceptance. It all depends on what we decide to do here and now."

She let go of him and nodded, acknowledging the regret surging inside her.

"What happens if you change the past?" Isabella asked.

Mick's eyes widened.

"It's honestly hard to say. Why?"

"I wonder if there's anything I can do to right my wrongs," Isabella said slowly, her eyes moving toward Nolan and making sure he wasn't eavesdropping on their conversation. She examined Mick deeply as if she was aware that he did, in fact, know of her sins in this world. "Without a doubt, I would do anything to fix them."

"Well, luckily, you don't need to change your past in order to do so," Mick said with a kind smile.

Chapter 47
The Governor

October 18th, 46 A.R.

Headaches plagued Colin more prominently at the beginning of his treatment, but even to this day, they wouldn't go away. His migraines never gave up—fiercely crossing his mind, taunting him insufferably. Colin found solace in only having two more months of the antidote left. He couldn't concentrate in his office at The Capitol Building lately and often found himself escaping to his home office. The space in The Capitol Building haunted him after Kathleen's death. He saw her everywhere, could even hear her voice. Sometimes, Colin believed he smelled the flowery scent Kathleen wore. He hadn't found the courage to replace her yet, despite the urgency and constant nagging from The Supreme and other members of The Legislature.

Colin's heightened sense of discomfort from his demanding schedule and lack of time management grew exponentially. Tonight, he and Julie were supposed to visit Celine and Martin and officially meet the newest addition to the O'Connor family, but he didn't see an end in sight to his drowning level of legislative paperwork.

Baby Henry O'Connor, Jr. graced the earth in July, but Celine had been hypersensitive to visitors. Colin was surprised to learn Celine named the baby after their father, a man who was so spiteful, especially at the very end.

"If you had a girl, would you have named her Melanie?" Colin had asked, looking straight into her eyes.

"No," Celine responded before turning off their video call.

Colin's hands lingered across the old mahogany desk in his study as he attempted to soothe his raging headache. The engraved wood was sentimental, the golden handles reminding him of a time of craftsmanship and power. A strange strong pull forced his hand to the bottom drawer. It glided open with an easy pull at the handle. He expected the bottom drawer to remain empty because he hadn't put anything there. Instead, a small unrecognizable cardboard box lay inside.

He grabbed the box carefully, placing it on top of the desk. In a state of complete curiosity, Colin lifted the lid and peered inside.

His discovery revealed a pair of strange objects. One resembled a peculiar pair of glasses and the other a tiny square but futuristic box. Upon closer observation, Colin determined this device looked similar—but less advanced—to the one Jones had in the carriage house. A time travel device.

How did this end up here? he wondered curiously. *It.*

Colin leaned back in his chair, completely perplexed. His fingers tapped the wooden desk, and he found himself smiling at the intricacies in the design, particularly the glasses.

Has anyone else taken the time to appreciate the artful details in this device? he wondered as his fingers caressed the engravings.

There were small dials that moved up and down, a spot in the center that was a bit stained and browned over time and usage. Small engravings encompassed the edges, resembling the outline of a phoenix. The mystery behind how It obtained such a clever piece of technology made Colin's eyes rise in curiosity. But an unsettling feeling in his gut grounded him in reality.

Did The Supreme give It . . . give me . . . this?

Colin heard Julie's light footsteps down the hall before she peeked her head hesitantly in between the doorframe of Colin's office. A small knock on the wooden door filled his ears.

Thump. Thump. Thump.

"Come in," Colin called out to her. He returned the device to his desk drawer and closed it gently.

Julie walked into the study smoothly, wrapping her arms around him from behind his chair and nuzzling her face into his neck.

"Are you ready? We're going to be late," she whispered into his ear.

Colin nodded, and they headed over to Celine's condo. Celine lived close to The City's river, the true border between The Hill and The River neighborhoods. Her home was decorated in a minimalist style, varying differently from her childhood at a warm and historic townhouse.

When they arrived, Celine opened the front door with a wide smile and large embrace. Her eyes looked worn and tired, the crow's feet more pronounced than Colin previously remembered. Martin also appeared tired, but his deep olive skin helped hide the bags under his eyes more so than his sister's. Colin shook his hand, the facade of being chummy with his brother-in-law didn't fool anyone, but he wanted to try now; this man had made him an uncle after all.

The baby boy was beautiful, and having a new member of the O'Connor family was a cause for celebration. Celine poured them all glasses of champagne and handed the baby to Colin. Baby Henry looked up at Colin with such wonder and amazement.

Colin assumed he'd already have children by now, but the timing had never been right. Colin blamed It for that; he never wanted to bring a child into this world knowing how It possessed him sometimes. What It could be, what It could do. But with It gone—or almost gone—Colin couldn't help but wonder at the possibility. Especially looking at the smile on Julie's face, the flushness of her cheeks.

The freshness and newness of the baby's skin, along with his big grin, touched a part of Colin's heart he didn't know existed. He handed the baby over to Julie, and he settled into her arms. The baby wrapped his tiny hand around Colin's pointer finger and grinned. Colin returned the smile and looked up at his sister. She smiled at him, her usual aloofness disappearing as the sunset shone behind her. Eventually, Celine and Martin took Henry Jr. upstairs, and Colin and Julie headed back home.

The night was warm, and between the short distance from Celine's condo to the townhouse and the quiet, dark streets, they indulged in walking back. Normally, Colin and Julie never went in public, afraid someone would recognize them together. Especially now that she was somewhat famous in The City.

Being with Julie outside, in the public streets of The City, felt invigorating and slightly wicked. A rarity and indulgence.

"Do you think children will ever be a part of our family?" Colin asked her.

The charming historic streetlamps illuminated softly against the freckles on Julie's face as she smiled, grabbed his hand, and interlocked her fingers with his.

"Yes, someday."

***

The nightmare was horrifying, the first nightmare Colin experienced since starting his treatment of the antidote.

He and Julie were at The Oceanside, meandering along the cliffs as she held on tightly to his hand. But there she was again, standing in front of Colin instead of by his side. He still felt her hand in his, so he looked over, only this time, it was his mother staring back at him. Colin felt like a small child about to witness something unexplainable, something horrible. Like the child on the beach that day his mother died.

In the nightmare, the woman holding his hands became Julie again. Her face continued morphing, jagged across her cheekbones. Blood poured out of her ears, her nose, and her eyes before, suddenly, her face returned to its normal state again. Colin turned his head and looked away, the sight of her too gruesome for him.

He faced the other Julie, the one standing in front of him. This Julie's face wasn't mangled but instead, her abdomen bled. Stab wounds covered her, and her hands gripped onto herself tightly, as if to hold herself together. To keep her organs from falling out of her.

Colin let go of Julie's hand, allowing her to wander forward without him. She approached the other Julie, and the two eyed each other intently. The throbbing sound of waves crashing against the cliffs intensified, and everything began to spin.

Right before Colin's eyes, one of the Julie's pushed the other right off the ledge of the cliff, her body dangling in the wind as it viciously crashed below.

Colin's eyes whipped open with a shockingly strong force, his breath panting rapidly. The room was dark, but he was in The City, not The Oceanside, and Julie was resting beside him, sound asleep and oblivious. He observed her naked body. Her skin was untouched, no wounds accounted for. He laid his head back down on the pillow, hoping to eventually find sleep. The night sky broke into a morning blue, betraying him as the sunlight filled the room.

God, how I wish I could have taken one of those sleeping pills instead of enduring a restless night, Colin thought selfishly.

He felt Julie curl into him, her body tiny compared to his underneath the sheets. She was a bit chilly, cooler than normal. Her arm wrapped around his chest, pulling herself closer to him. He loved the smoothness of her skin, the way she fit with his body.

"How did you sleep?" she asked without opening her eyes, her lips planting soft kisses along his shoulder.

Colin didn't answer her and instead ran his fingers through her hair. He was afraid to tell her he had a night terror and that his headaches worsened.

He was afraid this meant the antidote wasn't working.

***

Colin forced himself to concentrate inside The Capitol Building. Luckily, wanting to avoid thinking about his nightmare allowed him to accomplish much on his to-do list that day.

Kathleen would have been proud, he thought as he finished writing up his comments on the latest piece of legislation The Representatives of The People put forward.

A knock on his door made him lift his eyes up in uneasiness. Colin was surprised Joel Kennsington stood in the entryway of his office. He secretly missed their messy confrontations and decided to indulge his wicked side.

"Come in, Representative Kennsington," he called toward him.

"How are you holding up, Governor?" Joel asked, taking a seat without being told he could.

The man really has no manners.

"I'm doing fine, considering the circumstances," Colin replied, leaving it at that. He needed to remain strong and confident in front of the face of the Humanizer party.

"Are you at least taking care of yourself during these difficult times?" Joel asked, leaning his body closer to the edge of Colin's desk.

"I'm not sure what you're implying there," Colin started before Joel interrupted him.

"I want to make sure you're okay. Sound of mind and all."

Colin knew instantly The Supreme was using Joel Kennsington as a pawn on her board against him. Joel never thought about these nuances. She hated Joel with every fiber in her being, but this wasn't beneath her. Colin refused to fall for this façade.

"Really, Representative Kennsington, I understand and appreciate your concerns. But I'm fine. Things are still moving forward; our legislature is actually in a very healthy balance right now. Thanks to all of us."

Joel sat back and grinned. He slapped his hands on Colin's desk before getting up.

"Don't worry, Colin, making a social call doesn't mean I actually give a shit about you. Nothing has changed there. I'll continue my mission to make sure you don't get re-elected. Your time in The Capitol Building is limited," Joel spat back.

"You really think that's the case? I slaughtered you in the race." Colin's voice escalated in annoyance. "I humiliated you in that gubernatorial election."

"I'm not speaking about myself; I'll stay in The Legislature," Joel said with a menacing laugh. "There's a bigger picture, a bigger plan at play."

"I don't know what else to tell you other than I have a good twenty or so years left in me to run this office, to run The Constituency. The people love me. I care about them. Unlike you," Colin said through his teeth.

"You'll be old news by the next election cycle. There's younger blood thriving at COLI*GO. The people will eventually see you for what you are: old bloodline scum. You're not relatable, and there's no affiliation you have with the public." Joel grinned like a small gleeful child. "There's a nobody who finally has a say in The City. A nobody who finally has power. The people will love her more than they love you. She's made herself a somebody—albeit by using you. I don't blame you, Colin. She's enticing. I probably would have fallen for her seduction, too."

Joel strutted out the door, his disgusting and piggish laugh echoing deafeningly in Colin's office chamber.

Oh Joel, The Supreme has misguided you. She doesn't know what Julie and I planned together.

***

Tonight was worth celebrating. Tonight, Julie would administer Colin's last dose of the antidote.

Colin barely had time to greet her as she came home, her eagerness almost greater than his own. Julie pulled out the tiny vial of COL23 and the syringe.

The antidote.

Her hands shook slightly with excitement as she filled the final dose and walked back over to him.

"Wait," Colin said, smiling up at her.

Julie looked at him intensely with eagerness. She was truly stunning to him with her messy bun and the wrinkled crease marks stretching across her work blouse and skirt.

"I wanted to tell you something first."

"Okay . . ." she said slowly and tentatively, gently placing the syringe down on the coffee table.

"I can't describe my gratitude, Julie. You've shown me nothing but love throughout all of this. And you not only showed me love but also gave me the greatest gift of all. Myself," Colin said, grabbing her free hand. "You stayed through my darkest moments and believed in me."

He breathed all of Julie in as he embraced her, a sense of complete relief filling him with indescribable joy. She held back soft tears and kissed him. He was ready for the last dose of the antidote.

Julie pierced his skin one final time with the needle. Something about the sensation felt different, but Colin realized it was a trick of his mind in the complete delight of this evening.

They didn't do anything overly elaborate to celebrate. He lit a fire in the fireplace, the warmth and crackle relaxing around them as he held her in his arms.

When he woke the next morning, Colin didn't physically feel any different than he had the night before and was surprised to find himself on the couch and not in his bed. The fire had simmered down on its own, and Julie was where she belonged: curled up beside him. He cleaned up the coffee table and held the vial gently in his hand. The lettering was crooked on the bottle, a slight defect in the printing of the label. His heart accelerated in his chest, and an unsettled feeling crept in.

Colin shook his head and rubbed his eyes slowly, kissing Julie's forehead before leaving the living room. He brewed coffee for them in the kitchen and wandered over to the first drawer in the island. He hadn't thrown away any of the vials since they began his treatment. A sick but sentimental memento of this time in his life.

He placed all the bottles next to each other on top of the marble. Some of the bottles resembled the vial on the coffee table and others looked perfect with no label printing defects. Colin's thumb traced the lettering, concealing everything except the two numbers: twenty-three.

His heart stopped in his chest. Twenty-three. June 23rd killed his soul and his mother. Twenty-three stab wounds killed his victims. And now, the number twenty-three saved him. Cured him. So, why were some of the bottles different from the others?

Colin shook his head. Julie had to sneak vials out of the lab in the COLI*GO building to treat him. He didn't know how she sourced the antidote, but he trusted her.

Maybe some are manufactured in the lab and others are manufactured in the production facility. Colin took a deep breath and put the bottles back in their hiding spot. *I really need to stop being such a control freak. No more second guessing with those I love and those who love me.*

Chapter 48
It

November 3rd, 46 A.R.

It hated this dark room. He'd been trapped in here for months and months on end. Or at least he assumed he'd been stuck here for months. Time was difficult to understand in this strange place.

When he first arrived, the door was covered in a sticky substance he couldn't identify, blending into the walls and becoming one with them. The element resided everywhere around him like a growing slippery fungus. He hated the feeling across his body; he was concerned the stickiness would get inside of him, infect him, and turn him ill.

It wasn't sure how he came to the room, other than remembering waking up here. It couldn't see very clearly at first. Shadows surrounded him, and he had no idea what time it was. Even more troubling, he was alone. There was no sound except for the echo of his own footsteps pacing back and forth impatiently for days on end. He also wasn't sure how much time passed before the silence and darkness drove him mad. Or if the madness was in fact, from breathing in this mysterious substance surrounding him. He couldn't concentrate and felt suffocated, with only his thoughts to keep him company.

He needed an escape.

It tried banging his way out, his fists pounding the oddly dark, flesh-colored walls.

Thump. Thump. Thump.

After giving up, It took the time to fully appreciate his entrapment. He was mesmerized by this exotic room he was detained in. Then he grew terrified.

The soft, pulsating pinks hinted toward a purple tone as the wall continued up and out of his line of vision. The walls went on forever; there was no ceiling. Sometimes, everything around him was glowing, peaceful. Other times, the colors vibrated viciously, mocking him as a prisoner inside them.

No matter how often or how ferociously his fists beat the soft, squishy walls, there was no response. He continued pounding harder and harder. Still nothing.

Eventually, It grew tired, but sleep was not an easy task and his mind played tricks on him. When It closed his eyes, he sometimes saw the outside world. Not always, but sometimes, which gave him a false sense of hope. They were only flashing moments, and he could only believe what he saw was real.

Colin's desk at The Capitol Building. The full legislature in session. The reporter's sleek device shoved into Colin's face outside The Courthouse. Isabella's hand grasping desperately at Colin's. Kathleen's mother's embrace and the tears uncontrollably escaping her. Colin's gentle words of condolence. The waves crashing against the cliffs at The Oceanside. Julie falling over the edge only to end up beside him moments later in bed. Celine's newborn baby and his bright steely blue eyes gazing up with all the curiosity in the world. Another O'Connor. Joel Kennsington's disgusting laugh. A sensual moment of Julie's lips on his neck, her tantalizing legs wrapped around him. Around Colin, that is.

And the vial. It saw the shiny syringe once or twice in her delicate hands. The crystal-clear drug inside.

The fucking antidote.

None of these visions made sense to It. He never experienced them in full; as quickly as he observed them, he found himself back inside this room, this horrific prison. The one pulsating around him, the one too quiet that the noiselessness became so intensifying, so loud. Now the walls were alive, beating rapidly, constricting It in on himself. Vein-like ripples protruded vividly throughout, taunting him before disappearing and resurfacing elsewhere unpredictably.

This was worse than any night terror, any nightmare.

The space continued shrinking each day. Soon, It could barely maneuver around the room except for a few strides. He wondered what would happen to him: Would the walls crush him together, splinter his bones into thousands of pieces, and force his eyes to pop out of their sockets? Or would this place simply eat him alive?

When bashing his hands along the walls didn't work, It screamed. All the madness bubbling up inside of him erupted instantly: the vicious, ugly sounds of anger exploding from between his lips as his whole body unearthed venomous reverberations.

That didn't work either. But It was resilient.

In complete desperation, It bit and clawed at the walls. The spongy feeling lingered between his teeth, slipping out the corners of his mouth like greasy ground meat. He cleaned out the gooey substance from underneath his fingernails each time he dug into the incisions he made in the wall.

It persisted. He would always persist. And luckily for him, today, after so many uncountable days in his imprisonment, a light shone through the bottom of the walls.

It lay down, wanting to see if the outside world was really just beyond this room of hell and had been inches away from his fingertips this whole damn time. He reached out, clawing at his former dents made into the wall, ripping them apart as energetically as he could. As he attempted his grand escape, the bright light blinded him. It closed his eyes, shielding them from the painful sensation searing through his body.

When It opened his eyes, he was back in the O'Connor townhouse. He smelled the remnants of a fire, the remnants of Julie.

His eyes widened, taking in the sunlight again, basking in the warmth. It strode over to the staircase and climbed with a lightness and ease despite his wobbly legs. He made his way to the master bedroom and paused. He approached the window curiously as a flash of movement crept across the courtyard.

The figure of Mick Taylor in the carriage house captured his attention. But as suddenly as Mick appeared, he was gone.

***

"I'm glad to see you, my friend. You've been gone far too long," The Supreme said from across her desk at The Capitol Building.

"Did you have no faith in me? Didn't think that I would escape that hell, that prison you sent me to?" It viciously spat at her.

"Oh," she said, taken aback, "you think I sent you there? No, my friend. I'm the one who rescued you. I guaranteed your safe return. Who do you think switched out the remaining doses of the antidote with a placebo? The poison that trapped you in that hell hole?"

"The antidote? The antidote did this to me?"

"Yes. Julie realized by poisoning you, she could control Colin. The weaker you are, the stronger of an influence she holds on Colin. I discovered her intentions halfway through but was afraid my intervention was too late. But you're right, I underestimated you."

It sat back for a moment, taking all this fresh information in.

"I have to destroy her."

The Supreme laughed lightly. "What if I told you I could control her?"

"You can control her?" It asked with interest, leaning closer to her.

"Well, when I activate the microchip I put in her brain, yes. I haven't activated the technology yet. But when I do . . ." The Supreme's fingers curled around one another with a glimmer of satisfaction running across her face. She was terrible at hiding her understanding and feeling of emotions today, It noted.

It thought for a moment.

The one advantage he had over The Supreme was her not knowing he hated her. He spent his life leading her to believe they were friends, allies conspiring against Colin.

In reality, It always looked out for Colin. And Colin trusted Julie. Colin rarely trusted anyone. It did not want The Supreme to succeed in their sick, twisted game. That's why he convinced Colin to kill all those women. They reminded The Supreme of his tenacity, his viciousness. They also posed a threat to the delicate peace Colin spent years of his life building.

At all costs: The Supreme cannot succeed.

Now The Supreme put It in a difficult position. Colin would not want to kill Julie. He actually wasn't sure if Colin had the wherewithal to complete the task. But if The Supreme could control Julie, The City would crumble. Julie was too influential now; people believed in her. A dumb, irresponsible man like Joel Kennsington even recognized Julie's potential. Androids believed in her.

People believed in her. The City believed in her. And belief was infectious and dangerous. If The Supreme could control Julie, all their dreams for a better society would crumble.

Now It wondered if Julie used Colin for her own advantage, or if The Supreme had a hand in that as well.

Why else would she have tried to weaken me instead of accept me? It wondered. *Unless she wants to control Colin, much like every other person before her.*

Julie was now a threat, not a partner. It needed to take back control. He needed to save Colin.

And The City.

Chapter 49
Mick

December 19th, 46 A.R.

Mick returned from the past, having utilized Isabella's blood. He felt a bit guilty doing this under false pretenses, but he'd been so enthralled to have someone besides The Supreme or Jones to discuss time travel with.

Isabella listened to him and provided a sense of ease and comfort. Mick was addicted to something about her, something he couldn't quite place. She was stunning, but his attraction was less sexual and more like a raw, unidentifiable emotion.

He told Isabella if she gave him a sample of her blood, he would travel to the future to see what her future looked like.

But that was a lie.

Instead, Mick used her blood to go to the past. He was too intrigued by what such a wholesome and generous woman could be regretful for. And now he understood.

His next journey was not about the past; this next journey was about the future. Mick put this trip off for too long, and at this point, there were too many versions of himself wandering around in multiple dimensions. He needed to get rid of them, and he needed Jones's insights.

Mick pulled out the small tube containing Colin's blood. There was only enough inside the tube for one more journey in time.

Now or never.

Mick never feared not returning from an expedition in time travel but this time, he wasn't so confident. He pulled out his device and typed a quick note to Jones, expressing how much he loved Jones, how he was doing this all for him.

Sighing, Mick placed his device down and sent the encrypted

message with instructions to read it in two months if he didn't come back. Then, he placed the drop of Colin's blood on the device and leaned back. He clicked the dial on the side in an upward motion, indicating he wanted to go forward to the future. The small chrome box buzzed wildly with enthusiasm.

He was on his way.

***

Mick knew when he arrived in the future that The City would be in complete disarray. He wasn't discouraged by this notion; the scenes of empty streets, people rushing to get indoors before nightfall, were all too familiar to him at this point. And so were the androids dressed in complete red, roaming the streets as the glow of their scales intensified.

He walked with an urgency in his steps, making his way across The Hill toward The Bay. When Julie's building came into sight, Mick relaxed. Inside the safety of her apartment, Mick locked her door and activated the deadbolt before placing a chair underneath the handle. No one was breaking in without a fight.

Next, Mick approached the large bay windows, pulling the blinds down and drawing the drapes. The room became very dark, but he only turned on one lamp.

So much of Julie remained in her studio. Her clothes were dusty but still hung up in her closet in color order—light to dark. Her bed wasn't made and still felt warm. Mick smelled her perfume in the air around him. Her emerald engagement ring was placed safely in the nightstand beside her bed.

Some version of her is still here, still using her home as a hideout.

He didn't have much time.

Mick stopped and looked at himself in the long mirror opposite of Julie's bed. The trip here completely changed him: His skin was visibly thinner, and lines spread across his forehead and around his eyes—aging him by at least ten years.

He shook his head—he couldn't change these effects time travel had on him, so there was no use in obsessing over his appearance for longer than he had to.

Mick hurried over to the kitchen and approached Julie's refrigerator hesitantly. His heart pounded in his chest, and his breathing became deep and heavy. He took a few deep breaths before mustering up the courage to open the door.

After pushing aside the few bags of frozen fruit and vegetables, Mick sighed with relief.

The journal was there.

Wrapped up carefully, the journal was treated with kindness in the way Mick knew Jones was the one who left it there. Julie hadn't noticed it.

Mick slowly removed the coverings protecting the journal and brought the notebook to his chest. He hugged it so tightly that he thought for a moment that it might explode and disintegrate in his arms.

He lay down on Julie's bed, afraid to read what the contents contained. He wasn't ready to face some of the truths Jones had discovered. But Mick needed to know everything in order for his plan to work. For The Supreme's plan to work.

Mick waited for the journal to warm up to room temperature before opening it.

PART NINE

Mick's Journal

"A great fire burns within me, but no one stops to warm themselves at it and passers-by only see a wisp of smoke."
-Vincent Van Goh

Entry Seven:

Dear Mick,

I'm unsure if I will uncover the answers to all your questions. But I will try. There is no other option—I must help you save The City if I can. I must help save you.

I'm not sure who "It" is exactly, but you write of this being as if I already know his identity. I do not at this point in time know him, but this assumption you made is tremendously useful to me.

Another useful insight from your journal: I now strongly believe It is The City's infamous serial killer.

I do not like what time travel has done to you. Not only the harm to your physical body but also your mental state.

I ask, What has happened to you? Beyond what you've shared in your journal. What has really happened to you as you've traveled through time?

<u>Entry Eight:</u>

Dear Mick,

I can help you answer some of your questions.

Colin is It. It lives in Colin's mind. I don't understand the human mind in the same ways as doctors, but I transcribed Colin's confession of It as another personality of his. This connects the clues around Melanie O'Connor's death. I'd gather Colin's brain developed "It" as an escape, as a "person" who would always be there for him from the trauma he experienced. A defense mechanism his own brain created gone wrong. If this is true, the neuroreceptors in his brain will forever be riddled with abnormalities from trying to heal itself and failing.

Unless the antidote can fix it. Colin admitted telling Julie of It. And that Julie is going to help him. This also explains how It knows about the carriage house. Colin told me he has seen you there. That is where he actually confronted me. There is nothing that can be done about It discovering your "safe haven." That is an inevitable situation. So, please, future Mick, be smart about where you go. Maybe consider finding an alternative place to hide. May I suggest Julie's apartment?

I suspect The Supreme told It of time travel, and this confirms the connection between the murders and The Supreme. It/Colin has your device. That is how he time travels.

Colin gave me It's blood, or rather his blood. I've left the sample in the very back of Julie's fridge. Get the sample to yourself at some point, Mick. You need to travel through It's time. Also, interesting enough, Colin taught me a new emotion, a new concept: conflict. I've never experienced that before today. That feeling, that emotion never coursed through my body until now. I don't know what to do with this information I know. Anna was correct, but I suppose technically so was I. Do I say something? Do I tell Julie that Colin is the serial killer?

Or do I let things play out the way fate intends them to? As if I don't know. I ask because if Colin is revealed as the serial killer, won't he be convicted of all those crimes? Won't he be imprisoned as you described in entry three? And won't that cause disarray in The City? Make The City crumble? Cause chaos and uncertainty amongst people and androids alike?

Entry Nine:

Dear Mick,

I have a strong suspicion that It is going to try to kill Julie if she isn't successful in treating Colin with the antidote. And if Colin/It does kill Julie, he will be sloppy with her murder because he loves her. He was extremely sloppy with Kathleen's murder compared to the others. Colin was careless with Kathleen because he loved her. A different kind of love than his love for Julie but still a love. And if there is one thing I've learned about human emotions, it's when you love someone that you are your most vulnerable, most uncontrolled.

If It kills Julie, Anna will catch him. She already believes Colin to be involved. Sitting on top of her list were the governor and The Supreme. Initially, I thought that can't be right. Both the governor and The Supreme would have been too young to kill Melanie O'Connor. And you even saw Colin as a boy on the beach, traumatized. You wrote about that.

But then I remembered. It has traveled in time.

If It succeeds in killing Julie, Anna will reveal Colin as the killer. Colin will go to jail. And then The Supreme will use this as an advantage to take executive power over The Representatives of The People along with her leadership over The Representatives of The Androids. And that future you speak of, the one from your third entry, that will all come true.

You've written about how you can't find Julie in the future or travel very far with her blood. Even when she should still be alive. There's a reason for that Mick: Julie is dead in the grim future you have experienced. I think you could save Julie. But even if you cannot, if you don't want the events in entry three to occur, then you will need to get rid of her body.

You haven't shared a future with that outcome. An outcome where we live in peace, where there isn't insanity across The City. That makes me wonder: Does it not exist at all, or does it not exist because you try to fix it? Would not doing anything instead cause a better future outcome?

I ask you to consider: Do we, does society, deserve the risks of us playing with the past? Should you try to change the future?

I certainly can't make that decision for you. I ask you to consider it.

PART TEN

The Present

"And oftentimes, to bring us to our harm, the instruments of darkness tell us truths."
-K.J. Parker

Chapter 50
The Supreme

December 28th, 46 A.R.

It was back, and The Supreme was glad. She was surprised by the amount of time that passed between It's entrapment and his return. The power of the antidote was stronger than The Supreme initially thought.

As The Supreme entered a meeting room inside COLI*GO, she noticed Julie Walsh first. Julie's hair was pulled back into a tight neat bun, and she dressed in a blazer that was a bit too large on her lanky frame. The Supreme narrowed her focus on Julie's long elegant neck. She understood It and Colin's fascination and attraction for a moment.

Her eyes widened at the scar creeping down Julie's neck, one that obviously didn't bother the scientist enough where she left it blatantly obvious for all to see.

Is she mocking me?

The Supreme never experienced the feeling of dread in this capacity before, but she felt it strongly now, coursing through her as she instinctively looked down at her scales.

Her serum worked, masking any impression that she was strongly feeling human emotions.

"Madam Supreme, let me provide you with the latest briefing document." She heard the familiar voice of Peter Schneider from behind her.

As she turned, he placed his device above her own and transferred the updated file. Peter smiled up at The Supreme before realizing she donned a grave, serious expression. She looked away, took her seat, and continued watching the rest of the room.

A very distracted Martin sat in the corner, clearly not acquainted with life back in the office from his short paternity leave.

Mick Taylor stood near the large sleek monitor mounted on the wall in the front. He fidgeted at the sheer number of employees in the room, swaying back and forth on his feet.

Mick has such potential. He could be as successful as Julie if he had the confidence, The Supreme thought as her eyes drifted back to Peter. He had a brute body, making Mick appear fragile and weak. She had future plans for Dr. Schneider.

Julie took a seat next to The Supreme with a swift motion. She smiled at The Supreme as if egging her on.

"Are we finally going to understand the stalls and severity of the situation with the COL23 trials?" The Supreme asked Julie in a hushed tone.

"I hope so. I honestly haven't read the full brief, but the team thinks they've identified the issues in the extension study on bipolar patients," Julie answered, a slight tone of uncertainty in her voice.

She should be afraid.

"Can we speak in my office after this briefing? Or are you too important to make time for me now?" The Supreme asked lightheartedly.

Julie chuckled in response before nodding.

Peter and Mick began their presentation, showing interesting findings from both the regular bipolar patient study and the extension study. The two men explained how the technology worked most of the time, curing patients and allowing them to finally live their lives with minimal effects from their psychological conditions. There was a small subset of patients who didn't see the intended results, and in these few cases, some got worse after their treatment.

"Mick identified the root of the problem. Trauma," Peter said, clicking to the next slide. The room grew very quiet. A few jaws dropped, and an unsettling feeling floated throughout the room.

"Trauma?" Julie asked, breaking the silence in the room and asking the question everyone else was too afraid to ask.

"Alzheimer's is not caused by trauma. At least, not the same type of trauma. That's why we aren't seeing this issue with patients in that arm of the study. But many psychological conditions are rooted in trauma. We know trauma causes damaged neurotransmitters in the brain, but beyond that, we don't know enough. Throughout the treatment journey, a patient might experience trauma, and that causes a relapse. The relapse is rooted in the damaged neurotransmitters pulsating and strengthening inside the brain. The antidote mistakes those damaged neurotransmitters for healthy ones and replicates them instead if patients are not far enough along in their treatment journey. Sometimes it's too late."

The Supreme was intrigued by this development. This meant It was correct—he was resilient. He could have come back without The Supreme's intervention.

Julie looked as if someone stabbed her directly in the heart. The silence in the room began filling with murmurs.

"We have good news," Peter said. "We can fix the antidote. We've already figured out how. The team believes that with the database of trauma-damaged neurotransmitters from the clinical trial, we can add an extra item of coding and teach the antidote to distinguish between trauma-damaged neurotransmitters and healthy ones. With that improvement in the antidote's technology and having doctors monitor their patients more proactively, we can help patients."

"When can we implement these changes?" Martin asked from the back of the room.

"With approval from The Board of Directors, as soon as possible," Peter answered with a charming grin spreading across his face.

"And Peter," Julie looked up at him from her seated position, "what about patients who finished therapy? Are they going to experience a relapse or regression if they experience trauma again?"

Peter and Mick looked at one another. It was clear to The Supreme they could not answer Julie's question.

"We don't know," Mick answered.

The Supreme noticed fear spreading across Julie's face before she took in a deep breath and nodded. They spent almost another hour answering questions before allowing everyone to shuffle out of the room. The tension was palpable, but there was a sense of relief that the damage could be fixed. For new patients, at least.

The Supreme tapped Julie's shoulder, signaling they still had other matters to discuss in her office. When they made it back to the 101st floor, an uncomfortable silence vibrated between them.

"I've noticed you're very present in more meetings than Celine ever was," The Supreme said as she closed the door to her office.

Julie didn't answer right away, clearly distracted by her own thoughts. The woman lingered over to the windows, looking out beyond The River.

"Is that such a bad thing?" Julie asked without looking at The Supreme.

"No. But I find it peculiar that you're so invested in all of Marta's financial meetings and all of Martin's research meetings. Others have noticed your presence besides me. They wonder if you don't trust them." The Supreme walked toward Julie.

"I trust Marta, and I trust Martin," Julie said, turning around and facing The Supreme head on.

The Supreme cocked her head to the side, daring Julie to finish the rest of the sentence: *but I don't trust you.*

"I assume you're still trying to make a decision from our last conversation? About your loyalties to Colin," The Supreme asked.

Julie looked over at her as a great sadness filled her eyes.

"I trust things will play out the way they're supposed to," she said as her fingers grazed lightly over her stomach in an awkward manner.

The Supreme almost felt herself shiver at Julie's words. She created a monster out of Julie—this was exactly what she wanted. And like everything The Supreme created, she made sure she had a way to destroy those creations, too.

I'll destroy you, Julie. Or, at least, I'll destroy your soul.

***

The elevator doors opened, and The Supreme found herself in the lower lab. Being here after her conversation with Julie felt risky—as if Julie somehow knew what went on in this place.

"Doctor?" The Supreme called out.

Isabella was seated at one of the small desks, her small fingers typing quickly on her device. She looked up at The Supreme and glanced her eyes sideways as if The Supreme inconvenienced her.

"I thought I told you to not leave a mark on Julie's neck. That was imperative." The Supreme was angry, and the words flustered out of her in a violent manner as her scales shimmered a shade of honey amber.

Isabella stood from her chair. "I didn't leave a visible mark. There was barely a scar left on Julie's body after the operation. You would really have to be looking for it to find it," Isabella said calmly as she approached The Supreme.

"Then why was it that just an hour ago, I was able to see a large silver and red marked scar creeping down from behind her earlobe and down her neck? Much larger than most?" The Supreme yelled, her face inches away from Isabella's.

"I can confirm that there was only a small faint scar left on Dr. Walsh's incision site," Nolan said from the corner of the room.

"This has gotten way out of control. I can't do this anymore," Isabella said, hurriedly pulling her personal effects out of the desk drawer.

"Why do you care so much about Julie?"

"You think I hate her?" Isabella asked, stopping what she was doing to look over at The Supreme.

When she didn't answer her, Isabella shook her head and laughed nervously.

"You think I hate her because Colin loves her? I don't. There are different types of love, Madam Supreme. Colin and I, we loved one another differently. Like people who understood our responsibilities to society. Yes, there were romantic feelings from time to time, but that love is vastly different. I wouldn't expect an android to completely comprehend those feelings, but I thought you were programmed more intelligently. I guess you're like the rest of them."

Anger flew through The Supreme in that instant. Her golden scales flashed a rough amber, the colors pulsating across her body. Isabella noticed and backed away, surprised by The Supreme's outward admission of her feelings.

"I understand 100 percent of human emotions, of feelings. You fool. You think you can escape this? Do you know what I could do to you?" The Supreme mocked her.

"What are you going to do? Have Colin and It kill me? Kill Julie? If you do, Anna will convict Colin for the murders. I know of It. Colin shared that with me. Surprised? Don't be. I know he won't kill me."

The Supreme stepped aside and backed away from Isabella. The Supreme realized, It killing Julie wouldn't be so bad after all. Anna knew—she had said so to The Supreme at Jeb's sentencing. How could The Supreme have not seen this opportunity sooner?

"I don't want our relationship to end on a sour note, Doctor."

"It's too late for that," Isabella said as the elevator doors closed in front of her.

Chapter 51
The Governor

December 28th, 46 A.R.

"I need to talk to you about something," Julie said to Colin as she walked into the townhouse. She pulled her hair down out of her bun and allowed it to topple over, covering her neck and framing her face in a golden-red hue.

Julie wasted no time; she was an observer, a trait perfected from her years of training as a researcher and scientist. A characteristic Colin realized he never fully appreciated.

Julie pulled up her notes and identified abnormalities and inconsistencies with a sharp level of accuracy. Colin wasn't shocked to see her squiggly handwriting consuming the surface of a piece of paper that emerged from her bag.

She collected a list of projects and neatly drew a box around each of them: The mess came from all the lines extending from one box to another. They all connected to The Supreme. This whole time, Julie quietly pieced together a case against the android leader. There were missing financials, absent reports, money shifted to a particular unidentified project.

"So much has been an oversight with the lack of fresh eyes on it. Now the layers are thinner. We must stop her. I think I'm close to having enough evidence against her, to bring her before The Legislature and The Board of Directors at COLI*GO. The Supreme is money laundering, pocketing funds so she can finance and profit off her illegal drug ring she started with Jeb Taylor," Julie said, slowly looking back up at Colin.

Colin felt his jaw drop as he looked over the scribbles and the lines. All the dots were connecting in his mind.

This must be the posse hominems. The human-android hybrids, he thought. Colin placed Julie's notes gently down on the kitchen island and passionately kissed her. Her hands grasped at him longingly, more so than he ever experienced before. Colin didn't want to finish discussing the issue at hand but knew they needed to. He pulled away from her lips and smiled.

"I need you to not be angry with me when I tell you something," Colin said slowly. "You know the rumors about how COLI*GO is creating human-android hybrid creatures? I think that is where the missing money is going."

Julie's eyes widened. "That's always been gossip."

"Rumors are always rooted in a bit of truth."

"How did you know about this?"

Colin could hear the hurt in her voice as she asked this question, but he still couldn't bring himself to admit to killing Lexi or Kathleen.

"Right before Celine had Henry, she and I were trying to look into the inconsistencies happening in the lower lab. We discovered that your colleague Lexi wasn't in any database and suspected the rumors were true. We didn't have enough evidence to prove it. But now we do, thanks to you."

Julie drew in a sharp breath and covered her mouth with her hand. The severity of how long this occurred finally sank in for her. She sat down on one of the barstools, her eyes scanning the entirety of her paper trail.

"We need to expose The Supreme. But you said she knows about you, about It. She won't go down without a fight. She'll frame you for being unstable. I wouldn't put that past her."

No, Colin thought. *She'll expose me as The City's uncaught serial killer.*

"Let me worry about that," Colin said to Julie, cupping her face in his hand. "Let's keep building this case against her. You're incredible. I hadn't realized you were investigating her."

"I told you, Colin. I have a vision for COLI*GO. That vision doesn't include corruption. My vision doesn't include people or androids who try to take control of others, take advantage because they can. I want to help society."

Colin walked around the kitchen island and away from Julie, the woman he loved. Together, he and Julie could make an impact. They could silence The Supreme once and for all. But that would come at a cost he wasn't sure he was willing to pay.

"We can do this together, but we have to strategize correctly or our plan will never work. Androids are not malicious beings, but The Supreme is. We need to bring down evil."

***

Julie left to pay a visit to Jones and then wanted to spend some time catching up on projects and messages she missed during the day.

Colin didn't mind some time alone and used the space to organize his own loose ends. The night grew darker, and Julie hadn't returned. He found sleep wouldn't come easy to him without her. He drifted in and out, awaiting her return, the warmth of her body against his. The creaking sound of the door opening downstairs registered in Colin's ears. He noticed Julie quietly enter the room, careful not to wake him. She didn't turn on a light as she changed into an oversized sweatshirt. Her body crept into the bed, curling up close to his.

Or at least, that's what Colin thought he saw, but he later wondered if he dreamt it. He experienced a strange dream that evening. This wasn't a nightmare or any kind of night terror. That gave him a sense of relief, but there was something so real about this dream, something so odd and misplaced, that he couldn't let go of it.

In the dream, he kissed Julie and pulled her toward him, wrapping his warm body closer to hers. She swatted his hands away as they crawled underneath her sweatshirt. He kissed her lips, convincing her to allow his other advances. Something passed between them as they made love; something different happened beneath the bedsheets—but nothing negative.

Colin felt invigorated. Reborn.

He couldn't describe the exact sensation, but this night was special, different. He felt closer to Julie now more than ever before.

His fingers crawled up her hips, and he nipped at her waist as he held her above him. Eventually, she grabbed his hands in hers, but before she did, Colin's fingers felt a strange sensation of different types of softness on her body.

Zigzagging lines crossed her skin: healed scars and so many of them. Scars she never had before.

He counted them as inconspicuously as he could. *One . . . two . . . three . . . four . . .* and finally, the count stopped at twenty-three.

He held her afterward, and she turned to him with a look of sorrow in her eyes. Julie rolled over to the nightstand and grabbed an envelope.

"This has everything you need against The Supreme in case anything happens to me," she whispered in his ear.

"I'll never let anything happen to you," Colin said, grabbing her face in his hands.

"Please, keep this somewhere safe."

Colin didn't like the look that registered across her eyes, a look of terror. As if she knew something he didn't, had some kind of insight into the future.

He grabbed the envelope from her hand and rose out of the bed. His naked body crept across the silent halls of the townhouse toward his study. He opened the bottom drawer, the one with the time travel device, and placed the envelope inside.

Colin returned to bed, and Julie stretched her arms out. He entered her embrace, and she held on to him tightly, as if this was the last time she'd ever hold him. They both fell asleep easily, tangled in one another.

When Colin woke in the morning, he heard the shower running. Julie's sweatshirt was tossed on the floor in the corner. He crawled out of bed and joined her in the shower. Julie kissed him gently, and his eyes lingered down her body: nothing was out of place; everything was normal. There were no unusual marks on her skin.

No scars. No strange softness. Just her.

Colin let out a large sigh of relief. When he experienced strange dreams, he was afraid this meant the antidote hadn't worked.

Of course the antidote worked. It is gone.

Months had passed since Colin's last treatment, and in April, he would celebrate a whole year of no It. His headaches finally stopped weeks ago, and he hadn't experienced any night terrors since earlier in the fall.

Things were normal for once in his life.

Colin basked in Julie's presence that morning, wanting to make the most of the short time they had before real life and responsibilities plagued them. He grabbed Julie's hand and twirled the emerald ring around her finger before kissing her forehead.

"Let's spend the weekend at The Oceanside," Colin said. "There's something kind of magical about that place in the wintertime."

"I'd love that," Julie said.

They drove out shortly after.

The estate looked vastly different during the winter compared to the summer, painted daintily from the heavy snowstorms that shook The Constituency over the last week.

Colin built a large fire in the fireplace and grabbed all the heavy blankets out of the storage containers, and together, they were themselves.

***

"Did you really think you could get rid of me forever? You do know that I'm not only smarter than you but also more resourceful."

Colin knew the voice without having to open his eyes. When he finally had the courage to, there in front of him sat the familiar vision of It. Colin looked around for Julie, seeing her out of the corner of his eye wrapped up in all the blankets. The fire was still going but had simmered significantly. They had fallen asleep on the couch.

"You're not real," Colin said slowly, steadying himself in hopes the confidence in his voice could shine through. That his confidence could get rid of It.

"I am real. Not the normal kind of real, but you already knew that," It said, staring back at him.

Colin couldn't bring himself to say anything. There were many emotions, many thoughts running through his mind. He was angry. The antidote hadn't worked.

Or did it not work because I hadn't really received the drug? he wondered, thinking back to the strange misprinted bottles.

"Clearly, you didn't get the antidote," It said as if reading his mind.

Colin shook his head. Of course It could read his mind. It was his mind. A part of his mind at least. Colin's biggest fears consumed him. He tried to shush the thoughts away, knowing they weren't safe against It. It could and would use anything against him. He couldn't allow himself to reveal any fear or doubt.

It looked over at Julie.

"She used you. What do you think will happen when you bring to light all The Supreme's crimes? The Supreme will reveal what we've done." It looked over at Julie, who slept soundly as he tucked a lock of hair behind her ear.

A very faint line flashed behind her earlobe, one not recognizable if he hadn't been looking. Unlike Kathleen's and Lexi's, Julie's marking was healed and blended in almost impeccably with her skin.

"No . . ." Colin said quietly.

"Yes."

He couldn't believe he hadn't noticed the scar before.

"Not her fault, really. The Supreme's work all along. Julie has no idea," It answered quietly.

Colin's heart completely dropped in his body, the sensation of heartbreak consuming him in an ugly and raw manner. He had an idea of what It would soon suggest.

"Julie has gained so much since she's been with you. She'd never be at the top of COLI*GO without you. She used you. A nobody who became a somebody. She's more relatable; isn't that what Joel said to you? Why was Julie speaking with that prick anyways? Think about all this, Colin."

Colin's thoughts focused on his heartbreak instead. He never experienced heartbreak before, except for when he lost his mother. This heartbreak was different, mixed with subconscious betrayal. He didn't want to believe any of this was true.

Julie loves me. She didn't use me.

"You know . . ." It began, but Colin glanced at him, a look that sliced silence even in It.

"No."

It looked at him, shaking his head. It was always disappointed in him, much like his father.

"This will only end badly if we don't do what needs to be done."

"She would never hurt me. She loves me," Colin said sternly.

"You're right. Julie wouldn't do this to you. But this . . . this thing; she isn't Julie anymore. The Supreme ruined that for us. For you," It said with a sadness in the tone of his voice.

Colin realized It was struggling with this too; It did care about Julie and Colin to some extent. It cared about Colin's happiness and how Julie accepted Colin and him. Colin desperately wanted all of this to be a bad dream. He'd risk telling Julie his night terrors returned if only his eyes would open and It was gone.

It sighed. He knew Colin's desires, Colin's thoughts.

Of course he does, he doesn't pity me.

It didn't understand Colin's desire for peace, for control. It thrived on chaos.

"I hate you."

"I hate you, too. But admit you hate The Supreme more," It said before leaning back from his seated position on the coffee table.

"I do hate her. I made it my dying promise that she goes down for everything she's done to destroy our society."

It looked back at the fire smoldering behind him. He grinned a remorseful smile as if the plan he constructed harmed him, too.

"You know, I was quite fond of Julie. For you. For us," It said, his eyes softening at the sight of the woman Colin loved.

"After this, there is no 'us' anymore, It." Colin couldn't look away from the vision of It in front of him. It betrayed him, even if It hadn't intended to.

"Sure," It responded. It rose quietly from his position and walked over toward the French doors overlooking the cliffs, the never-ending ocean beyond them. There was always something about this place; Colin should have known better than to think he could find solace here.

"I won't strangle her. She's too important to me."

"Fine, I think we can make that compromise. You made compromises before for me," It said without looking his way.

Colin closed his eyes, avoiding the pain that crept into his body. His hand affectionately brushed Julie's golden-red hair.

"Not right now, no. I will let you know when," It responded slowly. "At least I can give you the gift of time."

"When?"

"I won't tell you when, exactly. But you need to be ready, Colin. When I return, there is no other option. Clearly, you understand?"

Unfortunately, Colin did.

***

A month passed since Colin's encounter with It; since It told him they would kill Julie. He never told her It haunted his mind, that It had returned. Instead, Colin tried taking advantage of the time they had together, knowing it wasn't much longer. Since the microchip was in her brain, confusion and distrust ate away at Colin's mind. If Colin thought about this fact he knew about Julie too much, he began doubting her. The inability of knowing if he trusted her drove him insane. Each day, Colin spiraled more and more out of control. The hidden pills underneath the sink taunted him, teased him.

He took them, and always with a full glass of Scotch.

Colin could almost hear It chuckle at his madness, It's nasty scowl smearing across Colin's brain.

That bastard. Colin went so far as wondering if he could simply confront Julie about the microchip instead. *Maybe together, we could find a solution. No.* It told him Julie didn't know. She wouldn't believe him, or worse, The Supreme would do something rash.

The Supreme was up to something larger. By sabotaging Colin and by gathering her creations, Colin realized The Supreme had a grand plan to overthrow The City. The Supreme wanted power over the whole legislature. To do so, she needed Colin out of the picture. She was waiting for a moment to expose him.

He would not give her that satisfaction; he would not allow The Supreme—he would not allow Emilia—to eliminate all the progress in society, the peace between humans and androids. Colin would not allow her to ruin everything for the sole purpose of wanting control.

Control or retribution, the line is clearly thin.

The Supreme deliberately played her checkmate in their infinite game of chess by using both It and Julie against him.

But Colin refused to let her succeed. There was only one chance to stop The Supreme: he needed to catch her in the act. Then Colin could invoke The Legislature to arrest her.

That night, Colin and Julie cooked dinner together. He preferred thinking he and Julie could go on forever this way, a notion that made him vulnerable. They sat down, her eyes twinkling and her hair brushed against her shoulders seductively after she released it from her ponytail. A long day for her at the office, a long day for him at The Capitol Building.

As he and Julie sat across from one another in the dining room, he saw It's looming figure stalk behind her chair. Colin remained silent, and It leaned over, his face inches away from Julie in her seated position.

She did not see It. She did not feel It's presence.

But It's presence overwhelmed Colin.

It inhaled deeply, breathing in Julie as Colin held his silverware, gripping the knife tightly in his hand. This knife was not the same knife he normally used, but it glistened off the reflection of the chandelier, taunting him. Mocking him.

To distract himself, Colin picked up the empty bottle of wine. He grinned at Julie but couldn't look away from It.

Maybe if I continue smiling, she won't realize something is so terribly wrong.

It loomed behind her, his fingers hovering Julie's neck, not quite touching her skin but so close . . .

So damn close.

Colin rose from his seat, a chance for him to do the thing he didn't want to do. He found another bottle of wine in the kitchen and popped the cork. The sound echoed in the quiet room. He poured her a glass, slipping the tranquilizer in with the ruby red liquid. He walked back to the dining room, placing the bottle on the table. His fingertips lingered, touching hers as he handed her the glass. When Colin finally let go, she moved quickly, grabbing his face in her small hands.

As if she knows.

Their kiss was filled with passion and desire, a feeling Colin reciprocated but so desperately wished didn't exist in this moment.

He almost hated her for it but realized he could never hate Julie. She wanted him, and he believed she had no ulterior motives. She was simply just a casualty in his and The Supreme's game of chess.

My queen. I must sacrifice the most powerful piece to save everything.

Regret and pain filled his heart. This moment would haunt him every day for the rest of his life. Had Julie kissed him earlier in the evening, she might have convinced him to give up on finishing dinner all together. They could have faced the repercussions of It, could have faced him and The Supreme together.

But this was not the way he and It operated.

Julie pulled her lips away from Colin and took a large sip from her wine glass. Her eyes never left him.

She knows.

Reality set in as the words floated in his mind.

Colin needed to act quickly. Julie would be asleep within five to ten minutes. Then he would only have about an hour to take her somewhere—the woods outside The City—and do the unthinkable.

Chapter 52
Julie

January 28th, 47 A.R.

Julie's body was still, but her brain raced uncontrollably. Terror filled her instantly, and she wasn't sure where she was or how she got here. Her fingers twitched from the bitterness of the winter air surrounding her. Her body ached as the sinking feeling crept in her mind: She couldn't move. She was paralyzed.

Open your eyes, Julie thought before her body listened.

When she did have the courage to open her eyes, she realized she wasn't anywhere familiar. Julie had no recollection, no memory of how she went from being in Colin's arms to being in these isolated, dark woods.

How did I end up here?

Julie was interrupted by a sharp, jarring pain coming from her abdomen. Her eyes glanced down, and her worst fear hit her. The snow around the left side of her body wasn't white; instead, a bright red seeped through the moisture. Her eyes rolled back into her head from pure shock.

Fight or flight instinct immediately took hold, and adrenaline coursed through her body. She forced herself to open her eyes once again and looked up at the sky. There were no stars visible, only the moon.

So, I am close to The City at least.

Logically, Julie understood if she didn't act quickly, she would die. These woods were thick, the forest seemed endless.

But Julie would not allow herself to die in these woods.

The searing pain spreading across her body grew sharper as each minute passed. She moved her right arm, surprised at her own physical strength, and placed her hand tentatively on her stomach. The gravity of the situation sunk in.

Stab wounds scattered across her left ribcage and abdomen. Julie closed her eyes as she counted the small shallow stab wounds on her body.

Twenty-three.

The same number of stab wounds reported in Kathleen's murder. The same number of stab wounds reported in Kendra's. The markings distinctively belong to The City's serial killer.

Julie continued moving her hand up her body. Her fingers grazed her own neck, lingering at her jawline until she made her way behind her ear. Blood wasn't flowing profusely from this spot, but she still felt the stickiness trail down her skin. To her surprise, Julie felt the opening of a small incision tucked behind her left earlobe.

This concerned Julie more than her other stab wounds.

The same location where the androids' microchips were placed into their processors. And the same with posse hominems.

Julie wasn't an android; she was a human. But the rumors wallowed in her brain.

The lower lab. The fraudulent financial accounts.

She was one of these hybrids.

You can do this, Julie said to herself, trying to find the confidence to confirm her suspicions. She took in a sharp breath as she allowed her index finger to touch at the entrance of the incision. Julie screamed in complete pain before she blacked out.

When she came to, her finger was still jammed inside the wound, the fleshiness of her skin leaving way to the edges of a microchip and its wires.

Suddenly, the sound of branches breaking on the ground echoed loudly around her. The noise alarmed Julie, ringing hauntingly through her ears. Rolling on to the right side of her body, Julie struggled for a few moments as she attempted to get off the ground. The pain was so blinding that she had to close her eyes again. She didn't want to.

"Hello?"

She couldn't see the stranger calling out to her from her position, but the sound of boots in the snowbanks grew louder and louder. Without warning, tears and sobs escaped Julie. The pain across her body was unbearable at this point, and she knew she was losing a lot of blood. Julie opened her eyes and analyzed the man looking down at her. He moved around her, examining her wounded body. The man was lanky and scrawny with kind eyes. He looked so familiar to her, and Julie felt she could trust him.

Miraculously, he lifted her up with ease, supporting her as he walked toward a lightness that appeared behind a cluster of trees. Julie wondered if she was hallucinating in the woods as her body bled out.

"I'm Mick. A slightly different version of Mick but still Mick," the old man said.

I am desperate to hold on to something, she thought. That would logically explain this situation.

"Do you trust me?" Mick asked her.

Julie nodded, not sure if it was because she actually trusted him or because she had no choice. This version of Mick sheltered Julie's eyes with something resembling a pair of glasses. She couldn't see anything through them in the darkness and that brought her an inner peace. The obscurity calmed Julie, allowing her to breathe and forget about the pain in her body. She heard a sound click into the side of the glasses and then a sensation vibrated through her; it wasn't violent or unpleasant, but it was noticeable. Julie felt Mick remove the glasses from her eyes, and the skyline of The City emerged.

There was something amiss about The City. The streets were bland, and an unforgiving amount of garbage and debris scattered across the streets. Reality crashed around Julie as the pain from her wounds reemerged in this future reality. Mick quickly placed the glasses and chrome box in his pocket and looked up at her.

"Are you okay if I pick you up and take you down the hill? The path is too steep for you in your condition, and we need to move quickly before the bots come out and enforce the curfew hours."

Julie nodded. She was surprised at how Mick strode through the streets at a steady pace, especially considering how frail and old he appeared to her. No one batted an eye at them, as if they weren't really there. Mick explained how no one could see her because they were in the future, and in this future, Julie was dead.

Mick did not answer any of Julie's other questions and his silence spoke volumes. Panic crept back into Julie's mind. She saw how her fingertips and hands were now a shade of pale purple from a combination of the loss of blood and the cold. She needed to conserve her energy, but she couldn't stop asking Mick questions.

What year is it? Where were they? How was he going to help her? Where was Colin? Could Colin help? Through her uneasiness and blabbering, Mick remained silent.

Eventually, they reached a paved lot, and Mick opened the back door of a sleek vehicle with a quiet command. Everything in Julie's line of vision became blurry, and she felt herself fading in and out of consciousness.

The vehicle drove closer to The City and sadness overcame her physical pain. A thick viscous cloud of pollution lined the tops of skyscrapers, and buildings appeared abandoned. People and androids on the sidewalks wouldn't look at one another, as if they were afraid and untrusting of everyone around them. The common gardens and greenery were replaced with cold gray cement.

"This is the future. Humans have no control here anymore," Mick finally said from the front seat.

The vehicle turned corners gently, and they approached a part of The City so familiar to her she felt a small beam of comfort in all her agony. The beautiful brick, the black iron fences and gates calmed her. She was relieved that in the future, The Hill still held. Julie recognized Colin's townhouse instantly as they pulled into the garage.

"How did Colin let any of this happen?" Julie asked aloud after enough silence passed between her and Mick.

"Let's not talk about Colin, yet," Mick answered while maneuvering her out of the vehicle.

The townhouse hadn't changed much. Some of the furniture was different, but the place was immaculate and organized meticulously: the way Colin always kept it. The chandelier was the same, the artwork and fixtures were all identical to her memory from earlier. The home even still smelled like him.

Mick carried her toward the back of the house and placed her delicately on the dining room table. When Julie's eyes concentrated again, a familiar shadow loomed above her.

Isabella Garcia.

"Shit, Julie," Isabella swore, very uncharacteristically. Her small tiny hands hovered over Julie's stab wounds, taking in all the damage to her body. Isabella did not waste any time. She yelled over to Mick, asking him to hand her various instruments. The wounds hurt so badly at this point that Julie wasn't surprised to come in and out of consciousness on the makeshift operating table.

The place she ate dinner earlier. Dinner with Colin.

"I don't like the amount of stab wounds here," Isabella said as she worked speedily to stitch up Julie's wounds before dealing with the larger problem: the microchip in Julie's brain.

Then Isabella moved on to the location of the microchip. The original incision had been reopened and the skin festered an irritated red. An infection was forming.

Julie stirred, unpleasant sounds coming from between her lips as Isabella finished stitching her body. Isabella looked over at Mick and then frowned down at Julie.

"This new incision will leave a horrendous scar, along with the other scars littered across your body."

Mick's voice broke the tension. "But those were Colin's doing, something he will have to answer to, if ever given the chance."

***

When Julie awoke, her head hurt, and her body ached an unforgivable soreness. For a moment, she wondered if everything had been a terrible nightmare, but her hands felt the stitches across her body. She allowed the tips of her fingers to barely trace all of them. A complete disaster, a warzone of twenty-three scars.

The horror filled Julie's mind when she remembered what actually happened, and tears formed in the corners of her eyes. Being in the townhouse without Colin was strange. Being in his bed alone was strange, foreign even. Julie felt completely lost.

Mick never told her where or why he took her from the woods. She imagined they weren't too far in the future because some of Colin's things were still in the master bedroom.

His device lay on top of the dresser, the coffee mug he always drank from remained left behind on the small stand beside the chase lounge in the corner. An envelope, one torn open in haste was left by the bed, and Julie recognized her terrible handwriting on the outside.

Dear Colin—

She spotted another peculiar object in the room: Mick's journal. Beside the journal were various pieces of jewelry: random bracelets, earrings, and necklaces. Julie reached over the jewelry for the journal, a throbbing pain coursing through her body once again. She clenched her teeth and fought through it.

Memories of when Mick accidentally dropped the journal in the café flooded Julie's mind. She had chased him all across The Hill and ended up here at the townhouse. The very beginning of her and Colin. Julie now understood it was a Mick from a different time, not the Mick she knew. And he was aware of what could happen; he was aware what his small actions could do to change the future.

How differently would things be if I read the journal then? Julie wondered. *If I hadn't ended up in Colin's embrace, letting myself give in to my emotions? That indescribable pull?*

Julie opened the journal and read. She was stunned to find both Mick's and Jones's writing inside. A declaration of horror, a confession of truths. Terrifying truths.

Colin tried killing me, she realized.

A few moments after Julie finished reading the journal's contents, a hushed knock sounded on the door. Isabella's petite frame shadowed in the hallway.

"Come in," Julie called out.

Isabella entered the room with her usual grace. Unlike Mick, Isabella hadn't aged. She sat down at the corner of the bed, her hand outreached to affectionately grab Julie's leg.

"How long have I been asleep?" Julie asked.

"A few days," Isabella answered as she stood up to look over Julie's wounded stomach and the scar on the side of her neck. Isabella was a diligent doctor, a caring woman. Julie was grateful for her kindness.

"I removed the microchip from your brain."

"I didn't know there was one in there. How did that even happen?" Julie asked

"Drugging your coffee wasn't difficult, unlike performing the surgery on you," Isabella responded. "You woke up right after we operated. I can hardly believe you don't remember, but I'm glad you don't. I don't like being in the lower lab, and I can't imagine the horrid nightmares it left you. We performed all the operations on the posse hominems at COLI*GO."

Julie's terrible dream that night at The Oceanside returned to her. *That wasn't a dream; it was a memory.*

"I never realized you were behind the posse hominems," Julie said in awe. "But I'm fairly certain you worked with The Supreme?"

"Yes," Isabella answered sadly.

That happened right beneath me, right under my nose the whole time, Julie thought with remorse. How had Celine not known? *But she did know,* Julie thought as Isabella interrupted her.

"I'm not proud of what I did. I knew I needed to make amends at least for my own conscience. What broke me was performing the operation on Kathleen. But I was too afraid of The Supreme." Isabella's kind eyes told the truth.

Julie doubted the woman would lie to her; Isabella was everything but insincere.

"And when she asked me to put a blank microchip in your brain, I couldn't understand why. I knew about you and Colin. I think she believed that would make me hate you. But I could never hate you, Julie, even though I was jealous. I could never hate Colin, even after everything he did." Isabella closed her eyes and held back tears. "Your screams still haunt me. They will haunt me forever."

Julie looked away from Isabella softly. She felt betrayed but sympathetic. The Supreme had a way of using people in her own disgusting games.

"What about the microchip . . . the microchip in my brain?"

"I wasn't sure what to expect when I took the microchip out of your brain, but it still remained turned off."

"Off?" Julie asked in disbelief.

Isabella said nothing.

The pieces clicked together in Julie's mind. *There was a purpose behind why Colin tried killing me. He believed I was a true hybrid. Yet . . . had he really tried to kill me? Or did he purposefully give me a chance?* she wondered, her hands hovering over her shallow wounds. Instinctively, Isabella grabbed Julie as if to stop her.

"You need to let them heal," she scolded. "Honestly, I couldn't tell you why the microchip wasn't activated. I don't understand all The Supreme's intentions."

Isabella stayed for a little while longer. She answered some vague and unassuming questions Julie had regarding the night of her attempted murder. The perplexing realization didn't cross her mind until Mick entered the room.

Jones. Where is Jones?

Chapter 53
Jones

January 29th, 47 A.R.

The interior of the O'Connor townhouse shocked Jones. He wasn't sure what he was expecting but seeing a mixture of old world and new world threw him for a surprise. Jeb's paintings lined some of the walls, classical pieces paired next to them as if counteracting the wickedness that possessed the room.

He thought back to when Julie stopped by a month ago, her presence in his and Mick's apartment awkward, grim, and cold. Julie's hands went digging through her bag and out emerged a handful of COL23 vials.

"What is this?" Jones had asked her, holding out his own hand to take the drugs away from her grip.

"The antidote," Julie stated simply as if he should have known. "Early in the morning on January 29th, before the sun rises, go to Colin's townhouse. Wait for him in the main living space. Bring these doses of the antidote."

"Why January 29th? Will you be there?"

Julie didn't answer but she looked up at him with watery eyes. Dark circles were underneath them, and she looked paler than normal. A scar stretched down her neck, half-hidden by her hair. Jones backed away from his friend, fear consuming his processor.

"Who are you?" he asked, his eyes darting across her body.

"It's me, Jones. Just not the me you're used to."

Jones paused and took in this version of Julie. Finally, he spoke, "I wish Mick never discovered time travel."

Julie closed her eyes, the tears escaping her, too. "I wish he hadn't either. But, Jones, I have to correct Mick's wrongs. I really do; you don't know yet. You can't know. I have to make it so Mick never tried to change the past."

Julie wouldn't divulge more, and Jones knew, as Julie did, that was for the best. He wasn't sure if he was surprised Mick attempted to change the past even though he advised him specifically not to. Mick always followed the beat of his own drum.

Now, Jones was standing in the residence of the most important and powerful man in The Constituency: Colin O'Connor.

He heard rustling and movement upstairs. Colin was awake, and Jones wondered where Julie was. Moments later, as if in a violent manner, Colin's figure rushed down the grand staircase. The man stopped dead in his tracks and looked at Jones.

Colin O'Connor was a tall man, a man of stature. There was something simply intimidating about him in this particular instance. He wasn't dressed for the day, donning a plain shirt and boxers. In his grasp, he held an envelope, torn aggressively at the top edges. Many pages were stuffed within its contents.

Jones and Colin stared at one another for a very long time, and Jones pieced together everything in those moments of silence.

Julie wasn't here, but she had been recently.

Julie had traveled from the future even though she clearly wasn't sure she wanted to, to give Jones the antidote.

Colin's face was filled with grief. The presence of harsh drugs and alcohol spread across his skin like an infectious disease eating him at his core. Jones remembered again that Julie was not here. The place where she should be.

"You tried to kill Julie, didn't you?" Jones asked while firming his stance in the living room.

"Is she not dead? Please tell me she's not dead," Colin asked, an odd hint of optimism in his voice. "I didn't want to kill her. I tried not to."

"She isn't dead."

"Because of Mick?" Colin asked.

Jones didn't need to respond and looked away. Conflict—the feeling Colin taught him—lingered inside Jones's body.

"I'm hoping you can explain why she gave me these."

Jones held out the vials of COL23. He needed to hear the words from Colin's mouth. He needed Colin to make the right decision after making so many wrong decisions.

How could you? How could you do this to her?

Jones approached Colin cautiously, sensing the man was a bit afraid of him. An odd feeling overcame Jones: satisfaction. His scales gave away his true self, glowing instinctively as Colin closed the gap between them. Colin's hands grasped his own face in an attempt to hide his vulnerability but lifted the sleeve of his shirt as he approached Jones.

Jones placed the vials on the coffee table except for one, drawing the contents of the container into the syringe. Colin did not flinch when Jones injected him with COL23: the antidote. His eyes didn't leave Jones's, not even for a second.

"How many doses did I miss?" he asked. Jones looked at the remaining vials and did a quick inventory.

"Half. You had a few months of successful treatment, I'd say. Or, at least, based on the number of doses Julie provided to me."

Colin rose quickly and walked over to the kitchen. Jones heard him open a drawer, and after rummaging around for a moment, the governor returned holding empty vials. Jones took one from him, noticing the label was printed unevenly.

A barely noticeable flaw.

"But I read the reports on COL23 on Julie's device," Colin said hesitantly. "There's a chance even if I receive the full dose, this won't work. Something about experiencing trauma."

"This is the best we can hope for. What other option do we have?" Jones asked.

Colin didn't respond; instead, he shook his head. Then the man sobbed in Jones's presence, the sound unbearable in Jones's ears. He had rarely heard a human man cry, let alone the coldest and most aloof man in The Constituency.

Jones put his arm around Colin, plagued by the memory of this gesture from when Julie's mother died.

"I'm only here for Julie. And because you admitted you tried *not* killing her," Jones emphasized.

"How did she look when you saw her?"

Jones took a deep breath. He wanted to hate Colin in all these moments, but he couldn't, no matter how desperately he desired this feeling.

"I knew she came from some other time, but I didn't want to fully admit that to myself," Jones answered. "She looked tired."

"Was she a posse hominem?" The words lingered between them for a moment.

"Not anymore. She removed the microchip."

Colin's eyes widened, and he furrowed his brow in confusion.

"The scar behind her ear was much larger, much uglier, and more pronounced than any I've seen. The incision was reopened. But, Colin, she cared for you. She risked everything for you, and she still believes in you. I don't know what drove you to kill her. Based on your other kills, you thought she was a threat to society. But Colin . . . Julie never would have betrayed you."

"This was always The Supreme's doing. From the beginning. Everything," Colin said. "I should have done something."

"You never thought about going back in time and fixing it? You have the device," Jones asked him.

Colin shook his head.

"I do have a device. The device was It's," Colin said. "I never considered going back in time and changing the past. There's a reason why I voted 'no' on Mick's time travel research when he presented at The University. Changing the past isn't the answer. Courage is. Confronting and admitting to my own demons is the answer."

Jones nodded.

They sat in silence for a long time. Jones embraced the warmth from the fireplace as Colin wandered into the kitchen and picked up the envelope off the island. Colin pulled out the contents of the envelope, unfolding the papers gently, his fingers running across the creases. Paper was a novelty, such a strange thing. Jones appreciated this sentiment of old-fashioned ways—he understood this feeling when he had possession of Mick's journal. Paper was the only form of communication that simply traveled through time.

Julie's handwriting scrawled across the pages from the note left for Colin. Lines, arrows, scribbles, names, and numbers covered sheets of paper. The Supreme's name was circled, as were Mick's, Jeb's, and Celine's. Jones consumed the contents of the page with incredible ease, logging everything safely into his processor.

A personal letter was addressed to Colin on the very last piece of paper. Jones refrained from reading the note—a letter not meant for him. Colin read Julie's words carefully before cautiously folding the paper back into thirds.

"I know what I need to do," Colin said.

Jones questioned at that moment if It or Colin would prevail.

Does that really matter? he finally wondered.

***

The carriage house was lonely. Dust accumulated over the obscure objects Mick normally kept inside this odd place. Jones was drawn to the carriage house after leaving the O'Connor townhouse. A part of him hoped he'd cross paths with the complicated human man he loved, so he wasn't surprised to hear the creaking sounds of the floorboard.

"Which Mick are you?" Jones asked, turning to face him.

"Do you want me to be honest? I'm never really sure," Mick said as he approached.

"Where is Julie, Mick?" Mick looked out the bay window, his eyes longing at the O'Connor residence. The silence only solidified what Jones assumed.

"I sent her back," he answered plainly.

Jones wished he had the ability to take this all away, this moment of betrayal. He wanted to hide his true feelings, his true thoughts.

"Did you even care about what I wrote in the journal? About tinkering with the past? How that might cause more harm than good?" Jones asked, hearing his voice rise.

"Colin attempted to kill Julie, thinking she deceived him. That seed of doubt, in combination with not finishing his treatment with COL23, drove him absolutely insane. The man is already a little bit mad, and exasperating It wasn't a difficult task under the correct circumstances."

"You wanted Colin to kill Julie all along?" Jones asked in shock. "She was your best friend."

"Not kill her but attempt to. I knew I could save her," Mick said, looking at Jones in a pleading manner. "There's a purpose for everything. The Supreme taught me that. I care about Julie and didn't want her to die, so this felt right. I went back and saved her. I brought her to the future, but I needed to send her back."

Jones felt an uncomfortable heaviness in his body. *What is this feeling?* he wondered as it festered inside of him. Jones wasn't angry, at least not yet. Instead, he wished to close his eyes and pretend these words hadn't escaped Mick's lips.

"I know he loves her. And so does It. The stab wounds were mostly shallow, but there were so many of them. He stabbed her twenty-three times. I'm sure you could have already guessed that one for yourself, knowing what you know."

"I gathered as much," Jones answered simply, hiding any sense of emotion in his response.

"You're not really going to forgive a man who killed so many innocent young women? A man who tried to kill Julie?" Mick's voice rose in anger, and he hit his palm flat against the wall loudly.

Jones wanted desperately to look away from Mick, but his eyes were glued to him. *This is complete madness.*

"Why did you send her back in time, Mick? That's dangerous!" Jones spat back at him, unwilling to admit he didn't hate Colin O'Connor because it was Mick who tried to kill Julie.

Mick looked away. "You're right. She doesn't understand how all of time travel works. I didn't explain the time loops to her. I played to her wishes. I told her about how The Supreme replaced the last half of Colin's doses with a placebo. If she wanted to save Colin, wanted to save The City and everyone who lives in The Constituency, she'd have to go back. I knew she'd fall short in her quest. That she would be too late."

Tears formed in Mick's eyes, creeping down his face in slow wallowing motions. Jones wanted to reach out and embrace Mick, but he fought the urge. Finally, anger fueled inside him.

"You knew she would fail," Jones said.

Mick didn't answer; instead, he turned away from Jones.

Jones smiled slightly. Julie knew Mick helped The Supreme all along, and eventually, she pieced together the final line: Mick was willing to help The Supreme because he wanted something so natural, something so honest. He wanted a world where he and

Jones could be free. He felt The Supreme could provide that. And even though Julie felt hurt by this, she understood.

"There is a vision," Mick said, looking at Jones, reaching out and grasping his hands inside his own. "The Supreme has a vision of a society that would allow for all kinds of beings. And all kinds of equality. A society where you and I could live together, out in the open. We could be free. That was the real purpose behind the posse hominems. Not because she wanted androids to travel time. I did this for us. I did everything for us."

Oh, Mick. You fool, Jones thought. Mick was willing to go this far for a belief that was strong but a belief that was misled.

"So, where's your microchip, Mick?" Jones asked him crossly. Mick's eyes widened with recognition, realization.

That's right, you don't have one. Betrayal, Jones decided. *Betrayal is this feeling inside of me.* He let go of Mick's hands and slowly walked toward the main entryway.

"Well, Mick," Jones said looking at him, analyzing his frame, his face, the lines spread across his forehead. The sorrow in his lonely, desperate eyes. Jones took Mick in for the last time. "You ruined any chance of the future you planned for us by doing what you did."

***

Jones moved his things out of his and Mick's apartment the next day, not wanting anything to do with the space they shared. He wasn't sure where to go at first. He thought about Julie's studio apartment, knowing she wasn't occupying it, but that didn't feel right. The journal and Colin's blood would still be in her refrigerator, and that knowledge alone would haunt and mock him to no end. He eventually found himself at the doorstep of someone he least expected.

"Did you hear that Julie has gone missing?" Anna asked when she opened the door.

He nodded his head and allowed himself and his one bag inside. Her apartment hadn't changed much since the last time he'd been there, except the place was finally tidy and clean. He looked at her. Over the last few months, Anna finally gained a bit of her old self back. She wasn't frail or damaged looking, her face a bit plumper and her hazel eyes glowing.

The wall was still covered in the photos of all those women Colin had killed. Jones felt a strange sensation in his body as he tore them all down and handed them to Anna.

"I don't want to talk about it. I need a place to stay for a few days because I don't know where else to go. I promise I won't be in your hair for long. If you don't want me here, I understand but, Anna, you're my friend and I need you. Things ended sourly between us, so I understand if this intrusion isn't okay."

Anna didn't say anything at first. She took in Jones. They had grown close, shared secrets with one another. There was no doubt that they cared for each other even if they were still angry and bitter.

"You can stay Jones. For as long as you'd like," Anna answered, grabbing his bag and walking it over to the couch. "If it's any consolation, I resigned. I know who the killer is, but I don't know what to do about that knowledge, knowing how evil The Supreme is, too. So, I quit. As far as I'm concerned, that is all the past, and it should stay there."

Jones appreciated Anna. They shared an understanding: Neither was happy with either choice, but there was one clearly better than the other. He wondered if this was normal for humans, the ability to set aside differences for those they cared about.

Yes, that is doable, Jones thought. *Julie did this and, in a way, so did Colin.*

Anna's eyes filled with uncertainty and a hint of fear as she gazed toward her device. Jones followed her eyes to the news anchor on the screen outside The Capitol Building. Behind her, chaos erupted, and Jones recognized human and android representatives alike.

"Breaking news from The Capitol Building this evening. The Legislature has placed one of our leaders under arrest."

Chapter 54
The Governor

February 1st, 47 A.R.

Colin looked out the window toward The River. The sun was setting, and the golden dome from the top of The Capitol Building cast shadows in the courtyard. He made out the skyline of the buildings across The River. The COLI*GO building in particular stood out: an ominous place. It was something about the floor-to-ceiling glass windows. The complete exposure was such an opposite of what truly happened there. At least, here in The Capitol Building, the cold marble showcased reality.

Secrets and invisibility. Lies.

The Supreme's office in The Capitol Building was minimal, and she had no personal mementos on her desk. No paintings hung on the walls except for one: a canvas of Jeb Taylor's. The paint strokes mocked Colin with its presence: a woman wearing an emerald engagement ring similar to his mother's—similar to Julie's—being strangled by a large set of hands.

Colin thought of Julie. Now he realized his grasp on reality wavered for a reason. He wondered if, by her time traveling, his dreams were really dreams or if they were reality.

Or even memories.

Jones was correct when he told Colin that Julie would never betray him. From her note, she instructed Colin to trust Jones and encouraged him to admit to Kathleen's murder before handing over the evidence against The Supreme.

Celine's reflection in the window beaconed as she entered the room.

"Colin?" Her voice echoed around him, shocked and surprised.

"Hello, Celine," Colin said, turning to look her straight on. "Did you not expect to find me here?"

The color drained from his sister's face before regret colored it back up. Her skin grew blotchy, patchy shades of red. She opened her mouth to answer him but quickly retreated.

"You knew about this, Celine. You lied."

Her eyes were blinking rapidly, trying to hold back tears. "You don't understand, Colin. I didn't really have much of a choice."

"You know, I've learned recently that's not true. You always have a choice."

They continued to look at one another, neither moving from their strong stance.

"You knew about time travel? You knew of the human-android hybrids all along, didn't you?"

"Of course I knew about time travel. I helped finance the project. I wasn't overly involved in Mick's research, but I helped shuffle some funding for The Supreme. And eventually, yes, I knew about the human-android hybrids, too. I allocated funds needed for the miscellaneous projects that took place in the lower lab. The Supreme told me this would help you and hurt Joel. You have to believe me, Colin. I thought this would help you."

"Did you know The Supreme uses time travel against us? Against people?" Colin asked her, afraid to address the larger issue of human androids. "Did you know she sent It back in time to kill Mom?"

Celine took a sharp breath. "What?"

"Yes, Celine."

"Who is It?" she asked, confused.

"A complicated subject, one I could explain if you'll let me," he answered honestly, but Celine looked angry, her shoulders squared and distanced.

"Father was right. You are dangerous. Do you know how much it hurt me when I learned that it was you who killed Kathleen? Don't you understand? There was no way to ensure the safety of our family legacy with you still in the picture. You are unstable. I told you, I have to protect my legacy, the one I worked so tirelessly to build. You were only concerned about yourself."

The words hurt Colin, sliced through him in a way he hadn't anticipated. Especially from his sister.

"Yes, I killed Kathleen. But I killed her because she was going to destroy COLI*GO and The Capitol Building, all at the hands of The Supreme. All the terrible things I've done have been for this family. It will always be a part of me, I suppose. But Julie tried to fix that. She cared. Unlike Father. Unlike you. And, of course, The Supreme had to kill Julie to keep her quiet. Who is the real villain here, Celine? Me? Or The Supreme?"

"I'm fairly certain you were the one who killed Julie, Colin. Not me." The voice that spoke was not his sister's but The Supreme's.

"Julie isn't dead. I didn't kill her."

The Supreme's presence was all consuming among them. She was not alone. Colin wasn't surprised that behind her, he saw The Representatives of The People and The Androids congregated together. They were here, divided. His transgressions against The Supreme provided to The Legislature of The People. He assumed her transgressions against him were provided to The Legislature of The Androids.

"You killed Julie when you put a microchip in her brain. The creation of a new species, new beings wasn't enough for you, was it, Emilia? And obviously, you had to kidnap humans and perform those experiments on them yourself. How many have you created? Dozens? Hundreds? Or Thousands?" Colin asked, feeling as if they were the only two in the room.

She didn't flinch, didn't make any motion to give away her secrets and transgressions. The sensation between them felt noticeable in the room. Everyone held their breath, waiting and watching.

"You were too caught up in your own greed, Madam Supreme. And why is that? Shouldn't you not feel the human emotion of greed? Or is that because you know too much? You feel too much?"

The Supreme's eyes widened at Colin's accusation. Colin and The Supreme caught Joel Kennsington's eyes as he pushed forward through the group and stood in the front. The Supreme looked at Colin directly, her eyes barely moving or blinking.

"We cannot allow this to go on in our society. We are placing you under arrest," Joel Kennsington said on behalf of The People and The Androids holding up his device with the decree.

The Supreme and Colin stared at each other with intensity: The silence ricocheted around them. They both realized, at this moment, there was no unity. Maybe there never would be among society. Unity was an obscure concept.

This was the last time they would face one another.

Checkmate.

PART ELEVEN

Six Months Prior

"Missing is the sure mind. It bends to whomever it wishes. It is now them in a different body."
Apostle of Eventide

Epilogue

Julie

June 23rd, 46 A.R.

Dear Colin,

In my experience with time travel, changing the past usually provides an inconsistency of outcomes. I need to keep the past as pure as I possibly can. Regardless of those outcomes, I can say with struggle that I wish Mick never discovered time travel. So much wouldn't have happened, but I suppose we wouldn't be who we are without his invention either.

Imagine a world where you (well, It) didn't travel back in time and murder your mother. You never would have even been introduced to that demon in your brain. I wish that never happened, but the experience shaped you. It shaped both good and evil in you.

Would you have ever become the governor? Would you have done so much to help people? Help androids, too? Would you and I have ever fallen in love, let alone crossed paths?

Probably not.

Was that worth all those lives?

Also, probably not.

But I've grown tired of trying to hate you. It will always be a part of you even after you finish the actual treatment with the antidote. Jones will give you the last doses of treatment you need while I'm not here. Through all of this, Jones is the only being who has never betrayed me. Please, trust him as I trust and believe in you.

I really do believe in you. I believe you will be strong enough to acknowledge and face your trauma, because what I've learned through all of this madness is: You can still choose the future, but you cannot destroy or change the past, no matter how hard you try. You can never forget what happened in your past, but you need to be confident in yourself to face It head on.

And I know you are. I know you can.

Coming back is wrong of me. But in my attempt to keep the past as pure as possible, I have to create this infinite time loop. I don't know what will happen to me when I kill myself in the past. Will I go back to the future? Back to the past? Will I finally die for good? I hope that wherever I end up, I hope that includes you and only you.

And even if that doesn't happen, always remember that I not only believe in you but also accept you.

Love,
Julie

***

The device hurt Julie's body when she used it. She wasn't sure if that was due to the scars on her body or if this was the consequence of such an innovative technology using something as primitive as blood. Regardless, Julie knew to expect this unwelcome pain.

This wasn't her first experience with time traveling.

When Julie removed the device, she recognized the familiarity of summertime. The summertime in The Oceanside with Colin. The warm weather felt welcoming on Julie's fair skin. She had spent the last few weeks recovering from her wounds, hiding out in the O'Connor residence as The City crumbled outside around her. The people and androids were divided.

Julie knew Mick lied to her, was well aware Mick aided The Supreme because she convinced him of a world that involved freedom: a world where humans and androids and half-humans half -androids could live in harmony.

The Supreme wasn't sincere. She wanted control.

Julie wanted to believe there was another way to fix the future situation at hand. Mick told her the only way to avoid a future of complete chaos was to travel back.

"What happens when I do that? What happens when you change the past?" Julie asked him the next time he came to visit her.

"I'm not sure," Mick answered, but this was not an honest answer.

Julie formed her own plan in what little time she had left before Mick sent her on this mission. A false mission.

"And what happens when there are two of me in one dimension?" Julie had asked him once.

"There's always going to be something off about the dimension when there are two of you in it. The only way to avoid that is to kill yourself in that current dimension and take over as the only 'you' there," Mick said.

Julie didn't ask Mick the question that burned in the back of her mind: *Had that been what he was doing all along? I don't want to know the answer.*

Julie returned to The Oceanside. June 23rd, 46 A.R. She and Colin would be at the O'Connor family estate.

The waves were loud below her, hitting the sides of the rocks with a strong force. The sky was a clear blue, not a single cloud in sight. After giving Colin his dose, Julie knew her past self would be unable to sleep and venture outside for a walk to quiet her mind. This future Julie waited and watched her feet dangle over the edge. Eventually, Julie stood and angled her back against the edge of the cliff.

Seeing herself was a breathtaking moment. The other version of herself was startled, rubbing her eyes as if she was experiencing this like a dream.

Julie observed the woman standing in front of her. She wore one of Colin's undershirts and a pair of gym shorts, her hair haphazardly tied in a messy bun on top of her head. She was so familiar because it was a part of her that Julie held dearly.

"Am I dreaming this?" she asked her future self, lifting her hand to Julie's face in shock. Her fingers traced Julie's atrocious and crooked scar, the one elongating down from behind her ear to the beginning of her neck.

"This is a bad dream you're having," Julie answered. "Instead of remembering this dream, you will remember your next one."

Her past self faced her future self before the words left her lips.

"Push me." Horror spread across her face.

"No!" the Julie from the past yelped.

Future Julie sighed, a bit aggravated but unsurprised. She had already gone over the scenario in her mind a thousand times. The only way to keep the past as true as possible would be to create a time loop. There could only be one Julie and she could never allow herself in the future to act like Colin hadn't killed her. Even though he hadn't.

By killing Future Julie, her present self would continue on and eventually Colin would attempt to kill her. Mick would bring her to the future and inevitably send her to the past. A loop would be created. A loop that may play out again and again, but at least she wouldn't be changing what the past had intended itself to be.

Julie peered over the ledge, wondering if she had the courage to jump herself. She did not. That didn't matter anyways. Mick confided in Julie how he killed himself in the past, but he woke back up. Some kind of invincibility and inability to kill oneself while traveling time.

"Then I'll push you," she threatened even though this was an empty promise, one she knew she wouldn't actually do.

At least these words sparked her past self.

Julie's own delicate hands shoved with a shockingly strong force. There was complete confusion in her eyes, but Julie knew at least the memory would not stick. There would be no remembrance of this moment because she'd have an equally terrifying dream of death later.

Stumbling off the ledge, Julie looked up, her eyes wide and fixated on the O'Connor estate. She underestimated the height of the cliffs. They were further up from the ground than she anticipated. Or the act of free falling off them lasted longer than she assumed. Had time slowed down, realizing what happened?

She hit the rocky, sandy bottom of the beachside with a painful thump. Julie's eyes opened and closed, but at least the moments weren't too long in between. She finally closed them once again, the freezing lingering sensation of the ocean consuming her.

An image haunted Julie in her last few breaths. While falling off the side of the cliff, she noticed Colin watching, leaning over the side of the balcony from the second floor.

Was this Colin or It who saw this horrid scene?

She couldn't be sure.

And will this be traumatic for him to witness—to see two of me—one pushing the other like this?

Yes.

Julie hadn't accounted for this in her plan.

In her best intentions to keep the past as pure as she could, she may have in fact ruined the future anyways.

Coming Soon

UNITAS

Book Two of The UNITAS Series

Summer 2022

For more information, please visit:
LeeSHannonBooks.com

A once peaceful society has turned violent and chaotic. The Legislature and newly appointed Commissioner Jones must decide their next move in regards to Governor Colin O'Connor and his counterpart, The Supreme—and quickly—before society completely crumbles.

Across The River at the biotech company COLI*GO, Celine O'Connor is ready to make amends with her brother. She tasks her new CEO, Peter Schneider, to find a missing and presumed dead Dr. Julie Walsh, the inventor of an antidote that could save them all. But Peter soon discovers he isn't the only one searching for Julie as his journey intersects with the dangerous time traveler, Mick Taylor.

Determined to remain hidden until she can figure out a plan to save both The City and Colin, Julie escapes an infinite time loop she created. One thing stands in her way—a looming uncertainty from the person she needs as an ally: It.

Acknowledgements

This was a journey like no other. The idea for COLIGO was born from a particularly cold night in Boston, in February 2020, when I poured myself a nice glass of red wine and sat down to read a research study titled "G Protein-coupled time travel: evolutionary aspects of GPCR research." My brain wandered to: What if time travel wasn't reliant on physics and instead propelled by the mechanism of human blood? I left the thought—scribbled in my notebook—alone for a few days but couldn't ignore it for too long.

But on to the best part of acknowledgements: The people who helped make COLIGO an actuality.

First, thank you to my readers. I can't believe I created a world and characters that people not only believe in, but enjoy. I hope you stick around for the full UNITAS Trilogy. I'm glad to fast-release this world and these characters for you.

There were many points in this process where I wanted to give up and I'm glad I didn't. Without the encouragement from one of my closest friends (and the beautiful cover artist), Tori Mulhern, I'm not sure I would have made it past Chapter 48. Yes, even that close to the finish line. She encouraged me to keep writing. Tori created a cover design I couldn't have ever imagined and each time I look at COLIGO's cover, I fall more and more in love with it. Truly, you're an amazing friend, thank you.

Thank you to my parents, Geoff and Linda Smith, you were my first readers when this book was over 30 percent larger. As in, 190,000 words. Yikes. Wowzers. Thanks for reading the first draft and its insanity. And then diving back in again multiple times. You're my number one supporters and I love you. Thank you for everything.

I can't thank my beta readers enough; your opinions, enthusiasm and honesty helped shape the whole UNITAS Trilogy. Special shout out to Barbara, Cathy, Dana, Kira, and Kirstie. Additional thank you to other beta readers who read bits & pieces where needed but not all of COLIGO in its entirety. I hope you get to enjoy the story now that it's complete.

I would also like to thank the designer of The City's map, Keir DuBois. Without him and his genius creativity, I wouldn't have been able to illustrate the world I envisioned for my readers.

It takes a village to get a novel from draft one to the finish line. I couldn't have done this without my fantastic editor, Jenny. Thank you for all you do, and for helping get rid of my imposter syndrome.

I took various creative liberties while writing about specific topics but I would like to acknowledge the research, studies and papers that enlightened and educated me in areas where I'm not a subject-matter-expert in. Especially, those within neurological disorders, the wild theories of time travel, and psychological disorders. You can find links to the full references on my website.

Thank you to my grandmother, Idella White. I miss her every single day. She always enjoyed reading my stories as a child and supported my dreams. Dedicating my publishing company to her felt perfect.

Lastly, thank you to everyone who relates to someone in this story. Even It. I see you, I believe in you, and I accept you.

I hope to see you on the other side of UNITAS, Book Two of The UNITAS Series. I can't wait.

Sincerely,
Lee S. Hannon

www.ingramcontent.com/pod-product-compliance
Lightning Source LLC
Chambersburg PA
CBHW020304030826
48979CB00027B/2099/J

* 9 7 9 8 9 8 5 1 1 7 5 3 0 *